WHEN

YOU

AND I

COLLIDE

WHEN YOU AND I COLLIDE

BY **KATE NORRIS**

PHILOMEL BOOKS

PHILOMEL BOOKS
An imprint of Penguin Random House LLC, New York

First published in the United States of America by Philomel Books,
an imprint of Penguin Random House LLC, 2021

Visit us online at penguinrandomhouse.com.

LIBRARY OF CONGRESS CATALOGING-IN-PUBLICATION DATA
Names: Norris, Kate, author.
Title: When you and I collide / by Kate Norris.
Description: New York : Philomel Books, 2021. | Audience: Ages 12 up. |
Audience: Grades 10–12. | Summary: Sixteen-year-old Winnie, who can see
alternate realities, finds herself transported to one and must now find
her way back to save the man she loves.
Identifiers: LCCN 2021009715 | ISBN 9780593203033 (hardcover) |
ISBN 9780593203040 (epub)
Subjects: CYAC: Space and time—Fiction. | Love—Fiction. | German Americans—
Fiction. | Science fiction.
Classification: LCC PZ7.1.N644 Wh 2021 | DDC [Fic]—dc23
LC record available at https://lccn.loc.gov/2021009715

Manufactured in Canada
1 3 5 7 9 10 8 6 4 2

Edited by Liza Kaplan
Design by Ellice Lee
Text set in Dutch823 BT

*Dedicated to all the readers
who need other worlds to escape into,
and to the libraries and librarians
who keep this escape free and accessible.*

PART ONE

The optimist thinks this is the best of all possible worlds.
The pessimist fears it is true.

—J. Robert Oppenheimer

CHAPTER ONE

LATE OCTOBER 1942
NEW YORK CITY, UNITED STATES OF AMERICA

Late afternoon sunlight poured through the classroom windows, and Winnie watched the light dapple her lab bench in a dancing pattern of oak-leaf shadow. Freedom was near. It was the final period of the day, and Mr. Claremont, her physics teacher, stood at the front of the room leaning heavily on his wooden podium.

"Consider an archer's bow," he said. "The perfect example of potential energy! When the archer pulls back the string, he loads the cocked bow with potential."

Maribel, a classmate in the next row, yawned at Winnie dramatically and mouthed, "Boring!"

Winnie smiled back, and the girl gave her a confused frown.

Oh. Maribel's pantomime must have been meant for Winnie's lab partner. Winnie's cheeks went hot with embarrassment.

Communication was a funny thing. Winnie was fluent in German—her first language—as well as the English she'd learned when she and her father immigrated to the United States eight years earlier. And Mr. Claremont's science-speak came naturally to her; she'd been surrounded by such talk since childhood. But the effortless, unspoken teen-girl language her classmates shared? Winnie didn't think she'd ever master *that*.

Would she have been such an outsider if she and Father had stayed in Germany?

The dismissal bell rang, and Winnie quickly slid her heavy physics textbook into her knapsack, eager for escape. She was normally happy to consider the bow—or the mechanics of any machine, simple or otherwise—but even Winnie sometimes got sick of school. The past week had been full of clouds and cold rain. Who could be immune to the lure of a sunny fall day after all that?

"Miss Schulde, do you have a moment?" Mr. Claremont asked gruffly.

Winnie gave a startled look in his direction, squinting in the glare reflected off the cabinets along the side of the room. All the sciences at her small, private girls' school shared one lab, so the cabinets were full of an odd cross-disciplinary assortment of beakers, barometers, and taxidermized animals. Few students there studied the hard sciences—and fewer still stuck with them through physics, the most advanced course offered. Winnie was one of just seven students in the class.

"Of course," she answered.

Some of the other girls shot her gleeful "oh, you're in for it now" glances, probably hoping this meant the "class pet" was about to be taken down a peg. Winnie had only one true friend at school—Dora—a girl both fierce and fiercely liked, and if she had been there, the girls wouldn't have dared give Winnie those looks. But of course Dora wouldn't be caught dead enrolled in something as drippy as a physics class.

Winnie put on a smile to show those girls she wasn't worried. Although the smile was forced, it was true that she wasn't afraid of Mr. Claremont. Other students complained about what an ogre he was, but if they thought *he* was a strict taskmaster, they should try working with Father.

After the classroom emptied of stragglers, Mr. Claremont cleared his throat. "Barnard College is going to establish a physics department," he said. "They contacted me in hopes of recruiting scholarship students with aptitude in the field. May I give them your name?"

Winnie was stunned.

"But I'm just a junior," she stammered.

And she was a young one at that—Father had Winnie skip third grade when they moved, since she was working above her grade level in all her classes. Keeping her schoolwork up on top of trying to become fluent in English had been quite the challenge, but Father firmly believed that there were two ways of doing things: you were either pushing yourself to the limit, or you were being lazy.

"I know what year you are," Mr. Claremont said with a snort. "But you could graduate early. It would require a few extra classes this semester and next, but it's early enough in the year to change your schedule."

Winnie said nothing.

"You aren't afraid of a bit of hard work?" he pressed, frowning in that way that made some of the other girls tremble.

"No—of course not."

"And you do want to go to college?"

Well, yes. She did—very much. But did *Father* want her to? He never said anything about it. And she never asked.

Father sent her to the best girls' school in the city and demanded nothing but the highest grades from her (not that she'd ever struggled with that). So, Winnie had always hoped college was in her future . . . but she could also imagine Father telling her it was a waste, since he could teach her anything she needed to know.

What if he didn't want her to go to college?

What if he meant for her to keep working with him, for her to continue their experiments forever?

The prospect made Winnie's breath catch.

Surely he'd want her to go to college. Mama had gone to university, and it had been much more out of the ordinary then. If she were still alive—

Winnie stopped herself. No. No point thinking about that.

But still, she couldn't help but wonder: What would it feel like to have a life you didn't long to escape?

"Miss Schulde?" Mr. Claremont pressed. "You *do* intend to go to college?"

"I—I'd *like* to—" Winnie began.

"Well, good!" he interrupted briskly. "Have your father call and set up a meeting so we can discuss it."

Winnie shook her head. "I can't."

"What do you mean?"

Mr. Claremont had expected excitement, she imagined. Effusive thanks. Not to see his brightest pupil transformed into a stammering dope. Well, it irritated Winnie too. But that didn't change anything.

If she asked Father now and he said no, that was that. Dream, dead. Hope, over. She couldn't just spring this on him. It would take finesse. It would take *time*.

"It's too soon," Winnie said.

Mr. Claremont shook his head in annoyance. "Miss Schulde, what are you afraid of?"

Wanting.

The answer just sprang into her head. Was it true? Of course not. She wanted all the time. She wanted this very thing—her, at Barnard. This wasn't her first time thinking about it. Of the Ivies, only Cornell admitted women, but Barnard was at least the sister school of an Ivy—Columbia, where Father taught. Now they would have a whole physics department there, just across the street from the world-renowned one at Columbia! Wouldn't that be grand?

Winnie didn't just love physics because it was Father's chosen field, and hers by default. When Japan had bombed Pearl Harbor the year before, an awful feeling of "if *that* could happen, then *any* awful thing could" had taken hold of everyone. This sinking feeling of "my god, what next?"

For Winnie, quantum mechanics was an antidote to that despair. Not because it was clear or rational. It wasn't. There was an uncertainty *principle*, for heaven's sake. But physics offered a window into the true weirdness of the world—a way to understand the unexpected not as chaos or tragedy, but as mystery. And mysteries were easier to withstand.

Quantum mechanics governed the behavior of subatomic particles—the very heartbeat of existence. And that heartbeat was *strange*. It made simple rationality seem childish by comparison, and Winnie's own awkwardness and oddity somehow okay.

Things didn't have to make sense. They could just *be*. And scientists could discover ways of describing and utilizing those odd occurrences, even when they couldn't explain them. Winnie longed to do more than just read about these scientists and do dumbed-down versions of their experiments. She wanted to do more than work with Father, where they were doing authentic research, but research in which she would never really have a say. Winnie wanted to be a scientist herself. Attending Barnard could be the first step.

And Barnard didn't just mean education.

Barnard meant *freedom*—freedom wrapped in a package that Father might just accept.

So yes, Winnie wanted to go to Barnard. Was "want" even a strong enough word?

But she understood that life was a series of equal and opposite reactions. To want wildly was to risk wild disappointment.

Winnie had to approach this desire the same way she approached everything: with caution.

"It's too soon," she repeated.

"Fine. I'll ask someone else. Miss Grafton would jump at this opportunity."

Oh, Henrietta certainly would! Winnie felt sick with jealousy for a moment, which she knew had been Mr. Claremont's intent.

"She would be an excellent choice," Winnie said evenly, proud she was able to keep the envy out of her voice.

There was a fine line between caution and cowardice.

Sometimes, Winnie didn't know which side she was on.

Mr. Claremont let out an irritated huff. "Fine." He waved his hand at her. "That's all."

Winnie stepped back, but before she turned to go, she paused. "I do appreciate you thinking of me," she said.

His face softened, but before he could say anything more, Winnie hurried from the classroom, eyes stinging.

DORA WAS WAITING FOR HER WHEN SHE GOT TO HER LOCKER, TAPPING her foot playfully in put-on irritation at having to wait.

"Sorry!" Winnie said. "Mr. Claremont kept me after."

"I heard! To shower you with praise?"

"Something like that."

Dora frowned. "Anything wrong? Sally thought—"

"No, no, everything's fine."

Winnie loaded up the books she needed to take home that evening and put on her coat, then the two girls headed toward the exit.

At school dances and parties, Dora was always surrounded by her whole gaggle of friends, but after school it was almost always just the two of them. Winnie preferred it that way, but she'd never say so. It was just a wordless little agreement they'd reached, and in exchange, Winnie put up with the chaotic slumber parties and other social outings where she faded into the background, lonely in the crowd.

Dora threw the school doors open. "Bus?" she asked. "Or walk?"

"Let's walk," Winnie said. "It's so pretty out."

They set off down the sunny street. The air was full of that special fall scent, sharp but warm, and seemed to thrum with possibility. The city was as loud as ever, but beneath the bleat of traffic and the chatter of pedestrians, Winnie seemed to hear something else: the voice of the season itself, offering her a taste of its signature alchemy. *It's fall! Fall!* the wind tantalized in her chilly ear. *Everything is changing, and so can you!*

If only it were that easy. If only she could be made flashy and fantastic by the same magic that set the maple leaves ablaze! But no. Winnie was small and dark and plain as a sparrow, and imagined she always would be. Winnie was a girl who had just rejected an offer for the one thing she wanted most.

Well . . . second most.

"Say, let's go to a show!" Dora said.

Winnie shook her head. "I've got homework to do, then Father needs me in the lab."

Dora sighed heartily, a robust sound from a robust girl—Dora never did anything by half measures—and said, "Can't he take his own notes for once? What's he even working on that's so important, anyway?"

Winnie let out an airy little sigh herself. Sometimes she wished she could tell Dora everything.

Father's official research was on wave mechanics, and his work continued at home with Winnie's help. She did more than take notes, and Winnie was proud of the work they did . . . mostly . . . but she couldn't talk to Dora about any of it. The daily work defied discussion because it was boring by Dora's standards and complex by *anyone's* standards. It required things like helping Father's assistant, Scott, set up experiments, cleaning and mending laboratory equipment, and yes, taking notes. But their other work—those occasional terrifying, exhilarating sessions Winnie tried to wipe from her memory once Father had sobered up—those could not be discussed because, for those experiments, Winnie was the subject.

One of the war posters that had sprung up everywhere caught Winnie's eye, pasted on the wall of the movie hall next to advertisements for current shows: *Careless Talk Costs Lives*. Winnie didn't need the reminder. She knew sharing secrets came at a cost. Dora had always been so accepting of Winnie, but even she must have her limits.

Winnie could never tell Dora the truth, not about Father's work and not about herself.

"Gosh, you know even I barely understand Father's experiments," Winnie lied, kicking at a pebble on the sidewalk. "But you know how he is." She forced a grin. "As far as he's concerned, an afternoon off would turn my work ethic to rubbish."

Dora offered her a sympathetic elbow and began to swing their twined arms. Then she smiled so broadly her dimples showed. "Are you sure this devotion to your father's work doesn't have anything to do with that handsome assistant of his? Stan?"

"Scott," Winnie corrected automatically. "And I never said he was handsome." She tried not to blush.

Dora laughed. "I suppose you didn't. Just that he was *so* brilliant, and *such* a good worker, and that you can't *believe* how much he knows, considering he's just an undergraduate and all. And then your eyes went all heart-shaped and you swooned dead away!"

"I have a lot of respect for him, is all!"

But Dora was right—"respect" wasn't the only thing Winnie felt.

In fact, if Winnie were to make a list of what she wanted, Scott would be at the top. Above Barnard, above *everything*.

"Uh-huh."

Winnie knew she must be blushing now. "I don't have time

for a movie, but we *could* go to the library," she suggested, desperate to change the subject. "I need to get some books for our English project."

"You know what you're writing about already? Miss Hart just assigned that this week!"

Winnie nodded.

"All right, then," Dora said, "*if* you agree to help me pick a topic."

"Sure," Winnie said with a shrug. Dora would probably be calling her up the day before it was due, begging for her help to get started. Better to have something interesting to write about.

"Then let's go!" Dora said, tugging at Winnie's arm.

Winnie returned her friend's bright smile with her own faint one and allowed herself to be pulled along.

CHAPTER TWO

The trip downtown to the library ended up taking longer than Winnie expected. As soon as she entered the mudroom of their Sutton Place brownstone, their housekeeper, Brunhilde, was on her, unburdening Winnie of her schoolbooks and helping her out of her coat.

"So late! Vhere vere you?" Brunhilde exclaimed, in the same thick accent Father had been intent on banishing from his and Winnie's speech. Though Winnie had worked hard to lose the language that would out her, even now, she couldn't keep it out of her voice when she was nervous or annoyed. Although they had all been in America for nearly a decade, Brunhilde left the house only to buy groceries from Herr Wagner, the German greengrocer, or to take the train all the way to Queens to attend German mass at St. Matthias, so she had easily maintained her accent. "Your vater is already in the laboratory," Brunhilde added in hushed tones.

Winnie felt her stomach drop. "This early?"

Brunhilde gave her a dark look.

"I'll go straight down."

"Yes," Brunhilde said. "But stop in the kitchen and have a few cookies on your way," she added, dropping her voice to an almost-whisper, as though Father might overhear.

Winnie headed down to the basement laboratory immediately. Her stomach grumbled a small protest, but the last thing she wanted to do was make Father wait any longer.

As soon as Winnie entered the lab, Father fixed her in his sharp gaze.

"Winifred, how kind of you to join us," he said, voice slow and sarcastic.

Father always spoke carefully to conceal his accent, but it had the side effect of making him sound bored by everyone. If it weren't for that voice, based on looks alone, a person might make the mistake of thinking him friendly. He had eager blue eyes, boyishly blond hair, and a lanky physique, and even though he was her father, Winnie could recognize he was handsome. She saw how this surprised people any time someone who'd first met her later met him. They probably assumed that her mother had been plain, but that couldn't have been further from the truth.

Winnie could only wish that when she looked in the mirror, she saw some bit of Mama looking back at her. But no.

Through an unkind quirk of genetics, two attractive people had parented someone ordinary, and she saw Mama only in her memories.

Scott was in the corner, adjusting the knobs on a massive, boxy generator. He glanced over at Winnie and smiled warmly. Winnie smiled back, then quickly looked away. If her feelings about Scott were obvious to Dora, who had never even seen them together, were they obvious to him too?

Father had enlisted Scott as his assistant two years earlier, when Scott quickly distinguished himself as Father's best student during his freshman year. Winnie didn't know how Scott could stand to work such long hours—daytime at the university, and then evenings here—especially for a man as demanding as Father. But Scott's company had become so precious that she prayed he never came to his senses.

Sometimes their eyes would meet across the lab with what Winnie could swear was complete understanding. He would look up from whatever work he was doing, fiddling with a mess of copper filaments or taking notes, and then—*pow!* Like the best sort of sucker punch. These moments filled her with hope—not just that there might be something more between them one day, but that there was more to *life*, and that one day she would experience it.

It was so strange. This subterranean laboratory was home to both her brightest moments and her darkest.

"What kept you so late, anyway?" Father asked sharply.

"I stopped by the library after school," Winnie said, keeping her lowered eyes on the slightly scuffed leather of her Mary Janes. "I'm sorry."

Father accepted her apology with a nod and went back to his calibrations, occasionally barking instructions at Scott, who always answered with an easygoing "Yes, Professor Schulde." Winnie understood that she was supposed to stand there and wait patiently for her own orders, so she did.

The floor beneath her feet was packed earth. It gave the lab a primal feel, more like an alchemist's lair than a state-of-the-art laboratory despite the array of shiny, meticulously maintained equipment. Here, anything felt possible. Her eyes drifted to the large Faraday cage in the corner, where Father locked her—for her own safety—during their other work. When she thought about their night experiments out in the waking world, they seemed mad. But down here? Down here, she was forced to consider that much of quantum mechanics seemed impossible, right up until it was proven true.

What would Scott think if he knew about the other work that went on in that lab?

Winnie risked a quick glance at him, and noticed that his curly, butterscotch-colored hair was a little overgrown. She smiled. Of course Scott wouldn't notice he was overdue for a trim. He was completely unlike the preening boys she saw when she and Dora went to the soda shop, boys who were always trying to catch a glimpse of themselves in the flat black of the dark windows, seeming more interested in their own images than in their dates.

Winnie never would have confessed this, not even to Dora, but Scott was always with her at the soda shop, or when they went to see a picture, or even just when she was putting her hair up to go to bed. He was a constant companion in her own imagination. When Winnie lay in bed at night, she would imagine telling him anything and everything. The taunts she endured at school when Dora wasn't there to threaten to sock anyone who so much as looked at Winnie cross-eyed. The way that sometimes the strangest things, like the smell of Brunhilde baking pfeffernüsse at Christmastime, could make her miss her mother so badly it felt like her stomach had contracted to the size of a pea. That even though she feared she would never be anything but a disappointment to Father, she wanted to please him so badly that on nights when he dragged her down to the lab for those other, secret experiments, alcohol hot on his breath, what she prayed for wasn't for him to stop, but for them to succeed.

"Winifred!" Father said, snapping his fingers and motioning to the cabinet a few feet to his right. "The cathode ray tube."

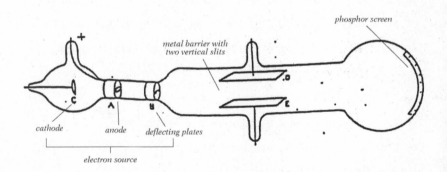

You're closer, she thought sulkily, but silently fetched it for him nonetheless. Was she a good daughter for obeying? Or a bad one for wishing she didn't always have to?

"Tonight," Father said, "I want to try something with photons—a bit of a twist on the double-slit experiment. I know Scott is familiar with it. You've heard of it too, I presume?"

Father saw her grades. Did he really think she might not be familiar with Young's famous experiment? If only Father were as confident in her scientific aptitude as Mr. Claremont was, she thought with a pang.

"Of course I have," Winnie said, a touch of sharpness creeping into her voice.

"Oh?" Father raised his eyebrows and paused just long enough for Winnie to know she was in trouble. "Then tell me, where did he publish his first account of the experiment?"

Winnie had no idea. This was why it was better to just smile and nod and keep her mouth shut. Father was already irritated with her for being late. She knew he wouldn't just let this go.

"Well, I know he first performed the experiment in the early nineteenth century. *Very* early. 1801, I believe—"

"Correct," Father said coolly, "but not what I asked."

"Sir, I believe it was—" Scott began, but Father silenced him with a look.

"I asked Winifred, not you."

Winnie thought for a few more moments, then finally admitted that she did not know.

"Astonishing," Father said. "And here I thought you were the expert. Go up to my study and find the journal where it was published. We'll wait."

If she'd learned meekness too well, Winnie thought bitterly, it was because she had an excellent teacher.

UPSTAIRS, WINNIE PUSHED OPEN THE DOOR OF THE CONVERTED SECOND-floor bedroom that served as Father's library. She cringed out of habit at the loud creak of the door hinges, nervous to be entering Father's personal sanctuary, even though he was the one who'd told her to.

Father kept his periodicals in a bookcase of their own, un-fortunately but unsurprisingly organized by title rather than year. She stared at the shelves for a long moment, imagining having to page through hundreds of scientific journals, the task taking hours while Father grew angrier and angrier . . .

But it was only a moment before she came up with a simple solution. Young had performed his experiment more than a hundred and forty years ago; Father didn't have many jour-nals that were that old. All Winnie had to do was scan the spines to find the ones that looked shabbiest and check the in-dexes of those. After checking fewer than a dozen, she found Young's "Experimental Demonstration of the General Law of the Interference of Light" in an 1804 volume of *Philosophical Transactions*.

"How fantastically *edifying*," Winnie grumbled to herself.

She knew she should rush back downstairs, but she'd found

the article so quickly. Why should she hurry back? She hated that Father had embarrassed her like that in front of Scott . . . and she hated even more that all she could do about it was spend a few extra minutes upstairs pouting.

Winnie began scanning Father's bookshelves absentmindedly. She pulled an old issue of *Annalen der Physik* off the shelf, curious to see how her German was holding up. She took a seat in Father's desk chair with a delicious feeling of rebellion, then flipped to an article that had been dog-eared.

Winnie was surprised to find that someone had filled the margins with notes. Not Father, certainly. He wasn't the type to write in books, and it wasn't his handwriting besides— although she could swear she recognized the slanted, elegant script. Winnie's heart began to pound, but it took a few hurried beats for her conscious mind to catch up with her body.

This was her mother's handwriting.

Winnie quickly flipped to the inside of the front cover to confirm it. There it was, in careful block print: her mother's name, Astrid Keller, as well as a Swiss address that Winnie assumed was the boardinghouse where Mama had lived while attending the University of Zurich.

Mama must have studied this article there, when she barely older than Winnie was now, but with less than a decade to live.

Winnie brushed her fingers over the ink. She could just barely feel the divots her mother's pen had scratched into the paper. Did Father realize this scientific journal had been his wife's—that it was sitting on his bookshelf, full of her notes?

Maybe he did. Maybe he had all sorts of mementos he kept from Winnie, while she didn't have even a single photograph.

Some days, no matter how hard she tried, Winnie couldn't picture Mama clearly. Other times, when she *could* picture her, it was only the awful image of Mama slumped over in the front seat of their car, dead. What the windshield had done to Mama's forehead. The blood all over Mama's pretty yellow dress.

Normally she pushed those awful images aside, but this time she couldn't help but let the memory linger—there, in Father's library, fingers tracing Mama's words.

Winnie dreaded her father's night experiments, but she felt their pull too. It was all tied together. Their experiments. Mama's death. The experiments were Father's twisted way of trying to make up for what had happened to her.

Because the accident that killed Mama was his fault.

Well . . . his—and Winnie's.

It had all happened at once. They lost Mama. And they found out what Winnie could do.

CHAPTER THREE

Mama died in 1934, on one of the first days of the year that finally felt like spring. The frost had broken, the ground was clear of snow, and songbirds could be heard in the morning. They spent the day at Mama's parents' house in the city, but what should have been a lovely afternoon was tense from beginning to end. It didn't help that Father started drinking before lunch.

Winnie's parents started arguing the moment they got in the car to drive home.

"You know, when my father asks you how the job search is going, it's just that—a question. He's making conversation."

"Making conversation? Did you see the look on his face when I told him I won't apply for that Berlin posting?"

"Surely you can understand how it looks to him. It's a good job, and you *would* apply, if not for . . ."

Here, Mama trailed off. Winnie wasn't sure exactly what

they were arguing about, but at seven, she was old enough to understand that their financial situation was precarious. She'd heard enough of these fights to know that Mama and Papa each thought that these problems were caused by something that the other one either had or hadn't done.

"Exactly!" Papa said, then mimicked Mama in a high-pitched voice. "*If not for* . . . ! So, the least you could do is say something when he brings it up, not just sit there."

Winnie bounced violently when the car hit a large bump in the road, which was still winter-rough.

"For goodness' sake, Heinrich! Slow down."

"And then he smiles and tells me, 'You might want to take a job, even one you think is beneath you, before you let these girls of yours starve.' Like I'm turning positions down, like I'm not trying . . ."

Her father's voice began to fade in Winnie's ears. She felt sick to her stomach, which was odd, because she didn't normally get carsick, although Papa was driving a bit erratically.

Then it happened. Winnie saw her first splinter, although she had no idea what it was at the time.

First, she saw herself asleep in the back seat of the car. Stronger than a daydream—more like a *dream* dream. She was inside it, experiencing it. But at the same time, she knew she was awake. Was this really just her imagination? Why imagine herself asleep in the car? Sure, it would be nice to not hear Mama and Papa bickering, but—

In this vision, a deer leaped in front of the car.

The car swerved, spun, and that sleeping version of Winnie woke screaming as her father managed—barely—to right the car and keep it on the road.

Winnie screamed along with that other dreamlike version of herself. "Papa! Papa, watch out!" Yet when she looked around, the deer was gone. It seemed so real! But it wasn't.

Was it?

Papa turned in his seat. "What? What's going on back there?"

Just then a deer leaped in front of the car. Here. *Now*. In her waking world.

Papa was looking back at Winnie, and they hit the thing head on.

WINNIE CAME TO COVERED IN BLOOD. FATHER WAS WRAPPING HIS SCARF tight around Winnie's upper arm.

"Ow! Papa, stop!"

"Hush, and stay still!"

Winnie saw the blood gushing from the gash in her arm, and everything went black.

WHEN SHE WOKE AGAIN, ONLY MOMENTS HAD PASSED. WINNIE COULD tell because Father was still right there, pressing on her arm.

"Mama?" Winnie whispered. She could see the outline of her, folded over in the front seat. "Mama?"

Louder now, wailing.

She leaned forward to get close, to see, but Papa pulled her back. "No," he said roughly, "don't look."

But it was too late. She saw. Mama's gold hair black with blood. The slash on her forehead peeled back to the white skull. And her eyes, terribly open. She might have wondered if Mama was still alive, if only they'd been closed.

"Why did you shout like that?" Father asked, shaking her. She could smell the malt of beer on his breath. She knew he didn't mean to shake her so hard. "If I'd been looking ahead and seen the deer, I could have stopped! Why did you yell? What did you see?"

What *had* she seen?

She'd seen—herself. She'd seen what would have happened . . .

If she fell asleep.

Then Father saw the deer.

Then he swerved the car.

Then Mama lived.

And Winnie knew—she *knew*—that it really had happened like that. Somewhere else. For some other her.

And somehow, she saw it.

DAYS PASSED. WEEKS. THE MEMORY OF THE CRASH THAT HADN'T HAP-pened was eclipsed by the aftermath of the crash that had. Winnie's odd vision became just another nightmare facet of that awful evening, and made just as much sense as any of it—which was to say, no sense at all. Grief blunted all meaning. Mama was gone. Shut up in a box and buried. *That* was the impossible thing, not whatever she had or hadn't seen.

But then, it happened again. She was out in the yard with Father, trying to bring some order to the little vegetable garden—Mama's garden—and failing. Winnie saw a fox chasing a thin, young hare and flinched away from the sight but still saw it captured, neck snapped and limp, behind her closed eyes.

"You can look," Father said, with that hollowness his voice always held now, "she made it."

Winnie opened her eyes. The fox stood at the far end of the field, long snout buried in the little hole the rabbit had escaped to. She picked up a stone and threw it at him, knowing she would fall short but get close enough to startle the fox into trotting off without his dinner.

"See?" Father said. "Nothing to fear after all."

This was Father's new habit—vague assurances, delivered with an insulting lack of conviction.

We're going to be okay.

Mama is in a better place now.

As if foxes didn't catch hares. Didn't kill them. As if foxes wouldn't die themselves if they didn't.

As if Mama weren't dead. As if anything could ever be all right again.

These assurances—these lies—mocked Winnie's own grief and shut her off from her father's.

"*This* rabbit lived, but another one died. I saw it."

Father opened his mouth, about to say something dismissive, but then stopped, brow furrowed. He stared at her with narrowed eyes, and Winnie felt like he was looking at her—*really* looking at her—for the first time in weeks. It was a relief, even though he looked at her like she was a diagram in one of his scientific journals, not his daughter.

Finally, Father shook his head and scoffed.

"I don't like this new imagination of yours, Winifred," he said shortly.

"I didn't imagine it," Winnie said, jutting her chin out. "I didn't imagine this, and I didn't imagine what I saw the night—"

Winnie fell quiet at the sight of Father's suddenly furious face. He threw his spade in the dirt and stalked off in silence.

But later that night, he shook Winnie awake. "You think she lived? In some other world, she lived?"

Winnie said nothing. She was half-asleep and scared. She couldn't tell if Father was angry or excited.

"It's absurd. Other worlds! But some scientists believe it— that there's an infinity of different realities. Why should you be able to see them? And yet . . . perception is just the first step, you know. What if you could have prevented the crash that night, instead of . . ."

His voice trailed off, but she knew what he meant anyway: what if she could have stopped the crash, instead of causing it.

From then on, Father became obsessed with the idea of

alternate realities. He read everything he could get his hands on. It seemed that Winnie had a miraculous gift. He had to understand it. Father made Winnie report every time she had a sense of an alternate reality breaking off from their own, and the details of what she saw in the split. For the most part, he was content to observe and record, but other times, late at night, drunk . . .

He began performing his experiments. What if Winnie's visions were just the beginning? What if she could hone this gift until she could not only *see* but *shape* the possibilities? And what if he could harness that power?

And so, Father's desire to create the splinter machine was born.

According to multiverse theory, anything that happened both happened and did *not* happen, and these different outcomes gave rise to different realities. The splinter device would allow Father to control which possibilities occurred in their own reality. It would let them live in the best of all possible worlds. The next time tragedy came for her and Father, they could just . . . turn it away.

Winnie certainly understood the appeal.

But she hated the experiments.

All those electrodes, Father shouting, the pain, the continued failure. Her early splinters were like peering at an altered landscape through a dusty window—*real,* but remote. As she and Father continued to experiment, the details became sharper, and the splinters occurred more frequently. But even as she honed this sixth sense, Winnie never could gain any control over how things played out in her own world.

At least she and Father had something they were working on together. But as Winnie became the focal point of all Father's attention, she grew ever more distant from his affections. He hired Brunhilde, and all of Winnie's daily care was outsourced to her dutiful hands. Winnie was everything to him in the lab—and nothing outside it. It had been that way for nearly seven years now.

Did he even love her anymore? Or had all Father's love died when Mama did? If nothing else, at least he needed her. Winnie was essential to his work on the splinter device.

Several months after Mama's death, Father was finally offered a job—in America. His work at Columbia kept him busy, and the splinter research faded into the background, except for those occasions when Father would feverishly pick it up again—times that seemed random until Winnie recognized their general pattern over the years. Mama's birthday. Their anniversary. At least once sometime over the holidays. And always, always on the first day of the year that felt like spring.

Father raged during these "experiments," but only once, years ago, did she think he might actually hit her: when Winnie had the gall to say, "I miss her too, but can't we just stop this? She's gone."

Father had raised his hand to slap her, but after a few heaving breaths, dropped it without striking. He wouldn't answer her question. Father wouldn't talk about Mama anymore. Only the splinter device.

Winnie had lost more than just her mother in that terrible crash. She'd lost Father too. And even if they somehow, miraculously, designed a working splinter device, it could never bring either of them back.

CHAPTER FOUR

Winnie wiped away an errant tear and sighed. The past was never really the past, was it? It happened, and happened, and happened, rippling alongside the present. Inside, there would always be a part of her that was still seven years old, scared, and trying to learn how to live without her mother.

A light knock at the study door startled Winnie away from her gloomy thoughts and out of Father's seat. He couldn't find her like that, sitting at his desk, crying over Mama's notes!

"Winnie?" a voice called softly.

Scott.

Of course—Father wouldn't have bothered to knock. Winnie felt a moment's relief, then a different sort of discomfort. She didn't want Scott seeing her upset like that either. She should have just brought Young's article to Father as soon as she found it. But then she wouldn't have stumbled across this reminder of her mother. Winnie quickly tucked her mother's copy of

Annalen der Physik into the waistband of her skirt, took a few more swipes at her cheeks, then told Scott to come in.

"Professor Schulde sent me to help you," he said, shutting the study door behind him.

Scott glanced around the office, and Winnie saw him spot the copy of the journal Father had asked her to find, lying right there on the desk. He gave her a gentle look. Winnie was sure he could tell she'd been crying.

When Father had first hired Scott, Winnie dreaded working with him. He was too young. Too handsome. The last thing she needed in that lab was another thing to be on edge about.

But then she got to know him. He wasn't the brash, do-no-wrong star pupil she'd expected. And that was worse, in a way. She could find no reason to dislike him, no flaw to inoculate herself against falling for him. Winnie wouldn't have chosen to have these feelings if she could've helped it. Scott was spectacular, and Winnie was—well, *her*. What could he possibly want with his boss's mousy daughter? He was unattainable.

But Scott *saw* her. He was smart and he was kind and his eyes were the color of honey fresh off the comb, and he saw her. That made him irresistible.

"He's just as hard on his students, you know," Scott said. "If that helps."

Father's treatment wasn't really what she was upset about, but also, in a way it was. It made not having a mother harder, having a father like him.

"He isn't my professor, though," Winnie said. "He's my dad."

"I just mean that it isn't your fault that he's this way," Scott said with a helpless shrug. "It's just the way he is."

"I don't know," Winnie said, shaking her head slowly. "If *I* were different, maybe he would be too."

"Different how?"

"Just more—" Winnie shrugged. "I don't know."

But she did.

If she were more lovable, maybe Father would love her more. She knew he was capable of it. He had loved Mama, after all.

But there was something wrong with her. It wasn't just the splinters that set her apart. There was something in her that was closed off, something that left her always on the sidelines, listening, observing, but never fully part of things, never all the way in the moment and out of her head. It made her seem standoffish at school, she'd been told. Winnie was just grateful Dora didn't seem to mind—if anything, it delighted her, since it was so different from Dora's own chatterbox nature, Winnie supposed. *I never know* what *you're thinking!* Dora had told her soon after they met, seeming thrilled by the novelty. But if Winnie were jolly or warm, maybe Father wouldn't find it so much easier to relate to her as the subject of his experiments—or at best, as a lab assistant—instead of treating her like a daughter.

"Sometimes I don't think he even likes me," Winnie said. "Much less loves me."

"Winnie, of course he loves you."

Winnie frowned and met Scott's eyes. "What makes you so sure?"

Scott adjusted his glasses nervously, and Winnie immediately realized she was staring at him too intensely. God, he must think she was certifiable! Perhaps she should interrogate him about her scrawny frame and lack of friends too, since apparently she'd decided to put every anxiety on display.

"I'm sorry—" Winnie began, but Scott was already speaking himself.

"Look, I wanted to—" he said, then stopped. "I'm sorry. Go ahead."

"No, no," Winnie said, cringing. "I've said enough already."

"Not at all!" he said earnestly.

The two of them smiled at each other, and for once Winnie didn't break his gaze. It was a moment straight out of her fantasies. His smile seemed to say all he wanted was to listen to her blather about her silly insecurities all day.

But then Scott frowned. "Your father didn't really send me," he admitted abruptly. "I volunteered. He was getting agitated about how long it was taking—"

"Oh god, we'd better go," Winnie said, swiftly brought back down to reality. She took a step toward the study door, but Scott stopped her by placing a hand on her naked forearm. His touch sent thrills radiating up and down her skin.

"Wait—I said I'd come get you because I wanted the chance to ask you something. There's a physics department mixer tomorrow night. Will you come with me?"

"Yes," Winnie said quickly, "of course!"

She could feel a goofy, child-at-a-birthday-party grin on her face—not exactly a hallmark of the sophistication she wanted Scott to see in her, but she couldn't help it. And anyway, he didn't seem to mind.

Scott smiled back in a way that made her enthusiasm feel less silly. "Great!" he said. "Now all we have to do is ask your father." He gave her a raised-eyebrow grin. "Should be easy, right?"

Winnie had been so excited about the invitation that she hadn't even thought about the logistics.

"Oh," she said, deflating. "But he'll never say yes."

"Then we'll just have to convince him," Scott said firmly.

How he could understand Father so little even after working with him these past two years?

Scott's expression turned serious. "You see, I don't just need your company—although I'll be happy to have it," he added quickly. "My friend James is missing." Scott frowned. "Or—maybe he's not. They say he dropped out, but he would have told me if he was planning on leaving Columbia. At least, I think he would have . . . Anyway, the department mixer is at his mentor Professor Hawthorn's house. James was working with Hawthorn on this government project of his. Project Nightingale. Everyone is talking about it, but no one seems to actually know what it *is*. Something seems off to me, but I don't know. I'm afraid I've lost perspective. But you, Winnie—you see things, right?" he asked, a bit breathless.

Winnie's stomach did a nervous flip. "What do you mean?"

"I've noticed it in the lab. You're incredibly observant, and your instincts—they're amazing. I could really use that now."

Winnie let out a breath. She realized with relief that Scott didn't suspect the truth about her ability.

But he wasn't actually asking her on a date. He needed—well, an assistant. Naturally he would think of her. Assistant in the laboratory, assistant in life.

Of course, that didn't change her answer.

"I'm happy to help," Winnie said, struggling to keep at least the ghost of a smile on her face despite her disappointment. "If I can."

Even though Winnie was crestfallen, she was eager to help Scott solve this puzzle.

Why would a promising young student drop out of Columbia and not tell his friends?

One possibility immediately jumped to mind. Winnie walked past the East River Navy recruitment office on her way home from school sometimes, and lately she had been seeing more and more young men—some barely older than her and her classmates—walking out its doors, enlistment papers in hand and faces flushed with excitement. James could have been one of them, spurred to action by the Nazis' sinking the civilian SS *Caribou* off Nova Scotia, or the latest news from the Pacific theater or Stalingrad.

"Would James be afraid to tell you if he enlisted?" she asked.

Scott considered a moment.

"I hope not, but it's possible. It's something we students talk about—how scientists are more useful to the war effort at home than on a battlefield."

Winnie must have raised her eyebrows. It was rare to hear *anyone* say something like that amid a sea of posters and radio ads decreeing that all able-bodied young men should be eager to join the fight.

He sighed and said, "I know, I know—it's half genuine, and half the sort of thing we have to say to feel less guilty for staying home. So, it's true that if James had brought up enlisting, I would have tried to talk him out of it. I'll check in with some recruitment offices."

Winnie nodded.

"See?" said Scott. "You're helping already."

Winnie was happy to help—but it wasn't pure altruism. She wanted Scott to see the girl behind the physics aptitude.

Winnie could feel the crisp, dry paper of her mother's old notes cool against her skin. She shared her mother's scientific interest and aptitude, but as far as Winnie could tell, that was all they shared. Mama had been as blonde and robust as Winnie was dark and slight; and although her mother's face wasn't always clear in her memory, Winnie remembered enough to know it was a singularly beautiful one. Even as a child, she had understood that the reason Father totally erased any trace of Mama from their lives after her death was because of how much it hurt to remember her. Winnie longed to inspire that sort of passion herself.

And the mystery of James's disappearance—it was like an equation just itching to be solved.

What would it mean to Scott if she could be the one to solve it?

"No," Father said briskly. "Winifred is too young to date."

Winnie knew that plenty of other sixteen-year-olds went out with boys, but she also knew that in this case, Father wouldn't be swayed by statistics.

"There couldn't be a safer place for her, sir," Scott said. "The event is at Professor Hawthorn's townhouse. We'll be surrounded by colleagues, and you could even—"

Father scoffed. He attended the department lectures sometimes, but never the parties, which he considered "a shameful misallocation of university resources."

"No," he said again. "Consider the subject closed."

But as he said this, something opened inside Winnie: a peek through the door his answer had cracked. She caught a glimpse into an alternate reality where Father said yes. Sometimes, a splinter would escape her grasp before she got a chance to see it properly. Not this time, she vowed. *This* she had to see— despite how physically uncomfortable it would make her feel to do so.

Blood throbbed at her temples, and her mouth flooded with saliva. She felt sick with the effort. But there was a crack, and Winnie knew she could push it open if she just gave in to the feeling. Even so, it wasn't easy. It was like grasping a sparrow: hold too tight and the vision was destroyed, slacken her grip too much and it would fly away.

So Winnie focused her mind. A vise squeezed her temples; nausea yanked at her stomach.

This feels awful.

And that's okay.

She was intent on experiencing this splinter in its entirety.

Winnie's internal vision was watery at first, the colors all whispers of themselves. Then it clicked into focus. She saw the three of them clearly—her, Father, and Scott—all together in the laboratory basement, just like they were at this very moment in her own reality. She saw Father agree to their date.

"You may go to the mixer only," he said, giving them each a firm look in turn. "And have her home by ten o'clock."

Winnie was shocked that there was actually a world where Father said yes. What went into that choice? Was it, just maybe, the thought that saying yes would make Winnie happy?

But if Father could say yes, why couldn't he have said yes *here*?

Seeing a better world made it so much harder to live in this one.

Before Winnie could get sucked in by her self-pity, she was distracted by a shift in her vision. The split-scene changed. Now she was in a different laboratory, not the familiar basement one at home. A lab on campus, maybe? She and Scott were wearing different clothes from the ones they were in now.

It must be the same splinter, but sometime in that other world's future.

Winnie and Scott were not alone.

The two of them were talking to an unfamiliar boy. No, not a boy. A young man Scott's age, although he was slight, and there was something boyish about him even beyond that—a certain softness to his face and the quirk of his smile, tinged with worry, that made Winnie feel instantly fond of him with the strength and senselessness of emotions that spring up inside dreams.

And although Winnie didn't recognize him, in that splinter future she knew who he was, and so she knew here too: this was James. When he reached out to shake her hand—they must be meeting for the first time—he saw her notice the bruises that ringed his wrist. He hastily pulled down his sleeve.

The bruises looked like fingermarks to Winnie, the ghost of someone's too-hard grasp.

Then her vision was over. Winnie's awareness was back in her own world, which carried on now without skipping a beat.

But what on earth had she just seen?

Winnie usually just caught a little peek at the "what if?" of another world. Her glimpse had never extended so far before. Why now? What had changed? Sometimes, Father called her ability to see splinters her "gift." This was the first time it actually felt like one. James was in trouble; she was sure of that now. But if she went to that mixer—if she defied Father—it would set her down a path that might allow her to help him.

The thought of disobeying Father made Winnie's stomach tremble with nerves, but this was what their night experiments were all about, wasn't it—Winnie using the splinters to shape her own reality?

She'd never felt such a clear way forward from a splinter before. Maybe her ability defied the artifice of Father's experiments. Or maybe Father was right. Maybe she'd never wanted it badly enough. But now . . . she longed to help Scott—to impress him into loving her.

Those bruises on James's arm—how far into the future was that? Was someone hurting him right now? What was Project Nightingale, and why did Scott suspect their involvement?

Winnie hoped some of her curiosity would be sated at the party the next night, but she had a feeling that this mystery would deepen before it unraveled.

CHAPTER FIVE

They finished with their experiment for the evening soon after.

"Father, you look tired," Winnie said. "Why don't Scott and I finish cleaning up?"

She wanted an excuse to talk to Scott alone, but the suggestion didn't come out as casually as she had hoped. Winnie started disassembling the cathode ray tube with intense focus so she wouldn't have to meet her father's eyes.

She mentally braced for Father to reject the idea, or worse, to question her motivation, but he just said, "Fine. Give that a good dusting and pack it with the chamois when you're done." Then he left.

Once Father was up the stairs and out of earshot, Scott smiled and said, "Oh well. It was worth a try."

"But what about James?"

Scott's face grew serious. "I don't want you to worry about

that—I might be jumping to conclusions. In any case, I'll get to the bottom of it myself."

For a moment, she was tempted to tell Scott that she could see splinters and explain what she'd just seen. But although she often fantasized about confiding in Scott, the reality of sharing her oddness with anyone was terrifying. What if he didn't believe her? Or worse, what if he *did*, and started looking at her the same way Father did—like a scientific mystery, or a tool for his own ends?

And that wasn't even considering the danger she'd be in if more people found out about her ability.

The world was at war, and every action was now measured on a single scale: did it help the Allies, or hurt them? The groceries you bought, how often you drove your car, even how you disposed of tin cans and bacon grease—all of it was a weapon, either against the Germans or for them.

As a German immigrant, those scales were already set against Winnie. If people knew about her ability, they might expect her to be able to control the splinter possibilities, just like Father did. They might expect her to sway the war in the Allies' favor. When she told them she couldn't, that she had never seen a splinter beyond the scale of her own small life, what would people think then? What if they thought she was choosing not to help? Or worse—what if they thought she was trying to help the Germans?

No. Her ability had to remain secret. Besides, it wasn't like she'd seen anything that would help them find James. She'd just seen enough to know that for once she needed to be brave.

"I'm going to the party with you," Winnie said. "Sometimes my friend Dora and I go see a picture on the weekend. I'll say I'm doing that, but I'll go with you instead."

"I can't let you—"

"Scott, I know you," Winnie said, cutting off his objections. "You wouldn't think your friend was in danger if he weren't. You wouldn't think there was something suspicious about this Project Nightingale if there weren't. So, I'm going with you, and we'll get to the bottom of this together."

He looked at her for a moment. Winnie could see uncertainty on his face, and gratitude—and some other feeling she couldn't quite name, one that made her heart jump into her throat with giddy excitement.

Finally, Scott smiled and spoke.

"You're risking a lot for some kid you don't know."

"Not for a kid I don't know," she said. If she could work up the nerve to defy Father, then she could say this. "For you."

I would do anything for you. Winnie thought this so strongly that she felt like maybe he could hear it, even though she didn't dare speak it out loud.

Scott looked at her so intently, and they were standing so close to each other, that for one wild moment, Winnie thought he might be about to kiss her. But instead of leaning in, Scott took a step back and allowed the moment to harmlessly discharge.

And yet, there was a little hitch in his breath that let Winnie know he'd felt that electricity too.

THAT EVENING, WINNIE HAD DINNER IN THE KITCHEN WITH BRUNHILDE while Father worked in his study, as usual. She might have seemed calm from the outside, chitchatting with Brunhilde and eating mashed potatoes, but inside Winnie thrummed with excitement. She was going to defy Father! She was going to a party with Scott!

After they finished eating, Brunhilde retreated upstairs to get ready for bed, and Winnie set about washing their few dishes. She had just finished drying the last glass when Father came in, footsteps nearly silent in his suede-soled slippers.

Winnie's stomach gave a nervous twist. Father usually worked in his study later than this. Was Mama alive for him tonight too? Would this be a night of splinter experiments?

"I'm making some tea," Father said. He sounded calm enough. "Would you like a cup?"

Winnie nodded cautiously. "Yes," she said, then added a hasty "Thank you."

He gestured to the kitchen table, and Winnie took a seat. She watched as he took a tin of loose-leaf tea from the cupboard—some herbal concoction their German greengrocer swore by for calming the mind—and measured a few scoops into the pot, then set the kettle to boil.

Once it was ready, he put two cups of tea on the table, adding a heavy pour of kirsch to his own.

"You think me overly strict, I imagine."

Yes! Of course she did! But she couldn't just say that.

Winnie added a small spoonful of sugar to her cup and

stirred, trying to buy time as she considered how to respond.

"It isn't like we want to go out dancing. It's just a university event."

"I'd rather see you at some nightclub than around those people. These professors are all vultures—and Hawthorn is one of the worst."

But it was fine for Scott to take their classes? Fine for Father himself to work with them? Winnie was certain that if she were male, he would already be planning which courses she should take when she was inevitably admitted to Columbia.

It wasn't fair.

"When she was my age, Mama was allowed—" Winnie stopped when she saw the look on Father's face.

He took a breath, seemingly to calm himself, then a long sip of his tea.

"I know you don't understand the dangers young women face in this world. I consider it a triumph that you don't. Honestly, Winifred? I hope you never do." He shoved his chair back. "Goodnight," he said, then left without another word.

Winnie frowned. He wanted to protect her. He wasn't trying to make her unhappy; he was trying to keep her safe. But his concern was misplaced. She wasn't the child he seemed to think she was.

Winnie picked up the kitchen telephone and dialed Dora.

"Vandorf residence," Dora's housekeeper, Louisa, answered briskly. "May I ask who's calling?"

The woman had been Dora's nanny when she was younger,

but with Dora's parents gone so frequently (and a bit helpless even when they were there), Louisa had been kept on, becoming something like the household sergeant, managing the various drivers and cooks and maids needed to keep daily life luxe for the Vandorfs.

"Hello, Louisa! It's just Winnie. Could I talk to Dora for a minute? I promise I won't keep her long. I know it's late."

Louisa got Dora on the phone, and Winnie explained what Scott had asked her to do.

"You'll help?" Winnie asked, a bit breathless with the excitement of it all. "I can pretend we're at the movies together tomorrow night?"

"Oh! Oh yes! You can even get ready here. This is so exciting! I'm sure Mother has a cocktail dress you can borrow. She's tiny, like you."

"She won't mind?"

Dora gave a sad little laugh. "They're abroad, as usual. I don't remember where. Switzerland? Somewhere Mother wanted to bring her furs. So no, I don't think it'll be an issue."

Dora never let this sadness show at school. She glossed over the loneliness of her parents' travels, and focused on the freedom their absence allowed her. It was different with Winnie. She supposed it was because she could commiserate somewhat. Both girls knew what it was like to miss their mother.

"Okay. Thank you, Dora."

"It's finally happening! I'm so excited for you, Winnie!"

Winnie smiled. "I'll see you tomorrow, okay?"

It felt wrong to be this excited when Scott's friend was missing. But tomorrow, Winnie would see Scott out of his lab coat. Out of the lab! They would walk down city streets together. The two of them would be partners out there in the world.

It felt like the beginning of something.

It felt like the beginning of something *wonderful*.

CHAPTER SIX

Winnie and Dora walked up bustling Second Ave. on Friday night, heading toward the soda shop where Winnie had agreed to meet Scott.

"Nervous about your date?" Dora asked.

"It's not a date," Winnie said, reminding Dora for the nth time that day. Reminding *herself*. "It's an investigation."

Dora's excitement about what she insisted on calling a date made it hard for Winnie to keep her own jitters in check, but Winnie was still glad she'd told her friend. There were so many things she had to keep inside. She didn't want to add another.

"I'll take that as a yes. But you shouldn't be! Just be yourself. How could Scott not adore you then?"

Winnie reached out and gave Dora's arm an affectionate squeeze. For as long as Winnie'd known her, Dora had always had a soft spot for the underdog.

"That's sweet," Winnie said, then looked around nervously. "But don't say his name so loud!" She knew it was silly to worry that a friend of his might overhear, but she couldn't help it.

Dora wrapped an arm around her shoulders. "You aren't really mad?"

"No. But how I feel—it isn't a joke to me."

Dora gave her a squeeze, then let her go. "I know, doll-baby."

But Dora didn't really know. How could she? Any boy would be thrilled to find out Dora liked him. As sweet as she was to say that Winnie would charm Scott just by being herself, there had always been people who had no problem disliking the authentic Winnie.

Dora couldn't understand because she had an ease with people that Winnie did not share, and beauty as the cherry on top. Winnie took time to warm up to people, and they to her. She knew her shyness sometimes made her seem cold, even judgmental, but being aware of this flaw didn't bring her any closer to being able to fix it. In fact, she wasn't sure it *could* be fixed—that it wasn't just part of who she was, for better or worse.

They reached the soda shop, and Winnie could see it was packed with the typical Friday night crowd. She paused outside the door.

"Well, I guess this is where you leave me," Winnie said, rocking back on her heels nervously. "Thanks for your help."

Dora laughed. "Not a chance!" she said. "If you think I'm leaving without even laying eyes on lover boy, you're crazy."

Winnie sighed. She knew Dora well enough to know there was no point arguing.

The girls walked into the soda shop and pushed through the crowd of people milling around, sipping drinks, to order at the counter.

"Chocolate egg cream for me," Dora told the soda jerk, who hurried off to make her drink without even checking to see if Winnie wanted anything.

This sort of response was so typical that it didn't even register with Dora, but Winnie always noticed.

"What are you going to have, Winnie?" Dora asked cheerfully. "Some fries? A chocolate malt?"

The mention of food made Winnie queasy. Although she had skipped dinner, her stomach was all raw, roiling nerves.

"I'm not hungry."

"Well, then don't do it for your stomach—do it for my ego. That little waist of yours does a number on it."

Winnie rolled her eyes. "Oh, sure—because *your* shape just drives the boys away."

Dora had curves like Mae West. She often got double takes from boys and grown men alike, and she knew it.

"Keep in mind, I have help," Dora said. "As Mother always says, you can't land a first-rate husband with a second-rate girdle!"

The soda jerk returned with Dora's drink. When she paid, he tilted his paper hat back to a jaunty angle and said, "Enjoy!" with a wink.

The girls turned their backs to the counter in search of a table, but none were free. A pair of boys at a corner table saw them scanning the shop. One got up and sauntered over. He was wearing a varsity sweater, and his blond hair was immaculately brushed and shiny with Brylcreem. Winnie took an immediate dislike to him.

"You're welcome to sit with us," he said, "if you want."

Winnie gave Dora's arm a little squeeze of protest. She was ignored.

"Well, sure!" Dora said, batting her lashes prettily. "That's awful nice of you."

They followed him back to his table. Dora slid into the booth after him, and Winnie sat across from her, next to a bored-looking boy who glanced over at her for a second and nodded an unenthusiastic hello. Apparently, he was as thrilled to be there as Winnie was.

"I'm Matty," the blond said, "and that's Roger."

"Dora, and Winnie."

"What's a girl like you doing out alone on a Friday night?" Matty asked Dora.

Winnie resisted the urge to point out that Dora hadn't exactly been *alone*.

"I figure any girls who need dates to have a good time must be pretty dull themselves," Dora said. "And we don't have any trouble having fun just the two of us, right, Winnie?"

Winnie nodded and glanced over at the clock behind the counter, cursing herself for being so nervous about being late to her rendezvous with Scott that she had instead arrived quite early.

"What, you bored?" the friend, Roger, asked her.

Winnie shrugged, aware that she was being a bit rude, but not really caring. She wished Dora had just left her to wait alone. No boys would have approached *her*, and she could have waited for Scott in peace.

"She's a quiet one, isn't she?"

"She can hear just fine, though," Winnie said icily, trying unsuccessfully to keep the slight German lilt from creeping into her voice.

"Say, you aren't a Kraut, are ya?" Roger asked suspiciously.

"I'm an American citizen," Winnie said haughtily, then reluctantly added, "who immigrated from Germany."

"So . . . yes?"

Winnie could think of no quick comeback, so she just glowered at him.

Dora gave Matty an annoyed look, and he quickly said, "Aw, leave her alone, Roge."

"I'm just going to go wait for Scott outside," Winnie said.

"Stay!" Dora said. "Please?"

"Yes," Matty echoed disinterestedly, "please stay."

Winnie shook her head and stood.

"Fine," Dora said, glaring at her. Then to the boys, she said, "It was nice meeting you." She paused for a moment—waiting for Matty to ask for her number, Winnie suspected—but the boys just nodded goodbye.

"Gee, thanks a lot," Dora said, once they were out on the street.

"They were obnoxious."

"Why can't you ever just laugh things off? A couple of decent guys want to spend time with us, and at the slightest misunderstanding you become Little Miss Sourpuss."

"You heard what his friend called me!"

"Your mind was made up before he said a peep. It would be nice if we could just have a good time sometimes, talk to a few boys without you frowning at them."

Winnie crossed her arms over her chest. Stuff guys like that. Dora could have them. Those were the kind of boys who'd smashed up Herr Wagner's store windows just because he was German, who tooled around Brooklyn in beat-up cars and threw cabbages at the immigrants in their telltale baggy clothes and heavy-soled shoes.

Still, she knew that Dora was right about one thing: her disinterest in those boys had little to do with being called a Kraut. Dora wanted a boy like Matty—or better yet, two or three of them—to take her to drive-ins and dances, and maybe to neck a little bit. Winnie wanted . . . well, she wasn't sure exactly what she wanted from Scott, but something different. Something more substantial.

She tried to find the words for her dissatisfaction. "The world's a huge place, filled with interesting people," Winnie said, "so why should I waste any time smiling at a couple of jerks?"

Dora sighed. "Couldn't you just be a little friendlier next time?" She nudged Winnie's arm and pulled a funny face. "A little nicer, just for me?"

For Dora, being friendly was the most natural thing in the world—it was like her dimples had formed from smiling at everything and everyone. It wasn't so easy for Winnie. She could no more fake friendliness than she could fake flu, which Brunhilde had *never* fallen for.

Winnie felt a sickening jump in her stomach, like the feeling when an elevator begins a speedy descent with a lurch, but much more intense. She tried to keep her face neutral as a split played itself out in her head. *I hate that, for me, being out with you is fun enough, but you're always scanning the crowd, looking for something better to come along,* Split-Winnie said.

In some other world, she was bold enough to confront Dora. But here, all Winnie did was nod and say, "Fine. I'll try to play nice next time you make us sit with a couple of dull strangers."

Dora chose to ignore Winnie's tone. She smiled brightly and said, "That's all I ask."

Yes, all Dora wanted was for Winnie to be the one making concessions yet again, Winnie thought, but of course, she said nothing.

IT WAS ONLY A FEW MORE MINUTES BEFORE SCOTT ARRIVED, BUT IT FELT like an eternity. When Winnie finally saw him walking toward them, she waved enthusiastically—too enthusiastically—and then quickly dropped her hand. His wool overcoat was unbuttoned, so Winnie could see that he was dressed rather formally too, in a gray suit and a crisp white shirt with a dark tie knotted at the neck. Were the department mixers at Columbia such a dressy affair, or had he taken extra care with his clothing for her?

It was intimidating to see Scott looking so handsome—dashing, even—but then he grinned at her, and the expression made him look like the boy she knew again. She smiled right back.

"Hello, Winnie," he said. "This must be Dora," he added, offering his hand. "It's a pleasure to meet you."

"Likewise," Dora said.

She gave Winnie a significant look—a look that plainly said *well done*. Winnie blushed a little, but she was pleased by Dora's obvious approval too.

"Were you going to join us for the party?" Scott asked uncertainly. "I'm only really allowed one guest, but I'm sure—"

Dora laughed. "Thank you, but no, that's quite all right."

Scott smiled in return. "It's not how most girls prefer to spend their Friday nights, is it? Surrounded by a bunch of pontificating professors."

"Pontificating professors! Our Winnie will love that, though, won't she?"

It seemed a horrifying overstep—that *our*—but Scott didn't laugh nervously or show discomfort of any kind. He just smiled, and said, "Hopefully!"

"We should probably . . ." Winnie said, trailing off.

"Yes," Scott agreed. "The party starts in less than an hour."

Dora pulled her into a hug. "I want you to tell me *everything*," she hissed in Winnie's ear.

When Dora pulled away, Winnie could have sworn Scott was grinning like he'd overheard.

She would *kill* Dora! She would simply kill her—if she didn't die of embarrassment first.

Scott offered Winnie his arm. "Shall we?"

Winnie tucked her hand in the crook of his elbow. She could feel the wiry muscle of his forearm even through the thick wool of his coat, hard under her fingertips. Any annoyance she felt toward Dora vanished. She suddenly wished it were spring, so Scott would be wearing a lighter coat.

But she shouldn't forget the true purpose of the evening—to learn more about James's whereabouts. If she let herself be distracted by her attraction to Scott, she might never figure out what had happened to his friend.

She imagined how grateful Scott would be when she helped him find James. Then, maybe the next time he invited her out, it really would be a date.

At least, she could hope.

CHAPTER SEVEN

Professor Hawthorn was the chair of the physics department at Columbia, so Winnie had expected him to have a nice home. But even years of friendship with Dora, who came from the kind of extreme wealth that left its imprint on every aspect of her life, hadn't prepared Winnie for this.

Hawthorn lived in one of the "Millionaire Row" townhouses on Fifth Avenue. When they entered, a butler—wearing a tuxedo complete with white gloves!—took their coats at the door. Winnie smoothed her borrowed dress nervously and looked around in a daze. The parquet floors were polished to a high gleam, and every wall was covered with oil paintings in ornate gold-painted frames. She'd never been in a house with such high ceilings. It felt like a church.

She wondered what was worshipped here.

"Wow. I didn't expect—all this," Winnie said, gesturing around vaguely.

"Hawthorn's family is in munitions. They did *very* well during the First World War."

Winnie was glad that Dora had insisted on dressing her. She was wearing a peach brocade cocktail dress with cap sleeves and little jeweled buttons. It wasn't really her color and was a bit too long as well, falling to mid-calf instead of right below the knee, but at least it was appropriately formal.

"You look lovely," Scott said.

Were her nerves that obvious?

"Thank you," Winnie said, then nervously added, "So do you. Um, handsome, I mean."

Scott smiled. "Say, do you mind if we get the formalities out of the way?"

Winnie nodded, although she wasn't sure what he meant.

Scott took her arm and began guiding her toward the center of the room. The purposefulness of his steps and the gentle pressure of his hand on her elbow gave Winnie a thrilling taste of what it would be like for the two of them to really be together. She felt a sudden pang of wanting so strong it almost frightened her. *This* was what it would be like to not be alone.

Scott led them toward a tall man with swan-white hair. He appeared to be holding court—was this Professor Hawthorn?

He noticed Scott and waved to him warmly.

If Winnie had been expecting a mustache-twirling, cinema-villain sort of man, she would have been sorely disappointed.

"Ah, Scott!" he exclaimed. "Glad you could make it. There

are some people here I'd like to introduce you to. But first, who's this?"

"Professor Hawthorn, this is Winnie Schulde. Winnie, Professor Hawthorn."

Hawthorn gave Winnie a courteous handshake. His grip was strong, but not aggressively so, and his fingers were dry and warm. So why did his touch send a nervous ripple down her spine?

She had expected Professor Hawthorn to be old, both because of his white hair and because of his university position, but the more she studied him, the younger he seemed. His shoulders were wide and straight beneath his fine suit coat, and his pale blue eyes were sharp. He was maybe ten years older than Father, but no more than that.

As Winnie returned Hawthorn's smile, she realized his own didn't reach his eyes. It made him look quite calculating.

Winnie swallowed awkwardly. "Nice to meet you, sir."

"You as well, my dear," Hawthorn said, then raised his brows. "Ah—Schulde? Could this sweet little thing be our dour Heinrich's daughter?"

The party was suddenly too loud, the lovely parlor too bright, as Winnie was pierced by anxiety: Would Hawthorn mention their meeting to Father?

No, no, no! If Father found out—

Winnie was hit by a lightning-quick flash of splinter.

"Heinrich?" splinter-Winnie asked innocently. "No. He's no relation."

Was the lie as obvious as it seemed to her?

It seemed unwise to lie to this shrewd man unless absolutely necessary. But how it went for her in that other world was a mystery. This splinter provided no glimpse of the outcome, unlike what she'd experienced the other night when she'd "met" James.

"Are you all right, Ms. Schulde?" Hawthorn asked, eyes narrowed with sharpened interest.

Winnie's heart stuttered as it skipped a beat, then caught up with a quick-thudding crash.

No one could ever tell when she experienced a splinter. Not even Father, who knew they happened.

No one.

As far as she was aware, no matter how involved the splinters were for her, they passed in an instant for the outside world, and Winnie had a lifetime's worth of practice making sure she never showed any surprise.

But Hawthorn seemed to suspect something was off. How?

"Thank you, sir, but I'm fine."

She felt anything but.

She met his icy eyes, and wondered if the bruises she'd seen on James's wrist came—or would come?—from him.

Something in her felt certain the answer was yes.

As the group surrounding Professor Hawthorn continued to chat, Winnie watched and took mental notes.

A waiter brought over a tray of champagne flutes. The fizz of tiny bubbles made each glass seem to sparkle enticingly.

Hawthorn must have noticed her looking. "Go ahead—take one," he said. "I'm sure your father wouldn't mind."

Was this a sly reference to Father's drinking? There was no way to be sure. Winnie grabbed one of the flutes by its delicate stem, although Father almost certainly *would* mind.

Father disliked Hawthorn, and this animosity was clearly mutual. Did they dislike each other because they were so alike?

Hawthorn was the only man she'd ever met who reminded her of her father. She had a lifetime of experience observing *him*. He was the original mystery in her life. She watched him closely. Anyone who lives with someone volatile must.

She'd realized long ago that Father was a powerful man. Authoritative, and deeply invested in logic and reason. But as she'd gotten older, Winnie discovered that was just a mask. Underneath, he was propelled by the chaos of grief. And Winnie had no problem understanding that.

But it would be a mistake to think this meant she understood Hawthorn.

TALK TURNED, AS IT ALWAYS DID, TO THE WAR EFFORT. EVERY PUBLIC conversation had to include a bit of war talk—penance they paid for being safe and warm while the *New York Times* shared grainy pictures of rain-soaked US soldiers besieged by night raids on the Solomon Islands, or headlines proclaiming that Congress would soon be lowering the draft age.

One man joked about his wife's recent attempt at war cake:

a milkless, eggless, butterless concoction which, by his telling, was about as edible as a brick.

"Did you know they're rationing coffee now too?" another professor said with a heavy sigh. "Or word is they're about to. Our cook said they were completely out of the stuff on her last grocery trip. I don't know how we're supposed to get any work done."

A few of the men chuckled, but the sound died when they caught sight of Hawthorn's face.

"Fighter pilots. Tank men. I suppose we should let them stay groggy so you can—what is it you're even working on now?" Hawthorn asked, face utterly blank.

Father did that too. His mood turned on a dime. Things were fine and then, all of a sudden, they weren't.

The professor who'd been speaking about rations visibly paled, and Winnie realized that these men didn't just respect Hawthorn. They feared him.

"Ra-radio waves," the professor stuttered, "how they—"

"And yet you haven't published on the topic in three years."

The man's mouth hung open for a moment. He looked like a gutted fish.

"I'm happy to skip my morning cup if it helps the Allies," a young professor—or perhaps another graduate student—cut in eagerly.

Hawthorn met this bootlicking with disdain.

"We should all be doing more than that. But I suppose that's all some are capable of."

He gave the coffee-loving professor one last disparaging look before turning his attention to Scott. Winnie had a feeling that man wouldn't be a professor at Columbia University much longer.

Had *that* been James's fate? Some small misstep, then dismissal from the university by Hawthorn?

"Now, Scott, I wanted to introduce you to Erwin—Erwin Schrödinger, that is. He's visiting to give next week's lecture. Where has that man gotten off to?" Hawthorn asked, scanning the room. "Ah, well, there's Fermi. I bet he can help me track Erwin down."

Even in the midst of Winnie's concern about Hawthorn and about James, she couldn't help but be starstruck. Fermi! Schrödinger! Both men were Nobel Prize winners. Father spoke about his colleagues only to complain about departmental politics, so Winnie hadn't quite realized that the same people who were famous names to her were familiar faces to Father.

Hawthorn motioned to Fermi to invite him over, but the man pretended it was a wave, waved back, and kept walking.

Hawthorn's eyes narrowed. "My god, he's got a big head. We welcomed him after Italy became . . . inhospitable. You'd think he'd show more gratitude. If his bomb's a success, he's going to be insufferable."

Scott blinked a few times in surprise. "I didn't realize that project was common knowledge, sir," Scott said, a hint of disapproval in his voice.

"What, the Manhattan Project? Oh, it's terribly secret, of course! But surely there are no secrets *here*," Hawthorn said, with a slyness that made Winnie worry. Did Hawthorn already know that Scott was suspicious of him?

Winnie finished her champagne in one anxious gulp, stifling a cough when the bubbles tickled her throat.

"The whole department has been abuzz about it, 'top secret' or not," Hawthorn continued. He grabbed another delicate flute of champagne off the tray of a tuxedoed waiter. Hawthorn was obviously concerned with the war efforts, but apparently didn't buy into the idea of loose lips sinking ships.

To Winnie's surprise, Hawthorn silently handed the champagne to her, exchanging it for her empty glass. It was a courteous move—ah, what a considerate host—but Winnie wondered if the gesture masked another message: *You've captured my interest. I'm watching you, girl—even when it seems like I'm not.*

"Ms. Schulde, I'm sure your father must have said something about it to you, even," Hawthorn said.

Winnie shook her head. "No, sir. He hasn't mentioned anything."

"Ah, well, the government has been recruiting the university's finest minds, but perhaps Schulde wasn't invited."

"Professor Schulde's own research keeps him busy enough," Scott said briskly, and Winnie felt a flush of warmth at how quick he was to defend Father. "Besides, he would never work on a weapon."

Hawthorn gave a slight raise of an eyebrow. "You'd think a German would be more eager to show he's on the right side.

Although the idea of an atomic bomb *is* rather crass. Like using a telescope to pound in a nail."

Scott frowned. "But I thought your work was related?"

What was Scott doing? Hawthorn had just dressed down a professor for complaining about coffee. Surely he wouldn't tolerate a student interrogating him!

Hawthorn smiled—a genuine-seeming one this time. Scott must know what he was doing. "Only tangentially. My own work is much more—" Hawthorn looked into the middle distance and scratched his chin, pretending to think. "Esoteric," he concluded smugly.

Scott waited a moment, an expectant look on his face, but if he was hoping Hawthorn would say more about Project Nightingale, he was disappointed. Hawthorn was happy to chitchat about other classified projects, but it seemed he was tight-lipped about his own.

"I hope to learn more about your work someday," Scott said finally, smiling faintly.

"I'm sure you will," Hawthorn said.

Winnie couldn't tell if she was imagining the edge in his voice.

"So, what do you make of him?" Scott asked, once the two of them had left Hawthorn to "go mingle."

"He seems clever—and very impressed by his own cleverness. I don't trust him."

"You sound like Professor Schulde," Scott said with a grin. "Your father can't stand Hawthorn, and—as I'm sure you've guessed—the feeling is mutual."

Winnie remembered—Father had called him a "vulture."

"Hawthorn seems pretty keen on you, though."

Scott shrugged. "He's always seemed to like me well enough—probably because liking me annoys your father."

"You have a theory about what he's working on?"

Scott nodded. "I'll tell you my suspicions after the party— although you'll probably think I'm crazy," he said with a smile. "I don't want to bias your observations now, though."

"Scott!" a student called, waving at them from across the room. "Come settle a debate for us!"

Scott waved back. "In a minute."

"You go ahead and talk to them," Winnie said. "It'll give me a chance to eavesdrop."

"You'll be okay on your own?"

"I'll be fine," she said firmly. "It's what I'm here for, right?"

He took her hand and pressed it.

"Not just that."

The intensity in his gaze made Winnie's heart quicken, but before she could respond, he kissed her hand lightly, then dropped it and walked off to join his friends. Winnie was absolutely dizzy with glee—and more determined than ever to prove herself worthy of the faith he'd put in her.

What did the risk of Father's anger matter, when this feeling was the reward?

CHAPTER EIGHT

Winnie scanned the room. Although some professors were barely older than their graduate students, it was easy for Winnie to tell them apart. The students' clothes were generally shabbier, and they had a sort of glazed look. The combination of limitless refills of decent champagne and their first encounter with obscene wealth, Winnie supposed.

Columbia had no female students or professors, so all the women in attendance were either professors' wives or students' dates. There were small clusters of serious debate around the room; that was where Winnie wanted to be. But women didn't seem to be part of those conversations. Did they mind? Surely, some of them must, just like Winnie would. Smiling and nodding and sipping a drink while the men talked was fine for a night. But for a lifetime?

It wouldn't be like that at Barnard, which made her excited once more for the prospect, but she wished attending Columbia were an option for her. Barnard offered an amazing education, no doubt—one parallel to what the boys had at Columbia—but it was still separate. There would be no Fermi there, no Nobel Prize–winning guest lecturers like Schrödinger.

Well, for tonight at least, she was part of the Ivy League—as bystander, if not participant. Winnie began to drift through the room with feigned casualness, pausing here or there to grab a canape or gaze intently at a piece of art, all while listening to the conversations that swirled around her. For once, she was glad to blend into the background.

Winnie overheard plenty of the sort of sycophancy that Father complained about. There were students bending over backward to compliment their professors' latest articles, and associate professors congratulating the tenured ones for the grants they'd just secured (while not so subtly hinting that they would be great assets to the work). But there were also vibrant discussions about recent and controversial scientific developments, which Winnie had to remind herself not to get sucked into, since they had nothing to do with Hawthorn's secret project or whatever might have happened to James.

Then she heard a birdcall—or rather, a poor imitation of one. It might be nothing, but Hawthorn's project was code-named Nightingale . . . bird calls *could* be related. She looked around for the source of the sound and saw two students stationed near an hors d'oeuvres table, chatting and eating. Winnie got a bit closer, then bent over and began to fiddle with the ankle strap on one of her shoes to give her an excuse to linger.

"You do a good songbird," one of the students said, "but I think you meant to say *cuckoo, cuckoo!*"

The other laughed. "I know, I know—but if it's *that* crazy, why is the government footing the bill?"

This cemented Winnie's suspicion that the two students were discussing Project Nightingale. She hoped they didn't notice her there, pretending to fasten her shoe for much longer than necessary.

The first student gave a dismissive wave of his hand. "It's a bribe they threw him, so he wouldn't get too fussy about Fermi getting the Manhattan Project—and push for them to move off campus."

"Well, you have to admit Hawthorn has had some pretty amazing successes." The student glanced around the room meaningfully, as if each Tiffany lamp were as impressive as a Nobel Prize.

"This stuff? Family money," the other said. "And a few lucky patents," he admitted grudgingly.

Although Winnie was no fan of Hawthorn's, she found herself irritated by this student. Father had often told her that any good scientist must be a natural skeptic, which this young man certainly was, but Father had also taught her that great discoveries required a leap of faith. It was easier to be a critic than an innovator.

"Excuse me, do you need some help with your shoe?" the student who seemed to be a fan of Professor Hawthorn's asked.

Damn, she'd lingered too long!

"Oh, no, thank you—I think I've got it now," Winnie said, rebuckling her strap and standing up so quickly it made her dizzy for a moment.

The student who'd spoken to her didn't look at all suspicious—but of course, why would he be? Who could possibly imagine that she was there as a spy of sorts, or that she'd waste any time listening to students' chitchat even if she were? Winnie decided he would be the perfect person to probe for a bit of information. Scott probably would have heard any gossip they might share, but she might have a fresh perspective on it. That was Scott's hope, right?

"I was wondering," Winnie asked, "if you've seen my friend James anywhere? A friend of a friend's, really—of Scott Hamilton's. I met James at a party a few months ago, and with Scott off somewhere, well, James is the only other person I know here . . ." Winnie trailed off with a frown.

"I'm sorry, but no." The boy furrowed his brow. "Actually, I don't think I've seen him around lately."

"Oh, *James?*" the other student said, making some sort of limp gesture with his wrist that Winnie couldn't exactly parse, but which was clearly derogatory. "Didn't he drop out?"

"Did he?" Winnie asked, feigning surprise. "What a shame! Any idea why?"

The snide student opened his mouth to speak, but his friend silenced him with a sharp look and said, "I hadn't heard that James left, but it *is* a rigorous program. Sometimes it gets to be too much for people."

"I suppose Professor Hawthorn will be looking for a new research assistant, then," Winnie said.

"More like a new *subject*," the mocking student said, then ducked his eyes like he immediately realized he'd said too much.

"Look, there's Professor Rutledge," the other said nervously. "We should probably go chat him up a bit, eh?"

They walked off quickly, leaving Winnie once more alone in the crowd, head spinning.

Had that student really been serious in suggesting that Hawthorn was experimenting on James? That kind of ethical violation could potentially cost Hawthorn his reputation, his funding—even his job.

Although, experimenting on a student was perhaps more ethical than experimenting on a daughter. And Winnie knew firsthand that was a risk at least one scientist was willing to take . . .

Physics was the study of matter and energy, which were both inanimate. By definition, living subjects were almost never involved in any type of physics research. Some experiments dealt with the impact of a human observer—what it meant that all discoveries were viewed through a human lens—but Winnie couldn't think of a single line of inquiry in the field of physics that used human *subjects*.

Except her father's work, of course.

But whatever Hawthorn's work turned out to be, if the rumors were true and Hawthorn had been experimenting on a student who was now missing, then Hawthorn's work was a danger that belonged in a category all its own.

Winnie considered finding Professor Hawthorn's personal office so she could snoop through his notes, but decided against it. If she were caught, Scott would be implicated too. It wasn't worth the risk of Scott being dismissed from Columbia, especially since she might not find anything about James. Plus, Hawthorn seemed like a man intelligent enough not to leave incriminating papers lying around.

Winnie noticed that the conversation of one of the clusters of men standing near her was becoming heated and drifted closer to hear what they were discussing out of sheer curiosity—she wanted to know what contentious project or recent article in *Scientific American* was causing such a stir.

But it turned out the men weren't discussing science at all.

"The law's quite clear," said one man—a professor, Winnie assumed, based on his age. "Those bleeding-heart attorneys lost their case."

A student laughed. "Can you believe that man thought he could get a doctor to slice up his face and pass for Spanish! How stupid does he think people are?"

Winnie's heart jumped in her throat. She was instantly furious. They were talking about—*laughing* about—the Japanese internment.

Earlier that year, President Roosevelt had signed an

executive order decreeing that anyone with Japanese ancestry had to relocate to secure camps for the duration of the war. They were potential traitors, all of them. Even the ones who were naturalized citizens, just like Winnie. Even the ones who had been born in America! One of those American citizens had refused the order, been arrested, and sued.

He'd lost.

"It isn't settled yet," another professor said gravely. "The ACLU is appealing the case."

Winnie loved that he didn't even deign to look at the student who'd made the cruel joke about the plastic surgery the man had endured in his attempt to avoid arrest.

"Where they'll lose again," the first professor concluded bluntly. "Look, it's not like the Japanese are being sent to prison. They like to keep to themselves anyway, and this way we're all safe. You don't want another attack, do you?"

Winnie couldn't believe that a professor in the physics department at Columbia—a *scientist*—could have such a small-minded way of looking at the world. She knew she should bite her tongue, but just couldn't, especially since she had the bravery of anonymity.

"We'd better lock up Professor Fermi too, then, don't you think?"

Much to Winnie's gratification, the man couldn't have looked more shocked if she'd walked up to him and thrown her drink in her face.

"Excuse me?" he sputtered.

"Well, he's Italian, even if he did leave. They're no allies of ours, right? And what about me? I was born in Germany."

The man just glared at her.

"Or me?" said a man who Winnie hadn't noticed earlier. He had a muted accent—German, most likely, or maybe Austrian.

"Of course not," the professor said, in a much more respectful tone than he would have used were he responding to just her. "The Japanese are a completely different matter, obviously."

Winnie knew this was the common consensus, but it wasn't just because Japan had been the only member of the Axis to stage an attack on American soil.

It was because they looked different.

Winnie wasn't different in a way that showed, but she was different nonetheless. She knew she was lucky she had the option to hide. Her heritage didn't give itself away at a glance, and her ability—which was stranger and potentially more threatening to the government than any nationality—was invisible. So she couldn't help but sympathize with anyone who was treated cruelly for something outside their control.

Although Winnie could see from the looks on their faces that she'd done nothing to actually change any minds, she was pleased to have at least deflated the conversation. Perhaps, if she was really lucky, she had soured the night for the bigots in the group.

The small group of men broke apart then and rejoined the general flow of the party.

Well, all the men except one. The professor with the accent stayed behind. Winnie was glad—she wanted to thank him. She knew that his support had gotten her a more civil treatment than she might have received otherwise. But he spoke before she could.

"I wouldn't expect to see a beauty like you unattended at a party."

The man smiled at her wolfishly, and it took Winnie a moment to comprehend that this stranger who was old enough to be her father—older even!—was making a pass at her. She couldn't believe his nerve! So much for her new ally.

But the more Winnie looked at him, the more familiar he became. He was perhaps fifty and had a compact build, just a few scant inches taller than Winnie herself. His dark hair was pushed back from his forehead in one thick wave, and he had a straight mouth framed by parentheses that had likely been dimples when he was younger, but were now rather stately grooves. The overall effect was a handsome one, and he looked like someone who could play a scientist on film, not just in real life. Was that where she knew him from? Could the old letch be an actor? It would be odd for an actor to be at a physics department party, but Winnie had no doubt that Hawthorn mixed with a tony set.

It was the distinctive, perfectly round spectacles perched on the man's hawkish nose that finally made his identity click for Winnie—that, and his accent. Yes, she had seen him before—in photo spreads in *Scientific American*, *Popular Science*, and even

Time magazine. He was one of the most well-known scientists in the world—one of the Nobel Prize–winning scientists she had been surprised to hear Hawthorn reference earlier.

This was the famous Erwin Schrödinger.

But that didn't change Winnie's initial impression that he also seemed like a creep.

CHAPTER NINE

"Who are you," Erwin Schrödinger asked, "and what sort of idiot did you come here with, that would leave you alone?"

Winnie took a step back but tried to keep the revulsion from showing on her face. He could be useful to her investigation. The way that Hawthorn had smugly called Schrödinger "Erwin," like the world-renowned physicist was an antique pocket watch he could pull out, polish, and show off, made Winnie think it likely that he would have told Schrödinger all about Project Nightingale in an attempt to impress him. She would need to be careful how she went about things, but Schrödinger seemed like he might be a promising person to ask about Nightingale.

"Nice to meet you, *Herr* Schrödinger," Winnie said, offering him her hand. Formality seemed the best tack to take with such a man. She didn't want to encourage him *too* much. "My name is Winifred Schulde."

His hand went limp in her own, and his smarmy grin was replaced by an expression of shock. After an awkward moment, he said, "I'm sorry—Winifred Schulde?"

Winnie nodded, and tried to think of what she'd done to make him so instantly and intensely uncomfortable.

"And your mother—her name is Astrid Keller?"

Winnie frowned. "How do you know my mother?"

Schrödinger's eyes scanned her face intently, but although his focus on her was intense, the sexual charge was now gone.

"Oh, ah, from the University of Zurich," he said. "I was her professor there, for a time."

"Then you must know my father too. He's a professor at Columbia, although he isn't here tonight," Winnie said, hoping this detail would ensure that he wouldn't make a pass at her again. Surely the man wouldn't try to seduce a colleague's daughter.

"Heinrich Schulde?" she prompted.

Schrödinger was quiet for a long time, and Winnie assumed he was having trouble remembering her father—although he'd remembered her mother easily enough, based on Father's last name.

"Well, yes, of course," he finally said.

Schrödinger continued studying her face. He must have picked up on how uncomfortable this made her, because he suddenly said, "I'm sorry—it's just that you don't look much like her."

Winnie doubted that he meant any offense, but it hit on an

old hurt. She'd spent years unsuccessfully trying to find a trace of her mother's beautiful face in her own.

"But I must," Winnie said, "because I look nothing like my father."

Schrödinger smiled faintly. "No, you do. I see the resemblance."

Winnie felt a growing unease with this discussion of her mother, which surprised her. The day before, she'd been poring over her mother's old school notes, famished for any bit of information. Now, she was face-to-face with someone who'd actually known her mother—aside from Father, the only person in the entire country who had! And unlike Father, he seemed willing to discuss her. But more than anything, Winnie wanted to change the subject. Luckily, she had a more useful line of conversation in mind: Project Nightingale.

Winnie was no expert at charming men, but she'd been watching Dora do it for years. That had to be worth *something*.

Winnie tried to channel Dora as she put on what she hoped was her winningest smile. "Say, could you help me solve a mystery?" she asked.

Schrödinger blinked quickly and adjusted his glasses. "Perhaps."

To her surprise, he seemed to be on guard. Winnie was constantly underestimated. It would be just her luck if the one time she actually wanted someone to think she was nothing but a silly girl, they took her seriously! She tried to mimic the look Dora used when she wanted something from a boy, tilting her chin and trying to keep her expression harmlessly eager.

"Hawthorn mentioned this government project he's working on, but wouldn't say what they're doing. My"—Winnie considered referring to Scott as her boyfriend, but that felt like overstepping, even in service of this investigation—"friend is hoping to work for him. Do you have any idea what this Project Nightingale is all about? It will be easier for him to impress Hawthorn if he knows which topics to mention."

Schrödinger looked relieved. What had he been afraid she might ask?

"Well, I can tell you," Schrödinger said, laughing and shaking his head, "but I don't know if you'll believe it. Are you familiar with multiverse theory—the idea that this world is one of many parallel realities?"

Dread twisted her stomach. If Hawthorn was interested in multiverse theory, he would be *very* interested in her, and he didn't seem like a safe man to interest. But that would be an issue only if he found out about her ability. Father certainly wouldn't give up that information, and neither would she.

Winnie nodded her head and tried to keep her expression neutral. "I've heard of it," she said, "but isn't that pretty fringe?"

"Oh, it is! But if nothing else, wartime does encourage innovation."

Winnie didn't want to seem overly curious, but she'd already come this far—she had to know the specifics. Was Hawthorn trying to build a splinter device too, or something else? Should she tell Father about it? She didn't think he would take the news well.

"What, exactly, is Hawthorn trying to do?" Winnie asked.

He cocked his head at her, looking rather like some type of sharp-eyed bird of prey behind his spectacles. Did she seem too eager?

"Hawthorn is trying to develop a method of transportation between realities," he answered finally. "An interdimensional travel machine."

Talk about outlandish! Trying to travel between realities was a bold—and in Winnie's opinion, likely impossible—goal, and stupidly dangerous. If the machine weren't manned, how could you ever know where it had gone, or get it back? And if a person were to make the trip, who could anticipate the impact it would have on the human body—not to mention the impact it might have on the world you entered?

Of course, what did Hawthorn care for the danger, if he wasn't the one making the trip. She imagined that was where an eager lab assistant came in handy.

Poor James! Winnie could tolerate being an occasional specimen—barely—but only because it was Father's experiment. Had James gotten involved of his own free will, or was it possible that he was locked in a lab at that very moment, being experimented on, poked and prodded? It was an awful scenario to imagine, and Winnie could imagine it all too well.

Or . . .

. . . What if Hawthorn had completed his machine already?

What if James was missing because he was trapped in some other world?

But that was crazy. This was a government project. Surely there must be oversight. If James was involved, even as a subject, it was much more likely that he was out of communication with Scott because he had to keep his work classified, not because he was being kept prisoner or had—beyond all odds—crossed the barrier between realities.

"You know," Schrödinger said, "it was your mother who first led me to believe there might be something to all this talk of alternate realities."

This revelation startled Winnie away from her worries about James.

"Really? Why?"

"She had quite"—he paused as if to think—"*unique* ideas on the topic. That's what first attracted her to the field of physics, in fact—odd study, for a girl. I wonder if that's something she's shared with you? Those . . . ideas?"

If he was implying what Winnie *thought* he was implying—

No.

She couldn't think about that now.

The last thing she wanted was for Hawthorn to find out that she was a girl with any "ideas" about multiverse theory.

"We didn't talk about things like that," Winnie said firmly, which was true. Hopefully that would make it sound more convincing. "I was only seven when she died."

Apparently, it was Schrödinger's turn to be surprised.

"Astrid is dead?"

Winnie nodded. "She died in a car accident, back in Germany."

Schrödinger stood there blinking at her for a moment, like he couldn't quite absorb what she'd said.

Why was he so upset? Winnie's mother had been his student, but that was a lifetime ago, and they must not have kept in touch after she left school, or he would have known about her death before now.

"But if your mother's dead, who's been taking care of you?"

Winnie was confused by the question. "Well—my father, of course."

Schrödinger frowned. Could he could tell that although Winnie hadn't lied, it wasn't the full truth either?

Sure, her needs were met, but no one cared for her like Mama had.

"I knew Astrid was pregnant when she left Zurich," Schrödinger said suddenly, "but I wasn't sure a baby came of it until tonight."

What else would come of a pregnancy but a baby, Winnie wondered? Then she felt stupid. She was far from worldly, but even she knew that not all pregnancies came to term—some due to the mother's intervention.

Why had Schrödinger thought Mama might not want to keep her? She had been married, and in love. Unless . . .

Wait.

Mama had gone to school in Switzerland, then she and

Father had moved to Germany and married after his graduation. If Schrödinger was right, and Mama was already pregnant when she left Switzerland . . .

Winnie tried to make sense of it all.

She had always assumed Mama didn't finish her degree because she wanted to get married, and Father was done with school. But no. She'd had to leave because she got pregnant.

Winnie felt a twinge of shame in her chest, which she immediately tried to stamp out. So, she had been conceived out of wedlock. So what? Her parents had married before she was born. It was no business of hers, really, and certainly no business of Schrödinger's, nor anyone else's.

"If I'd known," Schrödinger said, "when Astrid passed, I would have . . ." He trailed off, shaking his head. "Well, I don't actually know what I would have done." He gave her a searching look. "Heinrich—he does take good care of you, though?"

Winnie nodded mutely. She felt her breathing pick up speed. She stared at Schrödinger for a minute more, trying to process everything, the meaning behind his words.

What he was telling her, she didn't want to know. But she couldn't un-hear what he was saying, and she could no longer ignore his eyes. Winnie had finally realized where she recognized Schrödinger from—and it wasn't just the odd magazine photo here and there.

Winnie saw bits and pieces of him every time she looked in the mirror.

"Does he know?" Winnie said, her voice sounding strangled in her own ears.

Schrödinger looked at her thoughtfully. He must be trying to decide which was better, the truth or a lie.

What criteria could he possibly use? Was it better if Father had no idea, and now she had to keep this secret, or if he'd known the whole time and never told her? It was awful, either way.

"Yes, he knows," Schrödinger said finally, laughing humorlessly. "Heinrich had words with me about it."

"And he married her anyway?"

Schrödinger gave her a gentle look. "I imagine he married her because of it."

"Because you wouldn't," Winnie said, practically spitting the words.

"Well, I couldn't. I was married already, and besides—Astrid had no interest in me."

Winnie just stood there, eyebrows raised. No interest in him! How could he say that while she stood right there, eloquent evidence to the contrary?

"I don't know how to explain this," Schrödinger said with a sigh. "Winifred, my dear, you're very young."

Each moment that passed, this shocking new knowledge sunk in a little deeper, becoming worse and worse. Winnie took a shaky breath, trying to calm herself. It didn't work.

"I'm nearly the age she was when—when you knew each other. I'm old enough!"

"Well, then maybe you can understand that there are things young women do sometimes not out of love, but . . ."

Here he trailed off, but he gestured around the room.

Winnie couldn't believe his gall. "You're saying it was for her career."

Schrödinger shrugged. "Look at me, then look at Heinrich. I think I would be flattering myself to say otherwise."

"That's disgusting."

"Perhaps. But that's the world."

If that was the world, she wanted no part of it.

Winnie looked at the others in the room. What was the point of all this? For Hawthorn to show off his fancy house? For underlings to laugh too loudly at their superiors' jokes? If Schrödinger was to be believed, Mama had made a terrible trade, trying to be part of this world—only to end up leaving the university with a pregnancy instead of a degree.

It all repulsed her. Was that how Father felt about it too? Was that why he stayed away from events like this? Perhaps she was his daughter in that, if nothing else.

This interaction with Schrödinger—this revelation—was *this* why Father wouldn't let her come? He'd wanted to protect her. Either from Schrödinger, or from men like him.

She had been conceived by the sort of man young women needed to be kept away from.

She felt like she was about to be sick.

Schrödinger took an elegant silver card holder out of his

pocket and clicked it open. "Here," he said, handing her a business card. "The world is hard on idealists like you and Heinrich. Even harder during wartime. If you need something, ask. I'm not a wealthy man, but I'm comfortable. I'll do what I can."

Winnie accepted the card. Embossed letters on heavy paper stock. She tucked it into her evening bag mechanically. She imagined the card itself was more substantial than the offer. The way he said it—what did he think she might need? A new dress? A trip to Europe?

The things she needed weren't the sort of things that could be bought.

It didn't matter. She didn't want his help anyway. She never wanted to see him again.

Schrödinger grabbed Winnie's hand and tried to look into her eyes, but she refused to meet his gaze. He put a finger to one of her earlobes. "I gave these pearls to your mother, you know," he said.

He took a breath as if he were preparing to say more, but Winnie didn't wait. She pulled her hand away and walked off without another word.

Had Schrödinger thought about Mama at all over the years? Had he thought about their child even once?

What did it mean to be the daughter of such a man?

. . . and what did it mean to be her mother's daughter?

She thought about what he'd said about Mama's "ideas" about multiverse theory.

How very little Winnie knew about what she might or might not have inherited.

And Father. Was she still his daughter too?

He had his flaws, but at least he had integrity. He paid Scott, not in extra credit or favoritism or vague assurances that he was part of important work—in *money*. Father would never use one of his students like Schrödinger had used Mama.

Thinking about Father now made her feel sick. She didn't know how she was supposed to face him.

Winnie had often wondered how he could treat his daughter the way he did, and now she knew. It was simple. She wasn't his daughter.

She'd solved a mystery that evening after all.

And she'd never felt worse.

CHAPTER TEN

When Winnie found Scott, he was standing next to Hawthorn again, talking to a group of professors. Winnie didn't dare approach. She felt sick. She didn't trust herself to act normal. Finally, Scott glanced over at her and she must have looked awful, because he immediately excused himself and came over.

"Winnie, what's wrong? Are you okay?"

"Could we go?" she asked. "I'm sorry."

He nodded. "I'll go say goodbye to our host, make some excuse—meet me by the door?"

Winnie was so glad Scott was Scott. He didn't immediately press her for details.

She went and got the butler to bring their coats. Once they were outside, away from the light and chatter, away from Hawthorn, away, thank god, from Schrödinger, Winnie felt like she could breathe.

She and Scott walked down the street in silence. After about a block, he stopped, looked at her, and began, "Winnie—"

She cut him off with a shake of her head. Winnie knew he wanted her to tell him what was wrong, but she wasn't ready.

Even so, there was one thing she'd found out from Schrödinger that she could share.

"I learned what Hawthorn is working on," she said, pleased that she sounded almost normal. "Project Nightingale is trying to build a device that can transport people between alternate realities."

Scott considered a moment, then nodded. "There's always been gossip about Hawthorn's interest in multiverse theory, so that makes sense."

"You're not as surprised as I expected. What does it have to do with building a bomb? I don't see the military application."

"Don't you? An interdimensional travel machine would be the ultimate bunker. If the government has one group of scientists working to make an atomic bomb—a weapon with the potential to devastate this planet—wouldn't they want a second group working on the escape hatch?"

It made sense, but a terrible kind of sense. She didn't want to believe it.

Winnie frowned. "I doubt any machine Hawthorn makes could transport many people."

"Most lifeboats don't," Scott said. "I doubt Hawthorn cares about any of that, though. He probably just wants to see if it can be done."

Scott seemed to think this interest of Hawthorn's was just happenstance, but he didn't know that there were people who *knew* alternate realities were fact, not theory. People like her. Were there others?

Was Hawthorn one of them?

Was that why he seemed to study her with extra care when she'd seen that splinter? Was he able to recognize that something was happening behind her eyes, though no one else could?

The prospect made her feel obscenely exposed. Like she'd been cut open, pink organs pulled out for Hawthorn to play with.

If he *did* know . . . what would he do?

Winnie gave herself a sharp mental slap. She couldn't give in to panic now. There was still more to tell Scott.

"I also heard a rumor—" Winnie began, then stopped. She swallowed nervously—she didn't think this would be easy for Scott to hear. "One of your classmates insinuated that James wasn't just Hawthorn's assistant, but the subject of his experiments somehow."

Maybe it was James who saw splinters, she thought suddenly. That could explain why she felt such a kinship with him in the splinter she'd seen.

Scott clenched his teeth and nodded. "He never told me that himself—not outright. But I think it's true." He gave her a gentle look. "I know it must be shocking," he said. "It's a terrible thing, but not all scientists share the same ethics. Some aren't above experimenting on humans."

Winnie felt a wave of shame on Father's behalf—and some shame herself. After all, she let him.

But why would James allow his professor to experiment on him? How could you do that, unless it was for someone you—

And then Winnie suddenly understood the mocking gesture that student had made.

"Is James homosexual?"

"Does that matter?" Scott asked sharply. He shoved his glasses up his nose and jutted out his chin, as if daring her to voice some disgust. "Do you think that means I shouldn't be his friend? Or that I shouldn't try to find him? Or do you think the same thing as everyone else in the department—that with a 'character flaw' like that, it makes perfect sense that he would drop out midsemester, tell no one, and just disappear?"

"No! Scott, of course not!"

Winnie's only experience with homosexuality was as an accusation giggling girls lobbed in the locker room when somebody didn't keep their eyes down while changing. She knew she was supposed to find it unnatural and repulsive, but she certainly hadn't chosen the way she felt about Scott, and she assumed there wasn't much choosing for anyone else either. Why condemn people for something out of their control?

Besides, how hypocritical would Winnie be if she judged someone for being different?

"I'm sorry," Scott said. "I shouldn't have snapped at you like that. It's just—people can be awful. I should have known you wouldn't be."

"It's all right—I understand. And normally I wouldn't think it was any of my business, but it seems pertinent."

"Why?"

"Because it makes him vulnerable."

Winnie thought about Schrödinger. And she thought about her mother.

Was James taken less seriously than the other students, like her mother had been—and forced to compromise himself as a result, like her mother had? Was that why he agreed to be Hawthorn's subject? Or was there something more still?

"Do you think he and Hawthorn were having an affair?" she asked.

Scott looked surprised for a moment, considered, then shook his head. "No, I really don't think so. Hawthorn has always treated him almost paternally. Why do you ask?" Scott frowned. "Winnie," he asked softly, "what happened in there to upset you?"

This conversation had been a welcome distraction from her earlier one with Schrödinger, but now that all came rushing back. Mama had slept with Schrödinger—and he was Winnie's real father. She had to tell Father that she knew, didn't she? But how?

"I—" Winnie began, but immediately faltered. "I had a—an upsetting conversation—with Erwin Schrödinger," she finished limply.

Then she burst into tears.

"That son of a—" Scott shook his head furiously, hands

clenched tight into fists. "Winnie, I'm so sorry. He has a terrible reputation. I shouldn't have left you to fend for yourself. I really didn't think anyone would bother you there, but I should have known better. Would you believe that once, at Princeton, he—"

"Stop!" Winnie said, arms fluttering up in a half-hearted attempt to block her ears. It was already bad enough. She couldn't bear to hear an inventory of Schrödinger's debauchery. What would that say about her mother—or about her?

Scott gently placed his hand on her forearm. Suddenly, she was tired of all that lay unspoken between them, of understandings that might or might not be one-sided. Winnie didn't want there to be any secrets between her and Scott—any distance between them at all. She resolved to tell him about the splinters too, sometime when there wasn't so much else they needed to talk about.

For now, Winnie took a deep breath. "Schrödinger told me he's my father."

Scott just stared at her. "What? No. He can't—"

Winnie stopped him with a look.

"It's true, Scott. I'm certain. It's awful, and it's true."

"Oh, Winnie, I just—I don't know what to say. I knew Schrödinger was Professor Schulde's mentor at the University of Zurich, and I knew Professor Schulde hated him, but I could never have guessed the reason."

"It wasn't an affair," she said quickly, through her tears. "It was before Mama and Father were married, I mean."

She didn't want Scott to think her mother was like that,

that she would cheat on her husband—but maybe that *was* what her mother was like. What did Winnie know? Before tonight, if someone had asked her to describe her mother, Winnie might have said she was smart, and certainly that she was pretty, but all she really had were a child's impressions of Mama as warmth and safety and all that was good and right. Her memories of that time were there but blurred, like a watercolor. Flat. Mama wasn't really a whole person to her after all these years, but an idea—an idea that was now in flux. She didn't really know her mother. And since Mama was dead, she never could.

Winnie sniffled indelicately and wiped her nose on her wrist because there was nowhere else to wipe it. She was surprised to find she wasn't mortified after breaking down in front of Scott like she thought she'd be. In fact, she felt a bit lighter.

"I'm sorry I made you leave early," she said.

"My god, don't give it another thought! And you managed to confirm what Nightingale is all about—that's huge."

She wished that were all she'd found out.

"But, Winnie," Scott continued, "right now I'm more concerned about you. Are you okay? That's just—it's such a shock. I can't even imagine."

She paused a moment, then nodded, even though she didn't feel remotely okay. At least she wasn't in danger—real, physical danger—like James seemed to be.

She didn't know anything about Hawthorn's experiments, but how awful it must be for him! Winnie, at least, had the consolation of knowing that Father would never allow her to be seriously hurt by their experiments. She wasn't just a subject to him. She was his—

That *was* how he thought of her, wasn't it—as a daughter, even though they didn't share blood? Winnie suddenly wondered if she would still have a home if she said no the next time Father demanded she join him for an experiment.

Was there any cage more effective than family? No lock needed. No chains either. It was a cage she carried inside her and feared she always would. She couldn't ever say no to Father now.

"Can we just go home?"

She had never been more tired.

"Of course," Scott said. "Are you going to tell your father what you found out?"

Winnie nodded.

"But not tonight."

THE HOUSE WAS DARK WHEN WINNIE RETURNED HOME. BRUNHILDE would have left the foyer light on for her. Father must have forgotten she was out and turned it off.

She made her way up the center staircase. A sliver of light under the library door was the only sign of life. Father was still awake, of course. Wrapped up in his work, she supposed.

Winnie heard a creak of movement behind his shut door and froze—like an intruder. The door opened and Father emerged.

"Oh," he said, rubbing at the bridge of his nose. "You startled me. I didn't realize you were still out."

"I'm sorry."

"Was it good?"

"Pardon me?"

"The film."

"Oh. Yes. Quite. A musical."

"Ah, that's nice."

He paused a moment, and the two stood there in the shadowy hall, looking at each other.

When he looked at her, what did he see?

In the laboratory, they had their fixed roles. There was comfort in that. Outside the lab? They each seemed on the precipice of calling out "Line!" to the prompter offstage. *Tell me, please, what I'm supposed to say to this person? This person I share everything with—and nothing.*

"I think I'm going to make myself a snack," Father said, smiling uncertainly. "Have you eaten? Would you like anything?"

"No," Winnie said. "Thank you."

It broke her heart, how careful his kindness was.

She'd seen family be casual with each other. The families of other students at school events. Families in movies. Father never felt more like a stranger than when he was kind. So solicitous, like a gentleman at a bus stop. *No, no—after you.*

He did try to be good to her. But all the *effort* of it showed.

And Winnie understood now how awful a work it must have been, being a father to her.

Imagine, loving a girl so much you jump at the chance to save her from unwed motherhood.

Imagine, she dies.

Imagine, being left to raise that child alone.

But he had never told Winnie the truth of her parentage, not even in some moment of drunken frustration. At first that had seemed like a betrayal—him keeping the truth secret from her.

Was it actually a kindness?

When Winnie was a little girl, Mama usually tucked her in, but sometimes he would come in too. Tousle her hair. Present his stubbled cheek for a kiss.

How right the world had seemed in those moments. The three of them, together.

Looking back now on that little girl—it was like looking at a stranger.

CHAPTER ELEVEN

It was a relief to get back to the dull routine of school on Monday. Winnie was able to brush off Dora's questions with a minimum of fuss or hurt feelings, and when she got home, she immersed herself in homework. The reverberations of her unsettling Friday evening still made themselves felt at her center, but she told herself that if she could just keep it all tamped down, eventually it would dissipate—it must.

She tried her best to focus, but thoughts of Mama and Schrödinger continually intruded on her work. Did she continue to pop up in his mind as he did in hers, or had she been gone from Schrödinger's thoughts as soon as she was gone from his sight?

Winnie was so distracted that when she heard a crash downstairs, it took her a terrified moment to parse the sound.

"Winifred!" she heard Father roar, "Get down here now!"

Winnie couldn't normally hear when Father got home from

all the way up in her attic bedroom; the crash must have been him slamming the front door.

Blankness overtook her, just like it always did during Father's rages. The fingers of her right hand unconsciously sought the pulse in her left wrist. It felt quick. She took deep breaths.

Father was angry. It couldn't be a coincidence. It must be about Friday—

"Winifred!"

She trudged toward the staircase. He must know she'd lied about going to the party. Someone must have mentioned meeting her there. But did he know the rest? That she'd spoken to Schrödinger, found out about him and Mama? That she'd discovered the truth, and said nothing to him? If so, how could she appease him now?

Her relationship with Father was, at its best . . . less than ideal. But how she longed to have the relative peace of even a week ago. How she longed to un-meet Schrödinger, un-know what he'd told her! Now that everything was out in the open, what if Father rejected her? She was practically an adult. He could ask her to leave. Maybe it would even be a relief to him, not having to pretend to be her father anymore.

"I want you in the lab, now!" Father shouted, and Winnie heard him stomping toward the basement. Vibration in his throat, in the air, in her ear.

Winnie's heart thudded hard and quick in her chest. That was not the sound of a "relieved" man. She tried again to turn her brain off, focusing on what was outside herself, not in. She was good at switching off when she really had to, and knew, in a detached sort of way, that this wasn't a skill to be proud of. Sure, it helped her get through the hard times, and the experiments with Father, but it was sad to want to not feel. It was sad to have a life that made you want that.

Brunhilde was in the kitchen, mixing waxy white oleomargarine with yellow dye as a substitute for rationed butter. She seemed to be straining for normalcy, but the bowl trembled in her hands.

"There are worse fathers," Brunhilde said suddenly.

"I know," Winnie answered, but she was pretty sure Brunhilde said it to comfort herself.

"Ah, Liebling—" she began, then stopped herself with a sharp shake of her head, exhaled heavily, and said, "Go on."

Once Winnie was on the basement stairs, she could feel the deep bass thrum of the generator in her stomach, a counterpoint to the hummingbird flutter of her heart.

When she entered the laboratory, Father had his back to her while he adjusted the generator. He appeared to be modifying it so that it would output a higher voltage than usual. Even from a few feet away, Winnie could smell the alcohol radiating from him. Had he really been drinking on campus? That wasn't like him.

Father was wearing heavy rubber gloves that protected him from fingertip to elbow, but it made Winnie nervous to watch him work anyway. He could be sloppy when he was drunk, and electricity was unforgiving.

Scott stood next to Father, and when he glanced back over his shoulder at the sound of Winnie's approach, his expression was bleak.

Winnie couldn't mask what she felt either. Facing Father alone was bad, but having Scott there would only make this worse. She didn't want him to see this version of Father—to see this darkness at the heart of their life together.

Winnie took a breath, hoping to calm herself, but she could feel electricity in the air, like the atmosphere before a lightning storm. It throbbed around her, setting her teeth on edge and raising the fine hairs on her arms.

Scott approached her. He paused like he was about to say something, but just exhaled. Winnie understood. What could he possibly say?

She didn't think he would ever look at her the same way again.

"You should go," she whispered hoarsely. This was her mess.

"There's no way I'm leaving," Scott said, indignant, and much too loud.

Father turned around. "Such loyalty! Loyalty like that I can't even get from my own daughter."

Angry as he was, Winnie was still so relieved to hear him call her that.

"I'm sorry I lied about going—"

Father cut her off with a glare. "This isn't about Hawthorn's vulgar parties. This is about your *father*."

That word was meant to cut her, and it did.

He peeled off his long rubber gloves and tossed them on

the lab bench. Father's normally immaculate golden hair was pushed this way and that, like he'd been running his fingers through it, and his eyes were wild. When sober, Father prided himself on control, but drunk, he was forever on the cusp of losing it. Winnie had to be the one who restrained herself, who took what he dished out in silence. She had found out Mama was a liar—Father was a liar—and what was his response? *He* was angry with *her.*

"Was it everything you hoped? Meeting *Herr* Schrödinger?"

"Oh, certainly," Winnie said, voice hard with sarcasm. "I always hoped to have a stranger announce he was my father at a cocktail party."

"You want pity? Lie down with dogs, wake up with fleas. That's what you get, going to that party, speaking to that man. The nerve of him! He comes to my office, this *Herr* Schrödinger," Father said, practically spitting the honorific, "with an opportunity. 'I'll help you secure a position working with Project Nightingale,' he tells me. 'The extra income will help you better care for my daughter.' *His* daughter! *His* daughter he calls you! I kept you out of that world. I stayed out of it myself, as much as I could. And you blithely wander in!" Father grabbed Winnie by both arms and jerked her back and forth. "What were you thinking? If Hawthorn finds out about your abilities—they'll take you from me, you stupid little—!"

"Sir!" Scott said sharply.

"This Nightingale Project," Father continued. "If they find out what you can do—"

"Sir, that's enough!" Scott pulled Father off her.

For a moment, the three of them just stood there. Winnie was afraid Father would turn his wrath against Scott, but he stayed rooted to the spot, heaving angrily.

Winnie rubbed at her arms. She was certain they would purple with handprints overnight.

"There's no way for Hawthorn to find out," she said, but her voice wavered.

Based on what Hawthorn had witnessed last night, he might already suspect. And Schrödinger had implied that Mama saw splinters. If Schrödinger suspected this meant she might see them too—he could tell Hawthorn about it.

Would he?

Winnie had no idea.

"Well, I'll be damned if Hawthorn's project progresses beyond our own. *I* will be the first to unlock the secrets of the multiverse." He glared at Winnie. "Which means that you need to start working much harder."

Scott gave Winnie a confused look. How strange this all must sound to him! As far as Scott knew, Father's only work was their own experiments on wave mechanics.

"Professor Schulde, listen to yourself," Scott said, speaking slow and level. "She's just a girl. What exactly do you expect of her?"

Father whipped his head toward Scott. "I could have you dismissed from the university for canoodling with my daughter." His voice sharpened. "Stay out of it."

"Winnie?" Scott said softly. "Let's go. We'll come back when—when things have settled down."

He grabbed for Winnie's hand, but she pulled it out of reach. "I can't."

Father—he wasn't perfect. But he was her only family. Without him, there was no one. They might not share blood, but their shared pain was just as tight a bond. Tighter.

"What do you want me to do?" she asked.

Scott took a few steps back, shaking his head, but he didn't leave. Winnie was glad for that.

"I've been thinking that what's holding you back is a lack of motivation," Father said, "but I've come up with a solution for that. We're going to try a version of an experiment I believe you're familiar with." He gestured toward the corner. "Winifred, get inside the Faraday cage."

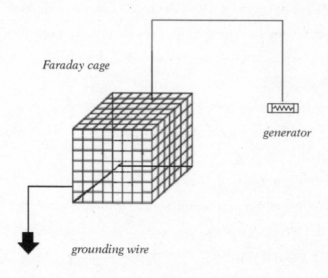

Faraday cage

generator

grounding wire

Winnie eyed the cage anxiously. It was for her own protection, but it still made her nervous—being trapped. She swallowed her fear and stepped into the eight-by-eight cage of heavy metal mesh. The walls of the Faraday cage were grounded, preventing any charge from accumulating on its outside surface. Father could surround Winnie with an electric field, which he theorized might act as a medium for her ability, and inside the cage, she would be perfectly safe.

Father was always careful to protect her from harm during their special experiments, just like he safeguarded all his difficult-to-replace equipment.

"Scott, there's a cardboard box upstairs in the hall. Bring it down, please."

Scott retreated upstairs. After a few moments, he still hadn't come back, and Winnie wondered if they'd finally reached his edge. She was relieved when she heard him coming down the stairs, but when he returned, his eyes were dark, and his mouth was set in a straight line. It was an expression she'd never seen him wear before.

Scott met Winnie's eyes through the mesh of the cage, and it was plain as day—he'd stayed for her. But he didn't want to be there.

"Well, bring it out," Father said.

Scott opened the box and lifted out a small black kitten. He cradled it to his chest and stroked its fur absentmindedly. The kitten let out a tiny mew.

This was too much.

She could easily guess the experiment Father had planned. It was awful. And how could she pretend it had never happened, with Scott there as witness?

Schrödinger's cat-in-a-box thought experiment was quite well known. Imagine a cat, a flask of poison, and a radioactive source in a sealed box. If a single atom of the radioactive source decayed, a monitor would register the radioactivity and the flask would be shattered, killing the cat. There was equal probability that an atom would or would not decay over the course of an hour. Within that time frame, the cat must be considered both alive and dead. It was all theoretical, of course, or at least that was what Schrödinger's paper supposed, and what other scientists assumed.

Winnie knew better.

This was a representation of how splits happened. The cat really was both alive and dead, just in separate realities.

"You're both familiar with Schrödinger's famous paradox, I assume?" Father asked.

"It's meant to be a thought experiment," Scott said, speaking through his teeth, "not an elaborate method of exterminating house pets."

Winnie braced for Father to explode, but he just laughed.

"Father, please—"

His smile froze, and he spoke flatly. "Perhaps this wouldn't be necessary if we'd had any measure of success—if you'd tried a little harder." Father turned to Scott. "Put it on the workbench," he said, pointing. "There is fine." He looked back at

Winnie. "We don't need any elaborate setup, do we? Geiger counters, uranium, and the like? Schrödinger always was more of a showman than a scientist, and there is, as they say, more than one way to kill a cat. As for our element of chance, a coin toss should work just fine."

Father had made her play this game before, but without such grim stakes. He flipped a coin, then checked the results without letting her see. After years of training her focus, Winnie could *usually* force herself to see the splinter of the toss, and then she would know that if it was tails in that other world, it was heads in her own, or vice versa. The next step—the one she'd never succeeded at—was changing the results of the coin toss that had already happened. After she tried to will it different, Father would look again, hoping to see a new result, and be disappointed.

Winnie didn't really think she could affect the outcome of something that had already happened like that. Then again, Father always told her that she was small-minded to cling to a linear idea of time. Space and time were a continuum, and relative to the observer. She was a different sort of observer, wasn't she? So, Father said, why wouldn't she be able to use her observations to influence time as well as matter?

Winnie glanced at the kitten, looking so forlorn sitting there on the workbench. It didn't know it should run away. It was such a baby, she didn't even think it would be able to.

Would Father really kill it if Winnie failed to change the results of the coin toss? She looked at him—the wildness in his eyes.

Yes.

He would.

Winnie would try her hardest. That was the most she could do.

"All right," Father said. "Put your hands on the receivers." Winnie took hold of the metal rods that measured the electrical activity in her own body. "Scott, the circuit, please."

Scott stood there a moment, looking at her, his expression one of confusion and pity—exactly what she'd wanted to avoid. She didn't want him to feel *sorry* for her.

Then he flipped the circuit, flooding the Faraday cage with current. Electricity would saturate the metal mesh surface, then harmlessly bleed back into the earth below through the grounding wire.

Father tossed the coin in the air, caught it, and placed it, covered, on the back of his hand. He glanced at the face of the coin himself without letting Scott or Winnie see, but Winnie didn't need to look to know. She'd caught the splinter as soon as the coin was tossed—it was heads there. So, tails in her own world.

"All right, Winifred. I want you to change the result. Now concentrate, and tell me when you're ready."

Even though Winnie thought she had no control over the coin, she still had to try. She closed her eyes so tight they hurt and focused as hard as she could. She could hear the kitten meowing on the bench a few feet away. Why did Father do these things?

But she knew. She knew.

Winnie squeezed the receivers in her hands and wished for a different outcome. *Heads, heads, heads,* she repeated fervently in her mind.

"Enough—five seconds and I'm looking, whether you're ready or not."

One of the machines began to whine, but she pushed the noise aside. *Do it,* she told herself fiercely. *Just force it to happen.*

Winnie could hear the cage humming. She felt a sort of pop below her breastbone. Her eyes flew open. Something was wrong. If something was wrong with the cage, all that current could touch her, stick out a forked tongue and take a taste . . .

"Scott?" Winnie cried shrilly, her head full of images of being electrocuted, burnt to a crisp. "Scott! I think something's wrong!"

Scott hurried close. "It's buzzing." He bent over to take a closer look at something, then immediately jumped up. "The grounding wire—it's frayed! Professor Schulde, cut the power!"

But it was too late. There was too much current to be contained, and with the grounding compromised, nowhere for all that energy to go. Electricity jumped off the Faraday cage in a blinding arc—how could something so dangerous be so pretty?—and Scott was right there, the quickest path to the ground.

Winnie saw Scott seize as electricity surged through his body. Then he crumpled.

Winnie's legs gave out beneath her almost in tandem with

Scott's, and she collapsed onto the floor of the cage. Its surface was still buzzing with charge, but she was safe inside. If the wire mesh had been damaged, she would have been at risk, but she should have realized immediately that wasn't the case. She'd been worried for herself, when she had been the only one who was safe.

Her nose was thick with the acrid smell of singed hair. Scott's hair. She shook her head ferociously, as if she could undo what she'd done through the sheer vehemence of her denial.

First Mama, then Scott. Was anyone who got too close to Father doomed, or was it just anyone she loved? Or was it the two of them, together, who destroyed all pure, good things they touched? She couldn't bear it. Everything was too awful. She couldn't bear it.

Father shut off the generator and stumbled over, looking like a ghost of himself. Pale, edges blurred—that was the smoke. "Are you all right?" he asked her, voice trembling.

Winnie didn't bother to answer. "Scott? Scott, can you hear me?" She pushed the door of the Faraday cage open and tried to run to him, but Father blocked her way.

"Stay here. I'll check on him."

Scott was crumpled on the floor like a discarded rag doll. She could see the scorched hole on the arm of his lab coat from where the electricity had struck. He was so still.

Father knelt by his side and shook him, shouting Scott's name right in his face.

But he didn't move.

Father looked back at her. He looked shell-shocked, and suddenly sober.

She hated him. She hated him like she had never hated anything.

Scott couldn't be dead. Her mind skipped away from the thought. She refused to live in a world without him in it.

Winnie's head buzzed.

Her vision tunneled, then went dark.

When Winnie came to, she pulled herself back up onto trembling legs, angry with herself for having fainted. The laboratory was full of smoke. Something must have caught fire. Her eyes searched the floor frantically. Where was Scott? Had Father even called for a doctor yet?

Winnie stumbled forward, waving smoke away from her eyes. "Father?" she called out. She couldn't see him for all the smoke.

A high-pitched whine—Father must have switched on the exhaust hood—and the smoke began to clear.

"Winnie, what on earth are you doing? Did you hear the explosion? I think it was just a circuit breaker, thank god," Father said. "Don't you know when you hear something like that, you're supposed to run *away* from the sound, not toward it?"

Winnie hardly registered what he said. She was looking past him, at Scott, who was throwing extinguishing chemicals on the small fire that flickered around the circuit box.

"Scott? What's going on? You're all right?"

He grinned at her and gave a small wave before returning to the task at hand.

"Oh, I see how it is," Father said. "You weren't worried about me. You just wanted to check on your darling."

Winnie felt herself blush, even though embarrassment was low on her list of concerns at the moment.

"No, I just . . ." Winnie trailed off.

What was going on? Had she imagined the whole thing? Had what she'd experienced been a powerful splinter that she'd somehow confused with her own reality?

"Everything is fine, so run back upstairs—and I'll forget you came down here if you forget I ever left the door unlocked."

Unlocked? The basement door didn't have a lock. It was the smoke, and the chemicals—it had to be. She was confused, or Father was, or they *both* were. She turned around, moving as if she were underwater, and climbed back up the stairs.

When she reached the top, she saw that the basement door *did* have a lock, and it had been bolted from the inside. Winnie was even more confused. Had she locked the door behind her and forgotten? And when had Father put a lock in, anyway?

She opened the door and fled into the bright light and fresh air of the kitchen. She leaned back against the wall and closed her eyes. Her head hurt from the smoke—or had she hit it when she fainted? What was going on?

She heard footsteps on the basement stairs, either Father or

Scott. She opened her eyes. Scott approached her, his face a mask of concern.

"Winnie, what's wrong? You seem, I don't know—confused."

Winnie didn't even try to stanch her tears. "Oh Scott, I thought you were dead."

He wrapped his arms around her waist and pulled her close. She pressed her face to his chest and let the thirsty cotton of his pristine lab coat absorb her tears.

"Shh," he soothed. "Here, let me look at you."

Winnie pulled back a little and tilted her face up toward his.

"I'm fine," Scott said. "It was just a little accident."

He leaned down and gently pressed his lips to hers. She was surprised by how soft they were.

How many times had she thought about exactly this moment, under the covers at night—her favorite bedtime story—or in a sudden unwelcome flash when he glanced over at her in the lab? It was her first kiss. It had happened a thousand times before, but finally—*finally*—it was happening for real.

In the movies, women kicked up a leg when they were kissed, or swooned, melting into their beloved's arms. Winnie stayed very still. The moment felt so perfect she feared that if she so much as twitched, it would burst like a soap bubble.

Still, the kiss was over too soon.

Scott pulled back, and adjusted his glasses, which had gone slightly askew. Winnie was electric with fondness for him—fully charged and dying to spark. She already wanted to kiss him again, and felt almost bold enough to do it.

But the expression on Scott's face wasn't fond. He looked deeply concerned—frightened, even. His eyes scanned her hair, her clothes, her lips. He backed away from her.

No! It hadn't been a mistake. Scott couldn't think it was a mistake!

Hadn't he felt what she felt?

He frowned, and Winnie braced herself for some argument—some excuse—for why he didn't want her after all. Her father. Her age.

But Scott said none of that. And still, his words knocked her flat.

"You're not Winnie," he said shakily. "Who the hell are you?"

PART TWO

Sorrow is concealed in gilded palaces, and there's no escaping it.

—Fyodor Dostoyevsky, *The Double*

CHAPTER TWELVE

S cott took another step back from her, looking stuck somewhere between horrified and awestruck.

Winnie was confused—but also oddly relieved. This was bizarre. Bizarre, she could handle. She could handle anything,
so long as it wasn't Scott saying something like *Oh, we can't do
this—your father* as code for *I don't want you after all.*

"I—of course I'm me," Winnie said. Who else could she be?
She looked down at her hands, turning them back and forth
like a magician—*see, no tricks here.*

She took a step toward Scott. He backed up until he was
pressed against the kitchen wall. His brows tightened in a
quick flinch of fear before he could compose his face.

"The smoke—I think you're confused," Winnie said gently,
in a tone she recognized as one learned from her mother. It
was the voice Mama had used to soothe one of their injured
hens—or one on the chopping block.

"I'm not," Scott said firmly. His gaze traveled up and down over her face like he was trying to analyze every detail. "It's uncanny!" he whispered.

"What's uncanny?" she whispered back. Was this just a terrible dream? Maybe it had all just been a nightmare—Father's anger, Scott's accident—and she was still asleep.

Then she realized. Why hadn't she understood sooner? The locked door. Father's smile. The shock, the smoke—it had made her stupid.

This wasn't her house.

That wasn't her Father.

This was a different reality.

And Winnie had no idea how she'd gotten here.

WINNIE LOOKED AROUND WILDLY. THERE WAS NO SHOCKING DIFFERENCE between this world and her own—not in the kitchen, at least. But as she looked around, she noticed a few small things. Cheerful yellow gingham curtained the windows, not just plain white blinds like at home. There was a little tray housing a napkin holder and salt and pepper shakers in the center of the table, while her own table was always cleared between meals. Dishes were left drying in the rack, not immediately dried and put away. It was all nice enough, and overall, pleasantly familiar.

But this wasn't her home. Was she safe here?

Not that her own home had been safe.

Scott—oh, Scott—if the accident *had* been real—

Winnie shut that door inside herself so sharply she could almost hear the slam. If she thought about that now—

No. She could not think about that now.

Scott's double stood in front of her, examining Winnie quizzically.

"You see it now?" he asked.

Winnie nodded. She saw.

Winnie closed her eyes for a moment and took a breath.

She needed to examine this new environment analytically, like a scientist would, to discover and avoid any potential dangers.

The first step of the scientific method was simple: ask a question.

Where the hell am I?

Winnie tried to work backward in her head. Although Father recognized her, he said she shouldn't be in the laboratory, and the door to the lab had a lock here. She existed in this reality, but she must not work with Father and Scott. What else was different here?

For one thing, this Scott was an unknown variable. Potentially dangerous, like all unknowns. Winnie looked at him, and she tried to believe this.

But she couldn't. Not now that all the fear had fallen from Scott's face as the shock wore off. He looked at her with the open wonder of a little boy.

She looked at him, and she saw *Scott*.

"I can see those wheels turning," he said. "What are you thinking?"

Even though Winnie knew she should be extremely careful until she got her bearings, she couldn't make herself distrust him. So she would gather as much information as she could and give as little in return as possible.

"I—I don't know. What are you thinking?"

Scott smiled and gave a little shrug. "Just the obvious. Project Nightingale must have had one hell of a breakthrough." He frowned. "Although they couldn't have intended to send *you*?"

Nightingale? Why would Scott's mind jump to Hawthorn's work? In her world, they'd only just learned of it—and it certainly wasn't something Scott had any *excitement* about.

"Nightingale has nothing to do with this," Winnie said sharply.

And she would have nothing to do with them.

Winnie didn't know where, exactly, she was, or how she'd gotten there, so it felt good to feel certain about *something*. To hell with Hawthorn. To hell with Father. To hell with any scientist whose work put other people's lives at risk.

Winnie had endured a lifetime of Father's poking and prodding. If she'd stood up for herself and put an end to the experiments earlier, Scott wouldn't have gotten hurt.

She would never let herself be experimented on again. Not by Father, and certainly not by Hawthorn.

From here on out, she would be designing the experiments herself.

"If not Nightingale, who?" he asked. "And what are you doing here?"

Winnie frowned. How *had* she gotten there?

"It was just—I don't know, exactly. An accident."

The color began to drain from his face.

"What is it?" Winnie asked.

"If it wasn't planned—how can I explain it?" Scott said the last part to himself, then bit his lip and sighed, eyes searching the space above her head as if there might be some answer printed there on the wall. "You see, matter can't just *poof!* into existence. That's been one of the challenges for us—trying to figure out how to balance the 'scales.' If we're going to transport matter, we need to absorb energy in return. There has to be exchange, not just transmission. It goes back to the first law of thermodynamics . . ." He trailed off, and gave Winnie an uncertain look, as if he was worried this was all over her head. "I'm sorry, is this making sense?"

"Scott, I know what the first law of thermodynamics is! 'Energy can be transformed from one form to another, but can be neither created nor destroyed.'" It was unsettling to have him talking to her like this, as if she were a silly schoolgirl instead of a peer. "You and Father—I take it you work for Hawthorn here? With Project Nightingale?" She was . . . not thrilled by this development. "Well, in my world, we don't. But I do work with you, and with my father. You can talk to me normally!"

"I'm sorry! But none of this is normal," he said, then shook his head. "Anyway, the first law of thermodynamics applies to matter too, of course. The amount of 'stuff'—of any kind—in our universe *always* remains constant. So, if you want to transport something to another reality—into another closed system—you have to receive something back too, or else . . . well, or else we have no idea what could happen."

He paused, and Winnie felt the full weight of his words. She understood his panic now. Her being there—it upset the order of things. The cosmos would strive to regain equilibrium. But how? And what would it do to their world?

. . . or to her?

"I understand," Winnie said. She understood all too well. "Go on."

Scott continued. "Hawthorn has been experimenting with— basically, they're a new type of battery. The idea is that they can be used to absorb energy from another reality to balance out the amount of matter we're transporting, so the total 'stuff' in each system remains constant. But you're saying there was no precaution like that during this—this accident?"

Winnie shook her head.

"We have to get you back home, Winnie. We have to get you back home as quickly as possible. I'm going to go get Professor Schulde. We have to take you to Hawthorn. However you got here, he'll be able to help you get back."

"No!" Winnie said sharply.

"Winnie—"

"You're saying Hawthorn has it all worked out? Really? He's able to transport people?"

Scott stared at his feet. He shifted his weight nervously, then looked back up at her. "No. Not yet. There have been some promising tests with inanimate objects. But the tests with living subjects . . . Hawthorn is still working out the kinks. They haven't gone great."

Winnie immediately thought of James, and her blood ran cold.

"Humans?"

"No! No, just animal subjects."

Winnie gave a shiver of revulsion. Better than testing on people, but gruesome all the same.

"I only met Hawthorn once," she said. "He—frankly, he frightens me. But you obviously know him better. Tell me, if he knows I'm here, and that some awful scales have become unbalanced—what's he going to do? Would he transport me the same way he's been transporting inanimate objects, even if he thinks it'll kill me? You know, to dispose of the extra 'matter'?"

Scott frowned. He bit his lip and looked away, considering.

"Well?"

He sighed. "I don't think he'd try to transport you if it would kill you. Not right away—not unless he felt he had to for some reason. But—probably he would want to keep you for testing. Figure out why it worked for you. How you survived. See if there's something different about you. And if there's a way he could use it."

Oh, there was certainly something different about her. And

Winnie doubted Hawthorn would ever let her go once he found out what it was.

She had to convince Scott that going to Hawthorn was the wrong move.

"Winnie is your girlfriend here, right?" Winnie asked. It made her blush to say it, but that was the least of her concerns now. "Is that something you'd want for her? Being experimented on by Hawthorn?" She looked at him and pressed. "Scott. Would you *really* hand me over to someone like that?"

She paused a moment, letting the question sink in. The uncertainty on his face gave her hope.

"We don't need Hawthorn," Winnie continued. "You know about his work; I know about the accident that brought me here. If we work together, we can figure this out ourselves. It will go much more smoothly with me as a collaborator than as a prisoner."

Scott's expression softened. Had she convinced him?

Before he could answer, they heard the front door open, then slam.

"I'm home!"

It was a voice Winnie recognized, but she couldn't immediately place it. Not Brunhilde, certainly.

Before she could think to hide, the girl entered the kitchen and saw her. Her jaw dropped, and her shocked expression was a perfect mirror of Winnie's own.

For a moment, Winnie couldn't process what she was seeing. The girl was dressed in a smart gray wool skirt with kick pleats, an inch or so shy of Winnie's school regulations, and a pearl-pink cardigan that made Winnie acutely aware of how grubby she must look from lying on the dirty laboratory floor. She wore her hair in a stylish, chin-grazing, gently curled bob.

But there was no mistaking it: This girl was her doppel-gänger, although they were hardly identical. Her double had rosy lips, artfully arched brows, sooty lashes—and in a sweater that snug, she actually had curves. Winnie had no idea this was waiting to be carved from the rough stone of her physique.

I'm beautiful, she thought, for the first time in her life.

Winnie would have savored the pleasure of this realization had it come at any other time, but as it was, she quickly moved past it to more pressing concerns.

This girl was *her*. If Winnie had an ally in this frightening world, she was it.

"You have no idea how glad I am to see you," Winnie said, laughing a bit with relief.

"Who is this?" her double asked Scott, sounding a bit pos-sessive. Then she seemed to notice how alike they were and began to tremble. "Scott, what's going on?"

Her double took a few steps closer. She reached a shaky hand toward Winnie's face, but stopped before she made contact.

Winnie inhaled sharply. Looking into this face that both was and was not her own—reality had cracked open to show its strange bones. All she could compare it to was the surreal feeling of déjà vu, but that didn't even begin to cover it.

"Is this some kind of joke? It's like—it's like looking in a mirror," this Split-Winnie said. She gave Winnie a doubtful once-over. "Well, almost. Who *are* you?" she demanded, voice shrill. Winnie recognized the ghost of her own German accent in the panicked tone.

"Shh! Your father will hear," Winnie said. "I'm your double. I came here from a different reality and—"

"Project Nightingale sent you?"

"No," Winnie said firmly. "They have nothing to do with this."

Winnie watched her double close her eyes, retreat into herself, and take a deep breath. When she opened them, she seemed a bit calmer. "We need to go tell Father. This is—this is *crazy*. You shouldn't be here."

This wasn't the response she'd hoped for from her double, but the girl was right. Not about Father—the girl's impulse to go to him was completely foreign to Winnie!—but that her being there was wrong.

Winnie had already realized that, but standing face-to-face with her double really drove it home. There was already a Winnie here. And from the look of things, Winnie thought with a pang, a better one. There was no place for her there. Not just in a cosmic, first law of thermodynamics way, like Scott insisted—but right there, in that house. Winnie was an inter-loper, and she was not welcome.

This girl had Scott. She had a life that didn't seem to be as unpleasantly tangled up in her father's work. She even had nicer sweaters! The two of them *must* also have some things in common, but Winnie couldn't guess what. At least when she was jealous of a girl at school, she could tell herself, *Oh, but she can't do X.* Or, *Everyone has different strengths.*

But this girl—what if she was Winnie, but just *better*?

She tried to push the thought out of her head.

"Yes, I need to go home," Winnie said. "As quickly as possible. But I'm keeping your father—and Hawthorn—out of it."

Winnie's double glanced back and forth between her and Scott in disbelief. "What? Why? Please tell me I'm dreaming, because this is all absurd. I'm getting Father. It isn't up to you!"

"No, Winnie," Scott said, putting a quelling hand on her double's forearm. "She's right. We have to help her. She's *you*."

For a moment, Winnie could hardly believe it. Her own double didn't want to help her, but Scott did. She felt a rush of gratitude toward him. He'd taken her side over his own Winnie! She'd never forget his kindness.

Winnie glanced at the dark expression on her double's face.

She wouldn't forget either.

CHAPTER THIRTEEN

"Scott?" Professor Schulde called from the basement. "If Winnie's all right, there is a bit of a mess to clean down here."

Her own father never called her Winnie.

This Father sounded nothing like the out-of-control man he'd been in her world minutes earlier, but Winnie's heart still pounded at the sound of his voice. Was this fear an animal instinct to be trusted? Or was she merely experiencing a conditioned response, like one of Pavlov's dogs?

Winnie didn't intend to find out. She needed to get back.

"Scott?" this world's Father called again.

She locked eyes with her double, the girl who looked so like—and so unlike—herself. How strange that she had no idea what this girl was thinking!

"Don't tell him I'm here," Winnie whispered urgently. "Please."

Her head began to pound painfully. She looked back and forth between her double and Scott. "If the two of you could just get him out of the lab somehow, I can go check it out, gather some evidence . . ." Winnie trailed off.

She had to see the laboratory before any sign of what had happened was tidied away.

Her double flinched and rubbed at her own temples. Yes, it was all too much to process.

Finally, Winnie's double nodded. "Fine. I'll help you." She sighed and shook her head. "I mean, *of course* I'll help you." She looked at Scott. "How are we going to get Father to come upstairs?"

Scott smiled. "Play along, okay?" Then he called down to Father, "Winnie's eyes are irritated by all the smoke. I'm going to take her upstairs to the bathroom to rinse them out. Could you come take a look?"

"Thank you!" Winnie whispered urgently.

Scott nodded in acknowledgment.

"Hide in the dining room," he said. "Once he comes upstairs you can go down to the lab, but you'll only have a few minutes."

"Thank you," Winnie said again, but although she was grateful that Scott's double was so willing to help her, she couldn't help but feel a bit betrayed by her own double's hesitation before. Of course, blind trust was hardly one of her own characteristics, so perhaps it made sense that she didn't find it in her double either.

"I won't say anything to Professor Schulde until we've

discussed things further," Scott added, "but I have so many questions! I hope that at some point, you'll have answers."

Winnie didn't know what kind of answers she could give him, but she'd worry about that later. For now, she was focused on enduring the present moment, then the next one, and the next . . .

The future was a terrifying blank, and the past—well, she didn't dare think about the past at all.

Something that had happened in the lab back home had led to her being transported here. If she could figure out what it was and how to re-create it, maybe that would be enough to transport herself back again. Not that there was anything so wonderful waiting for her there . . .

"Good luck," Scott said, pressing her hand in encouragement.

Winnie's fingers tingled at his touch.

Then Scott turned to retreat upstairs, bringing Winnie's doppelgänger with him.

He was just doing what she'd asked, but Winnie hated seeing him walk away. She wished he could go down to the lab with her.

Because even though the site of Scott's accident was a world away, Winnie still felt like she was walking into a tomb.

WINNIE NEEDED TO EXAMINE THE DAMAGE SHE'D DONE TO THE LAB WHEN she arrived, but first, she wanted to check out this Professor Schulde's notes. Even though Scott worked with Hawthorn too and would be familiar with Nightingale's work, Father was sure to have his own insights.

She headed over to Dr. Schulde's desk to see what she could find.

There was a small, leather-bound notebook lying open face-down on his desk. It looked identical to the one Father jotted his own thoughts in while they worked. Winnie picked it up, flipped to the first page, then began to skim his notes.

She stopped when she came across a particularly interesting passage:

There are two essential questions when it comes to traveling between alt-verses. The first: whether or not it is physically possible for matter to cross these barriers. We've answered that. Yes, it is. The second question—and in my opinion, the far more interesting and less certain one—is this: Could a person survive this transition? So far, animal subjects who make the trip seem physically unharmed, but suffer a mental deterioration that quickly proves fatal. Human beings have a consciousness that organizes and analyzes their experiences. Would this help a person's consciousness "manage" this transition? Or make the dissonance between worlds even worse? Hawthorn theorizes that certain individuals might have a kind of immunity to these ill effects, but it's unclear to me why or how this might be the case. As always, he is extremely guarded about his own reasoning and research.

So *that* was what Scott meant when he said interdimensional travel "didn't go well" for living subjects! The stress of the trip—what? Drove them mad? Winnie's mouth went dry. This was more frightening somehow than if they were just being killed directly.

Could that still happen to her? Or did she have Hawthorn's theoretical "immunity"?

Of course, maybe there was no immunity, and it was Hawthorn's method of transportation that caused that little side effect.

Still . . . Winnie doubted it was just a coincidence that she saw alternate realties and had now traveled to one. It seemed likely that whatever it was that allowed her to see splinters was also what had enabled her to travel between worlds.

Winnie wondered again if James was able to see splinters too. If he could, and Hawthorn knew about it—was that something that informed Hawthorn's cryptic theories about immunity?

Impossible to say. But Professor Schulde's notes confirmed that Winnie would be of particular interest to Project Nightingale. She was "special" somehow, although considering her situation, that word seemed comically inaccurate. "Uniquely cursed," perhaps.

What she couldn't understand was why her double's Father didn't seem to be experimenting on his Winnie, especially since he was working for Nightingale. Oh well—that would have to remain a mystery for another time. She had more than enough to worry about at the moment.

Winnie continued to scan the rest of Professor Schulde's notes. She didn't have time for a thorough study, but she learned that an ambient electric charge was crucial for interdimensional travel. It seemed that atmospheric electricity sort of "cracked the door" between worlds.

This made sense to her, particularly in light of the accident that had brought her here. Scott had been electrocuted because the Faraday cage's grounding wire was damaged. The lab would have been full of ambient electric charge.

After Winnie spent several minutes reading over the notebook, she reluctantly realized she needed to set it aside and begin her examination of the lab itself before Professor Schulde came back. She found the place where she'd "landed," for lack of a better word. The earthen floor didn't seem harmed in any way there, but she noticed the dirt seemed scuffed about ten feet from that spot—around the place where Scott had been electrocuted in her world.

She bent down to take a closer look. When she brushed her hand across the packed dirt, she was unsettled to find something hard there.

Bone? Winnie thought with a flash of revulsion, but no, of course not. She was letting her imagination get the best of her.

After a few minutes of careful excavation, she had the thing unearthed. It was a branching tube of jagged glass. It looked like—like frozen electricity.

Winnie pulled the name for it from some corner of her memory; it was a Lichtenberg figure. She'd seen illustrations in books, but this was her first time seeing one in person. A strong current had left its fingerprint there by melting something in the soil—silicon most likely.

Had the electric charge that shocked Scott in her own world left its mark in this one? How?

And if the current that struck Scott was powerful enough to turn dirt into *this*, Winnie thought, what had it done to Scott's body?

She knew the answer. She didn't want to face it, but she knew.

Scott was dead.

And it was her fault. Hers and Father's. Just like Mama's death had been.

Scott had wanted them to leave the lab together, but she'd insisted on staying. So he'd stayed too.

He'd stayed for her. He'd stayed for her, and now he was dead.

That was what was waiting for her back home. The lifeless body of a boy who'd had the misfortune of being loved by her.

WINNIE CONTINUED POKING AROUND THE LAB LISTLESSLY. IT WAS HARD to focus. It was hard to care. She just felt . . . helpless.

Then she heard it—footsteps on the basement stairs.

She'd taken too long. Professor Schulde was coming back.

Winnie's eyes darted around the laboratory. There was no way out; she had to hide. But where?

She took a few steps toward the lab bench, but no, that was too open. Under Father's desk? At least there was a chair she could hide behind there, unless he pulled it out and sat down . . .

The footfalls kept coming, ever closer, but she could not decide.

She'd seen scared rabbits freeze like this, out in the countryside. Darting back and forth but going nowhere. She always wanted to shout, *Just pick a direction and run!*

Now she realized what they must have felt in those moments: sometimes, there is simply no escape.

"Winnie?" a voice called.

Oh, thank god—it was Scott. He rounded the corner of the basement stairs and came into view.

"You scared me half to death—I thought you were Professor Schulde!"

"Don't worry. He's still upstairs. He sent me down for the saline from the eyewash station. We've rinsed Winnie's eyes with water, but I'll be darned if they aren't still irritated," he said, grinning slyly.

Winnie was grateful that even though her double had been against concealing her from Father, she seemed to be playing along now.

"Say, what have you got there?" Scott asked, gesturing to the lab bench where Winnie had placed the glass form she found.

"It's a Lichtenberg figure. I found it on the ground over there. There must have been some kind of electric discharge when I arrived. Do you think that could have caused the fire you and Fa—Professor Schulde—were putting out earlier?"

Scott stared at her in consternation. Had he noticed that she'd almost called this world's Dr. Schulde "Father"? An embarrassing misstep, to be sure, but . . .

"You know about Lichtenberg figures?"

Winnie sighed in frustration. He was surprised about *that*?

"I told you! I work with Father—and you. I'm going to be a physicist myself." *If Father lets me*, she thought, but did not add.

Scott picked up the glass rod and began to carefully examine it.

"Maybe," Winnie began, thinking aloud, "maybe this discharge of electricity was the universe, I don't know, snapping back into equilibrium?"

Scott raised his eyebrows.

Winnie was reaching. She knew she was reaching. She understood just as well as he did that when electricity discharged, it wasn't as if that energy vanished. It was just—she closed her eyes, and all she could see was her Scott, lying there on the floor. The jagged hole burned in his lab coat. The stillness of his chest.

That was the world she was supposed to want to return to?

Her chin trembled. Scott was right here! And completely out of reach.

"What is it?" Scott asked. He made a move forward as if to touch her, but then seemed to remember himself. He stopped short and stepped back. "Winnie, what's wrong?"

Winnie let out a trembling breath. "Right before I transported here, there was an accident. You were—" Winnie began, but cut herself off.

She wanted to tell, and she didn't. Keeping all this grief pent up inside her felt impossible. But saying it out loud would make it more real.

"An accident?" Scott pushed. "What happened?"

Winnie squeezed her eyes tight—not that it mattered. Eyes open or closed, she saw the same thing. Scott, coming close because *she* had called to him. And then the blinding bolt. And then Scott on the ground.

"Something went wrong with one of Father's experiments. Scott was hurt. No—not hurt. He—he's dead. He was electrocuted and he's dead."

Scott let out a shaky breath. "Oh, Winnie. That's awful. I'm so sorry."

She opened her eyes. "I read Professor Schulde's notebook. The animal subjects Hawthorn transports—they go crazy? Is that going to happen to me?"

"No! No, I don't think so. And it isn't—they don't 'go crazy,' per se. When they come back, it's like their brains have aged. But it happens very fast. If that was going to happen to you, we'd be seeing signs already. The rats immediately show signs of severe—fatal—dementia. Except when Hawthorn autopsies them, their brains appear normal."

Winnie didn't know what to think. "What if that happens to me when I go back?"

Her breath quickened. It was all catching up to her: Hawthorn's ghoulish experiments. Not being able to get home. What waited for her there if she *did* manage to get back.

And she was terrified.

Even if Winnie could somehow get herself home unharmed, what kind of experiments would Father subject her to, now that he knew it was possible for her to travel between worlds?

No. She couldn't do this.

"Scott, I can't go back! It's too risky. You say that me being here will upset the balance of things, but the first law of thermodynamics—it's like any other natural 'law': It's man-made. A theory, really. It could be wrong. Maybe me being here proves it's wrong. I don't want to go back, and you can't make me."

For a long moment, Scott didn't say anything. He just stood there, scratching his chin, looking at her. What was he thinking? That she was being a coward, probably. He must be so disappointed in her.

But even Scott's disappointment couldn't make her want to go.

To Winnie's surprise, when he finally spoke, it wasn't to rebuke her.

"Are you familiar with time dilation?" he asked.

Winnie frowned. She thought she'd heard the term before, but wasn't sure.

"It's a correlation of Einstein's special theory of relativity," Scott explained.

"Oh! Yes. I've read some of his papers, but they're . . . pretty dense."

Winnie had no idea where he was going with any of this.

Scott laughed softly. "Well, that's an understatement. And I'm certainly no expert myself, but Hawthorn is. Basically, the way he explains it is that time moves at different rates in different frames of reference. And alternate realities are *very* different frames of reference. So, traveling between worlds is always a sort of time travel. He thinks that's what's causing the animal subjects to experience a strange sort of aging. He's trying to figure out how to minimize that effect, but—"

"You think we could make use of time dilation—is that it?" Winnie broke in eagerly. "You think that when I go back, I could really go *back*—back to before Scott's accident?"

Winnie's breath went quick and shallow with excitement as hope took root. She could go back in time and prevent Scott's accident. The idea of time travel was crazy—but was it crazier than traveling to alternate realities?

Scott smiled. "Yes. Exactly. You could go back in time when you go back in space," he said. "At least theoretically."

The more she thought about it, the more sense it made. Father had always theorized that her ability could transcend linear time. That was the whole basis of his coin toss experiment— that she could change a coin toss that had already happened.

It all sounded pretty impossible.

But maybe she could do the impossible, if it meant saving Scott.

Without that hope, she had nothing.

Winnie gestured to the Lichtenberg figure. Its meaning was gradually becoming clear to her.

"I found that where Scott was standing when he was shocked. But that happened before I traveled here."

"Hmm," Scott said, considering. "Maybe it was like . . . a sort of echo. A reverberation that came through when the door between our worlds was open."

"Could it be a sign of the time dilation, though? Could there be an inverse relationship between time in your world and mine?"

Scott frowned. "I'm not sure I understand."

"Well, in my world, there was the electric blast, right there in the lab"—she pointed to the spot—"and then, *after* that, I was transported. But here, I was transported first—I must have been, or else there wouldn't be an opening between our worlds—and *then* came the blast. You see? The order is reversed. So, when time moves forward here—"

"It moves backward in your reality," Scott finished thoughtfully. "That could be the case."

"So, let's say it takes us a week to plan an experiment to get me back home—that would deposit me back in my world a week ago, right?" Winnie smiled wide. "Is—is that true, do you think? Because that would be *amazing*!"

Scott smiled. "It sounds logical to me. Of course, we can't know for sure. But it seems as probable as anything. So, you'll work on an experiment with me? To go back?"

"My god, yes! We should start right away!"

Scott gave a chuckle.

Winnie had been completely adrift since she saw Scott hurt and somehow transported herself to this strange place. Each new thing was a wave crashing over her, and she hadn't been processing things so much as just trying to keep her head above water. But now she felt like she could breathe.

Maybe she could see Scott again, and not just by proxy. Maybe she could save him. The thoughts were a life preserver, and she clung to them.

"What do we do first?" Winnie asked eagerly. She'd been in their world now for what—forty minutes? They were already plenty early enough for her to stop the accident if they began immediately.

"Well, let's not get ahead of ourselves," Scott said. "The experiment will take planning, and equipment—which means we need to find somewhere for you to stay in the meantime. You'll have to look like the *real* Winnie for that, so if someone spots you, it won't be suspicious."

"Don't call her that," Winnie said sharply. It made her feel like . . . like a cheap knockoff. And the worst thing was, she knew he was right. A glance at this world's Winnie revealed just how she measured up—or rather, didn't. "I *am* the real Winnie," she said, more for herself than him. "Just as much as she is."

"I'm sorry. I didn't mean anything by it. I wasn't implying that you're second-rate. Only—different."

Ah, yes. Different. He'd known she wasn't the "real" Winnie as soon as they kissed. There were much more important things to worry about, but unfortunately that didn't stop the petty ones from bothering her too.

She couldn't wait to get back to Scott. The *real* one.

SCOTT WENT BACK UPSTAIRS WITH THE SALINE SOLUTION, AND WINNIE retreated once again to the dining room to hide out until Scott and Dr. Schulde returned to the laboratory. Then she would let her double make her up, and the two of them would try to figure out someplace where Winnie could stay. Maybe with Dora? If the girl even existed in this world. She thought of her own Dora wistfully. How she would love to be part of Winnie's forced makeover! She was a little excited at the prospect of looking more like this world's prettier version of herself, and that feeling mixed uneasily with the awful events of the day.

Winnie knew Scott was dead, but she could undo it. She would go back—go back and wrest a happy ending out of that sad world, no matter what it took.

Winnie would remake reality and become Scott's savior, instead of his downfall.

Her body trembled lightly, still awash in adrenaline, an acrid taste in her throat. But despite that, a tentative shot of hope unfurled in her chest.

CHAPTER FOURTEEN

Winnie's double met her in the hall upstairs and silently led Winnie into her bedroom. Winnie was surprised to discover that the girl's room wasn't up in the attic like Winnie's, but in the large, bright bedroom next to Father's study on the second floor. It was the room that Brunhilde used back home. Did Brunhilde sleep in the attic in this world? Was there even a Brunhilde here?

Once the door was shut behind them, her double spoke.

"Well?" she asked. "What's the plan?"

Winnie's head throbbed dully. She didn't feel good, but supposed it would be stranger if she *did*, considering all that had happened. She glanced around the room, trying to get her bearings. Her double's room had no books. How could she sleep in a room with no books? Split-Winnie's bed was unmade, and yesterday's clothes were strewn on the floor, where they were a bit rumpled, but still in better shape than anything Winnie was wearing. Winnie glanced down at her dirty, wrinkled attire—she really did need to change.

When she looked back at her double, the girl was massaging her temple. Did she have a headache too?

"Scott says I need to be able to pass for you if I'm going to stay here," Winnie told her double.

"Here? With me?" the girl said, raising her eyebrows. "Easy for Scott to say! I'm not going to try to hide you in my room like a puppy or something."

Winnie recognized her own expression of incredulity, although she'd never seen it from the outside. There was an unexpected harshness to it. All those times Dora had begged her to be friendlier to their school acquaintances, to teachers who misspoke or just plain got things wrong, to stupid boys in soda shops, she'd thought her friend was just being pushy. But meeting herself, she had to wonder.

"No, I just meant here, in this world," Winnie said, trying not to sound irritated. "I was actually thinking I could stay with Dora. If . . . well, she is your friend here, right?"

"She is."

"Okay, good."

Split-Winnie just stared at her.

And was this what it was like to talk to her? She had never suspected her reserve was so . . . chilly.

"So," Winnie continued, "can I borrow some clothing?"

"Oh—yes, of course."

The girl opened her closet, and Winnie saw that her double

had easily three times the clothes she did, all of them as fine as could be. Her double took a pine-green cardigan with delicate pearl buttons off the hanger, passed it to Winnie, then searched for something to match, finally pairing it with a white blouse with a Peter Pan collar and a sharp plaid skirt.

"Thank you."

"I can cut your hair too," her double said. Then she regarded Winnie's face critically, with much the same focus and intensity Winnie imagined she herself showed when examining a broken-down piece of laboratory equipment. "And I'll need to make up your face, obviously."

Obviously.

Winnie tried not to let her annoyance show.

She took off her dirt-smudged shirt and skirt and caught her double giving her a sly once-over. The girl's curiosity wasn't exactly welcome, but it was certainly understandable. Winnie found herself wondering what "her" body might look like, not caught in the mirror or glimpsed up close in parts—a glance down at her knee as she lifted her leg to put on stockings, a peek at her elbow to look at a bug bite—but in full view, right there in front of her.

How odd that a person could live in a body for sixteen years, and still not fully know what it looked like!

Her double startled her by putting a gentle finger to the jagged scar on Winnie's upper arm then.

"I've got one too," she said, eagerly stretching the neck of her sweater to show a matching scar. "From the car accident, right? You really are me, huh?"

Winnie nodded, although it felt false. The two girls weren't really the same. Winnie suddenly felt shy standing in front of this person—herself, but somehow also a stranger—in her underpants.

Winnie couldn't take her eyes off her double's scar. When that shard of windshield pierced her double's arm, it had been *her* arm. Different as they might seem, they had been the same person then, in the same accident.

"Isn't it so strange?" Winnie said. "The worst thing that ever happened to me, and it happened to both of us."

Her double gave a little humorless laugh.

"The worst? Worse than *this*?"

Winnie blinked in surprise. Of course it was worse. Mama died in that accident. Unless—

"Wait—is Mama alive here?" Winnie asked eagerly.

If Mama was here—that wouldn't make Scott's accident *worth it*, but at least there could be some tiny speck of good. To see Mama again, to hug her again—Winnie's body thrilled with hope! She felt warm all over, like the sun was kissing every cell.

That must be where their worlds diverged. Both of them had been in the accident, but this girl—this confident, beautiful her—had a mother who'd survived it.

She grabbed her double's arms tight.

"Well, *is* she? I want to see her!"

Her startled double blinked back in surprise. "Let go of me!"

"Tell me! Tell me where she is!"

Her double stared back at her, eyes wide and mouth agape.

This must be what it looked like when Winnie was scared.

"She's gone!" her double said.

"Gone?"

"She died in the crash, just like yours!"

Her double must think she was completely unhinged. Winnie realized how tightly she was gripping her double's arms and tried to let go, but there was some strange resistance there, like her double was—sticky? No. *Magnetic*.

Winnie peeled her fingers away with difficultly and took a few steps back. She'd practically assaulted the girl. What was wrong with her? The flesh of her double's arms held the indentation of Winnie's fingers for a few uncanny seconds, like a couch cushion or florist's foam.

Both girls stared.

Winnie's double opened her mouth first. "What—" she began, but by then the flesh had sprung back to fullness. "What was that?" she finished shakily.

"I'm not exactly sure," Winnie said. "Scott said that me being here might cause some sort of energy imbalances, but . . . it's better now, right?"

Her double nodded slowly.

"I'm sorry," Winnie said, her voice small. "I didn't mean to hurt you. I just—well, *you* would understand." She looked at her double, eyes full of tears, but for once unembarrassed. "Can you imagine thinking for a second that you're actually going to see her again?"

Her double nodded grimly. "I understand."

• • •

WINNIE FINISHED DRESSING QUICKLY. WHEN SHE CHECKED HER RE-flection, she was both disappointed and relieved to discover that even in her doppelgänger's lovely clothes, she looked like herself.

Her double stood behind her, and it was beyond strange seeing both their reflections in one mirror. For a moment, Winnie was overcome with vertigo. She put her fingers on the dresser top to steady herself.

"What are you thinking?" her double asked. "It feels like I should be able to tell, but I have no idea."

"I really don't even know myself."

Words often felt inadequate to express her full feelings—it was part of why Winnie was so quiet in general—but they had never been *this* deficient.

"Here, go wash your face," her double said. She handed Winnie a washcloth, careful not to accidentally brush fingers with her.

"I don't think I'll really be able to pass for you," Winnie said.

Her double smiled faintly. "I guess we'll see."

AFTER WINNIE WASHED UP, HER DOUBLE SAT HER IN FRONT OF THE mirrored dresser and draped a towel around her neck. Winnie touched one of her long braids, which had been wrapped around her head to tuck them out of the way during the day. She hadn't cut her hair in years, enjoying the way it cascaded over her shoulders when she loosened her braids at night.

She could imagine herself Rapunzel up in her attic hideaway, trapped, but with the promise of escape. But now, seeing her doppelgänger, she thought her twin braids make her look silly, younger than her sixteen years. Why hadn't she realized it before?

Winnie watched in the mirror as her double carefully combed a section of hair straight and began to snip away. Wisps of dark hair fell and settled on Winnie's shoulders.

"Did you and Scott come up with a plan beyond hiding—a way to get you home?"

"Not yet. First we need to figure out how I got here."

Her double sighed. "I don't understand why you won't let us tell Daddy."

Winnie frowned. Father was clearly a different sort of man here. But in what ways—and why? She was curious, but not curious enough to risk meeting him, and maybe being given up to Hawthorn.

This wasn't something she thought her double would understand. How could she explain the tangle of hate and love, guilt and fear, she felt toward Father to a Winnie who called him "Daddy"?

To a Winnie who didn't even know he wasn't their father at all . . .

"I'm more worried about Hawthorn than your father," Winnie said, "but your father works for him."

"He *is* able to keep a confidence though. It isn't like he's so wild about Hawthorn anyway."

Winnie was glad to hear that, but ultimately, it didn't make a difference.

"I still don't want him to know. So, can *you* keep a secret?"

"Yes—if I understand why."

This frankness surprised a laugh out of Winnie. Of course her double would be the type of person who wouldn't blindly agree to something without knowing why! And although it was inconvenient, Winnie recognized they had at least that much in common, and if she were being honest, she'd be disappointed—and disconcerted—if her double weren't like that.

"All right," Winnie said, nodding her head resolutely. She would have to tell her double some slice of the truth, even though such openness went against her natural inclination. But she needed her double to trust her. And Winnie wanted to trust her double too. After all, she had to trust *someone* in this strange other reality, and who better to trust than herself?

"In my world, Scott's friend James has gone missing—and Hawthorn is either responsible, or he's covering it up."

Her double's eyes widened in concern. Winnie couldn't help but notice that it made her look even prettier.

"That's terrible! But how do you know Hawthorn's involved?"

"Well . . . I *don't* know. But Scott was sure of it. Do you need more evidence than that?"

Some things—most things—required proof. But not Scott.

After a moment, her double shook her head. "Okay. I won't tell Daddy about you," she said.

"And don't tell Scott about James—please. I'll explain it to him myself when we're planning our experiment."

Scott would need all the details, since it was likely that James's disappearance was linked to Hawthorn's experiments. When James disappeared, Scott had done everything he could to try to find him.

Would Dora do the same for Winnie? Would anyone else even miss her? Brunhilde, maybe. She wasn't sure about Father. Her life suddenly seemed very small, considered like that.

Scott had made it feel bigger.

Did her double know how lucky she was? Winnie had thought she appreciated Scott as much as humanly possible, but now that he was gone, she felt every wasted moment keenly. She should have told him how she felt. She'd assumed there would be more time. She'd thought they had a future together, perched out there on the horizon, waiting for them. As if futures didn't vanish as easily as fog!

Now that future was gone, and she'd never even shared the idea of it with Scott, the one person who could have made it real.

Winnie's chin began to tremble, and her eyes welled with tears.

"What is it?" her double asked, recoiling from her a bit. "What's wrong?"

"Scott died in my world," Winnie said. It was a little bit easier to say, this time. She took a few breaths to calm herself and waited for her tears to recede before she continued. "He died in the same accident that transported me here. We're going to try to figure out a way for me to go back in time to stop it, but . . ." Winnie trailed off with a helpless shrug. "As it stands now, he's gone."

"Oh," her double said softly. "That's—" she started, but then broke off. "If I saw Scott die, I'd want to disappear too," she finished simply.

"I didn't *want* to—"

Winnie fell silent. Hadn't she?

When she saw what happened to Scott, she remembered thinking that she didn't want to live in a world without him. And now here she was.

"Well, I guess I kind of did," Winnie said. "Father was doing an experiment, and something went wrong, Scott got hurt, and I couldn't bear the thought of losing him." Winnie took a shaky breath. "And the next thing I know, I'm here, and Scott's here, and he's fine."

"But he's not your Scott," her double said, her eyes narrowing slightly. "He's a different one."

"Yes," Winnie said, then shrugged. "But the two of them— it's not like with you and me. Scott here seems just like the one back home. It's as if they're identical."

Split-Winnie just stared.

Winnie realized how pathetic she must sound—speaking longingly of someone else's boyfriend. It would be bad enough in any scenario, made worse here by the fact that that someone else was a better-off version of herself.

CHAPTER FIFTEEN

Winnie's double continued her work on Winnie's make-over. Less than an hour later, Winnie looked in the vanity mirror, and her double's reflection stared back at her. But when she reached a hand up to tuck her hair behind one ear, the reflection moved too.

Split-Winnie had shown her how to do her makeup, coaching Winnie as she blended away the dark circles crying had left under her eyes and sketched in strong brows that seemed to change the structure of her face. They hadn't had time for her double's usual pin curls, so Split-Winnie had brushed out her own curls and styled them to match the waves Winnie's braids had left in her freshly cut bob.

Winnie looked sharp and mysterious, like someone who might have interesting secrets.

She smiled faintly at the thought. That was one thing she

did have—being from a whole other reality was one doozy of a secret.

"It's eerie," Split-Winnie said. "You look just like me, and it's like—who even am I?" She said it lightly, but the unsettled expression on her face belied her tone.

Her double seemed as disturbed by the success of Winnie's transformation as she was.

"You're still you," Winnie said.

The words were meant for both of them.

WINNIE'S DOUBLE HELPED HER PACK A BAG WITH ENOUGH CLOTHING TO tide her over for several days, then the two snuck downstairs. They stood, somewhat awkwardly, by the front door. What's a proper way to say goodbye to yourself?

"Well," her double began, "I'll call to let Dora know you're on your way."

"Do you think her parents will wonder why I'm spending so much time there? Although maybe they won't notice. Where I'm from, her parents are . . ."

Winnie trailed off. She couldn't think of a polite way to express what Dora's parents were: her father, a profligate heir seemingly bent on burning through the massive amount of money he'd inherited; her mother, a flighty, shallow socialite who seemed much more interested in jaunts abroad than her daughter.

Split-Winnie's expression confirmed that Dora's family

situation must be similar here. "Don't worry about the Vandorfs. They're on safari, or on a cruise, or skiing in Switzerland, complaining about what a bear it is to get their favorite caviar during wartime."

"Yes," Winnie said, cracking a grin, "that sounds about right."

She was excited to see Dora. The thought of staying with a friend, even if it wasn't exactly *her* friend, was comforting. And she felt reassured by the fact that Dora was friends with her in this world too. It seemed like a sign that maybe, at their heart, she and her double were more alike than different.

"I'll see you soon, right?" Winnie asked. "So we can start planning how to get me home?"

"Yes," her double said, returning Winnie's smile. "We can meet at Scott's after school tomorrow."

Her double pulled her into a sudden hug. Although Winnie knew it was meant to be a comfort, it was unnerving. Her double's body—*her* body?—felt both intimately familiar and completely foreign in her arms. Her waist was so small, and she could feel the curved cage of her ribs under the flesh. The delicate jut of her shoulder blades felt like calcified wings.

Looking at her double, touching her double—it was like coming home to find your bedroom full of a stranger's things. Winnie knew she was slender, but feeling the slip of herself right there in front of her, perfectly face-to-face, she was newly aware of just how vulnerable her body was. How vulnerable *everyone's* body was, she supposed. After all, she'd just seen Scott killed by nothing more than electrons.

Winnie extricated herself from the odd embrace. She met her double's eyes, and although she wanted to look away after a moment, she found she was unable. There was a jerk in her stomach—the feeling of falling—then a roaring in her ears. It sounded like the approach of an oncoming train. Split-Winnie began to look panicked, so Winnie was fairly certain that whatever was happening, her double felt it too.

Blood began to drip from Winnie's right nostril just as it dripped from her double's left. They each raised a hand to their nose to stanch the blood in eerie, mirrored unison. Winnie was finally able to tear her eyes away from her double's with great effort.

Her double retreated to the living room to grab a tissue for herself, and wordlessly passed another to Winnie.

"What was that?" her double asked in a shaky voice.

"Whatever it is, it seems to get worse the closer we are to each other."

"You should go," Split-Winnie said, her voice shaking. "We can figure it out later."

There was nothing to do but comply, although the thought of going off into this new world was terrifying.

Winnie left the house and her double shut the door behind her, averting her eyes as if from something monstrous.

Winnie heard her double throw the bolt behind her and knew she was really alone.

She was still shaken up about her and her double's nose-bleeds, and what had happened to her double's arms after Winnie grabbed her. Would they be all right if they stayed away from each other? Or would strange things keep happening to them for as long as Winnie stayed in their world? It was hard to believe she'd actually thought it might be a good idea to stay in this reality before she and Scott realized she might be able to go back and save his double.

When Winnie was thirteen, she'd gone to see *The Wizard of Oz* with Dora. It was her first time seeing a picture in theaters. How entranced she'd been—the music, the costumes, the spar-kling red shoes against the bright yellow brick road, all in vi-brant Technicolor! Dora sang the songs for months after, and Winnie sang along, even though her voice was never very good. She and Dora didn't know each other that well beforehand, but going to see that picture together and both loving it so much had cemented their bond.

When Winnie had teared up watching Judy Garland chant "There's no place like home," she couldn't have guessed that one day, she would find herself in a similar situation—mysteriously transported to a foreign world, at a loss for how to get herself home again. But Winnie knew that here, she couldn't go off on a quest to find some wizard to save her. Winnie would have to save herself.

She walked quickly down sidewalks that were disconcert-ingly familiar, half expecting to see something strange and awful around every corner—some other sign that this was a world entirely different from her own. She'd been transported to an alternate reality. The impossible had happened. Now *anything* might happen. If she bumped into a passerby, would their nose start bleeding too? Winnie quickened her pace.

Rush hour was long past, but traffic was still thick with canary-bright cabs. On the sidewalk, men in suits returning from a late workday mixed with couples heading out for the evening. Everything looked the same as it did at home, but rather than being reassuring, this similarity made Winnie uneasy. After all, which was more dangerous: the poisonous insect that announced its deadly sting with a bright-colored body, or the one that looked harmless?

The waxing moon had already risen and hung low in the sky. Was it the same moon she saw at home, or just one of a million others? And the stars, those pretty points of light people had navigated by for thousands of years, were they duplicated too? The vastness of the multiverse was too much to comprehend; just thinking about those infinite skies made her dizzy.

Soon, Winnie came to recognize at least one striking difference between her own world and this one: here, occasionally a young man would tip his hat at her with an expression that implied something more than simple courtesy.

Their attraction left Winnie flattered, but annoyed. Split-Winnie's fine clothes and a bit of makeup made her more appealing than her own character ever had. Was that really all that mattered to people in any world—the surface?

A part of Winnie enjoyed the appreciative glances she was

given, but mostly the attention made her nervous—like she was on display. She wrapped her double's coat more tightly around her body and shoved her hands deep into the satin-lined pockets. The coat, navy wool trimmed in rabbit at the cuffs and collar, the grown-up haircut—Winnie knew she looked more like a woman than ever, even though she hadn't felt this lost in the city since she was a little girl.

She was passing Central Park now. She was almost there.

She spotted some homeless men huddled on park benches. She knew her situation wasn't anywhere near as bleak as theirs, but even after just a few hours of being displaced, she looked at them less with pity than despair. You could lose everything—home, family, friends—so quickly. You could lose them in the blink of an eye.

Just like Winnie had.

CHAPTER SIXTEEN

Winnie was relieved to discover that the evening doorman at Dora's posh Park Place high-rise recognized her—or thought he did. He smiled and let her in.

"Good evening, Miss Winnie."

"Good evening, Ernie," Winnie replied, in what she hoped was a normal tone. Her fixed smile felt as stiff as a mask. She felt like a fraud.

Winnie stumbled a bit over the edge of the doormat. Ernie put his hand on her elbow to steady her and she jerked away, remembering the uncanny prints she'd left on her double's arm.

Ernie frowned. "Sorry, Miss Winnie."

She must seem like such a snob! But it was better to seem snobbish than to risk hurting anyone else.

Her ability had always been odd, and sometimes unwelcome. But she'd never been afraid of herself. Not until now.

The lobby elevator opened with a cheerful *ding* completely at odds with Winnie's dark thoughts.

"Penthouse, please," she told the operator.

He smiled a bit like he was laughing at her.

"Of course, Miss Winnie."

Winnie blushed. She hadn't been thinking. He wasn't the same lift man employed by Dora's building back home, but even though she didn't recognize him, of course he knew her. What would she do if the same thing happened to her out on the street—if some acquaintance of her double approached her, and Winnie had no idea who they were?

This world was a minefield of ways for Winnie to mess up.

Winnie reached the Vandorfs' penthouse duplex and knocked lightly on the door. After a few moments, it was opened by Louisa.

Winnie let out a breath; it was a relief to see a face that was familiar, but not in an emotionally charged way like her doppelgänger's or Scott's.

Winnie smiled tentatively, but this friendliness wasn't returned. It was odd; Louisa was a formidable woman, but she had always been fond of Winnie.

"Did Dora tell you I was coming?"

"Of course. Come in. I had Martha prepare you some food. Dora said you'd want something. She's waiting in the kitchen."

"She shouldn't have troubled you!" Winnie said, setting down her bag and quickly shrugging off her coat before Louisa could try to help her with it.

"No trouble at all," Louisa said. She gave Winnie an odd look, then picked Winnie's bag up off the floor and carried it upstairs to Dora's room.

It seemed like Louisa noticed a difference in her, which was disconcerting, although Winnie was confident Louisa would never in a million years guess what caused it. It struck her that she and her double had spent all this time making Winnie look like her doppelgänger, but there had been no mention of how she should act. Then again, how do you explain how you *are* to someone who doesn't know you?

Winnie could think of many words to describe herself— reserved, intelligent, hardworking—but had no idea how those lifeless adjectives actually played out for those around her. Many people were "smart" and "shy" without being anything like Winnie.

She didn't know her double, which in some way was to be expected, since they just met. But it made her wonder—did she really know herself?

It took Winnie a moment to recognize Dora. She was sitting alone at the kitchen table, wearing baggy jeans cuffed up higher than her bobby socks and a sweater made of some heavy knit that did her figure no favors. Winnie didn't care much about clothes, but Dora certainly did, and this was an outfit *her* Dora wouldn't be caught dead in.

This girl wore her best friend's face, but she was a stranger.

How was Winnie supposed to pretend to know her?

"Um, hello," Winnie said. She hoped her surprise at Dora's appearance didn't show, and that she sounded like her double.

Dora jumped up and hurried over to give her a hug. Winnie threw up her arms and cried "Wait!" but she wasn't quick enough—Dora already had her arms around her. Winnie waited for the headache, or nosebleed, but nothing happened. Even so, Dora pulled back and gave her a curious look.

"I'm sorry if I startled you!" Dora exclaimed. "When you—when she—called, I thought she must be joking. But obviously, you're really not Winnie, are you?"

For a moment, Winnie was too stunned to say anything. Her double had told! What was the point of the haircut, the fine clothes, all that silly makeup, if her double was going to give her away immediately anyway?

Winnie was an excellent secret keeper. *She* hadn't told her Dora about seeing splinters, even after being best friends for years. She was disappointed that her double couldn't keep this secret from Dora for even a day.

"She told you who I am?" Winnie asked finally. "What did she say?"

"Not much," Dora said, sounding a bit apologetic. "Just that you're here from another world by mistake, and that we have to try to get you back there."

It must have been some sort of misunderstanding. When she made Winnie promise not to say anything to her father, she thought it went without saying to not tell anyone else either, but now she realized she hadn't actually said that.

"She did tell you not to say anything about me to anyone else though, right?"

"Who would I tell?" Dora asked with a shrug, smiling. "But yes—she was quite explicit."

That, at least, was a relief.

Now that her surprise had passed, Winnie realized she was glad that Dora was another ally, rather than someone else she had to hide from. And this was her double's world, after all—Winnie had to assume she knew best. Although she doubted her own Dora would accept such a strange scenario with such little explanation.

Winnie pulled out one of the kitchen chairs and sat down. She wouldn't say she was *relaxed*, but this was probably the closest she'd come since arriving in their world. Winnie had always felt at home in that kitchen. Unlike the rest of the posh penthouse, it was utilitarian—since it was meant to be used by staff, not family—and all the spick-and-span surfaces and modern equipment reminded Winnie a bit of a lab. She reached up to cover her mouth as she yawned. Now that she'd stopped moving, she realized how tired she was.

"What should I call you?" Dora asked suddenly.

And just like that, Winnie was on edge again.

"Call me Winnie. It's my name."

"Won't that get confusing?"

Winnie shrugged. It probably would. But she had already given up enough of her identity.

There was a sandwich on the table for her, and Winnie took a tentative bite. It was a small thing, but she was deeply relieved to discover that Martha's roast beef and Swiss on rye tasted just like it did in her own world.

"You really do look like her," Dora said.

"I didn't when I got here. Do you really think I can pass for her now?"

"Absolutely! And I'll help however I can, of course—you just have to tell me what to do."

It was a generous offer—more readily given than the assistance from her own double, Winnie thought with a twinge of some feeling she could not yet name—but it left her unsettled. Back home, she never told Dora what to do, and Dora certainly never asked her to. In fact, Winnie had often questioned herself for letting Dora walk all over her, but she just told herself she went along with what Dora wanted because the stakes were never high enough to bother kicking up a fuss. What difference did it make to her what picture they went to see, where they went to drink their malts, who they sat with in the school cafeteria? This world's Winnie and Dora seemed to have a different dynamic.

Instead of being irritated that her double had told Dora the truth, Winnie began to question why her first impulse was always to lie.

Here she was with a whole new world to acclimate to, but she couldn't just learn about this new place and these new people without feeling like everything she encountered said something about her. It was already exhausting, constantly having what she thought she knew called into question. She thought back to that morning, getting out of bed, going to school—how blithely unaware she had been of what the day had in store! Had that really been the same day—the same *life*? Winnie set down the remaining half of her sandwich, her appetite suddenly and completely gone.

"I'm glad that you're so willing to help," she said. "But I don't even know what I'm going to do yet."

"Well, to start with, maybe get some sleep?"

Winnie glanced at the kitchen clock and was surprised to see that it was already after ten. She wasn't normally quite so tired by that time, but she didn't normally have evenings so jam-packed with revelation and disaster either. She nodded. "Sleep sounds good."

"Don't worry—I bet things will seem more manageable in the morning."

How many times had Winnie gone to sleep using that same sentiment as her own private lullaby?

You'll make friends tomorrow. They laughed at you today, but tomorrow is a fresh start.

Father will be sober by morning. You can both pretend none of this happened, and everything can go back to normal.

Tomorrow you'll be brave. You'll tell Scott how you feel about him.

It was never true.

How different this new world was—it disturbed her, but

it also proved that change was possible. Winnie thought she might be able to make different stuff out of her own life, given the chance.

But she was beginning to realize that chances weren't given; they were made. And now the stakes were higher than ever.

For Scott, you can do it. You can. *For him—and for yourself.*

She didn't fully believe it, but she believed it a little. And that was a start.

CHAPTER SEVENTEEN

Winnie awoke to the sight of Dora's frilly pink Swiss-dot canopy, instead of the sloped attic ceiling of her own familiar room. She jolted upright, momentarily disoriented.

Then it all came back to her.

If only it had all been an awful dream! But no. Scott's death, her transport, Winnie and her double's uncanny bloody noses—unfortunately, it was all real.

Today began the tough work of undoing it.

And Winnie had never been afraid of a bit of hard work.

Winnie and Dora ate a hurried breakfast, then headed off to school, just like normal—or so Louisa would assume. As soon as they turned the corner, away from Dora's high-rise, they parted ways. Dora really was going to school, but Winnie obviously couldn't join Dora—and her double—there.

"Good luck!" Dora said with a jaunty wave. "I'll see you tonight!"

Winnie gave a little wave in return. She was on her own.

She planned to hide out in the library for the day, hoping to do some research and begin figuring out how to duplicate the accident that brought her there—without the whole someone-getting-electrocuted part, of course.

It was a crisp, sunny day, and walking the eighteen or so blocks to the main branch of the library did wonders for Winnie's spirits. The sun seemed to say, *Anything is possible.* Winnie felt a warmth flowing through her. She had made the leap between realities once. She could do it again.

When she reached the library, she was happy to see the two massive lion sculptures, affectionately named Patience and Fortitude, guarding the library entrance there, just like back home. As she entered the building, she noticed a large, colorful poster hanging on the corkboard in the lobby. It was a carica-ture of Hitler, comically bucktoothed and in possession of a remarkable underbite.

for CARELESSNESS,

I gif nice MEDAL

the cartoon exclaimed.

This was a common theme: if we make the tiniest slipup, it's a win for the Germans. Winnie saw the logic of it. The United States and Germany were enemies; obviously, what hurt one helped the other and vice versa.

So why did posters like that make Winnie so uneasy?

She was German by birth, but that awful little man certainly wasn't her ruler. She hated the Third Reich, the same as Father did. Hitler was a conman, playing on people's fears until they agreed that oppression and aggression were not only acceptable, but necessary.

But Germany wasn't just Hitler's soldiers, and America wasn't at war with only the Third Reich—they were also at war with any innocent Germans along for the ride.

People like her grandparents.

She hadn't seen them in many years, but Winnie remembered them as kind, and they had continued to send her thoughtful letters and photographs over the years.

What did they make of Hitler, and of the war?

Did they see him as a violent dictator? Or as a noble führer—as Winnie was sure the German papers must paint him?

Maybe it was silly, but on top of all this, Winnie was bothered by that "gif." That was Brunhilde's "gif." It was her own accent, when she was flustered. Seeing it mocked on a poster was a reminder that no matter how much she considered herself an American, to some, she would always be an outsider.

WINNIE TURNED AWAY FROM THE UPSETTING POSTER AND WADED INTO the hushed lobby. The particular quiet of libraries always felt very full to Winnie, and almost holy. Entering a library felt like entering a church, especially when it had ceilings as high as this one's—a church of knowledge. Winnie wanted to believe that this was someplace she belonged, in any world.

She wasn't quite sure what she was looking for, so she skipped the card catalog and walked up to the reference desk.

"Excuse me," Winnie said, smiling brightly at the reference librarian, an older man in a tidy tweed suit. "I was wondering if you could help me find some materials about alternate realities?"

"Ah! Really? Funny reading for a girl!" he said, and gave her an indulgent smile. "I'm sure you could find something in one of the pulps, but we don't index the topics on those. Have you tried looking through *Astounding Stories*?"

"No," Winnie said, a bit frustrated by his patronizing tone. "Actually, I'm looking for something serious."

"Perhaps some classic science fiction, like Verne? Or Wells? Let me see . . ."

"No, something *scholarly*," Winnie said, annoyed. She heard her German accent creeping into her speech and grew even more irritated. The librarian's face lost its friendliness. Oh well—at least it lost its condescension too. "I'm looking for articles in scientific journals about the possibility of alternate realities—or better yet, the possibility of traveling between them. Articles referencing time dilation would be helpful too."

He narrowed his eyes at her. "Shouldn't you be in school?"

Winnie could have cursed herself. She wished she'd just gone straight to the stacks. She hadn't wanted to draw attention— and she was sure she wouldn't have, if not for her unwelcome accent. Winnie suspected that quiet, respectful, *American* teens could spend a day playing hooky at the library, no questions asked.

"We have the day off," Winnie said nervously, her accent stronger than ever.

The librarian looked not only unfriendly now, but suspicious. "I see," he said, then Winnie saw his expression become eager at some epiphany. "Now, what did you say your name was?" he asked with a poor imitation of nonchalance, grabbing a slip of paper and holding a pen at the ready. "Give me your information, and a better description of these materials you're looking for. I'll see what I can find and then I'll contact you."

He was going to *report* her, Winnie realized, stunned. For what, being German in the library? She had a feeling she was looking at the person who had hung that propaganda poster in the lobby.

Back home, it would have almost been comical. Winnie Schulde: schoolgirl spy! And even if someone *did* take the idea seriously, she knew that Father would bring the full weight of his determination and ferocity against anyone who tried to hurt her. He'd done as much before, threatening the school administration when a bully started shoving Winnie around after she showed up in third grade, awkward and small and foreign, dressed in the painfully out-of-fashion clothing Brunhilde had picked out for her.

But here, there was no one to defend her. And she couldn't afford the scrutiny. A girl with no family, coming from nowhere, bearing a sinister resemblance to the daughter of a scientist who was working on a government project? Winnie would seem *exactly* like a spy.

The only other possibility would be for them to believe her claim that she was from an alternate reality, in which case it would only be a matter of time until she was handed over to Hawthorn to "help" with Project Nightingale.

Winnie didn't know what would be worse: being a secret prisoner, kept captive for her uncanny abilities, or being a public enemy, imprisoned and tried for treason.

She took an unconscious step back from the reference desk, the shuffle of her double's heels on the polished floor echoing loudly in the cavernous space.

"Um, don't worry about it," she said. "I'll see what I can come up with myself in the stacks."

"It's no trouble," he said, but Winnie just smiled and turned to go.

"Miss?" he called after her, but quietly.

Winnie thanked her lucky stars this was a library. His soft call was easy to ignore, and she was able to duck into the stacks and get lost there before he could come after her. She doubled back toward the exit, shooting nervous looks behind her to make sure she wasn't being followed, and finally pushed out the door, where she stood panting on the portico for a moment.

Winnie descended the library's outside stairs at a good clip, then headed off toward Central Park—she could be anonymous there.

The night before, she had scolded herself for being slow to

trust and quick to lie, unlike her double. Well, she'd learned her lesson. If anything, she needed to be more cautious—cautious enough to combat the wartime paranoia. But what could she do—stay out of sight? Talk to no one? How could she possibly accomplish that when she had to stay away from Dora's apartment during the school day?

Winnie tucked her hands deep into the pockets of her double's coat and braced herself against a blast of chilly wind. Swirls of fall leaves danced around her feet. Central Park was beautiful this time of year, though far too cold for her to spend all day there.

Dora had pressed two crisp dollar bills into her hand that morning—it hurt Winnie's pride to have to accept them—but at least for today, she had more than enough money to linger over lunch somewhere, then move to a café later in the afternoon. And her double's fine clothing meant that she could spend hours window-shopping if need be, without seeming like an out-of-place ragamuffin. But goodness gracious, what a waste of a day—one that certainly wouldn't bring her any closer to getting herself home or saving Scott! It was unavoidable now, but she couldn't afford to make the same mistakes tomorrow.

Winnie cut across a grassy swath between the park sidewalks, heading toward one of her and Dora's favorite diners on West 68th Street. Suddenly, she began to feel—*heavy*. Her footsteps slowed. She felt like she was moving through molasses. It wasn't painful, just very strange.

Winnie lifted a foot with effort. When she put it down in

front of her, her foot sank into the ground an inch or two. What on earth was going on?

Winnie looked around the park. She saw a couple walking normally on the sidewalk a few dozen feet away, the wind rustling the remaining leaves on nearby trees, some starlings in unencumbered flight. Was this strange phenomenon only affecting her?

No.

Winnie noticed a little boy, perhaps five or six years old, standing stock-still ten feet away, holding a ball in two hands and staring right back at her. He had sunk into the earth up to his ankles.

"Get out of that mud, Willy!" a woman called from a nearby bench.

Then suddenly, Winnie could move normally again. The strange pressure was gone as quickly as it had arrived. The little boy ran back to his mama, and Winnie hurried on, unhurt but deeply shaken.

Scott had warned that her presence in their world could knock things off kilter, but could she really affect *gravity*?

Winnie was putting some kind of pressure on this reality, and the world—well, the world, it now seemed, was pressing back.

That little boy seemed fine, but if he had been hurt? Winnie gave a sharp shake of her head and gritted her teeth.

She had to figure out a way to isolate herself.

And she had an idea of just how to do it.

• • •

After school, Winnie met up with Dora a few blocks from her apartment as planned, and the two of them walked the rest of the way home together.

"How did your day go?" Dora asked. "Any luck at the library?"

"The librarian thought I was a German spy."

Dora laughed.

"I'm serious."

"Oh. That's . . . not great."

"Yeah," Winnie said dryly. "It's less than ideal."

She didn't say anything about what had happened in the park. She was still too rattled.

When they reached Dora's building, the daytime doorman was on duty. This time, he was someone Winnie didn't recognize. "Miss Dora," he said, nodding courteously. "Miss Winnie." Winnie felt consternation again at being recognized by someone she didn't know. All the more reason to keep herself out of the public eye.

"We're home!" Dora called out when they entered the penthouse.

Louisa came over and took Dora's knapsack and coat. She immediately offered them a snack, just like Brunhilde always did, Winnie thought with a pang.

Was Brunhilde worried about her back home?

. . . Was Father?

She was so angry with him! But she still wanted him to miss her.

• • •

DORA WANTED TO CHANGE OUT OF HER SCHOOL CLOTHES BEFORE THEY headed to Scott's, so Winnie followed her to her room. Winnie flopped down on Dora's bed—an absurdly spacious "queen" size, larger than any other Winnie had ever seen—then quickly propped herself back up again. This wasn't *her* best friend. Wasn't it rude of Winnie to be so casual with her?

"Gosh, I hate wool!" Dora said, pulling at her pleated skirt.

It was odd to hear her say this—her Dora wore wool all the time and never complained. Did it bother her too?

Dora finished taking off her school clothes and pulled on some tan trousers and a blue button-up shirt. Winnie noticed that this world's Dora didn't bother with any sort of waist cincher.

"No girdle?" Winnie asked. The words just popped out of her mouth, much to her embarrassment.

She was certain she must have offended Dora, but the girl just gave her a curious, indulgent little look and said, "They squish your organs, you know."

"I'm sorry—I didn't mean—it's just that the Dora I know wouldn't be caught dead without one."

Dora grimaced. "Poor girl." She grabbed a little brown pocketbook. "Ready to go?"

"Sure."

As she followed Dora out of the apartment, Winnie couldn't help but think about how wrong her initial impression of this split-Dora had been the night before. She'd been alarmed by the absence of her Dora's polished prettiness, but this girl

179

seemed comfortable with herself in a way that made her own Dora's flashy self-confidence seem, well . . . brittle. For the first time, she wondered why her Dora felt she had to try so hard.

And what kind of friend was she, that she had never wondered before?

Winnie didn't know where Scott lived, but her double had given Dora directions to his apartment. It turned out that he lived in Harlem, convenient to the university but farther north, well into the area where things started looking run-down. The first floor was storefronts: a locksmith, a repair shop, and a shoe store with a dusty window display that looked like it hadn't been changed since the Hoover administration.

The entrance for the apartments was sandwiched between two of the shops. Dora lifted the doormat and triumphantly retrieved a key. Winnie felt a twinge of guilt at the girl's bright smile. To Dora, it must feel like she'd been swept up in a thrilling Nancy Drew mystery, but this wasn't just a lark. When Winnie suggested staying with Dora, it hadn't occurred to her that she might be putting the girl in any danger. Now she wondered. After all, she hadn't thought Scott was in danger during Father's experiment either, and look how wrong she'd been there.

"His apartment is on the fifth floor," Dora said cheerfully.

There was no elevator, so the girls started climbing. Winnie was winded after the first two flights, but Dora didn't seem to have any trouble with them. The fuller-figured girl probably played tennis at the club. Her Dora did.

Winnie wondered how often her double climbed these stairs to his apartment, and what she and Scott did there together when they were alone.

Of course it was none of her business, but there was no assuaging Winnie's curiosity. She felt her cheeks grow hot, embarrassed to be thinking about the two of them together like that—but not embarrassed enough to stop.

She had fantasized, in a vague sort of way, about the kinds of things she might do with Scott, but it was nothing more than a scramble of images from the movies: the passionate kiss; his hands in her hair; them moving back toward the bed. After that it was just a fade to black, then a cut to the rosy afterglow: her smiling face and satin nightgown, him smoking a cigarette.

She knew what intercourse was, at least the basic mechanics of it. Father had her pediatrician explain the birds and bees to her after she'd had her first cycle. But that didn't mean it was something she could actively picture, even with Scott. Her double was probably worldlier than she was—but how much more?

Winnie's stomach lurched in embarrassment. Did it show? Could they all tell—that she was just a precocious child sitting at their grown-ups' table? She'd *just* had her first kiss, and it had come from a boy who thought she was someone else.

She and Dora finally reached the fifth floor. As they walked down the hall, an intense nausea struck Winnie. She tried to take a few more steps, then stopped. Her hand flew to her mouth. She was suddenly afraid she might throw up.

"What's wrong?"

"I'm feeling kind of queasy." She took a few shaky breaths and her stomach settled a bit. She shrugged uneasily. "Must be nerves."

They arrived at an apartment whose tarnished bronze numbers declared it 513, but before either of them could knock, the door flew open. There stood Winnie's double, white-faced and clutching her stomach.

"I could *feel* you coming," she said. "The closer you got, the sicker I felt."

Winnie frowned in dismay. It hadn't been nerves after all. But what should they do about it?

"Should I go?" Winnie asked.

"Go where?" her double answered with an irritated shrug. "Just come in already."

The girl didn't offer her a smile, but Winnie didn't take it personally. And this time, her double didn't grab Winnie, either; Winnie understood why.

She was scared too.

CHAPTER EIGHTEEN

Scott was pacing in front of a shabby, floral-patterned couch. It was hard to untangle the knotted mess of feelings Winnie felt when she saw him: relief that he hadn't somehow vanished overnight, grief over the him she *had* lost, guilt over the trouble she'd brought into his life. And pulsing under all of that, excitement (mixed with nausea). She was happy to see him, just like she always was. There were new feelings layered over it, but underneath, that same bedrock. Even if she could admit, at least to herself, that it was probably wrong for her to feel that way about him now . . .

Her eyes began exploring his apartment—that was safer than continuing to look at him. The place was small but uncluttered. A kitchenette occupied one corner of the living space, and there were double doors on the far wall, but judging by the empty space left in front of them, they concealed a pull-down Murphy bed, not another room. Although the apartment was modest, it was tidy and warm, exactly what Winnie would have imagined Scott's home to be: a clean, simple space for a busy student to sleep and eat.

"Have a seat," Scott said, and gestured toward a beat-up armchair.

Winnie's double went to take a seat on the couch, but Scott held up a hand to stop her.

"Not you," he said. "Dora, I want you to take Winnie home. Having her double nearby is making her sick. The other one can stay here with me, and we'll figure out what we're going to do."

Winnie winced at being referred to as "the other one," but supposed there wasn't really anything better for him to call her. It would be easier for them to talk once her double was gone.

But Split-Winnie made no move toward the door. "I'll be fine," she said, and sank down onto the sofa. "The nausea is going away already."

"You want to get another bloody nose?" Scott asked. "I wish you'd actually mentioned that bit yesterday—I would have told you to stay home."

"That's why I didn't tell you," her double grumbled, and Winnie grinned at her sass. After a moment, the girl returned her smile.

"Fine. Stay. But if you start to feel sick again—"

"I know, I know."

"I'm feeling better too," Winnie said, although she felt embarrassed a beat later, because no one had actually asked. "I wonder what makes it stop and start?" she added quickly, and took a tentative seat in the battered leather wing chair in the corner, the spot farthest from her double.

Scott frowned, thinking. "Maybe it's something like carsickness," he said. "Motion sickness is caused when part of the body—the inner ear, for instance—understands you're in motion, but another part—like your eyes—doesn't. Maybe when you're near your double, the parts of your body that orient you in space get confused—you're here, but you're there—and it makes you feel sick until your eyes catch up with your body."

Winnie did feel disoriented, but it had more to do with Scott than with her double. She saw Scott in her memory, on the floor, limbs at odd angles like a dropped doll. She saw Scott right there in front of her, tantalizingly close.

If she couldn't go back and save him . . . what would she do? What would she do without him? And how could she live with herself?

Scott caught Winnie staring.

They both quickly looked away, and Winnie noticed her double glancing back and forth between them uneasily.

What did she look like to Scott? Did the differences between her and her doppelgänger jump out at him? Or did he have to force himself to see them?

"Well," her double said, "we already know her being here is wrong. Scott, what did you call it? 'Violating the rules of space-time'? So, is it really such a surprise that it's messing things up?"

What her double said was true, but her words still made

Winnie feel like an unwelcome immigrant all over again.

"Why are we the only ones it's hurting, though? Dora hugged me last night—she was fine. And when I got here—before we realized what was going on—Scott kissed me. Nothing weird happened to him either."

"He *what*?"

Scott shot Winnie an irritated look.

"Honey, I thought she was you."

"Really? Did you think I'd just come back from a shopping trip at the Salvation Army or something?"

"All right!" Dora interjected brightly. "You each got a dig in. Are you ready to stop being shitty?"

Winnie and her double each let out a sharp bark of identical surprised laughter.

It gave Winnie an idea.

"Quantum entanglement! Or something like it," Winnie said. She looked at Scott. "Could that be causing it?"

"What's that?" her double asked.

"Basically, some particles are—they're linked," Scott said. "So, if something happens to one, it affects the other, no matter how far apart they are."

Winnie's double frowned. She didn't seem to like the idea. Suddenly, she gave her own arm a sharp pinch. "You don't feel that, right?"

Winnie shook her head.

"See? We aren't linked," her double said. "We aren't the same person."

Winnie found her double's unease extremely relatable. She was unsettled by the idea herself—but she still felt like she was on to something.

"Oh, I know we aren't," Winnie said. "I don't mean it like that. I was thinking on a quantum level—maybe all doppelgängers have linked particles, since we start out as the same person."

"So, it's not how we move our arms, but the orbit of our electrons or something?"

"Exactly! And maybe those energy fields throw each other off when they get too close to each other, like identical poles of a magnet."

Scott looked spooked.

"If that's true—Winnie, I don't think you understand how serious that is. If getting too close to each other puts pressure on your atomic bonds . . . well, you don't want to know what happens when an atom splits. Let me tell you, the whole city would feel it."

Winnie swallowed nervously. This talk sure made her and her double's petty jealousy feel—well, petty. She knew she had to mention what had happened at the park earlier, even though just thinking about it filled her with a queasy guilt.

"This afternoon, at the park—I think something went wrong with gravity."

"What!"

Winnie bit her lip—thinking back on it, it was as surreal as a dream. But no, it had happened. There was no denying that now, no matter how much she wished she *had* dreamt it.

"I got heavy—*really* heavy. It was hard to walk, and I sank into the ground. And it wasn't just me. It happened to a little boy playing nearby too. It happened out of nowhere, and then—it couldn't have even lasted a minute—then it stopped."

They all sat in silence for a moment, trying to absorb the shock of what she'd said, Winnie assumed.

"Well, that's . . . alarming," Scott said. "But whatever's going on, we need to focus on getting you back home as quickly as possible."

"Alarming? It was *terrifying*! Everything went back to normal after and nobody was hurt, but what if next time—" Winnie took a deep breath and tried to calm herself. She looked at her double. "She wasn't even there, so it isn't only us being near each other that's upsetting things. What are we going to do?"

"We're going to get you home," Scott said. He sounded calm, but Winnie noticed he had started bouncing his leg—one of his nervous habits. "That's all we *can* do. And, Winnie,"—he gave her double a stern look—"I don't want you involved after tonight. Whether this is quantum entanglement or who knows what, I don't want us to find out how serious these physical symptoms can get."

"I want to be involved, though! What am I supposed to do, just sit home alone and worry?"

Scott shook his head. "I'm sorry—I know it's frustrating, but I won't allow you to put yourself in danger."

His voice went a bit husky with emotion at the end, and Winnie felt a knot form in her throat. She'd seen that kind of protectiveness from Scott before. It was what had made him stay with her in the lab. It was what had gotten him killed.

He wanted to protect his Winnie—but who was going to protect him?

She had already gotten one Scott killed. And now, just by being there, she was putting the whole city—maybe even their whole world—at risk.

You will not let Scott get hurt, she told herself sternly. *You won't let any harm come to any of them*, she vowed.

But she already feared that wasn't a promise she had the power to keep.

Scott swallowed and shook his head, and when he spoke again, his voice was once more matter-of-fact.

"Winnie," he said briskly, now addressing her, "you can come here in the evenings, after I've finished my daily work with Professor Schulde. I told him I wasn't feeling well so that we could all meet early today, but I'll have to return to work tomorrow."

This was the moment. And Scott had given her the perfect opportunity to share what she'd been considering. "I was thinking," Winnie began nervously, "that it might be easier if I stayed here with you. I could keep working while you're away during the day, and there's less opportunity for me to raise suspicions if I'm not out and about. And less opportunity for any more . . . mishaps."

The safer she was from Nightingale, the safer they all were. And the fewer people she was around, the fewer people she could put in danger. Plain and simple. The thrill in her stomach was just the result of figuring out how she could stay safely hidden and find some answers at the same time, she told herself. Not because Winnie was eager to spend her nights with her double's boyfriend.

But before Scott could answer, her double said, "Absolutely not!" She looked a little embarrassed by her vehemence, and quickly added, "I mean, she'll be much more comfortable at Dora's," gesturing around the small space.

"I think it's better for her to stay here too," Dora said. "She has to leave the house with me in the morning, and—well, Winnie, tell them what happened at the library today."

Winnie hadn't intended to say anything about that. She'd been frightened in the moment, but now she wondered if she'd overreacted.

"Oh, it was just a silly thing," she said, waving her hand. Hadn't she given them enough to worry about? "I went to the library to do some research—"

Scott cringed and made a worried hiss.

"What?"

"Nightingale and the Manhattan Project have certain subjects at area libraries flagged. It's part of our security agreement to protect against espionage as government contractors. Any time someone makes an inquiry or checks out materials about nuclear fission, uranium enrichment, multiverse theory, interdimensional travel, et cetera, we get a report we're supposed to investigate."

Winnie sighed. "Oh. I guess I wasn't being paranoid, then."

"I should have told you."

"You couldn't have known I would go to a library first thing." Although, she was a bit surprised he hadn't guessed as much—wouldn't her double have done the same? "I didn't give them my name," she added. "Or anything like that. So at least there won't be much to go on. Just my description."

"Still, you should definitely stay here. The less you're seen, the better. This place is nothing much, but we'll make do."

Rather than being relieved at this, Winnie began to worry. She hadn't really thought about what it would be like, sharing such a small space with Scott for days on end. Where would she sleep? On the couch? No, of course Scott would be a gentleman and insist she take the bed . . . which, if her guess about the Murphy bed was correct, would be about five feet away from Scott on the couch. So, there she would be, wrapped in his blankets, head on a pillow that smelled of him, listening to his breath while he slept. It sent a tangle of feelings shivering through her stomach.

She was excited at the prospect of being so close to him, and ashamed of that excitement.

Winnie gave her head a brief shake. She was there to figure out how to save *her* Scott, not to think like that about his double.

"Well, that's settled—" Scott began, but Split-Winnie cut him off.

"No, it's not! I don't want her staying here. She can upset gravity just as easily here as she can at Dora's, and the only reason she's afraid of Hawthorn is because James is missing in her world, and their Scott thought Hawthorn was to blame."

"What?" Scott asked. "James went missing? Why didn't you tell me!"

"I was going to," Winnie said weakly. Her double just hadn't given her the chance.

Scott had never looked at her with such reproach before. Winnie felt a hot flash of righteous hatred toward her double for betraying her confidence. This feeling vanished as quickly as it had come, leaving behind confusion and shame. Was that the sort of person her double was when her back was against the wall—disloyal?

She and her doppelgänger were bringing out the worst in each other. The two of them weren't supposed to be in one world together, and with both of them occupying the same identity, just trying to exist made her feel like a dog begging for scraps. She couldn't just be Winnie anymore, even in her own head. "Winnie" was her, but also her double, who she had to dress like, even though she knew she could never really be her. She just wanted to be herself, but how could she, under the constant pressure of her own mirror image?

No. She had to stop thinking of her double as another self outside her body—as another "Winnie." *She* was Winnie. Let her doppelgänger be . . . Beta, at least in Winnie's head; she should get to be Alpha in her own mind, if nowhere else.

Winnie took a deep breath. Distancing herself from her doppelgänger made her feel calmer than she had all day. She was stuck in a foreign world, but she was Winnie, she was herself, and she was human. An individual, not just a poor copy.

"Well," Scott said slowly, "would you tell me about it now?"

"But that's the thing," Beta interjected. "It doesn't matter—it has nothing to do with *our* Hawthorn. Our James is fine. So, she doesn't have to stay with Dora, and she doesn't have to stay with you. We don't have to hide her at all. We can introduce her to Hawthorn and let Nightingale help her. Especially if they're just going to find her anyway."

Winnie being there might be upsetting the order of things and endangering people, but at least she cared. Her double didn't seem to care about anything aside from herself and her Scott.

"Hawthorn was using James as a test subject," Winnie said, pausing to let the horror of that sink in. "The kind of man who does that—he isn't a good man, not in any world." Winnie felt a lump forming in her throat, because what she said could apply to Father too. "But if that's the sort of person you're willing to turn me over to, then I guess there's nothing I can do to stop you."

"Of course we won't!" Scott said quickly. He shot her double a look of reproach. "We aren't going to make you do anything you don't want to do."

This felt like victory—but only for a moment. Beta immediately paled and clutched her stomach, which made Winnie realize that she was feeling queasy too. She lurched to her feet, eyes searching for the bathroom, but her double shoved past her and hurried that way herself, slamming the door shut behind her. Winnie could immediately hear the sickening sound of her double vomiting.

Dora took her arm and quickly guided her to the kitchenette, handing her a little wastebasket. Winnie's stomach heaved, but thankfully, it was empty.

She watched Scott as he waited for her double outside the bathroom. There was something so tender about the way his hand was pressed against the door that separated them, like he was eager to share even in her suffering.

Scott finally glanced back over his shoulder, sparing a thought for Winnie. But instead of inquiring how she was, he just said, "You should probably go. And maybe it's best if you just stay with Dora—at least for the time being. I'll see you tomorrow. We'll start planning then."

Even though Beta lost the argument, she still got her way in the end. Winnie wasn't surprised. She couldn't have really expected Scott to side with her over his own girlfriend. Still, it felt astonishingly unfair that her double's preference was given more weight than Winnie's safety.

She longed to see her own Scott then with an intensity she remembered from the early grieving months after her mother's death. That experience had taught her there was no escape from grief. Time would lessen it, but the only way out was through.

It wasn't an especially helpful lesson.

Winnie's legs felt increasingly weak as they descended the several flights of stairs to exit Scott's apartment building, but her nausea gradually eased. Once they were outside, a chilly wind lashed Winnie's cheeks, making her realize they were wet.

"Your stomach hurts terribly?" Dora asked, grimacing in sympathy.

Winnie nodded. It was easier to let Dora think that was why she was crying.

CHAPTER NINETEEN

The next evening, Winnie headed out for her rendezvous with Scott. As she walked down the block to meet him outside the five-and-dime store where Dora had said that Beta had said that Scott had said he would pick her up, she tried not to be annoyed that her life had become a game of telephone. If Beta had let her stay with Scott, communication wouldn't be an issue . . . but if Winnie was honest with herself, she knew that if she were in her double's place, she wouldn't want her staying with Scott either.

Winnie hugged her arms to her chest.

The weather had finally turned, and the night was downright cold, full of the promise of winter to come. She rocked back and forth, trying to keep warm as stiff fingers of wind pulled at her scarf and hair. Her hands stung. The skin at her knuckles had started to crack, and although Winnie knew it was almost certainly from the cold, it made her nervous.

She had begun to mistrust her body. Nausea, headaches, nosebleeds—what next?

She caught a glimpse of her own watery reflection in the glass of the store front window, illuminated in a cone of light from a streetlamp, the bright navy of her borrowed coat inky in the dark, eyes huge in her pale face, curls blown wild. It looked like she was fading away.

Scott waved at her from down the street, the other hand holding his hat tight to his head. He looked a bit enigmatic in his tightly belted trench coat. The light glanced off the lenses of his glasses, turning the expression behind them inscrutable.

Winnie found herself hoping she really could trust him.

"You haven't been waiting too long, I hope?" he asked, smiling lopsidedly. It was his nervous smile, and recognizing it flooded Winnie with an uneasy affection.

"Oh, no—I just got here."

He offered her his arm and began to escort her down the sidewalk, chivalrously walking on the street-side to buffer her from the press of traffic. It made Winnie feel odd—and guiltily pleased—that anyone who saw them would think they were a couple.

"How are you doing? Winnie's nausea stopped soon after you left. I assume yours did too?"

Winnie nodded. She was feeling a bit shy, just the two of them—but perhaps that was for the best. It wouldn't be right for her to be too comfortable with her double's boyfriend.

"I've been thinking about the connection between the two

of you," Scott said. "Quantum entanglement, or whatever it is. It's sort of—well, creepy. And then I think about *my* double, and what happened to him. It makes me feel like maybe I'm doomed and just don't know it."

Winnie was relieved that this, at least, was a worry she could ease. She knew that sometimes a person died in one world and lived in another. She'd known that since her very first splinter.

"It's not like that. Think about it—if there are infinite realities, we've probably all died countless times."

He thought for a moment, then smiled. "You know, that's actually comforting."

Winnie was glad she'd been able to make him feel better, but she wasn't able to return his smile. Even if Scott was likely dead in many worlds, and alive in still more, it was too abstract a reassurance for her unless she could get him back in her own.

SCOTT SET ABOUT MAKING WINNIE SOME TEA IN THE DOLLHOUSE-SIZED kitchenette. Once it was ready, he set the tea tray on the coffee table and sat down across from her. In addition to tea and cookies, he'd prepared a few cheese sandwiches, which he'd cut into tidy, crustless triangles. This touch of domestic flair surprised her, but on second thought, why should it? Surely someone capable of operating delicate, finely calibrated equipment wouldn't be at a loss when confronted with a kitchen.

"I thought that if you were skipping dinner at Dora's, I had better actually give you some food," Scott said, looking somewhat bashful, "although the pantry is a bit bare this late in the month."

"Thanks," Winnie said, grabbing her teacup and a triangle of sandwich, "I'm famished."

"So, where do you think we should begin?"

She knew that Scott wouldn't be able to help unless he knew everything, but it was hard enough for her to think about what had happened, much less talk about it. So, she had spent hours in a café writing down a full account of Scott's accident in what she hoped was meticulous detail—a truly horrible way to spend the day, but better that than trying to speak it all aloud.

"I wrote down everything I could remember about what happened in the lab that night."

That terrible night had been only two days ago. It felt like a lifetime. She only hoped that if they were right about the time dilation, and if she just hurried, she could be quick enough to undo it.

"But before you read it," Winnie added, "there's something you need to know. Or maybe you know already? But Scott didn't." Winnie swallowed nervously, but there was nothing to do but come out and say it. "Sometimes I see alternate realities. I get this glimpse of how things could happen differently, how that same moment plays out in a different world, but then also, sometimes—well, once, I saw a peek of the future that resulted too." Winnie could see he had questions, but pressed on. She wanted to get it all out. "So, it isn't a complete surprise—I mean, it isn't completely random—that I would be able to travel between realities too."

"That's—well, it's astonishing. I can't even begin to . . ." He trailed off, then said suddenly, "I wonder why Winnie doesn't see them?"

But surely Beta saw splinters too. Winnie's ability—it wasn't cosmetic, like her hairstyle or one of her double's lovely sweaters, something that could be taken on or off. Seeing splinters was part of her. Winnie didn't say anything, but her disbelief must have shown.

"No," Scott said firmly. "She would tell me something like that."

"I *wanted* to tell Scott, to tell Dora, even. But I never told *anyone*, outside of family. Don't think it means she doesn't trust you—I'm sure she does. But it's a scary thing, being different. And it's only getting scarier, with the war, being German . . . Growing up, seeing splinters felt like—I don't know, like a wart. I was embarrassed. What child wants to be different? But now it's worse. Now it feels like a target."

Scott nodded slowly. "I'm sorry. It's selfish, taking something so personal and making it about me. But it's just—it's so strange, for there to be something that significant about Winnie that I don't know. And Dr. Schulde! Why would he agree to work with Nightingale, knowing the risk if Hawthorn found out about her?"

Winnie was gratified to hear him acknowledge that the risk from Hawthorn was real, especially after Beta once again suggested handing Winnie over to him last night.

"I was surprised by that too," Winnie said, "but it seems like here, he keeps her out of his work. Maybe he felt like that distance was enough, or maybe he thought that him knowing more about Hawthorn's work would help keep her safe."

Or maybe, Winnie thought, her father was more worried about his own career than about his "daughter."

Winnie pulled the folded-up papers recounting the accident out of her purse and passed them to Scott. "Here," she said. "If you have any questions, just ask." She'd kept the account as dry as possible, but still felt as exposed as if she were handing over her diary. Scott began reading, and she took a nervous bite of her sandwich.

The evening of Scott's death had been awful, and it had been awful to relive it, which was part of why she'd written everything down. Printed words on a page couldn't waver. They couldn't betray her feelings by some inflection or glance. They couldn't alert Scott to the fact that the accident had been both the worst of her time in the lab and its culmination—not an anomaly, but the apex of years of awfulness.

Winnie watched his face as he read on. After a minute or so, she saw him flinch and knew what part he must have arrived at.

"A kitten? You were supposed to control a coin toss that determined whether or not Professor Schulde killed a kitten?"

Winnie nodded.

"But it was just to give you some extra motivation—a trick, albeit a cruel one. He wouldn't have actually killed it," Scott said. His voice sounded confident, but he was examining her face, looking desperate for confirmation.

Winnie shook her head. "He would have killed it."

She had known Scott would understand the physics of the situation, but she hadn't anticipated that he would struggle to grasp the psychology. When she considered leaving out those cruel details, it was from a simple desire to avoid airing the family's dirty laundry, not from any fear that he wouldn't believe her. Now she was glad she'd left those parts in. She needed Scott to understand it—*all* of it.

Her fate was at least partly in his hands now. She wanted him to know what that meant.

"The Professor Schulde I know—"

"You don't know him," she said. "Not like I do. And you don't understand how angry he was."

"Why? Why was he so mad? He sounds awful!"

Winnie frowned. Father wasn't a *monster*. She didn't want Scott to think he was.

"He found out that I found out that Erwin Schrödinger is my real father."

For a moment, Scott just looked at her. "But not here," he said. Then immediately shook his head. Beta and Winnie were identical. Obviously, they had the same parents. Winnie and Scott both knew that although there might be any number of differences between their worlds, the parentage of two identical selves wasn't one of them. "Are you sure?"

Winnie nodded.

"Still, the experiment, it's all so cruel."

"I don't think he does it to hurt me," Winnie said. "I—I think he does it to hurt himself. As punishment for the accident that killed Mama."

Scott raised his brows. "So, you're what—collateral damage?"

In a way, she was glad he didn't understand—glad that Scott had never been in so much pain that seeking out other, different hurts was a desirable distraction. Her double would understand. Wouldn't she?

"Don't tell her about any of this, okay?" Winnie said.

"Doesn't she deserve—"

"No. No good can come of it."

Finally, he nodded. "Fine. But I hate keeping secrets, especially from Winnie. And I'm awful at it."

"Then this will be good practice."

He sighed and shook his head, then he opened his mouth to speak—but instead, closed it again.

"What?"

He gave a heavy sigh. "Nothing. I—I'm just going to finish reading this, okay?"

Winnie frowned, then nodded. She wished she knew what he was thinking, but supposed he was entitled to his own private thoughts, same as she was.

SCOTT FINISHED READING WINNIE'S ACCOUNT AND SET THE PAPERS ASIDE.

"All right," he said. "I think I understand the premise of your father's experiment, and it's pretty clear how it went wrong. To start with, I think we need to figure out how to re-create the conditions of your first trip."

Winnie nodded. "There's some equipment we'll need—a pretty sizeable generator and a Faraday cage will be the most difficult to come by, I think—and we need more space than we have here."

"Don't worry," Scott said. "I know a place that has both the equipment and the space. Hawthorn's lab."

Winnie laughed out loud, although she had a sick feeling he wasn't joking.

"Winnie, you can do this. You didn't want to be in that world anymore, and because the conditions were right and you wanted out badly enough, you were able to travel between worlds. I think if we can re-create the conditions, you can will yourself back."

"All the way back, right?" Winnie pressed. "Back to Scott. Back to before the accident."

Scott nodded. "Yes. But you have to trust me. Scott wouldn't have done anything that could get you hurt. I won't either."

Winnie looked at him.

"Okay. I'll do it."

It was the last place she ever thought she would go, but if Scott really thought it was safe, and if this might be her only chance to get back and save her world's Scott . . . she supposed she would be paying a visit to Hawthorn's lab.

CHAPTER TWENTY

It was broad daylight, and Winnie was headed to the subway that would take her to the 116th Street stop—straight to Hawthorn's lab at Columbia.

Every step she took felt like she was moving through molasses. If she had trusted this world's Scott just a little less—or if she had been just an ounce less desperate to save her own Scott—she wouldn't have been able to do something so against her own instincts.

Yes, this was Scott's idea, and he swore it was safe, but it still felt like a *very bad idea*. Even if Hawthorn wouldn't be in his office.

There was a departmental meeting that afternoon, and Hawthorn was chairing it. Scott had assured her Hawthorn would absolutely be in attendance for the full two hours—and in fact, such things *always* ran long. All the other professors involved with Nightingale would be there too, including Professor

Schulde, as well as most of the other physics department staff, because skipping a meeting would put them in danger of getting on Hawthorn's bad side.

No one wanted to be on Hawthorn's bad side.

And even if—by some crazy chance—someone *did* see them in Hawthorn's lab, it would be unusual, but not unheard of. Hawthorn's personal laboratory was separate from the one for the project's common use, but they did occasionally share equipment, and if anyone asked about Winnie, well, Scott would just say they were going out to lunch, but he needed to finish some work first.

The safety of this plan relied on its brazenness. The least suspicious thing for her to do was waltz into the last place on earth she wanted to be and act like she had nothing to hide.

It seemed fairly safe, as far as completely insane plans went.

Still, Winnie very much wished her afternoon involved pretty much anything else.

SCOTT MET HER ON THE QUAD AS PLANNED AND WALKED WITH HER TO Pupin Hall, where the physics department and all related projects were housed. Winnie had been on campus with Father a handful of times over the years, but not often enough to have any real familiarity with the place. There was something extravagant about the expanses of tidy green lawn occupying so much space right in the middle of a metropolis. It was an intellectual oasis, and it reminded Winnie of how much she wanted a place like that of her own.

Of course, Columbia would never be that place for her. Students glanced at her as they passed by—not rudely, simply curious—but Winnie knew that if she weren't there with Scott, they would have stopped to ask her, ever so helpfully, if she were lost.

"Oh—I asked Winnie about the splinters," Scott said suddenly as they neared the physics building. "She doesn't see them."

Winnie almost stopped in her tracks. "She must. Maybe I didn't explain them properly. It isn't some trick I learned. I know we aren't identical now, but we started out that way. And this is something that was inside me at birth. In my chromosomes."

"How do you know that?"

"Well, I suppose I don't *know*, but I have pretty good reason to believe my mother saw them too."

"Hmm. Really? That is interesting." Scott made a small, considering sound and thought a moment. Then he said, "There are identical twins who are different heights."

Winnie just looked at him.

"I'm saying, what if it's a capacity—a potential? Not everyone has it, and you both do. But you, for whatever reason, fulfilled that potential, and it just never came to fruition for Winnie. Just like some twins don't get as tall as they might have."

What he was saying made sense, in theory, but it didn't *feel* right. A pretty, confident her with chic short hair and the boyfriend she'd always wanted? Yes, that was unsettling to see for many reasons, but none of those little differences cut against the core of her being like the thought of a self with no splinters.

Of course, the idea of having this ability all her own in a world where everything was Beta's had a certain appeal, but not enough to counterbalance how unsettled it made Winnie feel about who she was, and the role her gift played in her identity. She could travel between worlds! It was awful, but in that other sense too—she was awed by this ability that was as unconscious yet central to her as the beat of her own heart.

What did it mean if Beta didn't share it?

Would Winnie want to give up seeing splinters if she could?

They'd certainly caused their fair share of trouble over the years . . . but she still found herself unable to answer that question.

But it did raise another.

"Scott, wait—I just realized. I haven't seen one since I've been here."

"Really? Is that unusual?"

"Well, I don't know. They don't come on a schedule. I've been here"—Winnie silently counted; it felt like an eternity—"three days now. It wouldn't be *that* unusual to go without for even longer. But what if, for some reason, I can't see them here? Oh god—what if that means I've lost the ability to cross between worlds too?"

Scott furrowed his brow in worried consideration. "I can't begin to guess what all this might mean, but it doesn't seem like we need to jump to that conclusion yet."

Winnie's heart thudded panic, but she knew he was right. It was too early to guess what—if anything—was going on.

"Maybe we'll find answers in Hawthorn's lab," Scott finished.

Winnie nodded. "Maybe."

She just hoped they didn't find Hawthorn there. Or rather, that he didn't find them.

HAWTHORN'S LAB WAS A WINDOWLESS SPACE ON THE FIRST FLOOR OF THE building, meticulously clean and vaguely familiar-feeling from the glimpse she'd gotten in that splinter where she met James. It was just as empty as Scott had promised it would be, and the Faraday cage they would need for their experiment stood prominent and ominous in the corner. To Winnie, it looked like a cell.

Scott took some sheets of paper from his leather knapsack. "I wrote out a schematic for our experiment, based on what you told me about what happened."

He handed the papers to Winnie, and she began to look over them.

"I kept things impersonal," Scott said, sounding a bit embarrassed. "I'm the 'technician.' You're the 'subject,' et cetera. I just thought that even though it's unlikely anyone would find our notes, it would be a good idea to make them anonymous."

"I like it."

Scott's expression remained sheepish.

"Really, I do. It's comforting. Seeing it laid out like that, all stiff and scientific—it could be about somebody else."

She could almost forget that the life of the "prior technician" was on the line.

"I hypothesize that the panic you experienced when Scott— when he was injured—is akin to the fight or flight response. Your ability just affords you a unique exit strategy."

"That's an interesting theory."

"But it means we'll have to re-create that feeling. Which might be a challenge."

Winnie wasn't sure it would be. That grief, that terror—it remained right below the surface. Keeping it contained was the hard part. Letting it free would be a relief.

"I'm going to start getting the equipment ready while you—" Scott began, but he was interrupted by someone opening the laboratory door.

Winnie and Scott looked at each other in a panic. The breath caught in her throat as he stepped into view and—

"Oh—sorry." He looked surprised to see anyone there, then less surprised when he saw who it was. "Hi, Scott. I'm just grabbing some notes Hawthorn needs for the meeting."

He had dark hair and a sweet face that Winnie both did and did not know.

"Hello, Winnie," he added. "Nice seeing you again."

He reached to shake her hand, and Winnie saw the bruises

that ringed his wrist. He saw her notice them and quickly pulled his cuff back down.

It felt like the walls were pressing in around her. She couldn't think. Couldn't breathe. It seemed miraculous that she was even able to say whatever words she said—they disappeared from her mind as soon as they crossed her lips—to get out of that room and back to the hall, where she immediately pressed her back to the wall and slid down to rest on her haunches.

Winnie sucked in air in heaving breaths and tried to focus on the one concrete thing she was aware of: the cool tile against her clenched fists, braced against the wall on either side of her body.

She hadn't thought much about that splinter since she'd gone to Hawthorn's party. After that night, there had been so much more to think about.

Now Winnie realized that when she saw that splinter of James—bruised and seemingly in trouble—and decided she needed to try to bring it to fruition by going to the physics mixer at Hawthorn's, she'd gotten it all wrong. She had gotten a peek into the future, and she'd worked to bring it about because she thought it would mean finding James. But she hadn't seen herself meeting her own world's missing James. She had seen something else entirely, misunderstood it, and set herself on a path that led—*here*. To this stupid lab a world away. A place she had no business being.

Winnie had wanted to go to that party to help, but now she understood—everything that had happened since that party had instead led to Scott's death. Not because they'd been diverted from the course she'd seen somehow, but because Scott's death and her coming to this new world were stops on the path she'd set them on.

That splinter had been a glimpse into the future of another reality—and now she was living it. Now she was stuck.

It all just felt so pointless, so unavoidably *pointless*. She hadn't understood anything. She hadn't helped anyone. How could she possibly believe that was different now? How could she think she could save Scott, or even get herself home?

The door opened and, thankfully, Scott came out alone. Winnie tried to scramble quickly back to her feet, and Scott silently reached out an arm to help her.

"Winnie," he said softly, "you need to come back in, and you need to act normal. James is my friend, and he's trustworthy—but if we act suspicious, then we're involving him, and I don't want him involved."

Winnie gave a shaky nod. The more people involved, the more people she might hurt.

They walked back into the lab, Winnie wearing a bright and—she was sure—false-looking smile. "I'm sorry, James, I haven't been—" she began, but the words died in her throat.

James was holding Scott's experiment schematic. The expression on his face wasn't shocked, or confused, but sad.

"Scott, she can't be here," James said, shaking his head. He sighed heavily. "You must be the girl from the library," he said to Winnie. "Hawthorn's looking for you."

• • •

Winnie and Scott hurried off campus, but the feeling of being a fugitive remained even after she was back on the crowded city streets.

"God, I feel stupid," Scott hissed once they were a few blocks from campus.

Winnie did too—stupid for feeling hopeful. James was going to meet them at a diner in neighboring Harlem. He was going to help them—Winnie was positive, although she didn't know what made her so sure.

They found the spot James had suggested—Gracie's, on the corner of Lenox and 127th Street. It had been only perhaps a twenty-five-minute walk from campus, and Winnie worried they might run into other students there until they entered. She noticed that they were the only white clientele. Everyone in the physics department at Columbia was Caucasian too. No risk of running into any of them there.

They got some odd looks from the customers, but if the woman behind the counter was surprised to see them, she didn't show it. "Anywhere's fine," she said, and Scott led them to an open table in the corner, where they would hopefully be able to talk without being overheard.

They ordered Cokes and sipped them nervously while they waited. James walked in about twenty minutes later.

"Hey, sweetie!" the woman at the counter called, and brought him a coffee as soon as he was seated.

"Hi, Gracie," James said. "I wanted my friends to try the best burger in the city."

His smile looked strained to Winnie, but she supposed it would seem natural enough if you didn't know the stress they were all under.

"Oh, stop!" the middle-aged woman said, and slapped at his shoulder playfully. "Three burgers, then? I'd ask how you want 'em cooked, but you know Ralph only does medium-well."

She walked off to put in their order, and the air was immediately heavier. James lost his smile.

"You said Hawthorn is looking for the girl from the library," Scott said. "Does he already know it's Winnie?"

"No, no—just a split-sport."

Winnie gave him a quizzical look.

"You know, someone like you."

"Oh," Scott said, "a 'sport' like a genetic mutation."

"He sees them too, doesn't he?" Winnie asked eagerly, oddly gratified to have her initial suspicion about Hawthorn confirmed.

"Hawthorn?"

Winnie nodded.

James shook his head. "No—his mother does. Did. Only women can. Or, that's Hawthorn's theory, at least. It ran in his family, but it only affected the women."

Scott frowned. "He hasn't shared any of this with the research team."

"Well, you couldn't really expect him to."

Winnie bet there was a lot Hawthorn didn't share with the rest of the scientists working under him.

"James . . . what are those bruises from?" Winnie asked, gesturing toward his wrist.

Scott looked back and forth between them in alarm. "What bruises?"

James pulled at his sleeve, but they weren't showing at the moment. "It's nothing."

"James!" Scott pressed.

"You wouldn't understand."

"*I* would," Winnie said quietly.

James regarded her, brows knit, and Winnie thought he was about to speak when Gracie came by with some fresh Cokes for her and Scott, providing James with a convenient interruption.

"Thank you," Winnie said with a nod.

Scott fidgeted angrily on the bench seat next to her, and Winnie put a quelling hand on his forearm.

"You're better off than you think," James said suddenly, then sighed. "And worse than you know. Hawthorn hypothesizes that it's people who can see alternate realities who would be able to move between them—you being here proves as much. You've succeeded once. I'm sure you can do it again."

James stopped there.

"And the rest?" Scott pressed.

James closed his eyes for a moment, then shook his head. She could imagine how difficult it must be for him to betray his mentor's secrets.

"He's going to want her," James said finally. "He's already looking for someone by her description. As soon as he read the report, he knew that a girl researching alternate realities was almost certainly a girl who saw them. He's been working for years—before Nightingale, before the war—on a serum that would let him see them too. The serum requires genetic material from a split-sport. He used his mother's, when she was alive. He still has some, but—"

"Some?" Scott asked, voice thick with disgust. "Some *what*?"

James looked down at the table and began shredding his napkin. It was an anxious habit Winnie shared.

"Blood. Bone marrow. Some . . . tissue." He glanced up at them. "Everything except the blood post-mortem, of course."

"Oh. Of course!" Scott exclaimed. "James, you must realize how gruesome this is!"

"I understand how it sounds."

"He's testing the serum on you, isn't he?" Winnie asked gently.

"Not just me! On himself first, always. I'm the control, since he carries a recessive version of the mutation himself, and I don't. We don't know yet what difference that might make. He's not a bad man. But he's not . . . he's not always reasonable about this. He wouldn't hurt you, Winnie. But he wouldn't let you go either."

"Your wrist," Winnie prodded, working hard to keep her voice level—Scott's obvious indictment of the whole endeavor was getting them nowhere—"it looks like he grabbed you."

"No!" James said quickly. "Well, he *did*, but because I was falling. I was having a seizure—"

"What? Since when do you get seizures?" asked Scott.

"Just once. A side effect."

"Listen to yourself!" Scott said. "You have to stop this. You've got to—"

"You miss sleep for your work," James interrupted defensively. "You miss meals. Last spring, you came to class with walking pneumonia."

"That's not the same," Scott said with a furious shake of his head.

Winnie noticed the people at the surrounding tables were beginning to shift nervously and stare.

"This isn't the place," she said quietly, glancing around the diner.

"Look," James said, "give me a list of the equipment you need. I'll sneak what I can out of the lab for you and bring it by your apartment tomorrow."

Scott just glared at him, jaw set.

"Thank you," Winnie said. "Scott, could I take a look at your notes—and do you have a pen?"

He pulled out the papers detailing their experiment and passed them to her wordlessly, along with a notebook and pen. Winnie began making her list. They would have to build a Faraday cage themselves—it was obviously too large to transport—but everything else she wrote down, then she handed the paper to James.

He took a crumpled dollar bill and some change from his pocket and put it on the table.

"I need to get back to the lab. The meeting should be getting out soon. You two split my burger—they really are good."

He stood up, and without thinking about it, Winnie stood too, scooted out of the booth and gave him a quick hug. "Thank you. Is there anything—"

James shook his head. "Just do your experiment as soon as you can," he said. "And if it doesn't work, at least get out of the city. He'll find you if you stay here."

Winnie could hear the concern in his voice. And he didn't even know the half of it. "Where I'm from," Winnie said hesitantly, "you disappeared."

James gave her a crooked smile, but just like his mentor's, the expression didn't reach his eyes.

"Don't worry, Winnie. I know how to take care of myself."

She truly hoped he did.

CHAPTER TWENTY-ONE

That evening, after Scott finished his work at Professor Schulde's, they began building the Faraday cage with materials Scott picked up from the hardware store. Winnie wanted to say something that would make him feel better about how he and James had argued that afternoon, but she couldn't think of anything that would help.

She understood why James wouldn't just walk away from his work with Hawthorn; the tangle of emotions she saw in him seemed to mirror her own feelings about Father's work. She recognized the pride, the shame, the protectiveness—dare she say, the love—that had made it feel impossible for her to stop participating in Father's experiments.

But she could no more explain any of this to Scott than she could have made James understand that he not only could, but *must*, escape Hawthorn's project. Winnie hadn't realized escape was necessary herself until it was too late. Things always seemed bearable—until they weren't. James would have to come to the realization by himself, or not at all.

She could only hope that for him, it wouldn't take the same sort of tragedy it had taken her.

CONSTRUCTING THE FARADAY CAGE WAS MUNDANE WORK. THEY WERE building it with collapsible panels so that they could easily transport it to wherever they decided to attempt their experiment. It complicated things, but basically the cage was just a cube of wood framing with chicken wire stapled to it, so it was still simple enough to build.

Winnie and Scott worked together in companionable silence. It reminded her of those too-rare times when Father would step out of the lab for a bit and leave her and Scott to work together alone. Would she ever have moments like that with her own Scott again?

Winnie set the stapling gun down for a moment so she could brush a piece of hair away from her face. She liked the way her new hairstyle looked, but her pinned-up braids never got in the way like this. She wondered how her double could stand having hair in her face all the time. Then again, since Beta wasn't in the lab every night, assembling and cleaning equipment and leaning over to take notes, maybe it wasn't an issue for her.

Winnie finished stapling a panel, then pressed her hand to the chicken wire to make sure there wasn't too much give. The sensation of the fine mesh hexagons against her palm brought back a memory from long ago.

"We used to have chickens," Winnie said, "back in Germany." She closed her eyes for a moment, and it was like she could see their little cottage, henhouse out back, and Mama in a house-coat throwing down feed. She shook her head. "It feels like a lifetime ago."

Scott frowned. "Winnie never talks about her life before she moved here."

Winnie didn't normally talk about her time in Germany either. Partly because many people were unwelcoming toward immigrants, and partly because thinking about those days made her think of Mama, and the accident, and how wrong it had all gone in the end. When Father had been hired on as a lecturer at Columbia, he'd been adamant. America was a new life for them. A fresh start. She'd wanted that too. What was there to leave behind but pain? Of course, pain had no trouble traveling along with them.

But even though it wasn't something *she* mentioned much, Winnie was surprised her double never talked about her child-hood with Scott. She seemed more open than Winnie, and Winnie had longed to share all the details of her life with Scott, good and bad. Still, there was wanting, and there was doing. Maybe Beta wanted to talk to Scott about those times, but it wasn't so easy to actually do, was it?

"Well," Winnie said slowly, "not all the memories from that time are pleasant ones."

And some of those unpleasant parts, like Father's drinking, continued into the present. She had no desire for Scott to know about that, both out of protectiveness for Father, and a feeling of shame that she couldn't quite make sense of, since she wasn't the one who overindulged and then flew off the handle. She supposed it wasn't really possible to separate her own identity from Father's, seeing as how he was her whole family. They shaped each other. Maybe if she'd been different, he would have been too.

Scott was looking at her intently, and she knew he was eager for her to say more, but of course he was too polite to pry.

Winnie hadn't gotten the chance to share these things with her own Scott. She was shy at the prospect now, but she couldn't let herself miss this opportunity again.

"You have to understand, after Mama died, that house . . . it was like a picture she'd been cut out of. There was this massive, obvious hole, but around it everything just—stayed the same. You know Father. How meticulous he is. He didn't let the household fall to pieces. Before he hired Brunhilde, he did it all. Cooking, cleaning, scrubbing our clothes on the washboard outside and hanging them to dry just like Mama did."

"He's an exceptional man."

"No, you don't get it. I mean yes, he's exceptional. But it would have been better if he'd fallen apart. Not forever, obviously. But if we could have grieved—out loud, together—then maybe we wouldn't each have had to grieve in silence, alone, these past eight years."

That's what Winnie remembered most from those long

months in Germany after Mama's death, before Father received his job offer from Columbia: the silence. Her eyes filled with tears. Maybe her life was a bit lonely now, but nothing like it had been then.

Before Mama died, the house had been full of her chitchat. A woman who'd wanted to be a physicist talking to herself—possibly to fight the tedium of housework, Winnie realized now. Father tackled those same tasks after her death with a grim—and silent—determination. That, and the muffling effect of her own grief, had muted even the everyday outside sounds.

Only one sound remained crisp in her memory. The loud tock of her grandparents' sitting room clock, marking the seconds of every long pause during her and Father's continued Sunday visits with Mama's parents.

"I'm sorry it's still so—fresh," Scott said.

"Yeah, I think I'll always miss her. But maybe that's a good thing—remembering her. I just wish it didn't still hurt this much. For me or for Father. Your Winnie—she seems so much more *normal* than I am. She and this world's Professor Schulde—I think they must have done a better job of it. A better job grieving. A better job moving on. Father and I got stuck somehow. I wonder how they did it."

"Winnie, you shouldn't—"

"I know, I know. I guess I just can't help . . . wondering."

They were both quiet for a moment.

"Scott, with time dilation, do you think there's any way . . . ?" Winnie asked, trailing off.

Scott shook his head gently. "If you're right about the inverse relationship between time in our worlds, you would have to wait—what, a decade? Even then, I mean, you aren't even *you* there yet. You're just a little girl. You would be displacing the wrong amount of matter." He gave a heavy sigh. "I can't speak to the theoretical limits of time dilation, but practically speaking? I just don't think there's any way. And I don't think it's . . ." He shrugged and shook his head. "I think maybe it would be wrong, even if it were possible."

Winnie frowned, then shrugged. "I didn't think so," she said quietly.

It had been a mistake to dredge up this old stuff. She'd thought it would make her feel better. That it would make them closer. But his curiosity—it was really Beta's past he wanted to know about, wasn't it? Not hers.

If Scott thought *she* was going to be a tool for him to grow closer to her double, he was sorely mistaken. If he had questions about his girlfriend, he would have to ask her himself.

Scott opened his mouth to say something more, but just then a brisk knock on the door startled them both.

"The rent's paid," Scott whispered, "and I don't usually get many visitors. I don't know who it could be."

That was a lie.

He knew who it could be.

They both did.

How detailed was the description the librarian had passed on to Hawthorn and Nightingale? Apparently not so detailed that James had immediately thought of her . . . but clearly detailed *enough* that he made the connection after just a few moments of looking at Scott's experiment notes.

"Winnie," Scott said, "I think you should hide."

Winnie nodded and ducked into the bathroom. It wasn't a great hiding place. If anyone searched the apartment, they'd find her. She felt her stomach lurch.

She heard Scott's footsteps on the creaky bare floorboards as he crossed the room.

The knock came again, pounding this time.

"Who is it?" Scott asked without opening the door.

"It's me!"

The door muffled the voice, but it was unmistakably Beta. Scott opened the door, and Winnie let out a shaky breath and came out of the bathroom

"You were *hiding*? Isn't that kind of paranoid?"

Scott laughed, but it sounded a bit breathless, and Winnie could tell from his degree of relief that he had been just as scared.

"Now I feel silly," he said, "but I assumed it was something bad. I really couldn't think of a single person who might pay me a visit just because!"

Beta frowned.

"I would. Obviously."

"Well, yes, you of course," Scott said. Then he gave Beta a severe look. "But I thought we agreed it would be a needless risk for you to join us while we worked. What are you doing here?"

"I'm just stopping by for a moment—I wanted to drop off some dinner," she said, holding up a bag, "and see how things are progressing."

"Winnie—"

"Scott, I *need* to feel like I'm doing something. This affects me just as much as anyone." She gave Scott the sort of doe-eyed look Winnie had seen Dora use when she was trying to get her way with a boy, and Winnie saw him instantly soften.

"Not as much as it affects Scott—my Scott," Winnie interrupted angrily. *Or as much as it affects me*, she thought, fighting the feeling in her stomach. "He'll stay dead unless we figure out how to send me back. What is you coming here going to do to help, besides make us both feel sick?"

Scott and Beta gave each other a look, and Winnie saw them come to a silent agreement. That wordless communication was more intimate than any display of affection, and witnessing it was a harsh reminder that she and Scott had only ever been together as a couple in the flat space of her imagination.

"You're right," Beta said. "I'll go."

Winnie noticed as her double placed a hand on her stomach. Good. Let her be nauseated too.

"I'll tell you about how it's going later," Scott said. "I know I need to be better about that." He took the brown paper bag that Beta offered and walked her to the door. Winnie looked away, but she could still hear the peck he gave Beta's cheek.

Winnie hoped to never be alone with the two of them again, a voyeur to an improved version of her own life.

When Scott told her that Beta couldn't see splinters, she'd felt sorry for her double, but now, Winnie wondered if one reason Beta's life was so much better than hers was the lack of them.

"Wait," Winnie called, right as Scott was about to shut the door. "The splinters—you really don't see them? Not ever?"

Her double shook her head.

"Never."

"Not even the accident?" She could imagine convincing herself that some splinters were nothing more than an overactive imagination, but that one—that one couldn't possibly be ignored. "There was a world where Father swerved and missed the deer," Winnie continued. "I saw it. Didn't you?"

Bringing up the accident, such an important point of commonality between them, brought a gentler look to her double's face. "I was asleep when it happened," she said softly.

Maybe that was the initial splinter between their worlds, the one difference all others cascaded from. Winnie had seen a sleeping version of herself avoid the crash, but in Beta's world, she had been asleep and crashed anyway. Winnie wondered what this meant about the share of blame she'd been shouldering all these years, but couldn't let herself think more about that at the moment.

"I hope the work goes well tonight," her double said. "Enjoy the sandwich."

Scott stepped out into the hallway after Beta, and they stayed out there for a few moments, their voices an indecipherable murmur.

Winnie was used to feeling like an outsider. But being on the other side of that shut door, she had never felt lonelier.

It wasn't entirely their fault. At first, it had seemed harmless not to correct everyone's assumption that Winnie and Scott had been together in her world too, but now the omission was beginning to feel like an embarrassing lie, like she was a little girl playing dress-up in Beta's relationship.

Scott came over to the couch, opened the bag Beta had left, and handed Winnie a sandwich wrapped in wax paper. Winnie tore the wrapper open, but then set the sandwich down on her plate without taking a bite.

"I feel like I should tell you, Scott and I aren't—weren't—together in my world," Winnie said, forcing herself through the discomfort. "Things were heading in that direction," she hedged guiltily, "or at least I think they were. But we never had a chance to . . . make it official."

Scott looked like he was wondering what made her confess that right then, or at all. But rather than question her, he just gave her a gentle smile and said, "I'm sure it *was* heading in that direction. Us Scotts know things."

She knew she should just take him at his word, but found herself resisting the easy comfort.

"But how do you know? You and Scott—you're identical. But you knew I wasn't your Winnie immediately. You knew as soon as we kissed. I thought you were Scott, but you knew I wasn't her." She paused a moment to steel herself. "How could you tell?"

Scott looked at her for a moment, like he was trying to understand what she was really asking, and then he said, "I don't know. But it wasn't because the kiss was bad, if that's what you're thinking."

Winnie couldn't let the silence rest, afraid her relief would be too obvious. "What was it, then?"

He closed his eyes a moment, like he was thinking. "You seemed surprised," he said slowly. "I could feel you trembling." Scott shrugged. "It didn't feel like just another kiss. It felt like the first time."

He met her eyes, and the moment lingered a little too long. There was a charge in the air, almost like the one she'd felt right before Scott was electrocuted. They locked eyes, then both quickly looked away.

Another thought struck Winnie then. "Do you think there will be another me there?" Winnie asked. "When I go back— will I run into last week's me?"

She was terrified of the answer. Winnie didn't want to have to face herself again, even if it was her own true self of the recent past. She couldn't bear the thought of going home and still being an extra.

"No, I don't think so," Scott said firmly. He took her hand and gave it a reassuring squeeze. "There's still just one you. That isn't an alt-verse with a double in it. It's your home."

Winnie smiled at him uncertainly. It seemed too good to be true, but she wanted desperately to believe it.

CHAPTER TWENTY-TWO

Winnie had problems enough of her own, but she couldn't stop worrying about James. She would see him when he brought the promised equipment to Scott's apartment, and she resolved to say something to him then about getting away from Hawthorn. She saw many parallels between his life and mentorship with Hawthorn and her own life and relationship with Father. But all the relevant similarities *they* shared weren't things Beta had in common with James. It would all be coming out of the blue for him if Winnie were to suddenly tell him he simply must quit working for Nightingale.

So, she wasn't very hopeful that James would abandon his mentor on her word. But she resolved to try anyway.

She didn't get the chance.

"James wasn't in the lab today," Scott said as soon as he opened the door to let her inside the apartment.

Fear spread from her stomach in an awful wave, making her limbs tingle unpleasantly.

She bit her lip and shook her head. "What do you think happened?" A question just to say something. As if they didn't both already know.

Scott gave her a helpless look. "Hawthorn said he called in sick. God, if Hawthorn hurt James—" Scott stopped himself, jaw clenched, and shook his head.

Winnie didn't want to ask, as if speaking it aloud was the thing that would make it real, but she couldn't stop herself. "Do you think it's because of us? Do you think Hawthorn caught him stealing equipment?"

"I don't know. Maybe."

"We need to try to find him. Have you been by his apartment yet? We can go right now."

Winnie hadn't even taken off her coat. She moved toward the door.

"Winnie, no. Let me worry about James. What we need to do now is get you home."

"But—"

"It won't help anything if Hawthorn gets his hands on you too."

Winnie knew he was right. But she hated it. Protecting herself, being cautious—it felt so selfish when other people's lives were at stake too.

And she was the common link.

"I'm just . . ." Winnie paused so she could blink back her

tears. "All I do is get people hurt. I don't want to. I try not to. But I do."

"Winnie, this isn't your fault."

She raised her eyebrows. *Of course* this was her fault.

"James started working with Hawthorn long before you came into the picture."

She frowned. That was true—there, and in her own world. James had gone missing before she'd even known there *was* a James.

So at least this wasn't *only* her fault.

"I should have said no when he offered to get the equipment," Scott said. He paused and took a shaky breath. "And I shouldn't have fought with him."

"You just got angry because you care about him. I'm sure he knew that—knows that," she corrected quickly.

"He could be okay," Scott said firmly.

Winnie nodded. She had to believe James was alive, but *okay*? That seemed like too much to hope for.

It felt wrong to return to the preparations for their experiment, business as usual, but the fact of James's disappearance only made it more vital for them to try to get her home as quickly as possible. She didn't think James would tell Hawthorn about her voluntarily, but she did worry that he might be forced to confess.

Scott brought out a bulky canvas knapsack and began

unloading its contents onto the coffee table, parcels of varying size cautiously wrapped in gloves, knit caps, and some plaid scarves.

"The only thing I dared to take from Nightingale's labs was one of Hawthorn's special batteries. The lab has a huge supply, and I have no idea how they're made. But for everything else, I thought it would be safer to make do with these things from the general classroom equipment."

"Will anyone find out you stole this stuff? Will Hawthorn?"

Scott just shrugged. "I don't think so. But I didn't know what else to do."

Winnie picked up the largest piece of equipment, and carefully unwound the woolen scarf that wrapped it.

"A Leyden jar?"

Scott nodded.

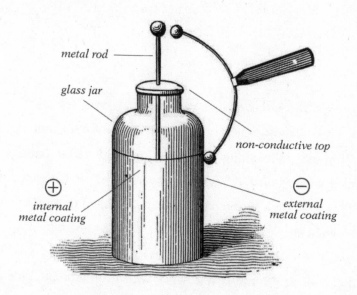

"We can use it to build a makeshift electrometer with some of the other things I took from the lab. There's only one electrometer, so someone would notice if it suddenly went missing, but no one will miss this."

They needed the electrometer to measure ambient electricity after they discharged the generator, so they would know when it was safe for her to come out of the Faraday cage without risk of electrocution.

"As for the generator," Scott continued, "there's one on campus that needs repairs. I'll say I want to fiddle around with fixing it and bring it home tomorrow. It's an old one we use in class, not one from Hawthorn's or Nightingale's labs."

"So we'll have everything in place tomorrow?"

"If everything goes smoothly, yes."

"Good," she said, trying to sound confident, but really wondering when—in this world or her own—things had ever gone smoothly.

THEY USED THE SPECIFICATIONS FROM AN OLD KELVIN ARTICLE TO CON-struct the electrometer. It took only a few hours, but it was much more painstaking than building the Faraday cage, and Winnie was exhausted when they were finished. Given all she had been through in the past week, it was hard to remember a time when she *hadn't* been completely wiped out.

And Scott must be even more exhausted than she was. He had classes at Columbia and work with Professor Schulde on top of their own experiment—not to mention the stress she'd brought into his life.

"I can't imagine how tired you must be," Winnie said.

"No, I'm all right."

Winnie gave him an incredulous look.

"Well, yes, I'm tired. But all of this—I mean, with everything happening in the world right now, there are certainly plenty of people who have it worse."

"Sure. But G.I.s aren't the only people who are allowed to get exhausted."

"No, no—of course not. It just feels silly to complain myself with all that's going on. Oh!" Scott exclaimed, a sudden light coming to his eyes. "But I must be exhausted, because I completely forgot to share this bit of good news: Winnie said she found the perfect spot for our experiment."

"Really?"

Winnie must have looked and sounded as incredulous as she felt, because Scott gave her a warning glance.

"I gave her a copy of our experiment design, and told her all the necessities—a wide, open space with high ceilings and absolute privacy—and today while I was at Professor Schulde's, she told me she found a place."

Winnie waited a moment, but Scott said nothing more. "Well, where is it?"

"We couldn't really talk there. I imagine she'll tell me tonight." Scott ran a hand through his hair nervously. "She's, um, going to come here."

"But—"

"I know—headaches and bloody noses. You'll leave when she gets here. Dora's going to come with her, so you won't have to ride the subway back alone."

"And you'll take Winnie home?"

Scott was glancing all around the room as if he were looking for something, but all their equipment was right there, on the table in front of them. She realized he was just trying to avoid looking at her.

"Well, normally I eat dinner at her house, but I've been skipping it lately to work with you. I haven't been able to spend any time with her." He glanced down at the table and his fingers began moving from one thing to the next like a picky bumblebee before finally settling. He sighed. "She told Dr. Schulde she's spending the night at Dora's, and she's going to stay here with me tonight."

Winnie strained to keep a neutral expression. "Oh," she said, "okay."

She had wondered how far things went between him and Beta, but she hadn't really thought they might go *that* far. He must think her such a child by comparison! She certainly felt like one, or like a country cousin come to town. Unsophisticated and immature.

Scott glanced at her, and suddenly his face went beet red. "I didn't mean to imply Winnie will be staying *with* me. I'll be sleeping on the couch, of course."

"It really isn't my business either way," she said stiffly.

"I don't want you to think I would take advantage. I wouldn't do anything that would . . . well, I wouldn't do anything."

"Like I said, it's not my business."

"It is and you know it. What happens between any two of us—it's all tangled up."

"We're each our own people," Winnie said, although she agreed that it wasn't that straightforward.

"I know you're not Winnie, exactly—but there *is* overlap. And I don't want you to think that's something I would to do to Winnie because that's not something I want you to think Scott would do to you. You want to feel one-of-a-kind," he continued, "and look, I get that—"

"You really don't. You can't possibly."

Scott was right that it was hard not feeling unique, but that was just one reason that Winnie preferred to think of her double as a sort of living shadow rather than a fully realized other self. The more she felt like Beta and she were two of the same person, the more it felt like anything that was Beta's was really hers too. She wore her double's clothes, slept in her double's best friend's bed, spent her evenings alone with her double's boyfriend. It was already too easy to feel like the clothing was hers, Dora her best friend, and Scott—well, she was jealous that Beta would be with him all night, and moreover, Winnie felt like she had a right to be, even though she knew she didn't.

"I know this is complicated," Scott said softly. "I would *like* to understand, though."

But Winnie knew that no, he really wouldn't like understanding it at all.

When she didn't respond, Scott glanced at his watch. "Winnie should be here soon." He started tidying up. "If the place she's found really works, we'll try our experiment tomorrow—I'll have Winnie let Dora know our plans, and she can pass them on to you after school."

There was a knock at the door, and Winnie's stomach dropped. She told herself it was just because Beta was near— that it had nothing to do with her feelings about Beta spending the night.

She turned to retrieve her coat from the armchair where Scott had placed it, until—

"Hello. Are you Scott Hamilton?"

Winnie looked to the door and saw two uniformed police officers standing on the threshold. She froze, one arm in the sleeve of her coat, and stared. If Hawthorn knew about her, he wouldn't send the police, would he? He would send someone from the military—or he would come himself. So why did the sight of them terrify her?

Well, when police showed up at your door, it never meant anything good—but on top of that, they were expecting her double at any moment. If Beta showed up while the police officers were there, they would lie. Pretend to be twin sisters. And that lie would be disproven immediately if the officers did even the most cursory investigation.

"Yes," Scott answered. "How can I help you?"

"Could we come in?"

Scott glanced over at her, then quickly back—it wasn't as if he could say no. Winnie hoped they could keep this short.

"Of course."

The four of them sat around the coffee table, and Winnie was struck by the odd mix of familiarity and formalness to the arrangement. Scott could have just invited some neighbors over for coffee—but all four of them were sitting grimly erect as if they were in church.

At a funeral.

That was why police showed up, wasn't it? If not to arrest somebody, or for an interrogation—then to tell you somebody was dead.

"What's happened?" Winnie asked, her voice cracking, unable to take a second more of waiting.

The officers didn't answer.

"I'm Detective McPherson, and this is Lieutenant Muldoon. And you are?"

Indecision flickered through her. Was it better to make up a false identity, or just tell the sort-of-truth that she was Winnie Schulde?

"This is my girlfriend, Winnie Schulde," Scott answered for her.

"Ah," Lieutenant Muldoon said. He took a notebook from his pocket and flipped through it. "Professor Heinrich Schulde's"— he glanced up at her—"daughter?"

Winnie nodded. Her mouth was too dry to speak.

"Has something happened to Professor Schulde?" Scott asked. If he sat up any straighter, he would spring right up off the sofa.

"No, no," McPherson said. He swallowed and gave Scott a grave look. "But something has happened. We have a body, and we have reason to believe it belongs to James Oswald. Before we have his family make the trip in from Chicago, we want to be sure. Would you be able to come down to the morgue with us?"

Suspecting, worrying—that had not prepared either of them for the awful knowing. She could *see* James, in her mind, sitting across the table from her at the diner the day before. His tapered fingers, restlessly shredding his napkin. *I know how to take care of myself.*

"No," Winnie said. She shook her head. Tears welled in her eyes. "No."

James had gone missing earlier in her world than he had here. Did that mean something different had happened to that James? Or was James dead there too? He might have already been dead when Winnie got involved in the whole mess, making the events that led up to Scott's accident even more pointless.

While Winnie was wondering all this, Scott was still just blinking at the officer, stunned.

"I'm sorry," Scott said. "You want me to identify a body?"

Muldoon nodded. "We tried to contact Mr. Oswald's boss first, but we're having trouble reaching him. Someone on campus mentioned you're his friend. Is that true?"

Scott's mouth was pressed into a straight line, making him

look almost angry, but he nodded once. "Yeah," he said firmly. "That's true. You want me to come now?"

"Sooner—well, sooner is better than later with these things."

Winnie wondered if Scott had ever seen a body before. Not that it mattered. It wasn't as if seeing her mother's body, for instance, had made seeing Scott's any easier.

The police officers stood, and Winnie and Scott followed their lead.

"Miss Schulde, we can drop you home on the way."

Winnie cursed herself for not realizing—she was still too shocked—but *of course* they didn't plan on taking a teenage girl along with them to the morgue. But she couldn't let herself be dropped off at Beta's house. What if her double was running late and hadn't even left yet? What if the police wanted to talk to Professor Schulde while they were there? She couldn't pass for her double in the girl's own home, with her own father! And she couldn't be dropped off on the doorstep possibly minutes after Beta had walked out the door, wearing a different outfit, being a different girl. Father wasn't stupid.

"Can she come with me?" Scott asked, saving her again.

Or so Winnie thought, until she looked at him. His shoulders were hunched like he was bracing against a biting wind, and his face had the slack-cheeked blankness of shock. Unless he was the best actor since Spencer Tracy, this was no clever maneuver. Scott didn't seem to be thinking about any of the practical matters. He'd just learned his friend was dead. He had to go see the body. He didn't want to face that alone.

Winnie reached for Scott's hand and gave it a squeeze. It took him a moment, but he squeezed back.

McPherson looked at their twinned hands. "She can ride with us to the morgue. If that's what you really want."

"And wait in the lobby," Muldoon finished.

"I've seen a body before," Winnie said, jutting out her chin.

She had seen two. She didn't want to see a third—she didn't even want to contemplate that the boy she'd met yesterday could be a body today—but for Scott, she would.

Muldoon gave her a look of sharpened interest. Winnie remembered too late that she shouldn't be calling attention to herself like this.

"Oh?" he said. "Well, you won't be seeing another tonight."

FEAR PULSED THROUGH WINNIE ON THE WAY OUT. IF THEY RAN INTO Beta, it was all over.

There was only one staircase in Scott's building. Winnie followed the officers down and hoped they didn't meet Dora and Beta coming up.

Scott's hand was lifeless in her own, but when she tried to drop it, he reached for her again. He must have felt her trembling—it pulled him out of the daze he'd fallen into. He glanced at her fingers, then at her face.

"Cold?" he asked, inquiring what was wrong in the only way that would seem innocuous to McPherson and Muldoon.

Winnie thought for a moment. She shook her head.

"Nervous. If people see"—she glanced at the officers—"what will they think?"

She hoped the police officers would assume she was talking about the neighbors, but Scott would take her real meaning—if the officers saw Beta, what then?

"That's out of our control."

He was right, but that did nothing to settle her pounding heart. It wasn't just discovery by Nightingale she had to worry about now. If the police learned Winnie had a doppelgänger, they wouldn't assume she was a transplant from an alternate universe, as Hawthorn or anyone else involved with Nightingale would. They would draw an explanation from the lexicon of their own experience: they would think she was a spy, groomed to resemble the daughter of a scientist working on a government project.

And they would suspect her in James's death.

"You seem awfully nervous," Muldoon said to her.

"You just told us our friend might be dead," Scott said, bristling.

Muldoon raised his eyebrows. "I didn't say she seemed sad."

CHAPTER TWENTY-THREE

The officers walked Winnie and Scott to the squad car parked in front of Scott's building. Winnie glanced down the street and immediately saw Dora and Beta walking toward them, less than a block away. She and Beta locked eyes, but Winnie quickly turned and ducked into the car. There was nothing she could do to let her double know what was happening, and she didn't want McPherson or Muldoon—especially Muldoon—to notice her looking at something and look that way themselves.

Winnie could only hope that Beta wouldn't try to go looking for them. And for all she knew, Beta *did* try to follow them to the station, in some other world. But Winnie didn't see a splinter. Even though she'd never thought the splinters were particularly useful—especially now that she realized she'd misinterpreted the splinter where she "met" James—she did feel blind without them. Would they ever come back?

It was Winnie's first time in a cop car. Looking through the metal grating that separated the back seat from the front re-minded her of being in the Faraday cage. She wondered if they would still be free to stage their experiment the next evening, and her chest went tight.

You are not trapped, Winnie told herself, and tried to take a full breath. *You aren't in trouble, and you are not a prisoner. You aren't a prisoner because you haven't done anything wrong.*

But she knew that doing something wrong wasn't the only way people wound up behind bars.

All those people in the internment camps—immigrants, like her. They hadn't done anything wrong. They were prisoners all the same. Young. Old. Citizen or not. Being at war made people eager to pigeonhole enemies, then lock them up so they could feel safe.

Muldoon was in the passenger seat. She could see him watching her in the rearview mirror. Was he suspicious of her because she was acting suspicious?

Or was it because of her German last name?

THE MORGUE WAS AN UNASSUMING BRICK BUILDING IN MIDTOWN Manhattan—it wasn't very large, so Winnie assumed the city must have several.

"Was the body found near here?" Winnie asked.

"No," McPherson said, shaking his head. "Somebody at Riverside Park saw it floating in the Hudson. Lucky we even found him, with these weird tides."

"Weird tides?" Winnie asked, although she dreaded the answer. Tides were caused by the gravitational pull of the moon. If her being there was interrupting normal gravitational forces somehow, that could affect the tides too.

"High tide has been *real* high lately—and totally off schedule. Don't you read the paper?"

Winnie felt queasy. What had happened in the park had lasted only a few moments, and it had affected only the small area around her. Did this mean the effects of her being there were getting worse?

Muldoon shot his partner a look.

"Come on—it's not like she's a reporter," McPherson said. "The kid was her friend. And the tides—well, that's sure not a secret."

Riverside Park was a block from Columbia's campus. If James had died in the lab there, it would be an easy place to dispose of a body—although not *the* easiest.

Professor Hawthorn was the head of the physics department, a brilliant man with access to a whole campus of resources and—if his lavish home was any indication—near-limitless funds. If Hawthorn really was the one responsible for James's death, the only reason his body had been found was because Hawthorn wanted it found. A body, Winnie thought, might raise fewer questions than a missing person.

"Don't worry," McPherson added, giving Scott a sympathetic look. "He wasn't in the water long."

It took Scott a few seconds to respond. It seemed like it was taking longer than usual for words to reach him, like he was underwater himself.

"Is that where he died?" Scott asked. "In the river?"

Muldoon raised an eyebrow. "What—was he a swimmer?"

"People don't die in the Hudson—unless they jump," his partner explained. "It's just where they're found."

"So then how did he die?" Scott pressed.

"We aren't sure yet," McPherson said. "But we don't think he jumped."

They showed Winnie to a row of stiff chairs against the wall of the small lobby.

"Wait here."

Winnie wanted to give Scott some last look of encouragement to lend him strength for the awful task to come, but he didn't even glance at her before Muldoon and McPherson walked him past the receptionist, through a door, where Winnie couldn't follow.

WINNIE DIDN'T WANT TO THINK ABOUT WHAT SCOTT WAS DOING ON THE other side of that door, or what a body might look like after it was pulled out of a river.

The hard wooden back of the waiting room chair bit into her own. It was an ugly room. Off-white walls, minty-green linoleum floor that evoked anything but freshness. It seemed like a poor choice to accompany death, but when she tried to think of a better color, she couldn't. The building would be ugly no matter what. Death was an ugly thing.

Winnie didn't know how to support Scott through this. Beta was the one who should be there, not her. Knowing Scott was suffering made her feel so helpless, and even though James had already been involved with Hawthorn before her trespass into this world, she felt a sick, guilty feeling surrounding his death, like it was another ripple of wrongness caused by her being there.

She had known James was missing back home, and it felt like carrying that knowledge with her had infected their world somehow. This was probably just the same ill ease and blame-seeking that accompanied any tragedy, but it was indisputable that Winnie's presence here made any bad thing worse. Her being there was another worry that got piled on top of any other.

She really wanted to go home.

She wondered if she would ever get to.

It was late, but Winnie supposed the morgue never fully closed. A body might turn up at any hour.

Winnie was the only person in the waiting area besides the receptionist. She was a steely-haired, whippet-thin older woman whose stern face gave Winnie the impression that she had the necessary nerve to spend her nights alone in a building full of bodies.

"How long does it usually take?" Winnie asked. The receptionist looked up from her book and met the question with a blank stare. "Identifying a body, I mean," she clarified.

It had been maybe forty-five minutes.

"It takes as long as it takes," the receptionist answered with a shrug, but not unkindly. "There's paperwork. And questions, sometimes. Depending on the situation."

Winnie was pretty confident that this was a situation that demanded questions.

There was a creak and then the *shush* of the building's revolving door being pushed open as someone entered the building. Winnie glanced over out of idle curiosity and saw Professor Hawthorn striding toward the reception desk. The heels of his dress shoes clicked sharply against the waxed floor. To Winnie, they sounded like certain doom.

"I'm here to identify a body," he said.

Hawthorn was so confident—and dressed with such class— that Winnie could swear the receptionist actually sat up straighter.

"Certainly, sir, but usually—"

"I was told the officers in charge of the case are already here. Detective McPherson and Lieutenant Muldoon. Page them, please."

The receptionist nodded and picked up the phone. "I have a—"

"Professor Seymour Hawthorn."

"—Professor Seymour Hawthorn here. Could you send McPherson and Muldoon up for him when they're finished?"

Hawthorn hadn't noticed Winnie sitting there. She supposed

some girl sitting in a morgue's waiting room was beneath his notice. But it would seem suspicious if he noticed her there later and she hadn't said anything, Winnie thought with resignation. Which meant that she would have to approach *him*. At least she didn't have to worry about trying to act "normal." There could be no normal under circumstances so awful.

Winnie stood and took a few steps toward the reception desk. "Hello, Professor Hawthorn," she said quietly.

He turned to look at her, a flicker of irritation at being approached was there and then gone like a bird ruffling its feathers. "Hello, Miss—?"

Shit.

Hawthorn didn't know her.

It hadn't occurred to Winnie that in this world, they might not have met—she had never even bothered to ask.

Winnie felt a flash of terror and immediately tried to mask it. She had been so sure, with Beta's father and Scott both working for Nightingale, that Hawthorn would have been introduced to Beta at some point, or at least seen her. Now she was stuck.

Winnie had put herself in the exact scenario she feared.

"Winnie Schulde," she said. It seemed too risky to lie about that now—the police could come out and call her "Miss Schulde" at any moment. "Heinrich Schulde's daughter."

"Ah," he said, and shook her hand. "I'm so sorry, but have we met?"

On second thought, Winnie didn't know enough about her

double's life to flesh out an honest response, so there was no choice but to try to bluff her way through it.

"Um, not exactly." Winnie tried to think of believable circumstances for why she would recognize him, but he wouldn't recognize her. "I—Scott took me to a lecture once," Winnie said. She knew the department hosted a monthly lecture series. It seemed at least conceivable that Beta would join Scott for one. "He pointed you out to me."

Hawthorn frowned, and Winnie could see that there was something about her story that didn't add up for him, but she couldn't imagine what—she couldn't have been vaguer.

"Well, it's nice to meet you," Hawthorn said, shaking her hand. "Although I wish it were under better circumstances."

There seemed to an unspoken question to this—*What are you doing here?* Winnie was thankful that this, at least, she had an answer for.

"I was with Scott when the police came. I guess they weren't able to reach you? They came to get him to—to see if it's James."

"Scott's in there with them now?" Hawthorn seemed agitated by this news, although he quickly tried to conceal it. "He shouldn't have to see his friend like that," Hawthorn explained hastily. "I would have saved him that if I could."

Winnie wondered what it was about James's body that Hawthorn didn't want Scott to see.

She wanted to hiss *"You did this!"* She wanted to shove him against the wall. She wanted him to be afraid of her like she was afraid of him.

"It's good you came," Winnie said. "The police will have questions for you, I imagine. Considering the experiments."

It wasn't all she wanted to say, but still, Winnie felt immense satisfaction in the implication—*I know you did it, and the police will too.*

Hawthorn reached a hand toward her face and—too quick for her to process what was happening and move away—tucked a piece of Winnie's hair back behind her ear, letting his thumb brush across her cheekbone. Winnie shivered in revulsion.

"You're a child," he said. "You don't understand anything."

Just then the door swung open, and Muldoon and McPherson escorted a pale Scott out to the lobby. If Scott was alarmed to see Winnie out there chatting with the head of Project Nightingale, he didn't show it. His expression didn't show much, in fact, but this didn't surprise her. That was grief. It blunted everything.

"Professor Hawthorn?" McPherson asked.

Hawthorn nodded, and the two shook hands.

"Mr. Hamilton here has already given us a positive ID on James Oswald. We tried to get in touch earlier—"

"Yes, yes," Hawthorn said impatiently. "I was at a trustee meeting for the Metropolitan Opera. I called the station as soon as I got home."

Winnie caught Muldoon rolling his eyes at the receptionist— a look that said *we get it, you're rich*—and was glad that she wasn't the only person the detective seemed to take an immediate dislike to.

"We appreciate that," McPherson said. "There's nothing

more for us to do here, but if you don't mind accompanying us back to the station, we do have some questions."

Annoyance flashed across Hawthorn's face, and Winnie once again had the sense that Scott identifying James's body was interfering with Hawthorn's plans somehow, but he said, "Of course."

"You'll be all right getting home?" McPherson asked.

Scott didn't seem to even hear the question, so Winnie nodded hastily and said, "Yes. We'll be okay."

Okay?

That wasn't remotely the word for their situation.

CHAPTER TWENTY-FOUR

As soon as the police detectives and Hawthorn left, Scott collapsed into one of the waiting room chairs.

"I just need a minute," he said. "It was James—it was definitely James—but also, it didn't look anything like him."

Winnie remembered that particular dissonance from her mother's death, seeing the corpse that both was and was not Mama. She could only imagine what James might look like now, and tried to shut the gruesome image out of her mind. She should have tried harder to make James understand the danger. She should have done more. Done *something*.

"I'm so sorry," Winnie said. It wasn't enough. It was never enough.

The silence stretched, and Winnie felt a growing itch to fill it even though she knew that wasn't a helpful thing to do.

"I saw Dora and Winnie on the street earlier."

This seemed to snap Scott back into himself. "What? Where?"

"Outside your apartment. They saw us getting into the detectives' car."

He nodded, then stood and walked over to the receptionist's desk.

"Pardon me—would it be possible to make a call? Local, of course. I wouldn't ask, but I don't have a telephone at home and there's somebody who's been worrying. I'd like to let them know."

The receptionist regarded him stonily for a moment, but something in his expression—perhaps the sad slump of his shoulders, which was breaking Winnie's heart—softened her. She nodded and handed Scott the receiver.

"What's the telephone number?"

Scott looked at Winnie. "What's Dora's number?"

Winnie gave the receptionist the digits that she hoped would connect to Dora in this world, and watched as the woman dialed.

"Hello, this is Scott Hamilton. Could I speak to Dora, please?"

Not five seconds later, Dora was on the line; she must have been desperately waiting for the call.

"Hi, Dora, it's Scott. Yes. I know you've been worried. No—Winnie and I are fine. But I'm at the morgue," he said, speaking that last word with a hint of question, as if he couldn't quite believe it was a word he had to say, or a place he had to be. "It's James. They pulled his body from the Hudson . . . No.

They aren't sure yet how. They don't know if it was an accident, or . . ." Scott trailed off.

She knew—James's death was no accident. Hawthorn was to blame.

Scott passed Winnie the receiver. "She wants to talk to you."

"Hello?"

"What's going on?" It was Beta on the line now, not Dora.

"We really don't know yet. Just that James is dead."

Her double was silent a few moments, then she said, "Well, I guess you were right," in a tight voice. "About Nightingale. About the danger."

"I didn't want to be right."

"I know," Beta said. She sighed. "Poor James. And poor Scott—James was his best friend."

"He seemed like a really wonderful person," Winnie said, and although she meant it, the sentiment felt trite and completely inadequate.

It was strange to witness people she knew intimately grieving for someone she had only just met. She felt the horror of James's death keenly, but knew her own feelings couldn't possibly compare to their own—just another way in which she was an outsider in that world.

"I'm staying at Dora's tonight," Beta said. "You'll have to stay at Scott's."

"Oh."

Winnie hadn't thought that far ahead. She'd been so jealous that Beta would be spending the night with Scott before, but she hadn't wanted to take that from her. Or at least, not like this.

"Put him on the line, please."

Winnie passed the phone to Scott. She didn't know what her double had to say to him, but apparently there was a lot—Scott was mostly quiet except for an "mmh hmm" here and there.

"I think you're right," he said finally. "I'll let her know. We'll see you tomorrow night." He sighed. "I love you." A pause. "Yeah. Me too."

WHEN THEY WALKED OUT THE REVOLVING LOBBY DOOR THE FIRST THING Scott did, much to Winnie's confusion, was take out his wallet and count the bills inside.

"You don't have any money, do you?"

Winnie shook her head.

"Of course not," he said with a bone-weary sigh. "Well, I think this will be enough for a cab. Assuming we can catch one."

"Scott, I'm so sorry," Winnie said. "James—"

"Not at sorry as I am," he interrupted fiercely, startling her. "You warned us! Not even about Nightingale or Hawthorn generally—you warned us that James was missing, and said it was Hawthorn's fault! I didn't take it as seriously as I should have."

It hurt her heart to listen to Scott blame himself. "There are enough differences between this world and mine," Winnie said. "We couldn't have known something would happen to him here too."

Winnie probably didn't sound very convincing, because she didn't really believe this herself. Even if they weren't exactly to blame, it still felt like they should have been able to prevent this.

Scott opened his mouth as if to argue but then his face crumpled. He took a shaky breath. "We saw him *yesterday*. The cops, they showed me these marks on his arms. Needle marks, from the serum injections, I guess. New, old. They think he was a dope fiend! It's just—how could it have been going on for so long, and I didn't even know? What kind of friend am I?"

Maybe that was why Hawthorn was upset that Scott was the one to identify the body. Hawthorn would want the police to think James was a drug user. There were all sorts of reasons an addict might wind up in the river, and none of them involved Hawthorn. But Scott must have sworn up and down that James wasn't involved with drugs at all, and Hawthorn would have realized that claim could blow his cover—if the police investigated further of course.

"James couldn't have been okay with what Hawthorn was doing to him," Scott said. "So why did he let him?"

Scott was looking at her so intensely that Winnie suddenly realized he didn't mean the question rhetorically.

She had the answer, but it wasn't packaged up all pretty. There were no words she could share with Scott that would actually help him understand.

James let Hawthorn do his work for the same reasons she allowed Father.

It was that look on Father's face when he offered up some new suffering for Winnie to endure—brandishing it like a dare—and she accepted without hesitation. Just a little flash of pride. It didn't matter that he didn't say "that's my girl." Because in those moments, Winnie knew he felt it.

It was looking at her classmates, and knowing that she might never be shiny and smiley and *normal* like they were, but she had this deeper purpose, this *secret*, and that made her life fuller and more mysterious than they could ever imagine.

It was feeling important, *being* important. And if you're vital to someone, isn't that love? How do you give all that up once you've tasted it? You don't. Even if it comes with a side of abuse. Not if you're so hungry for approval it feels like you'll never be full.

Her Scott, *he* would understand why James endured Hawthorn. She didn't know if this Scott could. It had been naïve of her to think the two of them were identical. It's amazing, the things we'll believe when we're desperate for them to be true.

She looked away and shrugged.

"Does it really matter why?"

Scott looked like he was going to argue, but then he pressed his lips together in a tight line and nodded twice.

"I want to make Hawthorn pay."

He barely sounded like himself.

"I do too," Winnie said. "But I don't think we can."

CHAPTER TWENTY-FIVE

Winnie's stomach was a tangle of nerves as soon as she and Scott got back to his apartment. She'd been alone there with him several times now, but it was different knowing that this time she was spending the night. The circumstances couldn't be less romantic, but she still found herself wondering what Scott's night would have been like if it had gone as planned, instead of taking its dark turn—if they hadn't just come from the morgue, and if she were his Winnie instead of herself.

Scott was holding himself together. He didn't look like he was about to collapse sobbing. But that was just as painful to watch, in its own way. He took off his jacket and hung it up. He helped Winnie with her coat. There was a stiffness to his movements that spoke of extreme restraint. She wished he didn't feel like he had to put on a brave face in front of her.

Beta would know what to say. Winnie was useless.

"We need to stage our experiment soon," she said abruptly. "Me being here just makes a bad situation worse."

"Yeah," Scott agreed with a nod.

She didn't blame him for agreeing, but it still hurt to hear.

Winnie wondered what would happen to the time the two of them had shared, once it ended? Would it be meaningless then? Was it meaningless to him now?

She sunk down on Scott's tired old sofa. The worn floral upholstery was rough against her hands.

Scott sat down next to her. Some things, you don't have to touch to feel. Magnets. Heat. Winnie felt Scott across those inches of air between them. She wanted him to touch her. What was wrong with her, that she could want that right then?

"I can't believe James is gone," he said, and shook his head angrily. "We have to get you home before Hawthorn realizes who you are."

Winnie grimaced. She hated to worry him more, but she had to tell him about her conversation with Hawthorn.

"I messed up, Scott," Winnie said. She couldn't look at him. "I didn't realize that Hawthorn and I don't know each other by sight here. So, I approached him in the lobby—I thought it would look stranger *not* to. But I don't think he believed the reason I came up with for recognizing him."

"What did you say?"

"That I went to a lecture with you one time, and you pointed him out."

Scott winced. "Yeah. I always go with James . . . and Hawthorn reserves us seats with the faculty."

"Oh." She figured she had messed up, but it hadn't occurred to her that such an innocuous-seeming lie would be so obviously untrue. "I should have just stayed quiet."

"You couldn't have known. Maybe he'll forget about it, with so much else going on . . ." Scott trailed off with a shrug.

"Maybe," said Winnie. But something told her that Hawthorn wouldn't forget her lie—that he would worry that mystery like a dog with a bone until it was picked clean. "Or maybe he'll connect it with the description he received from the library."

Scott nodded. "Maybe. Regardless, we need to get you back home. Winnie still thinks we should attempt our experiment tomorrow night, and I agree. She told me the location she found while we were the phone: your school gymnasium. What do you think?"

Winnie considered for a moment. The gym had tons of open space, no windows to show any suspicious lights, and a large surrounding yard to buffer any sound from reaching the street.

"I think it'll work."

But would their experiment? Winnie knew all too well how dangerous these things could be. If she died, like Scott had, would that at least restore the balance to this world? Or would the rest of them be left to fix it alone? She considered telling Scott that if she did die, he should dispose of her body by transporting it out of their world however Project Nightingale sent matter during their experiments, but decided against it. She was sure his thoughts were dark enough without her adding to his concerns.

"I don't know what we'll do if this experiment fails," he said. The nerves in his voice were raw.

How many times had Scott reassured her, both in her own world and here? She should have some kind of comfort for him—about their experiment, about James—but she had *nothing*.

"Well," he said finally, "I suppose we should try to get some sleep."

Winnie glanced down at her outfit: a pleated wool skirt, a button-up shirt, a cardigan, stockings, a slip.

"Do you have some pajamas I could change into?"

Scott bit his lip. "I've only got one pair, unfortunately," he said. "I mean, you can have them, of course—"

"I suppose I could sleep in my slip."

Winnie felt shy despite the absurdity of it. Scott had just identified his best friend's body, and Winnie had made a terrible misstep with that friend's killer. With all the grief and worry she and Scott carried between them, what did it matter if he saw her in her slip?

Winnie went into the tiny bathroom to change. She took off her clothing, slip, stockings, and brassiere, then pulled her slip back on. It was Beta's, so of course it was beautiful—blush peach satin, trimmed in ivory lace—not utilitarian like the ones in Winnie's dresser at home. She glanced at herself in the medicine cabinet mirror and decided that no, she couldn't walk out there like that, and put her cardigan back on so she would be at least somewhat covered.

Scott had pulled down the Murphy bed, and he stood next to it wearing a pair of plaid flannel pajama pants and an undershirt.

Seeing him in his nightclothes felt unnervingly intimate.

"Here. You take the bed," Scott said with a briskness that didn't quite succeed at covering his nerves. "I'll sleep on the sofa."

Winnie gave the couch—a loveseat, really—a doubtful look; it wasn't even long enough for her to stretch out on, much less Scott.

"No, I'm smaller. I can sleep there, and you take the bed."

"Winnie, I'm not going to take the bed." He smiled faintly. "What kind of host would I be? It's a terrible sofa."

She knew she wouldn't win this argument—Scott was too much of a gentleman.

Winnie climbed into his creaky bed, and Scott lay down on the couch and turned off the table lamp, plunging them into sudden darkness. Winnie shifted around, trying to get comfortable. She could hear the small movements of Scott trying to do the same on the sofa. She folded his thin pillow for a bit more support under her neck, and finally lay still.

It was quiet except for the sound of Scott breathing.

"You know," he said softly from across the room, "I believed you—but I didn't really *believe* you. Not like I should have. I didn't think Hawthorn was this much of a danger, even after

James told us about the experiments. Hawthorn cared about James! But that didn't stop him. I don't get it. How do you do something like that to someone you care about? I guess you would understand that sort of thing better than I can."

He meant because of what she'd told him about Father. Because of the things he put her through, even though he loved her.

Winnie supposed she "understood" like Scott "believed"—she did, and she didn't.

But that was too much to try to explain, lying there in the dark.

"I guess so," she agreed.

"But if that's the kind of thing Hawthorn will let happen to someone he cares about—Winnie, I will never let him get his hands on you. I promise. *Never.*"

Winnie was so touched by this promise that tears sprang to her eyes.

This was a promise he was making to *her*—not to his girl-friend's doppelgänger—and she clung to it.

Winnie knew Scott's promise wouldn't keep her safe, but knowing he wanted to, and that he would try—knowing he believed her, at last, about the danger—it was like sitting down by a fire after being cold for so long that she'd forgotten what it meant to be warm.

She marveled again at the sort of wonderful Scott was; even through his grief, his first thought was helping someone else.

The pillow under her head smelled like him. His soap, his

aftershave—it was almost like he was there in bed with her. And in her heart, she was holding him tight.

"I'm going to miss him so much," Scott said suddenly. "I keep thinking that, over and over—but I don't really feel it. I don't even know what it means. How can James be gone forever?" Scott repeated that word—"forever"—like he was sounding something out in a foreign language.

Winnie knew that no matter how much time passed, it would never make sense that the people we loved could be gone *forever*. Scott could turn it over and turn it over in his mind and get no closer to understanding. Winnie never had.

That was why people believed in things like being reunited with the dead in heaven—to give themselves some relief from that unfathomable forever.

Winnie wished she shared that belief, but she didn't.

Mama was gone, forever.

James was gone, forever.

"I don't know what any of it means," Winnie said. "But I hate it. I hate it so much."

"Me too," he whispered.

In the silence between them, Winnie's worries took over. What would things be like if she was able to return home? If Scott was okay, could he ever forgive her for causing the accident? And if she *did* succeed in getting back home, did that mean *this* Scott would be gone forever? That thought made her sad, but she knew the thing that mattered most now was making sure their experiment worked.

Even if it weren't for Hawthorn, she *had* to go home. She felt it more the more time passed, especially when she was still, and it was quiet: this feeling of dread. A silent reverberation, some kind of vibration she had set off when she came there, waves radiating through she didn't know what—through the ether, through something—that were waiting to strike the right material so they could sound.

She dreaded what noise they might make.

Winnie slept restlessly, but she did sleep. Each time she stirred, she was calmed by the rhythmic sound of Scott's deep, even breaths.

She wondered what he dreamt about—if he was dreaming.

When Winnie woke up, Scott was already dressed and heading out the door.

"You're leaving? Where are you going?"

She didn't know why this felt like such a betrayal—she guessed she just didn't want to be alone.

"I'm going to the lab for a little while," he answered.

"But Hawthorn will be there!"

"Probably. But it would be strange for me to try to avoid him. The last thing I want is for Hawthorn to think I'm suspicious. Besides, I need to stay busy. And I can use the phone there. I know the police probably talked to them already, but I should call James's parents."

Scott looked so lost, and Winnie felt guilty for resenting

him for leaving her alone. This was bigger than her.

He shook his head and continued. "I don't know what I'll say to them, but it feels like the right thing to do. And I want to stop by James's apartment—he keeps a key under the mat—and see if there's anything . . ." He trailed off.

"Like some sign of what happened to him?"

Scott shrugged. "Or just things he'd rather his parents not find."

Winnie hesitated a moment, but she wanted Scott to know he didn't need to skirt around James's sexuality for her sake—she already knew. "Like a letter from a boyfriend?" she asked gently.

He gave her a surprised glance, then nodded. "I mean, it wasn't a secret—James was terrible at keeping secrets." Scott frowned. "Although I guess in the end, he was better than I thought. But his parents . . . it was a point of contention be-tween them. And James—he's the kind of person who wouldn't want them to be even more upset during all this, even if it's something they shouldn't be upset about."

This gave Winnie an even stronger idea of the sort of person James was. It made sense that he and Scott would be friends.

"I wish I could have gotten to know him," she said.

Scott's mouth quirked into a sad half smile. "Yeah. Me too."

WINNIE FIGURED THAT WHILE SCOTT WAS AWAY, SHE COULD KEEP HER-self busy by reviewing their experiment design. She gave the plans a careful read and double-checked their calculations.

Everything seemed sound, but that couldn't set her mind at ease. Was Scott in the Nightingale lab with Hawthorn at that very moment? What if Hawthorn discovered what they were up to—when would Winnie even find out that everything had gone wrong? She hated being the helpless one, stuck home waiting. This was what her double must have felt like the night before. It was awful.

Winnie glanced at the small clock on Scott's side table. It was—eight thirty! How was that possible? Scott had been gone for a few hours at least, and the sun had been up when he left. She noticed the second hand was moving far too slowly, much to her relief. The clock batteries must be dying. Winnie walked over to the window and threw back the curtains to try to see if she could guess the true time from the sun.

She frowned. The sun was still too close to the horizon to be visible past the other buildings on the street. Could she really have gotten the time that wrong?

No. There was no way Scott hadn't been gone for hours. Her stomach told her it was nearly lunch. Bodies are clocks too, albeit imperfect ones.

What initially had just seemed odd began to feel frightening.

What was going on? Had time slowed down?

Winnie picked up the little table clock. She shook it—as if that could do anything! It continued to tick . . . tock . . . at a painfully leisurely pace. Winnie's own heart was beating frantically. She felt like she was losing her mind. Her breath came quicker and quicker—

Tick . . .

. . . tock . . .

She raised the clock above her head to smash it, but before she could throw it to the floor, Winnie noticed the sun.

She could see it in the sky now, above the buildings across the street, rising unnaturally fast.

To her horror, Winnie realized the hands of the clock had sped up too. The second hand now spun around the face, and the minute and hour hands sped up in turn. Hours were flying by in a few breaths.

Church bells began to ring down the street. Winnie counted the peals. Twelve. Noon. The hands of the clock rested at the top of the face, then began to tick at a normal pace.

Winnie set the clock back down as though it were an armed bomb. Her hands were trembling.

Gravity, tides, and now time itself.

Something was very wrong in their world, and Winnie was pretty sure she knew what it was.

Her.

CHAPTER TWENTY-SIX

S cott came through the door a little after eight o'clock that evening, right when Winnie was starting to fear he never would, and wondering what on earth she'd do then.

"What is going on?" she asked quickly.

Scott looked at her funny. "What do you mean?"

She explained what had happened that morning—that time had slowed down, then abruptly sped up.

"You didn't notice anything? Really?"

Scott bit his lip and furrowed his brow.

"I guess I felt like something was off, but I thought I was just out of it, because of last night . . . I figured I had just sort of lost time. A lot of time. I got to the lab, settled in at one of the workbenches, and it felt like I blinked and all of a sudden it was noon."

"Do you think anyone else noticed?"

"A couple people made jokes about how they barely got

anything done this morning, but I don't know if . . ." Scott trailed off, then shrugged. "Are you sure it didn't just feel slow at first because you were here all day waiting?"

"Scott, the clock? That could have just been some kind of malfunction. But the sun? I *saw* it speed up." Winnie frowned. "What I don't understand is, other people must have seen it too, right? It was uncanny! Why weren't people panicking about it on campus?"

"I don't know. But if you're right, there's no way anyone else saw it, because if they had, it would be all over the news."

"It *did* happen! I swear!"

"I believe you, I just—what if it only happened that way for you?" Scott paused, and seemed to think for a moment. "What if time skipped ahead for the rest of us? Like someone picking up the needle on a record player and moving it past a song they don't like."

Winnie considered this for a moment, but it didn't make any sense.

"Why would I be aware of what was happening if no one else was?"

Scott looked at her hard. "Because you're the hand lifting the needle." Scott sank into one of the tattered armchairs. He looked so exhausted. "I guess this is what happens when you violate a natural law."

Winnie hadn't meant for any of this to happen, but she was still full of sick guilt.

"Everything seems fine now, though," she said uncertainly.

"For the moment."

Winnie stood abruptly. She knew Scott was right, so she headed over to the kitchenette to brew them some coffee.

However "fine" this moment was, they had a very long night ahead of them.

THE STREETS WERE QUIET THAT NIGHT AS WINNIE, DORA, AND SCOTT walked to the subway station that would take them to the school.

If everything went as planned, Winnie would be home in a matter of hours.

It was very hard to believe that everything would go as planned.

The three of them made their way to the platform that would take them uptown, too nervous for small talk. After a few minutes, the train pounded into the station in an assault of screeching brakes, hot rushing air, and—was that the echo of a ship horn? Impossible. They were nowhere near water.

"Did you hear—" Winnie began, but Scott and Dora were already hurrying onto the train. Winnie followed them onto the mostly empty train car. Their odd bundles of equipment got a strange look or two, but no one said anything.

Winnie set her piece of the Faraday cage on the floor by her seat. She caught her reflection in the dark window across the aisle, cradling the delicate, carefully wrapped electrometer in her arms, and felt a pang of uncertainty. She looked like a little girl holding a doll, not like someone on the brink of solving a great scientific mystery, about to break the barrier between worlds and travel back in time to save the man she loved.

"What do you think it will look like when you go?" Dora asked suddenly.

Winnie was grateful to be distracted from her doubts. She thought a moment, but she had no idea. "Like magic," she said finally. "If it works."

"Don't say that," Scott said. "It's going to work."

She wondered if he was really as confident as he sounded.

Beta was waiting for them outside the school gate, as planned. She had stolen the groundskeeper's key ring earlier that day. It was strange to think of her double—this girl who shared her face—having her own separate part in the planning that Winnie knew nothing about. She imagined the girl sneaking into Mr. Bidwell's shop out by the track. Had she found this task thrilling or terrifying?

Beta gave Scott a quick hug, which was made a bit awkward by the Faraday cage bundle he carried. Winnie looked away, trying not to think about how she had fallen asleep with her head on his pillow the night before.

"You haven't been waiting long, have you?" Winnie asked, hanging back to keep a careful distance from her double.

"No, not too long."

Dora scanned up and down the street nervously. "Let's get inside."

After a bit of fumbling with her stolen keys, Beta was able to unlock the exterior gate, which she quickly locked again behind them. They entered the building itself through a side door sheltered from any possible prying eyes by an overgrown broom shrub. Once inside, the four of them walked the halls quiet as cat burglars, their flashlights cast at the floor in hopes that the rogue beams of light wouldn't draw attention from any passerby.

Winnie thought her double seemed the least nervous of them all. Seeing Beta stride the halls of her school so confidently made Winnie think about just how little of herself she ever let show there, even though she was an exemplary student. When she was around her classmates, in the cafeteria or during any social event, Winnie was always all folded in on herself, everything but her intellect tucked away. She envied Beta her apparent self-assurance, and wondered, not for the first time, where it came from.

Their worlds had diverged in the accident that killed Mama. Beta had been asleep when the crash happened. Could that tiny detail really be the crux of it all? Beta was her, minus a lifetime of guilt over crying out and causing the accident? Her, minus the splinters?

Seeing this other life, this *better* life, and knowing how close she had come to having it for herself made Winnie painfully aware that any moment could contain the seed of your undoing.

It was an awful thing to know.

They reached the gym, and Beta unlocked the heavy metal doors. Winnie found the panel of light switches and flipped a pair. Two of the caged pendant lights hanging from the tall ceiling switched on. After the dark of the halls, it was painfully bright. Winnie switched one of them back off.

"You're sure no one outside can see?" Dora asked.

"How?" Beta said gesturing around the gymnasium. "There are no windows."

Judging by Dora's furrowed brow, this didn't allay her fears. Dora had the least to gain from their venture, but she was still there with them, enduring just as much risk.

"Thank you for being here," Winnie said, with a smile she hoped didn't look as worried as she felt.

Dora smiled back. "I wouldn't miss it for anything."

Scott and Winnie carried the two halves of the Faraday cage to the middle of the room and set them down on the floor, right on the center line of the basketball court. The maroon markings showed up livid as blood against the honey-colored wood.

"You were brilliant to think of this place," Scott told Beta. "The court markings will make it even easier to measure everything out."

Winnie had to admit the location was pretty much perfect. She wished it had been her idea.

Winnie helped Scott prop up the sections of the cage, and she, Beta, and Dora all worked together to hold the sides in place while Scott soldered the open edges of chicken wire together. This was simple in theory, but the process took ages.

Winnie met her double's eyes from across the cage, then quickly looked away. She didn't want another bloody nose. More than that, she wished they could have connected somehow—been more direct allies without her double making Winnie doubt everything about herself.

If they succeeded and Winnie went back in time, would that be enough to make everything go back to normal for each of them? She had been so preoccupied with saving Scott that she hadn't really wondered what would happen to the world she left behind.

Once the Faraday cage was assembled, Scott set up the other equipment. Winnie left the arrangement of the electrometer and the generator to him. Scott had more experience, and he was the one who would be using them, so she wanted him to make sure they would be safe. Winnie would be secure in the cage, so if anything went wrong—

No. She refused to let herself finish that thought. Nothing would go wrong. Scott was sober and cautious, not in a drunken rage like Father had been when he set up the experiment that had been so disastrous. But for the first time, Winnie was glad Beta was there. She didn't think Scott would take undue risks with his own safety, or with hers, but with Beta there, he would be doubly cautious.

"I think we're ready to begin," Scott said finally, "if you are."

No matter how meticulous the experiment design or

elaborate her daydreams of returning home and rescuing Scott, Winnie found herself unprepared for this moment.

"So, I should just . . . get in the cage?"

"You can say your goodbyes first," he said. "Once the generator starts, it will all be set in motion, and then . . ." He trailed off with a shrug.

And then she would wait for his signal, and it would all be up to her.

"And then . . . poof!" Dora said, smiling faintly. "Just like magic."

Winnie smiled back at her. "I'll just click my heels together three times and think *there's no place like home . . .*"

She didn't know if the reference would hold the same significance for Dora as it did for her, but the girl's face lit up, and Winnie knew the two of them must have seen it together here too.

Dora leaned in and hugged her tightly. "Take care of yourself, okay?" she whispered.

"I'll try," Winnie said. She admired the way Dora had accepted her into her life and home, how the girl had been willing to roll along with such an inexplicable occurrence—it was an ease her own Dora shared, and Winnie reminded herself that she ought to appreciate her friend more. She intended to, if she got the opportunity. "Thank you so much, for everything."

Beta approached next for her goodbye, staying a half dozen careful feet away. The two of them stood facing each other.

"Will you grow your hair out?" Beta asked, surprising a laugh from Winnie.

"I honestly haven't thought about it."

"Well, you shouldn't. It looks better like this," Beta said. Then she added suddenly, "Are you afraid?"

She was. Of many things.

If they succeeded, she'd go back in time about six days before the accident. Before she had agreed to help Scott find James. Before she had met Schrödinger.

But even though she was going back, there was no *real* going back. She would still know her true parentage. And she couldn't keep going along with Father's splinter experiments.

If Winnie wasn't his eager assistant and willing subject, then what was she to him? Would he even want her in his house anymore? It was one thing to tell herself she was brave enough to stand up to Father, but what would happen if she actually did?

Winnie thought of her cozy room, her reading chair snug under the attic eaves. Rebelling against Father meant giving up the only security she'd ever known.

Even before she found out about Schrödinger, part of her had understood that things couldn't keep going the way they had been forever. But she'd known that for a long time, and still, she hadn't left. Was she really strong enough to stand up to him now?

"Yes," Winnie said. "I'm afraid."

Beta smiled reassurance. "Don't worry. You managed the trip just fine once before."

"It's not only the trip I'm afraid of. It's what comes after," Winnie said. "If you ever do see a splinter, never let your father know," she added, almost desperately.

Beta's smile faltered, then faded away entirely. She nodded, then walked away, back behind the line demarcating where she, Dora, and Scott would be stationed during the experiment.

And then there was Scott. The only farewell left.

Winnie gave him an uncertain look, not knowing if it would be appropriate to embrace him, unsure if he would want her to. She wanted to, desperately.

She was silly to have wondered.

Scott held her for a long time. Winnie was sure he would have to explain himself to Beta later, and she appreciated that their goodbye was important enough to him to risk her jealousy.

Winnie thought back to their first embrace, just a few moments after she made her way into this world. She thought about their kiss.

She couldn't be certain, but she would have bet anything that Scott was thinking about that kiss too.

He pulled away first. "I'll be seeing you soon," he said with a crooked smile. "Sort of."

Winnie nodded. She knew that if she tried to speak at that moment, she'd cry—not pretty tears either, but awful, racking sobs—and that wasn't how she wanted their goodbye to be.

"And when you see me," he added, "don't be shy about . . . you know. Okay?" His eyes had a mischievous glint.

"Oh, I don't intend to be."

Winnie had her doubts about what awaited her back home—what Father would do, what she would do in return—but she knew one thing for certain: Scott would know how she felt about him. When she saw him, she would hold him tight and never let him go.

"You're ready?" Scott asked softly.

She didn't feel even a little bit ready, but she nodded anyway.

Winnie entered the cage and shut the door behind her.

CHAPTER TWENTY-SEVEN

The generator was an old model Scott had taken from the campus laboratory. He'd given the old thing a tune-up, and then modified it to output 900 milliamperes, same as Father had done.

Scott switched on the diesel-powered generator, and Winnie could hear the engine start to strain almost immediately. It was being asked to output more amperage than it had been built for, so this was to be expected.

Father had always said how much he admired machines for their predictability. They always did just as they were asked. The laws of mechanics were so clean. A machine could break down, but it would never act out, and once you opened it up, there was no mystery to what had happened. Quantum mechanics were practically mystical by comparison—odd and contradictory. Why had Father decided to study unruly electrons? He would have been happier with bolts and gears.

Happier, Winnie thought darkly, with a clockwork daughter who never disappointed him.

The generator continued its work, feeding current onto the surface of the Faraday cage. Winnie began to feel the vibration in her teeth. Dora and Scott and Beta were far away from her, all the way on the other side of the gym—thank goodness for Scott's binoculars!—and while the distance was reassuring with regard to their safety, she felt terribly alone in the cage.

Winnie was completely trapped there. If she tried to exit the cage before the current discharged, she would be electrocuted, and Scott wouldn't even be able to turn off the generator, or he would be electrocuted too.

All she could do was wait. Wait for the overburdened generator to self-destruct. Then wait for the charge to dissipate enough for her to be safe, while still leaving enough charge in the atmosphere to approximate the conditions of her first trip.

"What's the reading so far?" Winnie called to Scott, who had his binoculars trained on the atmospheric electrometer.

"Nothing yet," he said with a frown.

"Should I start jogging?"

She was supposed to run in place in the cage while intentionally hyperventilating to simulate the physical effects of the fight or flight response. Given her anxiety about the situation, it should be no challenge to whip herself into a frenzy.

Scott's brow furrowed in thought. He looked terribly nervous.

"Yes," Scott said finally, "go ahead and start. But save a bit of energy for later. It might be a while before the generator blows."

"Maybe you did too good a job on that tune-up," Winnie said, smiling faintly.

Scott grimaced. "Maybe I did."

Winnie began to run in place. She kept her breath shallow and quick. She didn't follow Scott's advice to conserve energy. If she failed, it wouldn't be because she didn't try. As long as she didn't push herself so hard that she fainted, it would be fine.

Her ears began ringing almost immediately, and she began to feel dizzy. It was working.

"The generator," she called, panting, "is it louder?" The engine's whine seemed to have increased in pitch, but Winnie wanted to make sure that wasn't just because of her proximity.

"Yes—we're getting close, I think."

It was almost time.

Winnie surrendered to panic.

It was oddly freeing to give rein to her fears, rather than trying to tamp them down. In her mind, she took herself back to Father's basement laboratory, back to the night of Father's cruel cat-in-a-box experiment. Scott was right in front of her—he'd been electrocuted. She saw the scorched lab coat. Imagined the smell of the singe. Remembered the smoke—burning her lungs, burning her nose. She breathed even quicker—*in out in out in out*—through her nose until she felt the burn.

"I'm getting a reading from the electrometer," Scott called. "A high one. Be ready after the generator goes, but don't leave the cage until I say it's safe."

The muscles of her thighs were trembling. She wasn't much

of a runner. Her right calf began to cramp, but she ignored it.

Focus on Scott. He's dying! He's dead!

She timed her quick breaths to the bleat of that word in her head—*dead dead dead*. Tears flowed down her cheeks unchecked.

"Are you okay?" Dora cried, but Winnie ignored her. She knew she was scaring the girls, probably scaring Scott too, but she couldn't simultaneously reassure them and command her body to panic.

The poor generator was trying so hard. Such a diligent worker. The kind Father liked best. The engine screamed, the keen of a dying animal, then—abruptly—stopped.

"Wait!" Scott reminded her. "Wait until I give the all clear."

Their Faraday cage was intentionally ungrounded, like Father's had been that day by mistake. The charge on the cage would dissipate rather than arc, because there was no con-ductor close enough to arc to.

Or so they thought.

There was a loud crack, and electricity arced up to kiss the metal cage enclosing one of the overhead lights. They were plunged into darkness.

"What's happening?" called Beta.

For the first moment, Winnie's complete panic felt like a delicious success. But this wasn't part of their plan. She was no longer playacting fear to prep her body for its work. Their experiment had gone off the rails. It was in danger of failing completely.

"Damn!" Scott hissed. Winnie couldn't see him—she couldn't see anything—but she heard him take a few deep breaths.

"I can't read the electrometer now," Scott said, "so we'll just wait it out. Let's give it thirty minutes or so. The charge should dissipate long before then. We'll rebuild the generator, try again another time—"

"No," Winnie said. She was still panting. She couldn't seem to stop. The panic was still in her. Her heart felt shivery, her whole chest tight. The current on the Faraday cage had gotten its chance to discharge, but *she* hadn't.

The day before had brought James's death. Her being there was messing with gravity, changing the tides, and then that morning she had caused a complete disruption of time. What more would go wrong if they waited? She couldn't risk it.

"It's safe enough. I'm coming out. I'm trying now."

"*No*," Scott yelled. "Absolutely not. You could still get shocked!"

Yes, she *could*, but the chance was small. It was unlikely there was enough electricity remaining in the atmosphere to seriously hurt her, and in any case, the thought of being electrocuted wasn't as frightening as the thought of their experiment being a total failure without her even trying to get home at all.

She pushed open the door.

"Winnie, stop! Get back in the cage!"

She ignored Scott and took a few careful steps forward.

"It could still work! I'm just going to check the electrometer, then try to transport."

The darkness was still inky and oppressive around her, feeling like a physical barrier, rather than just the absence of light. But her eyes were slowly adjusting.

She took a few ginger steps toward the electrometer. She needed to know how much current there was in the atmosphere. If this didn't work, that data would be essential to plan their next experiment.

"Dammit, Winnie! What are you doing?"

"Just stay where you are," she said, her voice sounding loud in the dark. She was confident enough that it was safe to risk herself, but not confident enough to risk Scott. Again.

She moved slowly, sweeping her arm ahead of her, hoping to make contact with the electrometer—but gently. If she knocked it over, it would shatter, and that would be the end of that.

A few more steps, and her fingers brushed the glass of the Leyden jar. She leaned close. Her eyes would adjust, and she would be able to read—

Her knuckle bumped one of the metal plates she had so carefully sanded during the tedious construction of the thing. Static electricity sparked blue, bright enough for her to see the Leyden jar shatter. Winnie jerked back, the pain of the static shock sharp in her hand, like what she imagined a snakebite must feel like.

These weren't the conditions they had planned for. Winnie no longer felt the panic their experiment called for, just the irrational anger of sudden pain. And with the electrometer broken, she had no idea if there was still an atmospheric charge left after the discharge of her shock. Still, she had to try.

Winnie closed her eyes, and wished for home, for Scott. She tried to feel around inside herself for whatever it was that had allowed her to travel the first time, but—nothing.

It was like trying to wiggle her ears—she knew it was possible, because some people could. But she simply couldn't do it. She tried and there was nothing there.

Was the premise of their experiment wrong? Or did her attempt fail because they had messed up the conditions? It was impossible to know for sure.

Whatever the cause, one thing was clear: They had failed.

All their equipment was destroyed, and her hope along with it.

Compared to the disappointment, the pain in her hand was nothing.

"What's happened?" Beta called. "Winnie, are you okay?"

Scott rushed for the gym doors.

"Don't touch the metal," Winnie said, her voice sounding hollow in her own ears.

He kicked the door open, letting in a bit of moonlight from the hall windows. Now that they could see, Dora picked up the flashlight from the ground a few feet away from her and turned it on.

"Winnie?" Dora called. "Are you all right?"

The cone of light from her flashlight hit Winnie's face, and she flinched at the glare.

Dora gasped. "Your head!"

Winnie touched a hand to her forehead. It came away sticky

with blood that looked black in the pale yellow beam of light. She must have been cut by some flying glass when the electrometer shattered. A little shard of their hard work. One of the shattered pieces of Scott's chance for survival.

Dora aimed the beam of her flashlight at the center of the gymnasium, giving Winnie a chance to survey the damage.

The mascot painted at the center of the basketball court was completely obscured by a scar of charred wood. The circular burn was about ten feet across, surrounding the Faraday cage. If she hadn't been inside, Winnie was sure she would be dead.

The generator was still smoking. All of its plastic dials had melted. She turned around to look at the electrometer. Shattered glass and twisted shards of metal were all that remained.

"I suppose I can tell Martha not to worry about having my athletic clothes washed for tomorrow's gym class," Dora said faintly. She was trying to sound plucky, but her shaky voice betrayed reverberations from the shock of it all.

The way ears ring after a deafening noise, and everything sounds muted and far off—that was how Winnie felt. Not with her hearing, but with *all* of her. Her mind was deadened with the disappointment of their spectacular failure.

It felt like losing Scott all over again.

They would try again. She wouldn't stop trying. But what if they just kept failing? And what if the effects of her being in their world kept getting worse? How much time did she really have?

The cut on her head bled freely now. It hurt, and she was as nauseated as if she hadn't just lost a fair amount of blood, but swallowed it.

She stumbled over to Scott. His expression was completely shut down. Scott was still living in that moment between seeing the deep cut and feeling the searing pain that would follow—Winnie knew the signs.

When she met Scott's eyes, it was like he was just noticing that she was there. He didn't look pleased.

"Winnie, how could you? James—that was *yesterday*. You think I could stand to watch you die today?"

It was her life to risk, Winnie thought ferociously—but underneath, she knew that wasn't fully true. If he had done something similarly half-cocked and dangerous, she would have wanted to throttle him.

Winnie squeezed her eyes closed and kept them shut for a long moment. When she opened them, she saw her double standing there behind Scott, frowning at her.

"I'm sorr—" Winnie began to say, then fell silent in shock. A wound began to open itself on Beta's forehead, like her skin was being cut into by an invisible knife. Winnie didn't have to look in a mirror to know that this laceration was identical to her own.

"Scott," Winnie said shakily, "Scott, look."

He did, and his face went paper-white at the sight of Beta.

"Oh my god," Dora whispered.

Beta looked scared, but she had yet to realize what had happened. "What? What are you two staring at?"

Beta put her fingers to her temple then, and held them in front of her face in fascination, as if the blood on them were someone else's. "Oh," she said, and her knees began to buckle. Scott had an arm around her in a moment to keep her from falling.

Dora hurried over to the locker room with her flashlight and was back in a flash with a clean washcloth. She pressed it to Beta's wound.

"Hold it here," Dora said. "Tight."

"What are we going to do?" Beta said, almost wailing.

"Shh," Scott murmured. "It's going to be okay."

Her double folded in on herself and gave a hopeless sob. It was obvious that all that had allowed Beta to cope with the situation was that it would soon be over—but without that hope? Well, Winnie felt the awful weight in her own chest—a twin despair.

Winnie's own wooziness finally took hold, but no one was there to catch *her*. She stumbled down on one knee, pressing her bloody palm to the floor to catch herself before she fell completely. Dora and Scott were too busy examining Beta's forehead to even notice that Winnie had collapsed. She pushed herself back up and stumbled over to the bleachers, where she sank down to sit on the hard wood.

Scott pulled a clean handkerchief out of his breast pocket and knotted it tight around Beta's head. "I'll take care of Winnie," Scott said to Dora. "Get her home," he added, jutting his chin in Winnie's direction, tone clipped. "Tell your housekeeper she fell. She can help you get her scrapes cleaned up. Maybe she'll want to call for a doctor, but I don't think it needs stitches."

It shouldn't hurt so bad, having him angry with her. He wasn't the real Scott, she reminded herself. She had, what, a week of shared history with this person? He was a stranger. They were all strangers. Even Beta. Especially Beta! Beta, who made Winnie a stranger to herself.

"Let's go," Dora said softly.

Scott didn't say goodbye. He didn't say anything to her, just bent over and began picking up the pieces of their ruined electrometer.

Winnie didn't know why he bothered. It wasn't like there was anything salvageable.

Dora took Winnie's arm and gently pulled her into the hall.

But Winnie was still able to hear her double moan, "We have to get rid of her, Scott. We have to get rid of her."

CHAPTER TWENTY-EIGHT

The next morning, Dora nudged Winnie long before she was ready to wake. It took a moment for her consciousness to claw itself out of an unpleasant dream that immediately faded to nothing more than a vague impression of fear, needles, and James.

"What?" she asked groggily, glancing at Dora's alarm clock—6:45. They hadn't gotten in until after 3 a.m., and then they'd had to wake Louisa to look at Winnie's head, claiming she'd tripped carrying a glass of water back to Dora's room. Winnie would be surprised if she'd gotten two hours of uninterrupted sleep. "What is it?"

"School is canceled," Dora said. "We just got the call. I thought you would want to know."

Winnie's stomach sank. She'd hoped the mess they left in the gymnasium would pass as a failed prank, but they wouldn't close the school if they thought it was just schoolgirl shenanigans.

Winnie rubbed her temples. What was done was done. They couldn't change things now.

"All right," Winnie said. "I'm going to try to get some more sleep."

She rolled over, putting pressure on the cut on the side of her forehead. Tired as she was, it was a long time before she was able to fall back asleep.

WINNIE AWOKE AGAIN HOURS LATER TO A BRISK KNOCK ON THE DOOR. Louisa entered the room carrying a pale pink Bakelite phone on a shiny tray. Its long cord trailed off out the bedroom door.

"There's a call for you," she told Dora, setting the tray down on the bedside table.

Dora nodded mutely, and Louisa left the two of them alone again.

"Who do you think it is?" Winnie hissed.

"Maybe Mother, or Father?" Dora suggested uncertainly. "Maybe it has nothing to do with what happened." She lifted the receiver to her ear. "Hello?"

Winnie's eyes were trained intently on Dora's face, and she was surprised to see a flicker of irritation come and go.

"Winnie," Dora said, "you can't call here! You *are* here! Louisa knows your voice."

Winnie scooted closer to Dora on the bed, and Dora held the telephone out between them so she could hear too.

"I pretended to be Lucille. I had to call—some policemen

294

came by the house, the same ones we saw taking Winnie and Scott to the morgue. They had Daddy come home from work and they interviewed us together. They asked about James—no surprise there—but they also asked if we knew about what happened at school."

"What!" Winnie gasped. "How did they link that to you so quickly?"

That damn Muldoon had been suspicious of her from the start. But even so, it seemed unlikely that the police would connect the dots to her. Only Hawthorn would recognize the damage they'd left behind as a failed experiment.

"I don't know, but they seemed fairly certain a girl was there at the school when the explosion happened. They wanted to take my fingerprints, for some reason. Daddy wouldn't let them."

Winnie remembered falling on the gym floor, leaving a bloody palm print—a handprint that would be easily identified as belonging to a young woman just by the size, but the fingerprints would identify it as *hers*. Well, hers or Beta's.

"Scheiße!" Winnie cursed in German.

The police could have no idea what was really going on, of course—which, if anything, made them more dangerous. She thought about the facts of the case, as they would see it. A scientist—Beta's father—working on a military project. A dead student, best friend of his daughter's boyfriend, also part of the project. An explosion at this daughter's school, with a young woman present. A random jumble of evidence until you throw in this: the Schuldes—they're German. Now all this pandemonium coalesces, and a single cause emerges.

Espionage.

Suddenly, it's clear that the Schuldes must be German spies. They integrated themselves into a government project to steal American technology for the enemy. That student? He died because he knew too much—collateral damage.

Winnie let out a breath.

Even though there wasn't any truth to it, she knew far less evidence was required to make such charges those days.

That August, less than three months earlier, there had been a mass execution of German enemy agents. The six men had not carried out any sabotage, but they had *intended* to—or so the military tribunal claimed.

The details of the case had stuck with Winnie, for obvious reasons. The youngest of them had been only twenty-two, and a US citizen since the age of ten. He'd been abroad when Hitler declared war on the United States and wound up stranded in Europe. He claimed he'd only cooperated with the Germans as a way of getting home. When Winnie saw his mugshot in the newspaper, she couldn't believe how normal he looked— handsome even—and scared.

"That's not all," Beta said. "There was some other kind of accident last night, apparently. They asked if I knew about it, but wouldn't tell me *anything*."

"What do you mean? They thought you might be involved with something other than what happened at school?"

"I guess so."

What could it have been?

And was it possible that they *were* to blame for something else, something they didn't even know about?

Well, no, not "they."

Her.

"So, what are we going to do?" Dora asked. She spoke the question into the receiver, but she was looking at Winnie.

Winnie had no answer. What were they going to do? What *could* they do? Their plan had failed; their equipment was destroyed; police detectives were on their trail, closing in, and Hawthorn couldn't be far behind.

"I don't know," Winnie said, but her own uncertain words were lost beneath her double's confident reply.

"Winnie and I are going to restage last night's experiment tomorrow. Here, in Father's lab. He has the equipment," Beta said. "We can do it. Just she and I."

Winnie was surprised her double was willing to try again. The way Beta's forehead had just split open like that . . . thinking about it made Winnie sick to her stomach. Would something worse happen to the two of them the next time they were together? But the physical effects of Winnie's presence in their world were intensifying too. It was dangerous not to try.

"Scott won't like it," Winnie said finally. "What if we get too close to each other, and something goes wrong?"

"That's why we aren't going to tell him. He would just tell us not to. But nothing is riskier than you staying here. And what about your own Scott—you haven't given up on him, have you?"

"Of course not!" Winnie said.

"We don't have a choice. We have to try."

And for once, Winnie had to agree.

WINNIE SHOULD HAVE REALIZED MCPHERSON AND MULDOON WOULD come for Dora next.

That afternoon there was a loud knock on the door, audible even in Dora's bedroom. How was it that just a knock could convey so much authority?

"Mr. and Mrs. Vandorf aren't home at the moment," Winnie heard Louisa say firmly. "You'll have to come—hey, you can't just barge in here!"

There was the bass rumble of one of the detective's voices, but she couldn't make out the words. Winnie grabbed Dora's hand tight in her own. The two girls looked at each other, but neither said a word. Fear had pushed Winnie beyond the ability to speak.

Whatever the detective said, it must have mollified Louisa, because she said, "Here, I'll take your coats. Have a seat in the drawing room, and I'll go get her."

Louisa opened the door without pausing to knock.

"There are detectives here," she said quietly. "They want to speak to you, Dora. I told them your parents aren't here, but they insisted. Should I ring for Mr. Rockford? You should have *someone* here, but Dora, please tell me you don't actually need an attorney."

Louisa shot Winnie a dirty look, like she suspected that this trouble could be traced back to her. Winnie resented the unfairness of this for about a split second before realizing that Louisa wasn't wrong.

Dora shook her head mutely. Then, after a long pause, she said, "I'll speak to them. I—everything will be fine."

"You won't tell them I'm here?" Winnie asked Dora, but the question was really for Louisa.

"No, of course not." Dora frowned at Louisa. "It's just me and you and Martha here, understand?"

Louisa nodded, but she didn't look pleased about it.

Dora left to go speak with the men, but Louisa hung back a moment.

"I don't know what it is you've done, but I want you gone by tomorrow or I'll turn you in myself."

Winnie nodded. If the next day's experiment didn't work, she would have nowhere to go—but if the experiment didn't work, Louisa would be the least of her problems.

"It's okay," Dora said shakily when she returned some half hour or so later. "They just asked if I was at the school last night, or if I knew who was. They also asked if I'd heard about some kind of car accident? I just told them I'd been home all night. They asked if I knew James—there, at least, I could tell the truth. We never met. They must have found out I'm Winnie's best friend, but they don't know anything more yet."

Winnie frowned. "They might not know exactly what they're looking for, but they've already managed to get awful close awful quickly."

It was bad luck that there was an open investigation into James's death when they destroyed the gymnasium, and that she'd seemed somewhat suspicious already—to Muldoon, at least—when the investigation into the explosion at her school began. The two events weren't actually related, but of course they would seem that way, since Winnie had ties to both, and James and her father had ties to the same government project.

"You know, they might be watching Dr. Schulde's house," Dora said. "They might even be watching this building. Are you sure it's a good idea to go over there tomorrow?"

"No," Winnie said. "It's almost certainly a bad one. But it's the only one we have."

WHILE THEY WERE EATING THAT EVENING, LOUISA CAME IN, TOSSED THE *New York PM Daily* down, gave Winnie a glare, and stalked out of the dining room.

Dora met Winnie's eyes from across the table with a meaningful look, then cautiously picked up the paper.

"Oh," she said in a small voice.

Winnie pushed her chair back with a screech and hurried over to stand behind her friend so they could read together.

WARSHIP APPEARS—AND DISAPPEARS!—OUTSIDE BLOOMINGDALE'S

It was the kind of thing she'd expect to see on the cover of *Astounding Stories* or *Weird Tales*—some work of science fiction—not the evening paper. But there it was.

Winnie quickly skimmed the news article. Apparently, in the middle of the night, several bystanders saw a ship flicker into existence smack dab in the middle of the intersection of Third Avenue and 57th Street, remain there just long enough to demolish three parked cars, and for at least two witnesses to note the hull number and name on the bow—USS *Eldridge* 173—then vanish.

As if that weren't impossible enough already, the ship with that identification was planned, but it hadn't been built yet.

"What do you make of it?" Dora asked breathlessly. "It's just so strange! A hoax—?"

"Do hoaxes crush asphalt? Or cars?"

"What then?"

"I don't know. But I thought . . . I thought I heard a ship horn last night, when we were getting on the subway."

Dora frowned. "But that was earlier, and much too far away. The ship—"

"Appeared *maybe* half a mile from the school," Winnie interrupted. "Later. Right when we were performing our experiment."

Dora shook her head in disbelief. She seemed slow to accept what Winnie already had: This was her fault. It was another side effect of the energy imbalance Winnie had caused. She didn't know exactly *how* it had happened, but the why was no mystery.

"Maybe it was the Germans, somehow, like the paper says."

The article supposed that the Germans had somehow dropped a ship in the middle of Manhattan. What else could it possibly be? But that theory didn't account for the US hull number, or explain how the Germans could have gotten something so massive aloft—let alone how they could have possibly made it disappear after.

The whole article had a tone of barely constrained panic.

Only one thing is clear, it concluded—*our Axis enemies have a terrible new weapon.*

Winnie shook her head. "It was us. Me. Our experiment—somehow, I moved that ship. I must have brought it here from the future, from when it's done being built. Maybe even some other world's future. I'm jumbling everything up, twisting the natural order of things, and now . . . this. It's the only thing that makes any kind of sense."

"All these poor people!" Dora exclaimed. "Terrified of the Germans' 'new weapon.' I wish we could tell them they don't have to be afraid."

Winnie didn't say anything—she didn't want to worry Dora more—but people *should* be afraid. The real threat was right there, in their own city.

Winnie suspected it was the continued wrongness of her being there, concentrated somehow by the electric field they'd created, that had temporarily pulled a massive amount of matter into their system when she'd failed to transport herself. A small part of her was gratified. At least they were on the right track. At least they were doing *something*.

But what if there had been a person in one of those cars?

What if they'd staged their experiment at any other time of day, when that intersection would have been teeming with people, not just a handful of couples heading home from the Copacabana or whatever other nightclub. It was a tremendous stroke of luck that no one had died.

It was more urgent than ever for Winnie to try their experiment again.

And more dangerous than she'd realized for her to try again and fail.

"No call this morning," Dora said, "so I suppose school's reopened."

"Well, that's good," Winnie said uncertainly. "Maybe everything will blow over."

But she and Dora both knew that was just wishful thinking.

"Or maybe the police want to get all us schoolgirls back in one place, so they can keep an eye on us," Dora said.

Winnie felt a twinge in her gut and knew immediately that Dora must be right. She hated to think of her friend there all day under their ominous eyes, alone.

"Don't go. Come to Winnie's with me. We should all stick together."

Dora thought about it for a moment. "I think it's safest if we just act normal. Honestly, I wish Winnie wasn't playing hooky today." Her forehead wrinkled with concern. "The detectives last night—they didn't threaten me, exactly, but I got the sense that one of them, at least, would have been happy to cart me in even if I'm innocent, just to see if it put pressure on the right people. I don't want to give them any excuse."

"They wouldn't arrest *you*. Not without a good reason. You're—well, you're rich."

"This is wartime, Winnie. I'm not sure it matters who your parents are. And besides," she added, "it isn't as if my parents are here." Dora sighed heavily. "I'm sure they would have leaned on Winnie much harder if her father hadn't been there to tell them just where they could stick their inquiries. But me, I may as well not have any parents at all." For a moment, the pain was naked on Dora's face, but then she gave a weak smile and said, "I just have to hope they don't realize I know anything. So, I'll be going to school like a good girl. Now, if you'll excuse me, I'm going to grab my books."

Dora got up, pushed her chair in, and went off to her bedroom to put together her school things. Winnie tried to take a few more bites of breakfast, but the food turned to cardboard in her mouth. The fork dropped from her hand, and time thickened around her, like the air itself was so full of possibilities that it impeded the normally steady tick of seconds.

It was a splinter—the first one she'd experienced in this world. It hit with an unusual intensity, as if the energy of all the small splinters she would have normally seen in this time had combined into this one.

What Winnie saw was as real for her as if it were actually unfolding before her eyes: Winnie suggested Dora skip school and join them for the experiment at her double's house.

"Don't go," Winnie said, just as she had a moment ago. "Come to Winnie's with me. We should all stick together."

But instead of declining, Dora frowned, thought a moment, then nodded her head and said, "Okay. I think I will."

Then, time jumped.

Winnie saw herself and Dora with Beta in the shed at Beta's house, sorting through all Father's retired equipment. It was happening again. She was seeing a potential future, just like she had when she "met" James in Hawthorn's lab, although this one seemed awfully pedestrian. Dora went with her, and all seemed well.

Winnie felt a twinge of worry. Did that mean things would go well *only* if Dora went with her?

Then the other half of the splinter hit her. She felt a cramp deep in her belly, like someone had reached inside and was wrenching her organs in their tightly closed fist. Winnie doubled over in pain. She heard her plate shatter against the hardwood floor before she realized she'd knocked it from the table.

She saw her body alone on a dirt floor, a deep dent in her temple. Winnie started panting. Could it be she was just unconscious? No—not with an injury like that.

Was *that* what awaited her if Dora didn't go?

Winnie forced herself to focus on the here and now and tried to shut out the awful image of her dead body. She had seen her death once before. She had been crossing the street when a car sped around the corner, just barely missing her. In an alternate reality, it caught her. She heard the wet thump of the impact, like a thick slab of steak being tenderized with a wooden mallet, and saw her bloody body in the street. Although she was unharmed, it took her some time to realize it. Seeing the split had been so upsetting, things had gotten all jumbled. For a moment, it was like she *had* been hit. She collapsed, screaming. Once the gathering crowd realized she was uninjured, they decided she was having a hysterical fit. A man in a suit had knelt beside her and given her a sharp slap to bring her out of it.

Remembering this made Winnie hopeful for a moment. Perhaps this was like that other time, and she was confusing what happened in the split with what would happen here— perhaps it was some other Winnie who died on a cold, packed-earth floor. But the splinter seemed to be outlining two possibilities: If Dora came with her, she lived; if Dora didn't, she died.

Of course, she had *thought* she understood the meaning of the splinter she saw when Father told her she couldn't go to Hawthorn's party. She *thought* that defying him would lead her to James. But it had led her to the wrong James, in the wrong world, via a path that included Scott's death.

So how could she really know what to make of this splinter?

But the way it had come on, so intense—it also felt wrong to just ignore it.

Dora hurried into the room then, while Winnie was still struggling to decide what to do.

"Are you okay? It sounded like something broke."

Winnie nodded. She knelt down and began picking up the shards of porcelain.

"I'm afraid to go to Winnie's alone," Winnie said suddenly, the words popping out of her mouth before she even knew she was saying them. "Are you sure you can't come with me?"

Irritation flashed on Dora's face. "We were *just* talking about the danger of me skipping class."

But what if this was life or death? It very well might be, and Winnie was certain that Dora would say yes, if she explained that to her.

But what if Winnie was wrong? It wouldn't be the first time. How could she ask Dora to become even more mixed up in all this than she already was, when she wasn't even sure?

Asking Dora to skip school and come with her would be tantamount to demanding that Dora put Winnie's well-being over her own. And the thing was, she knew Dora would do it— which was exactly why she couldn't ask.

Of course, Winnie didn't want to die. She was sixteen! There was still so much she wanted to do. And, if she were to die, there would be no one left to try to save Scott. He would be dead for good.

So, she would try to be smart, and careful. Maybe with the

warning she'd seen, she would be prepared to save herself from whatever accident she'd seen the aftermath of, if it was truly the consequence of going to her double's alone.

Winnie made her goodbyes to Dora, thankful that any strangeness on her part would be dismissed as nerves about the impending experiment.

"This is our last goodbye, isn't it?" Dora said. "I mean, hopefully it is—if your experiment works."

Winnie forced a smile. "It is. Thank you for letting me stay with you. Thank you for everything."

She hugged Dora tightly. Then she made herself let go.

CHAPTER TWENTY-NINE

As soon as Winnie knocked, Beta opened the door, glanced up and down the street, then gestured frantically for Winnie to come inside.

Beta tucked her hair behind her ear nervously, baring the ugly gash on her forehead. Strangely, it startled Winnie more seeing it on her double than when she saw it in the mirror.

Winnie hadn't taken that close of a look at herself that morning. Were the circles under her own eyes as dark? Her skin that sallow? The girl was a wreck.

"Are you okay?" Winnie asked.

Her double laughed. It was a hopeless sound.

"No," she said. "Are you?"

Winnie shook her head. "No. I guess not."

"We should start in the shed, I think," Beta said, taking a few steps back from her.

Did the shed have a dirt floor? Winnie couldn't remember. Father used it to store excess lab equipment and things in need of repair, but she didn't go out there much herself.

"Why not the laboratory?" Winnie asked.

The floor of the basement laboratory was definitely dirt, but avoidance wouldn't save her—she had to hope that caution might.

"Father has a—what was that thing you broke? The glass thing that measures electric charge?"

"An electrometer?"

"Yeah, he has an electrometer out there, I think. And one of those cages too."

"Really? In the shed? Assembled and everything?"

"Um, I'm not sure. We might have to put it together. Let's go check."

Even though she knew they had to try to find a way to get her back home, Winnie didn't share her double's eagerness to get started. Their earlier failure hadn't left her with much confidence, and the stakes had only gotten higher. If all four of them together had managed to screw things up, what hope did just she and Beta have?

Beta turned and began walking toward the kitchen.

"Wait—" Winnie said. "Should we really be doing this? Maybe it would be better to wait for Scott."

Her double stopped and faced Winnie. Her expression was inscrutable.

"I didn't know James as well as I would have liked," she

said, brows furrowed. "But he meant a lot to Scott, and that means a lot to me."

"I feel the same way," Winnie said, although she wasn't quite sure what Beta was saying—or rather, she didn't understand the emotion underneath it, or why she was saying it then.

"Scott—" Beta began, but then shook her head. "He's been through enough already. He is going to be *so* mad." Tears welled in her eyes, but they didn't spill. "But I don't know what else to do. Do you?" She paused. "Scott sugarcoats it, but you and me—we know the truth, right? You're tearing this world apart."

Winnie couldn't disagree. It was dangerous to try their experiment again. Or rather, it was dangerous to *fail* again. But there was danger in all directions now, and retrying their experiment was the only direction that also had the potential for safety—and Scott.

Winnie nodded. Her double was right.

"This is what we have to do," Beta said.

Winnie nodded again and followed her double outside.

THE LARGE COURTYARD WAS HEMMED IN ON ALL SIDES BY THE NEIGHboring townhouses. A narrow, stone-paved path led to a small storage shed in the rear corner of the yard. Winnie began to walk toward it, and Beta trailed a few feet behind.

Winnie understood why her double was afraid to get too

close to her. She put a hand to the cut on her forehead—it looked worse than it felt, but she wasn't eager for any new injuries, and imagined her double wasn't either.

What traitors their bodies had become!

As Winnie approached the door, she saw that the padlock on the shed had been left open.

"Why don't you go in and see if the stuff we need is there, okay?" Beta said.

She looked miserable. Winnie felt a pang of guilt. She hadn't come to their world on purpose, but that didn't make her presence there any less difficult for her double.

"Okay," Winnie said. She entered the small shed, which was just as tidy as the one back home. All the tools were hanging in their designated places on a wall of whitewashed pegboard, and orderly shelves of laboratory equipment lined the back wall, either duplicates of things in the basement lab, or equipment in need of repair. The only thing out of place was a stool, pulled out from its spot in front of the workbench to sit in the middle of the room, with a bundle of rope sitting on top of it.

"I don't see a Faraday cage," Winnie called, "or an electrome—"

Her words were cut off when Beta rushed up behind her, grabbing her arms.

Winnie looked around the shed frantically—Beta was pulling at her—she must be trying to save her from something bad, but what?

Then she heard the snick of handcuffs clicking into place

around her wrists, binding her hands behind her back, and finally understood what was happening.

Beta wasn't trying to save her from danger—Beta *was* the danger.

Winnie realized immediately what her double must have planned, sure as if she'd conceived it herself.

Beta was going to turn her over to Hawthorn. Maybe he'd made some kind of threat. Or maybe Beta was just desperate to get their lives back to normal.

"Hawthorn needs a new subject now," Beta said quietly, "with James gone."

"You told him about me?"

She shook her head. "I didn't have to."

Hawthorn had found her so quickly, just like James knew he would—uncannily fast. Although, scientists were natural detectives, weren't they? That was why Scott had asked for her help finding James in the first place.

"He came by yesterday when Father was out," Beta continued. "Said it was nice to meet me—a trick. Of course, I didn't know we were supposed to have met at the morgue."

Winnie strained against the cuffs and tried to think. Beta had been in such a hurry to get them on that she hadn't secured them very tightly. The left one seemed like it just might be loose enough to squeeze out of.

"So that's that?" Winnie asked, hoping to keep her double distracted as she fumbled around behind her back. "Hawthorn knows about me, so you may as well hand me over?" She grasped the loose cuff in the fingers of her right hand and started to yank, ignoring the pain in her wrist.

"He said he can make the police think Scott did it—that Scott killed James."

"And you believe him?" Winnie asked, but she was stalling. She didn't think Hawthorn was the type of man who made empty threats. Still, there had to be another solution. "If you knew what it was like to be experimented on," Winnie added bitterly, "you wouldn't do this."

"Oh, please. Working with Father couldn't have been that bad."

Beta had no idea. Being dragged out of bed, kept up all night. Father looking at her, but not seeing her, interrogating her about the splinters, taking copious notes on every one—but skipping simple small talk like "Hey, how was school?"

Beta didn't know what it was like to watch Father at the breakfast table the morning after Winnie had been accidently shocked during their experiment the night before, eating his toast dry and drinking his coffee black like some kind of penitence. Even though Father wouldn't meet her eyes, it was like she could read his mind.

I'm a monster. You've made a monster of me.

She had to break the silence to let him know it was okay, so she'd told him, "Next time, let's try a Faraday cage," making herself an accomplice in her own torment—because it was either that or be a helpless victim.

Winnie couldn't do it again. She wouldn't.

It had been bad enough with Father, but with Hawthorn? He'd had James's body thrown in the Hudson like trash, and that was someone he supposedly cared about. He'd have no trouble disposing of Winnie.

"Hawthorn is a murderer," she said.

"Exactly! That's how we know he's more than capable of hurting Scott. If you really cared about him, you wouldn't fight," argued Beta.

"That's not true!" Winnie shouted. "Getting back home isn't just for me. It's to give my own Scott a chance. Prison is one thing, but my Scott is dead unless I go back. Let me try our experiment again! With what's in your father's lab, I'm sure I can make another attempt, and with me gone, Hawthorn won't have anything to gain by threatening Scott."

"Are you serious? Best-case scenario, you disappear, and *I'm* the one left with Hawthorn's threat. Now that he knows about you, he is going to get his hands on a Winnie. If it can't be you, he'll come after me instead."

Beta was right. But Winnie would rather it be her double. It was a ruthless thing to think, but it was easy to feel ruthless with her hands cuffed behind her back.

Not that it mattered. *She* was the one Hawthorn wanted.

"You're safe from him in a way that I'm not," Winnie said, "because you don't see them."

"You can't really be that stupid, can you?"

"What do you mean?"

"*Of course* I see splinters!" Beta said.

Winnie was stunned.

"I just know better than to tell people about it."

"But . . . really? Not even Father?" she asked, so surprised by this revelation that she momentarily stopped trying to yank her wrist free from the cuff. "Or Scott?"

She'd been so sure that not seeing splinters had caused the differences between them. But now . . .

"Not *anyone*. I know I'm a—a freak. No one else needs to know." Beta frowned. "I told Mama once," she said, "a long time ago." The far-off memory made her fade into herself for a moment. "She said to ignore them, and not to talk about it again."

Mama had been open enough about her gift once to tell even Schrödinger. Something had taught her that she should never do that again. It must have been a hard lesson.

So, she'd wanted to spare her daughter that pain. How could Mama have known that this command would plant the seed of such self-loathing in the girl?

Even Winnie had at least been able to share her ability with Father.

"Oh, Winnie—"

"Then you come here, and suddenly we're all in danger," Beta continued angrily, cutting her off. "Suddenly, Nightingale isn't the career break of a lifetime for Father and Scott, it's some shadowy threat—but Hawthorn was never a problem for us until *you* came along. I get too close to you and my nose bleeds, my forehead splits open—and ever since you got here, I see splinters *all the time!* Every day!"

That must be why Winnie had stopped seeing them. Both of them being in one world had caused some kind of interference, blocking Winnie's ability and flooding her double. It almost made Winnie feel bad for Beta—or it would have, if the girl hadn't handcuffed her.

"But somehow," her double continued, *"you're* the one we have to sacrifice everything to protect. And Scott will do it, too. He's too good for his own good. He'll put himself at risk for you, but enough is enough. I won't let him—and if you cared about anything except yourself, you wouldn't either. So, sit down," Beta said, gesturing at the stool, "and let me tie your ankles."

Winnie's double was a terrible funhouse mirror that showed her not squat and fat or stretched too thin, but stripped bare. Jealous, and broken, and capable of terrible betrayal.

This was the reflection of her own selfishness, wasn't it? When Winnie got there, Scott warned her that her presence put their world in danger. But her only concerns had been self-preservation and saving her own Scott.

Could she really be surprised that her double only cared about doing the same?

Winnie continued trying to pull her wrist free. She was making progress, slowly, until the cuff hit the lower joint of her thumb. The tight metal began to tear into her knuckle. Winnie fought to keep the pain off her face.

But trying to free her hands—it wasn't working. Winnie began to pant as she realized she wasn't going to be able to pull the cuffs off. They were too tight after all. She was trapped, and soon she'd be caged.

Would Hawthorn's experiments be like Father's, or completely different? How long would it be until her body gave out like James's had? Or would her ability allow her to endure Hawthorn's experiments for months—even years?

At least she knew she wasn't destined for the river. She had no family to miss her. No one to wonder. Even Scott would just think she'd gone back home. There would be no need for a body. When Hawthorn was finished with her, she would never be found.

Beta took a few quick steps over to the wall and grabbed a shovel that was hanging there. "Sit," she said again, waving the shovel in Winnie's direction. "*Now.*"

"If you hit me with that thing, you might hurt yourself too," Winnie warned her, but her double seemed desperate enough to try anything.

Beta glared at Winnie. "Just sit. It's over. Hawthorn's already on his way."

No. This wasn't happening. Winnie's eyes darted back and forth. If she let herself get tied down, it was over—but how could she possibly escape? Beta was standing between her and the door. It would be hard with her hands cuffed behind her back, but if Winnie could push past her—get free of the shed—then she would at least have a chance.

"What's Scott going to think?" Winnie asked harshly. "He won't forgive you."

"He won't know," Beta said, even though the threat made her eyes wide with fear. "Hawthorn promised."

"I think we both know he will."

It was a bluff, but the shovel sagged in Beta's hands, the head of it dipping down toward the dirt floor as she contemplated the awful possibility of losing Scott's love.

Winnie took her moment.

She rushed at Beta, shoving into her with her shoulder since she couldn't use her hands. The force of the impact sent them both flying. Winnie watched Beta's arms pinwheel for balance as she stumbled backward herself.

Winnie tripped over the shovel that had been in Beta's hands a moment before, and landed painfully on her back, on top of her cuffed hands, wrenching her shoulders and knocking her head against the dirt floor, hard.

She saw Beta fall.

She saw Beta hit her temple on the corner of the workbench. A glancing blow.

Winnie struggled to get up—she knew her double would be back on her feet in a moment, blocking her way again. It was difficult with her hands cuffed behind her back, but Winnie managed to stagger to her feet.

But when she did, Beta was still on the floor. Just lying there. Had she been knocked unconscious when she hit her head? Maybe that was why the blow hadn't hurt Winnie too—maybe when she was knocked out, it severed whatever connection existed between them.

Winnie eyed the door. How much time did she have before Hawthorn came to collect her? Was he waiting for some signal from Beta, or was he already on his way? She should go quickly, she should go right now—

But Winnie couldn't leave without checking on her double.

"Winnie?" she asked, approaching cautiously and nudging the girl with her foot.

Beta didn't move.

"Are you all right?" Winnie whispered, dread thick in her throat.

She nudged her double's shoulder harder, and the girl's head lolled bonelessly.

Winnie couldn't bend over to take her pulse with her hands cuffed, but she didn't need to. Her eyes fixed on the spot where Beta had hit her head. It was concave, and deeply purple.

Winnie stumbled back in horror.

That face, that ground, that awful dent in her skull. Winnie recognized this—it was what she'd seen that morning.

Her eyes unfocused. Her eyes blank.

Winnie understood now.

It wasn't her own death she had seen in that splinter. It was Beta's.

It was Beta's.

It was Beta's.

Her stomach heaved. She was afraid she'd be sick.

What had she done?

And what could she do now?

PART THREE

In each of us there is another whom we do not know.

—Carl Jung

CHAPTER THIRTY

Winnie would have to bury the body. Leaving it above-ground, where she could see it, where anyone could see it, where the smell—

She cut off the thought, breath trembling.

She needed to get out of there. Hawthorn was on his way. Was it already too late to avoid him? She could try to pass for her double and claim the other her got away, but not if he saw the body lying there, the blood pooled purple under the skin, her eyes—*oh god, oh god, her eyes*—

The handcuffs. The first thing Winnie had to do was remove them. Her hands were stuck behind her back, but it was better that way—it forced Winnie to turn around while she searched her double's pockets for the key. She didn't have to look at her.

After a few minutes' awkward fumbling, Winnie found the key and got the cuffs off.

She took a deep breath, then bent over and checked for a pulse. Nothing. Winnie closed her double's eyes.

She had to bury the body.

If she gave herself simple commands, she could function.

Winnie picked up the shovel her double had dropped and held it in her wooden hands.

Dig a hole, Winnie, she told herself.

And so, Winnie started digging.

The dirt floor of the shed was packed tight, but at least the ground hadn't frozen yet. She dug as fast as she could, through the screaming of the muscles in her back, as blisters formed and then burst on her palms and in the tender cradle of skin between her thumb and forefinger.

Finally, she had a hole—not as deep as it should be, but deep enough, and too much time had passed already. Hawthorn could arrive at any moment.

Drag the body to the hole, Winnie.

She grabbed the body's slim ankles and pulled. She moved it inch by slow inch until it toppled into the shallow hole.

The dead eyes had come open and they stared up at her, but she couldn't think of them as her double's eyes or human eyes or even eyes at all or she would lose it. So, she didn't bend down to re-close them. She covered them with a shovelful of dirt.

Before she finished filling the hole, she surveyed the shed to make sure she was getting rid of every trace of what had happened there. She wiped at the workbench with a bit of shop rag, then threw the rag and the handcuffs in with her double's body.

Now fill the hole, Winnie.

And this part was easy, because she wanted nothing more than to get the body out of her sight. She wanted this much more than she wanted her head to stop throbbing or her hands to stop bleeding or her back to stop aching or for that strange dull roar in her ears to go away.

She tried to think past the awful present. As soon as the body was taken care of, she would quickly pack some of her double's things, some food, then go. She didn't know where. Anywhere. Away. Take James's advice too late and flee the city.

Winnie hoisted shovelful after shovelful of dirt into the hole, moving mechanically.

Be a clockwork girl, she told herself. *Feel nothing.*

Once the hole was all full of dirt, she tamped it down with her feet, walking over it again and again, refusing to think about what lay below.

She was so focused on blocking it all out that she almost didn't hear the footsteps approaching on the paving stone path outside the shed.

Winnie froze. Could it really be Hawthorn so quickly? Maybe it was Father. Did he know Winnie had stayed home from school? Maybe he was coming to check on her.

The prospect of speaking to the father of the girl she'd just buried was maybe worse than the thought of facing Hawthorn.

Winnie surveyed the shed. No one would guess what had

happened there. All she had to do was pretend to be Winnie. Her hands were bloody, wrists bruised from the cuffs. If it was Hawthorn, it would be easy to explain her injuries—she and the Split-Winnie had fought; Split-Winnie had escaped—but what would she say to Father? There was no time to come up with a coherent lie. She would have to improvise somehow.

Winnie kept the shovel in her hand. She couldn't just rush at whoever walked through that door—her chance of being able to fight her way out of this was even worse than her chance of lying her way out—but she couldn't bear to set the shovel aside and stand there totally defenseless either.

The knob turned, and the door swung open.

Winnie held her breath.

"Winnie? And Winnie? Are you out here?"

No.

No, no, no.

It was Scott.

Tears began to stream silently down her cheeks. She would have preferred almost *anyone* else.

"Jesus!" he exclaimed as soon as he saw her, then rushed to her side. "What happened to you? And where's Winnie?"

Just the way he said that "Winnie" . . . she knew that he knew that she wasn't his.

Could she lie about what had happened to her double? She wanted to—she had the same impulse for secrecy as always, the one she had so recently realized her double shared—but all she could think about was the desperation on her double's face as she hissed that no, she never told *anyone* about the splinters.

A lie now would doom Winnie to lie forever.

And Scott deserved the truth, although she wished more than anything that she had a different truth to give him.

Winnie looked down at the ground, where her double was buried. She spoke her confession to the dirt.

"She's dead," Winnie said, her trembling finger pointing at the ground. "She's there. I—it was an accident."

"What?" His eyes darted back and forth between Winnie's face and the spot on the ground where she was pointing. "You *killed* her? You're not making any sense."

"She was going to turn me over to Hawthorn. I pushed her—trying to escape—and she hit her head."

"No. Winnie wouldn't do that."

"She didn't have a choice." Winnie reached up to rub her throbbing temple. Now that the panic and adrenaline that had fueled her double's burial was gone, she felt completely drained. "What I said to Hawthorn at the morgue—it gave me away. He showed up here and tricked Winnie into telling him the truth. It was only a matter of time."

Winnie noticed there was blood on her hand. When she fell and knocked her head on the ground, it must have reopened the cut on her forehead.

"I just don't—I don't understand," Scott said, voice thick with grief.

For now, confusion buffered his pain, but it was still torture for Winnie to witness. How much worse would it be once his shock wore off? How would he look at her once he felt the full weight of what she'd done?

The pain in Winnie's head was becoming increasingly insistent. First her injuries during the experiment at school, now this.

I'm about to faint, Winnie realized with relief—unconsciousness would be a delicious vacation.

The world tilted, then began to pass slowly before her eyes.

Pegboard . . . workbench . . . stool . . . lovely ground.

Winnie had space for one last thought before her vision tunneled in. She remembered what her stern paternal grandmother used to say, back in Germany, when someone endured misfortune after misfortune: *They must be living wrong.*

Then the world went dark.

CHAPTER THIRTY-ONE

When Winnie woke up, she was snug in her double's bed, head pounding terribly, but safe—whatever safety meant now that Hawthorn knew about her.

Hawthorn.

Had he shown up while she'd been unconscious?

She looked around. Everything was a bit blurry, but there was no sign of him. She recognized Dr. Gilbert, her pediatrician—in both worlds, apparently—with Father right beside him.

There was a stranger there too, sitting in the corner, hands knotted tight in her lap—a beautiful woman. Winnie's eyes stopped on the woman's face. She felt some mix of love and dread that she couldn't understand at first. She didn't know this woman. Why would looking at a stranger give her nose the telltale itch that meant she was about to cry?

The woman jumped up from her chair and rushed over once

she saw that Winnie had regained consciousness, pushing past the doctor.

"Oh Winnie, Liebling, how are you? Can you tell us what happened?"

The woman's features came into focus, and the truth sifted its way into her concussed brain.

"Mama?"

The woman was eight years older than her own mother had ever aged. She was dressed fashionably in a sharp gray wool gabardine suit that couldn't be more different from the plain cotton shirtdresses she'd worn as a young housewife in Germany, and her flax-colored hair was bobbed and curled instead of tucked into two braids and wrapped around her head—but she was still unmistakably Mama, and even more beautiful at thirty-four than she had been when Winnie was a little girl.

Her double's haircut—and therefore, Winnie's—was the brunette twin of Mama's own, she noticed with consternation.

But none of this made sense. What was going on?

Then Winnie realized—it must have happened again.

She had fainted and woken up in a new world, this one with Mama in it. She met this revelation with fierce determination.

She wouldn't ruin it this time.

She'd done an awful thing—she flinched at the pain of the thought; hopefully it looked like pain from her injuries on the outside—but this?

Mama, alive?

Winnie would be perfect until the end of time to deserve being there with her.

"Scott, she's awake," Father called. "Would you bring her some water?"

Scott was at the bedroom door in a moment. One glance said it all. His expression was steely, and he refused to meet her eyes. This was no new Scott.

She was in the same world, with its same problems.

The same Hawthorn was after her.

The same body was out there in the shed.

The body of a girl who had *lied* to Winnie about her own mother being dead. After all that had happened, she supposed she shouldn't be all that surprised by *that*.

But Scott had lied too, by omission at least. She'd poured her heart out about the pain of losing her mother. He'd said nothing about Mama being alive in their world.

Winnie stared at this woman. She was a stranger. And she was her mom.

Winnie had been without her mother for so long. She'd yearned to have even a picture of her—and now here she was in the flesh! All Winnie wanted to do was embrace her.

But how could she?

How could she hug the woman whose daughter she had just accidentally killed?

"What are you doing here?" Winnie whispered, half-afraid the woman was a hallucination brought on by her guilt.

"Silly girl," Mama said, smiling gently. "I came home from

Boston as soon as Papa phoned to say you'd been hurt. Of course I did! My presentation can wait." Her hand reached out as if she was going to stroke Winnie's hair, then pulled back, like she didn't want to risk hurting her. "What happened? Scott said something about an accident, but I still don't understand."

"I . . ." Winnie trailed off. She had no explanation. Awful enough, telling Scott what happened. But to tell Mama?

Why hadn't Scott said anything, she wondered?

Perhaps he wanted her conscious when he outed her as a changeling. It wasn't like Scott to relish anyone's suffering, but grief changed a person.

Rather than revealing who she was, Scott filled the lengthening silence with a convenient explanation.

"You don't remember the accident?" Scott said woodenly. "Being hit by a car?"

She hadn't expected him to turn her over to Hawthorn, but was he letting her pass for her double?

"Scott told us you called the lab and said you'd been hit by a car," Dr. Schulde said. "He *should* have told me straightaway," he added, giving Scott a dark glance, "but I was in the middle of a lecture, and you said you weren't hurt, just shaken up, so he came to check on you himself first. But then you were unconscious when he got here, so I called your mother and rushed over myself. You don't remember the accident?"

Winnie made the mistake of shaking her head and was immediately punished by a lightning bolt of pain pulsing temple to temple.

"It's not surprising," Dr. Gilbert said. "Memory can be quite jumbled after a head injury. More often than not, it comes back in time, though."

"Should she be in the hospital?" Mama asked.

"No!" Winnie said. She was probably in just as much danger from Hawthorn now no matter where she was—but home, even her double's home, felt safer.

"Shh," Father murmured. "Let's let Dr. Gilbert have a look at you. He'll know best. Now let's give her some privacy for the exam."

"I'm staying," Mama said.

Winnie closed her eyes and shook her head no, more carefully this time. She couldn't think, with Mama standing right there.

A look of confusion and hurt flashed across her mother's face, but she said "All right, little Mausi. We'll be right outside," and filed out of the room with Scott and Father, closing the door behind them.

"There, now let's have a look at you," Dr. Gilbert said, smiling at Winnie kindly.

He shone a bright light in her eyes, then had her clench his hands as tight as she could. He made her push his hands up, then press them down—testing for a brain injury, he explained. He gently probed her limbs, working up and down each arm and leg, then examined her trunk for any bruising.

The doctor finished his examination and gave Winnie an avuncular pat on the knee. "A concussion—but no fracture of the skull, as far as I can tell, and no other injury or blunt force trauma. It might not feel like it right now, but really you're quite lucky to make it out of a collision with a car without any more serious injury."

Was there something questioning in his expression? Winnie doubted the impact from a fall or the reopened cut on her forehead looked much like the injury that would result from being hit by a car, but at least he was keeping his suspicions to himself, if he had any.

Dr. Gilbert called her parents back into the room.

"What can I do for her?" Mama asked.

"She needs rest, rest, and more rest. She'll have a nasty headache, I'm afraid, and you'll want to keep her cut clean. Give her some aspirin for the pain. If she begins having any vision trouble, ring me immediately, and if there isn't decided improvement by tomorrow, let me know."

Mama thanked him and went downstairs to let him out, but she returned immediately.

"Do you need anything, Liebling?"

There was such concern, naked on her double's mother's face—such love. It made Winnie ache to see it.

She must be looking at the root of all the differences between their worlds. This world had splintered from her own when Mama survived the car accident. From her double's popularity to small things like the different elevator operator in Dora's building. Somehow, it all cascaded from that one dark day on a wet road in Germany.

No wonder her double's father seemed so different from her own. She and Father had been set down a bad path when Mama died. But Winnie had already known that. She didn't need to see just how good her life could have been if Mama had survived. She didn't need to see it, just to lose her again—if not when she found out the truth, then when Winnie went back home.

After Mama died, Winnie had dreamt about her all the time. Winnie would go to sleep early each night, hoping to see her. It was so wonderful to see her and speak to her—at first. But when she dreamt about Mama, there was always that awful moment when she woke up and realized none of it was real. Mama was gone.

Over time, the thought of sleep became more painful than restful. It hurt Winnie too badly to see Mama in dreams, knowing she would just have to give her up again when she awoke.

The woman put a hand to her cheek just then, and Winnie leaned into the cool touch and closed her eyes for a long moment. Then she sighed, and opened them.

What on earth was she going to do?

"Could you send Scott in, please? I need to talk to him."

"TELL ME WHAT HAPPENED."

Winnie eyed Scott nervously. She'd never seen him wound so tight. This was different from it had been with James, when something in him had just—unraveled. It made her frightened for him now. What would he do if he felt like he had nothing more to lose?

He would want to go after Hawthorn.

"I told you what happened," she said. "I don't know what else to tell you."

"You said it was an accident."

"Of course it was an accident!"

"I know. I know you wouldn't hurt Winnie on purpose." He sighed. "But I also know that Winnie would never agree to hand you over to Hawthorn. Especially considering what he did to James. It just—*why*?"

"Hawthorn threatened to frame you for James's death."

Even as she said it, she didn't know if being honest was the right thing to do.

It would help Scott make sense of her double's actions, but a terrible sort of sense. Did Scott really need to know that Winnie trying to save him was what had gotten her killed?

A complex combination of guilt and anger flashed across his face.

"But why wouldn't she come to us first? Why wouldn't she come to me?"

"She knew you would risk yourself to help me."

"Well—I mean, of course I would."

"She didn't want that."

Scott sat with this for a moment. She could see him turning this truth over and over in his mind, looking for the cracks—as if poking holes in the logic behind what had happened could bring Winnie back.

"We could have come up with a plan that kept us all safe," he said finally.

"Really? You think so? You know, so far our plans haven't gone great."

He couldn't possibly argue with that.

Scott pulled off his glasses and cradled his head in his hands. "What you're saying makes sense, but—" He let out a shaky sigh, and for a moment looked so forlorn that Winnie took a fistful of coverlet in her hand to stop herself from reaching out to touch him. "But then I just think of Winnie, dead, and think—how in the world did we get here?"

The pain Scott felt wasn't something Winnie had intended, but she was its author all the same. Would it ever stop? Winnie thought she had good intentions, but she just destroyed everything around her. Things had gone from bad to worse ever since the night of Hawthorn's party. Because Winnie ruined everything.

"I saw a splinter. Before I—this morning. I saw her dead."

"What! Why didn't you—"

"Because I thought it was me."

Scott just stared at her in silence for a moment.

Finally, he said, "Why didn't you do something? Tell someone? You were really just going to *die*?"

Winnie was quiet for a long time.

"It's like I didn't really believe what I saw. And the small part of me that did felt helpless to really change it. I wasn't even sure if I was seeing into this reality or some other one. I've been wrong so many times now. I didn't want to put anyone else in more danger."

Winnie paused. This was a harder thing to say, even to herself.

"And another little part of me thought . . . if I was *gone* gone, maybe it would be a way out—for all of us. You've heard of Typhoid Mary, right?"

Scott narrowed his eyes in confusion. "Of course."

"She never got sick herself, but the people around her"— Winnie shrugged her shoulders helplessly—"they all died. I think that's your real answer. I think that's your 'why.'"

"You can't possibly—"

She cut him off with a shake of her head, determined for him to understand.

"My mother. Scott. Now Winnie. All accidents. But we're scientists, right? How many 'accidents' have to happen before we start looking for a common cause?"

"Feeling sorry for yourself isn't going to get us out of this mess."

Winnie jerked back like she had been slapped.

Was that really what he thought—that she was being melodramatic? Self-pitying?

Winnie sat up a bit straighter, indignantly rearranging the pillows propped behind her back.

"I'm sorry I'm not handling all this with as much grace as

you'd like," she said acidly. "I'm a bit . . . hmm, out of sorts?" Winnie glared at him. Yes, he had many things to resent her for. But he wasn't blameless himself. "And to think you said you were bad at keeping secrets."

Scott sighed and massaged the bridge of his nose, leaving his glasses slightly askew.

"Winnie made me promise not to tell," he said. "She was afraid that if you knew your mother was alive here, you wouldn't want to leave."

"She was right."

Scott raised his eyebrows and shook his head as if to say "See?"

"That doesn't mean *you* were," Winnie said. "I had a right to know. You should have told me. How could you sit there and let me talk about growing up, about losing her—"

"It was torture! I wanted to tell you, but what good could that do? Make you feel like you had to choose between saving your Scott and staying with your mother? Especially when it wasn't like staying here was a real option!"

The desire had been rumbling through her unconscious mind, not daring to articulate itself—till now.

"Not then it wasn't." Winnie said. "But now . . ."

"Now that you've killed her, you mean?"

Winnie flinched, but she didn't back down.

"Yes. Now that Winnie is dead, I could actually stay. The two of us both being here, it was causing more interference than we even knew."

Winnie wondered if the only reason she'd been able to see the splinter that morning was because as soon as her double had made the choice to turn her over to Hawthorn, in a way, she was already dead.

"With her gone," Winnie continued, "I think the other . . . disruptions . . . might stop."

"Even if they do—you think I could look at you? Every day? Knowing what you did? You think we could *be* together?" Scott closed his eyes a moment and took a shaky breath. "Winnie, could you really live with her mother and father and never tell them what happened?"

"But she's gone. She's not coming back. Wouldn't it be kinder to them—"

"If you do this, you're doing it for yourself. Not them," Scott said icily. "And what about the people *you* left behind?"

Winnie thought about it for a moment. That had been part of the pain of leaving her own world: contemplating just how small a hole she left there.

"I don't think I'm missed there like she would be here."

"You can't really—"

"You still don't understand! Will Dora miss me? Will Brunhilde be sad? Sure. But all that's like—like a ripple. Their lives will close up around my loss like water around a thrown stone. Winnie's death will leave a wound here, and it won't heal. I know because I've lived with a hurt like that all my life."

Winnie began to cry. It terrified her. Now that she'd started, would she ever be able to stop?

"Oh, Scott, I could have met her. I could have met her and been—not her *daughter*, but I could have at least known her as me. Instead I'm meeting her as—as an imposter. As the person who led to her daughter's death! And I can barely look at her! I was so close, and I didn't even know it. Now I've lost everything."

"You have a father back home."

"Do I?"

Going home might mean finding out he didn't miss her at all. He might even be glad she was gone.

"Even if he does miss me," Winnie said through tears, "there's no way it's anywhere near as much as Mama and Father will miss Winnie here."

She could tell from the way he was looking at her that he wanted to reach out for her. To hold her and comfort her like he would if she were his own Winnie.

But he didn't.

When Scott opened his mouth to speak, Winnie said, "Don't. Don't say it. I haven't forgotten about Scott. But we don't know—"

"Our experiment design is sound—"

"Yes. And that ship is a good sign that I can manipulate time. But we don't really understand how it works. Obviously. And that ship—it's something that happened *because* of our experiment, right? It's just sheer luck that it didn't kill anyone."

"It happened when you and Winnie were both in the same place. Maybe that's what caused it. That's not an issue now."

"Maybe," Winnie shrugged. "Or maybe not."

"Let me get this right. You're saying you're done trying? We're giving up, and—what? You're just going to stay here and try to move on like nothing has happened? What will we do about Hawthorn? And do you really think Winnie's parents won't realize you're a different girl?"

Winnie put her head in her hands. "I don't know. I don't know. I just need some time to think."

Scott didn't say anything. Just looked at her.

She felt the weight of his disappointment settle over her. But she could carry it. She could carry it if it meant staying with Mama.

"Are you going to tell them about me?" she asked hoarsely, hardly louder than a whisper.

He stared off across the room, considering.

Scott had kept a secret for her double. Would he keep one for her?

"I don't know," he said finally. "I need some time too."

Scott went home, and Winnie told her double's parents that she didn't want dinner—that she just wanted to rest. She was bone tired, but lying there alone in her double's bed, sleep would not come. The horror of what had happened—of what she had done—had sunk into her and settled there. She didn't think she would ever really be free of it.

No matter how many times Winnie went over what had

happened in that shed, she couldn't imagine anything she could have done to force a less tragic outcome. What was she supposed to do, just let Hawthorn take her? But this was little comfort. How could something so awful be so inevitable?

What must it have been like for her double to see Winnie openly discussing what was, for her, her darkest secret? Both seeing her need for secrecy validated—Winnie's ability had put her in grave danger, after all, and Father's obsession with it was what had caused the accident that killed Scott and brought her here—but also seeing Winnie share something with Scott that she must have, at least sometimes, longed to share herself.

And the fear! She must have been so scared that now *her* secret would be exposed too. Winnie was a somewhat solitary person, but even she couldn't imagine being so alone with that much fear. How relieved her double must have been when everyone believed she simply didn't see them. But how terrible too, to miss the opportunity to share it with them, and to know that the people she loved would never *really* know her, not entirely.

She thought about the splinter she'd seen that morning and wondered if Winnie had seen it too—seen the death that was waiting for one of them, right around the corner—and soldiered on anyway, because there was nothing else to do.

Winnie watched through her double's bedroom window as the sun sank, turning the sky from a peaceful pink to the deep purple of a fresh bruise.

Just like the color of her double's fatal wound.

CHAPTER THIRTY-TWO

"How are you feeling?" Mama asked.

Winnie sat up, surprised to realize she must have fallen asleep at some point. Her head was pounding, and she could feel every muscle in her arms and shoulders tender from strain.

. . . the strain of burying her double.

The cut on her forehead stung, and every small movement of her hands pulled at the places where her blisters had torn open and were trying to heal.

Winnie might have slept, but her sleep had not been restorative.

Still, she said, "Better," because she didn't want to stay home from school.

Being alone with her thoughts all day sounded awful enough, but what if Hawthorn showed up, demanding to know why Winnie hadn't handed off her double as agreed? What if—god forbid—she stayed home, and Mama insisted on staying home with her? What if Hawthorn showed up with Mama there?

Mama did work outside the home, didn't she? A memory sifted its way through her foggy brain—Mama had mentioned something about a presentation. What did she do?

Winnie swung her legs off the bed and stood gingerly. She couldn't help but wince as all her aching bits cried out at once.

Mama's brow knit in concern.

"Perhaps you'd better not—"

Winnie's guilt mounted at this tenderness, feeling like someone marooned in the desert presented with a mirage of ice-cold water. Best to not even reach for the glass.

It wasn't for her.

"I'm okay," Winnie said quickly. "Really."

Mama left Winnie to dress. A glance in the mirror revealed that in addition to her ugly cut, there were half-moons of fatigue under her eyes, and she was winter-pale. She didn't bother with makeup. Perhaps her double would have had the art to make a presentable face out of all this mess, but Winnie didn't.

Winnie joined Mama at the breakfast table. Father was already on his way to the university. Winnie noticed a headline on the folded newspaper on the table. *MYSTERY TIDES*—she read, then eagerly opened the paper to read the other half—*RETURN TO NORMAL.*

It seemed like her double's death might have restored some sort of balance. Still, Winnie found it hard to feel relieved. That hadn't been her double's debt to pay.

Her double's mother presented Winnie with a plateful of eggs, sausage, and toast, but although Winnie hadn't had dinner the night before, she found she was unable to eat. She was hungry, but her hunger wasn't enough to overcome her repulsion. Her head was still full of corpses, and it seemed awful to be nourishing her own body when her double's was decaying out in the shed. What must it look like now? Those eyes, covered in dirt . . . they would go first, she thought. Winnie could not contain a little shiver at the thought.

"Winnie?" Mama said. "Winnie? You're a thousand miles away."

"I'm just not hungry."

"I'm calling Dr. Gilbert. You don't seem better at all."

"No, I am! Much!"

Winnie took a forkful of the eggs that had cooled on her plate and shoved them in her mouth—gelatinous, like eyes. She chewed and swallowed with as much enthusiasm as she could muster.

"I don't like this," Mama said. "You shouldn't be going to school, and you shouldn't be home alone. They can get a substitute in for me again today."

Mama must be a teacher, Winnie thought.

"I swear, I'm fine," she said, trying to inflect some annoyance into her voice, like she imagined her double would do in that situation. It was almost as difficult as pretending to enjoy her breakfast. It had been almost nine years since Winnie had a concerned mother cluck over her. Even though she had to convince Mama to let her go to school, she didn't think a mother's concern could ever really annoy her now. "I'm okay to go to school. Promise."

Mama sighed. "Well, all right. If you really think you'll be okay." She smiled wanly. "Goodness, I hope my other students are as excited to be in the lab as you seem to be."

Winnie felt herself pale as the words sank in. Mama wasn't just a teacher—she was a teacher at Winnie's school. From the sound of it, she was Winnie's own physics teacher. Better liked than Mr. Claremont, she was sure, although she wondered where he was here. Teaching physics at some other school? Working in a lab somewhere? Dead?

Winnie's heart was divided at the thought of being in class with Mama. She hadn't anticipated having to playact her double at school with Mama in the audience—it made the stakes of slipping up so much higher. But it also meant getting to spend more time with her, and Winnie would get to see her teach. Her own Mama would have liked teaching, she thought.

"You promise you'll go right to the nurse if you feel unwell? I'll take you straight home if being out and about becomes too much for you."

"I promise."

"I know you normally take the bus with Dora, but I'm driving you today. I insist."

This, Winnie readily agreed to.

Anything to delay telling Dora her best friend was dead.

"OH, WINNIE, YOUR FAAAAAAAAACE!" MARIBEL EXCLAIMED WHEN Winnie walked into homeroom. "What happened?"

Winnie froze a moment. She glanced around the classroom—to her relief, this didn't seem to be a period she shared with Dora. For now at least, she could assume that Maribel was a friend here, but how close? Winnie had no idea how her double would react to the girl in this situation. Brush off the concern? Package it into a flashy, exciting story?

It hit Winnie then—there was so much more she didn't know beyond just who her double was friends with. It was bad enough she hadn't a clue who she might be offending if she forgot to, say, smile at them in the hall. But she didn't know what her schedule was or who her teachers were either. How quickly might any little misstep add up to equal *This isn't Winnie*?

"It's not as bad as it looks," Winnie said. "But I do have a concussion. It's left me a bit . . . out of sorts."

Her injuries would help explain any odd behavior—for now.

Maribel frowned sympathetically. "You poor dear! But what *happened*?"

Winnie was relieved to have this conversation interrupted by their homeroom teacher.

"Girls, hush now," she said. "I have some announcements."

Mrs. Martin told them about upcoming bake sales and postponed intramural basketball games, and Winnie's attention drifted back to her own concerns.

She was safe from Hawthorn there.

But for how long?

• • •

Dora grabbed her arm as she was heading to lunch. "We have to talk," she hissed, then practically dragged Winnie to the nearest ladies' room.

They waited while the last girl inside washed her hands, then Dora shooed her out and locked the door behind her.

"Where is she? You were supposed to call me yesterday!"

Dora thought Winnie was her double.

Winnie just blinked at her for a moment, stunned.

"Oh!" Dora said. "It's you."

It hadn't occurred to Winnie to wonder before, but had Dora been in on her double's plan to turn her over to Hawthorn?

It was almost unthinkable . . . but after everything that had happened, maybe Winnie should expect the unthinkable.

Winnie leaned back against the wall. The little shelf under the wide mirror dug into her shoulder blades, but she hardly felt it.

"Dora . . . Dora, did you know?"

"Know what? What's going on? I expected to hear from her in the evening—I *hoped* I would hear good news, but I expected to at least hear something. Then you didn't even come home last night. Finally, I called, and Winnie's mother said that she'd been hit by a car?" Dora paused to take a breath, then frowned. "But that isn't true, is it?"

"No," Winnie said. "It's not."

She was so relieved that Dora hadn't known what Winnie was walking into yesterday morning . . . but that meant she had to explain it all now.

Winnie was accustomed to lying to her own Dora back

351

home. Lies like *No, I don't mind*, or *Don't worry—I just got here*, and of course she withheld important facets of herself, like her ability to see splinters. But she had never lied to Dora about something that really mattered.

Not that a lie could really save her now.

Scott knew the truth; it was only a matter of time before Dora found out too.

Winnie took a few darting glances up and down the row of toilets to assure herself no one was listening in. "Her idea to restage the experiment was a setup," Winnie said. "Hawthorn threatened Winnie, and she told him about me. She was going to hand me over to him for Project Nightingale. She thought that was the only way out for all of you."

Shock was plain on Dora's face, but she stayed silent, waiting. And Winnie could not form the words.

"But you're here," Dora said finally, "and Winnie is—not. Wait, did you trick him?" she asked angrily. "Did you turn her in instead?"

Winnie swallowed nervously and shook her head.

Dora's eyes scanned her face, examining Winnie's wounds. They drifted down to Winnie's bandaged hands.

Dora's face crumpled. "No," she whispered. She squeezed her hands into tight fists. A tear rolled down her cheek.

"It was—just awful," Winnie said. "It was an accident," she added quickly.

Winnie reached her hand toward Dora's shoulder, but the girl jerked away.

"So, now you're what? Playing her at school? Going to take some pop quizzes? You think you can just replace her now?" Dora paused a moment, panting, then whispered, "How did it happen?"

"She—she hit her head."

"And you thought, 'Hey, this is convenient! Why try to save my Scott, when I can just take this one?'"

Winnie was momentarily stunned by Dora's words, but her shock was quickly replaced by anger.

"You know what? You're right! Just staying here forever would be *so* much easier. I can't wait for the part where I get to tell Mr. and Mrs. Schulde their daughter is dead," Winnie said sarcastically. "I didn't ask for any of this!"

She fell silent when she realized how loud her voice was echoing through the tiled room.

"Yeah? Well, neither did Winnie."

"No. But she did decide she should tie me up and try to turn me over to the man who'd just killed Scott's best friend."

Dora's face softened. She closed her eyes a moment, and when she opened them, she was fully crying.

"I'm sorry," Dora said. "I'm sure you just did what you thought you had to do. But I can't be a part of this. What happened—I can't be your friend anymore."

Dora didn't even wait for a response.

She unlocked the door and left without a backward glance.

CHAPTER THIRTY-THREE

Physics was the last class period of the day, just like it was for Winnie back home. Of course, here there was one major difference: when she walked in the room, it was Mama standing at the front of the class. Winnie expected this, but still, walking in and seeing Mama there sent a wave of mixed worry and relief surging through her stomach.

Mama wore a tailored suit, and her hair was as perfectly coiffed as it had been when they left home in the morning. Winnie had assumed Mama would be well-liked as a teacher, but now, seeing her there, she had a feeling that students were just as intimidated by her as they were by Mr. Claremont back home. She felt a little flash of pride.

Mama's expression was tense, and Winnie felt a momentary jab of fear that Mama knew everything.

Then she noticed Hawthorn sitting in the back corner.

He had two men with him. The men weren't in uniform, but

they had a martial look to them, haircuts high and tight and posture perfect. These were military men; Winnie was sure of it. She had to get out of here.

But where would she go? And how could she leave now without looking incredibly suspicious?

For now, Winnie took a seat up near the front of the class. She wanted to be as far from their classroom observers as possible.

Of all the classes of hers Hawthorn could have shown up to, why this one?

The answer came to her immediately, making her feel stupid.

Hawthorn wanted to send a message. A message that said, "Look how easily I can access your family."

And "Think about how easily I could take them from you."

And "None of you are safe."

Winnie decided that if it came down to it, she would turn herself over to Hawthorn. She wouldn't let anyone else get hurt. But especially not them.

Winnie jumped in her seat when the bell rang. She could feel Hawthorn's eyes on her. How delighted he must be to watch her squirm.

"First, let's dispatch with the necessary," Mama said now that class had officially begun. "Yes, there are three strange men sitting in the back of the classroom. Yes, it's because of what happened in the gymnasium the other day. No, this does not mean we will be doing anything differently. Just ignore them. I've been assured they won't be a disruption.

"I was pleased to learn that you behaved yourselves while I

was in Boston. Mrs. Potter informed me that she was able to cover all the material I had hoped she would. So, thank you!

"Now, down to business. Today, we'll be recreating Alessandro Volta's 'crown of cups', an early electric battery. This will conclude our unit on electromotive force, and we all know what that means: there will be an exam covering this chapter of the text on Monday. So, if you have any lingering questions, make sure we address them this period.

"It was Luigi Galvani's work with 'animal electricity,'"

"Crown of Cups" Voltaic Cells

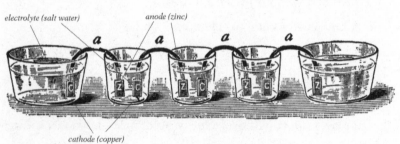

electrolyte (salt water)   anode (zinc)

cathode (copper)

Mama continued, "that led Volta to discover the electrochemical series—"

"I'm sorry, I'm a bit confused," one of the military men interrupted briskly. "You're having these girls build some kind of battery? I'm not sure that's a suitable—"

"If you have a question, I'm afraid I'll need you to raise your hand first," Mama said, cutting him off, "and the only question I entertain in the middle of a lecture is 'May I use the restroom.' But don't worry—the answer is always yes."

A couple of the girls tittered. Winnie stole a glance back

over her shoulder and saw the officer frowning while he jotted down a few vicious notes, but he kept his mouth shut. Next to him, the other officer—a younger, lanky man whose air of authority belied his age—was leaning back, smirking. There was something frightening in the expression.

Although it was thrilling to see Mama stand up to those Nightingale men, Winnie wished she would keep her mouth shut. These seemed like dangerous men to disrespect.

"Thank you," Mama said, continuing with her lecture. "Now, as I was saying, Volta's law of electrochemical series led to the invention of the voltaic pile, an early electric battery that operates by the same principle as the batteries we'll be constructing today."

She explained the setup of the experiment and what data they would be required to record, then set them loose to begin work with their lab partners while she circulated around the class, helping those students who needed it.

Winnie was working with one of her double's friends, so she had to conceal the fact that she could construct a voltaic cell in her sleep.

"Which metals do you think we should use?" Winnie asked, pretending to skim through the experiment parameters in her lab manual, although she knew very well that silver and zinc would produce the highest charge.

"What? You usually seem to have all the answers ahead of time," the girl sighed.

Shoot.

"Oh, um," Winnie said. "Not today. Say, how about we try silver and zinc? I'll go grab some."

Winnie hadn't thought about how close she would have to pass by Hawthorn to get to the equipment closet in the back of the classroom. She kept her head down, eyes trained on the ground, so she was taken completely by surprise when Hawthorn reached out and grabbed her wrist.

She made a little squeak of alarm and pulled her arm away.

"My, my, my, what happened to you, Ms. Schulde?"

Winnie's breath quickened, and Hawthorn's smile spread, like it fed on her discomfort. There seemed be an extra edge to him now. Was it a difference between Hawthorn here and the one back home? Or was he unraveling—something to do with James's death, perhaps?

He reached his hand out toward the cut on her forehead. Winnie trembled in revulsion, anticipating his touch, but she was frozen in place. Thankfully, Mama hurried up and slapped Hawthorn's hand away before he made any further contact.

"Get out of my classroom," she said. "Now."

"Ma'am," the older officer said, "you assured us that there was no way your students were involved with whatever happened in that gym, or with that ship. We're here to make sure that's the case."

"Really? You think schoolgirls dropped a warship outside Bloomingdale's? The three of you don't have anything better to do?" Mama shook her head in disgust. "I guess the real soldiers are on the front lines."

Winnie was astonished by Mama's audacity. She was afraid for her, but also impressed.

The younger of the two military men didn't so much as twitch, but his entire face went beet red in fury. Winnie watched in paralyzed fascination as the florid color crept over his face, feeling like a rodent captivated by the cobra that was about to swallow it whole.

Winnie was keenly aware that every eye in the classroom was on them.

Hawthorn laid a quelling hand on the young man's forearm.

"Let me speak with Ms. Schulde for a moment, then we can go."

Mama opened her mouth to protest, but the older officer cut her off. "Let him speak to her now, alone," he said, "or we can take both of you in to headquarters after class and have a chat there."

Winnie had a sinking feeling that if she ever set foot in Nightingale's headquarters, she wouldn't be allowed to leave after.

"It'll be easier if I just talk to him now, Mama. I'll be okay."

Then Hawthorn took her by the elbow—such a gentleman— and led her away.

HAWTHORN BROUGHT HER OUT INTO THE HALL, CAREFUL TO MOVE AWAY from the classroom door so no one could spy through the window.

If she cried out, Mama would be there in a moment, Winnie reminded herself, trying to keep terror at bay.

Of course, Hawthorn wouldn't do anything awful to her. Not there, at school.

But she had no doubt that if he wanted, he could have those officers arrest her.

And Mama.

They'd be able to do whatever they wanted to her and Mama then.

She wondered what was keeping him from doing it.

"You didn't call," Hawthorn said.

Winnie had hated him before she even had reason to hate him—from their first meeting at his party, when he had been playacting the genial host. How she hated him now! And what a blessing that hatred was. It helped drown her fear to nothing more than a dull roar.

"Things didn't go as planned," she said tightly.

She needed him to think she was the other Winnie, at least until she came up with a better plan. If Hawthorn still had hope of getting his hands on her, it would buy her some time.

"Your father said something this morning about a car accident. How terrible," he said dryly. "I take it the girl got away?"

Winnie nodded.

"Ms. Schulde?"

"Yes?"

"I hope you know I meant what I said. I've always liked Scott. But that won't stop me."

Winnie's stomach flopped, and she tried to bury that fear under a wave of authentic indignation. "Just look at me! Obviously, I tried."

"I didn't ask you to 'try.' I told you to get the girl," he said viciously. Then his nastiness was gone in a flash, replaced by a subtler one. "I miss James—he was such an asset to me, and so eager to prove himself." He paused a moment. "Did you know that some people thought he and Scott were lovers?"

"People should mind their own business."

"Maybe, but they don't. I wonder . . . do you think that's why Scott did it?"

Homosexual Student Slays Secret Lover—it was exactly the sort of salacious thing people would be dying to believe, and the worst kind of papers would love to print. Winnie was confident that Hawthorn would have some contrived hard evidence to back it up too.

"I'm not playing this game with you," Winnie said, straining to display a confidence she didn't really feel. "I know you aren't going to get Scott arrested."

"Oh?"

"At least not yet. You still want her, right? I can get her for you."

He was silent for a moment, lips pursed, thinking.

"Fine," he said at last. "Bring her to me within twenty-four hours. If you don't, I go to the police. No more second chances."

"What are you going to do with her?" Winnie whispered.

She asked without thinking. Probably he wouldn't answer. Probably it would be better not to know.

"I'm not going to hurt her," he said with an irritated sigh, "if that's what you're thinking."

"You hurt James."

"*I* didn't hurt James. Experiments mean risk. James understood that. But I know more now. The serum doesn't work—but that doesn't matter. I won't need it anymore. I'll have her."

If only she really were as powerful as Hawthorn seemed to think she was.

Unless . . . maybe Hawthorn knew something they didn't—something that would help her get home. Or maybe he was crazy. His voice had that feverish inflection Father's used to get sometimes during their night experiments. Father had always thought he was a hairsbreadth away from a breakthrough. But they'd never made any progress at all.

"Your parents," Hawthorn continued, "they really don't know anything, do they?"

"No, they don't," Winnie answered quickly.

"You do realize what that means, don't you? If they get wrapped up in this, they'll have nothing to bargain with. And, Ms. Schulde? I know that this ability of yours—yes, dormant or not, you have it—is genetic. So, if you can't find your double, don't worry. I could always use your mother. Do you have any idea how easy it would be to convince people your mother and father are German spies? Who would care what happened to them then?"

Winnie opened her mouth to protest, but Hawthorn turned back to the classroom, pulled open the door, and called for his men.

"Oh, and I apologize for bringing my dogs," Hawthorn murmured slyly. "I promise they're well-trained. Mostly."

As soon as the three men walked down the hall and turned the corner, Winnie rushed to the bathroom. She flung the first stall door open, knelt down, and vomited up every last bit of her lunch.

She and Scott had one day.

. . . but a day to do what?

To get her home?

Or to figure out a way for her to safely stay?

As soon as Winnie reentered the classroom, she set off a flurry of whispers among her classmates. Some seemed excited by all the drama, but others looked worried or scared.

"Back to work, girls," Mama said sharply.

She pulled Winnie back into the materials closet, leaving the door just barely ajar.

"Are you all right, darling?" Mama asked softly. "Damn those Hosenscheißer! They think they can come bully us here, in my own classroom. Well, let them just wait until Papa finds out."

"Don't tell him," Winnie said, "please."

Hawthorn had already threatened their family.

She would keep Mama, and Father, and Scott, and Dora all safe—somehow.

Mama grabbed her hand and pressed her fingers reassuringly. "I don't want you worrying about all this. Just leave it to me and your father."

In a way, she should be grateful that Hawthorn and his "dogs" had paid her a visit. She understood the stakes more clearly than ever. But she needed Mama to understand them too.

"Eight minutes," Winnie said.

Mama gave her a questioning look.

"Don't you remember the headlines? Those men convicted of being German agents? They said it took them eight minutes on the electric chair to die."

Mama pulled her into a hug. "Shh," she whispered. "Papa will be fine—we all will."

Winnie knew the embrace was meant to be reassuring, but Mama was holding her too tight—she could feel the trembling in Mama's arms.

Winnie was certain of one thing. She would do *anything* to make sure Hawthorn didn't get his hands on Mama—even if it meant surrendering to him herself.

CHAPTER THIRTY-FOUR

When Winnie and Mama arrived home that evening, Scott was waiting for them on the stoop. He had a bundle of equipment next to him, including wood and chicken wire, which Winnie recognized as the disassembled remnants of their Faraday cage.

"Now isn't the best time," Mama said briskly. She jutted her chin at the pile of materials. "What's that?"

"Something I'm working on for class. Professor Schulde'll be late tonight—staff meeting—but he said I could use the lab, and I was hoping to get started on this."

"Oh. All right—but Winnie needs to rest."

Mama unlocked the front door, and Winnie and Scott followed her inside.

Scott gave Winnie a meaningful look and gentle nudge while Mama's back was turned.

"I'm not tired," Winnie lied. "Can't I please help Scott in the lab for a bit before dinner?"

Mama frowned. "Winnie—"

"Please?"

She sighed, then shook her head and cracked a reluctant smile. "I suppose I do remember being your age. Just don't tire yourself out too much, all right?" She fixed Scott with a stern look. "I'm thinking she 'helps' by sitting down there and chatting while you work."

Scott grinned. "More than fair."

As soon as Mama turned away and headed upstairs, his grin faded.

"Let's head down to the lab," Scott said softly. "We have a lot to talk about."

They certainly did.

EVEN THOUGH WINNIE STILL FELT A FLUTTER OF ANXIETY ABOUT touching Father's things without permission, she rolled his upholstered chair over to the lab bench and sank down into it. Her head throbbed, and she felt like crying. Not even *about* anything in particular. Just about everything—from the sheer exhaustion of it all. She felt like a sad old pencil sharpened down to the nub, beyond any practical purpose.

"Hawthorn showed up at school today. He says I have one day to turn over my double."

Scott squinted at her suspiciously.

"You're thinking of turning yourself in. Aren't you?"

"He threatened you. He threatened Mama and Winnie's father. He showed up with officers, so I'd know he means business and has government backup. Obviously, I don't want to give myself over to him. But I will, if we can't come up with a better plan." She gestured to the cage he'd begun to reconstruct. "*You* obviously mean to try our experiment again. You should know that if it works, and I vanish, Hawthorn will make good on his threats."

The fate of her Scott still hung in the balance. But if she ran away now, what would happen to Mama and this Scott? How could she leave them in such danger?

"I'm not afraid of Hawthorn," Scott said harshly.

"Well, thanks—that terrifies me! You *should* be afraid of Hawthorn. He already killed James. What are you going to do—tell the police? You really think they would believe you over him? He has military officers at his beck and call."

"Hawthorn isn't petty—he's practical. Ruthlessly so. If—when—our experiment works, well, then I've witnessed a successful attempt to travel between worlds. Hell, I'm the one who designed the experiment. I'll be valuable to him. There won't be any reason for him to want me behind bars."

Winnie thought for a moment. It wasn't exactly a guarantee that everyone in her wake would be all right—but it wasn't the certain doom she'd been afraid of either.

"What about Mama, though?"

"I've been working for Dr. Schulde for three years now, so

I've known Mrs. Schulde for that long. Winnie, I promise you she's a woman who knows how to look after herself. And Dr. Schulde will do anything to protect her."

"But not knowing what's going on puts them at risk. We could just tell them everything. There haven't been any weird occurrences since Winnie . . . now that she's gone. I could stay. We could all work together, figure out what to do about Hawthorn, and keep each other safe."

Scott walked around the lab bench and crouched down in front of her. He took both her hands in his.

"Do you really think you staying here makes your mother safer?"

No. She knew it didn't. Her being there made Mama another piece of leverage for Hawthorn.

She shook her head.

"I need you to leave. I don't know how else to say this. I look at you, and I see her. I need you safe . . . but I also need you gone. Winnie, I'm begging you—please, just try."

When she met his eyes, staring up at her own so intensely, she knew.

She loved him.

And not because she looked at him and saw her Scott.

The feeling didn't replace what she felt for her own Scott either, but lived in uneasy cohabitation with it in her heart.

She didn't want to leave him.

She didn't want to leave Mama. How could she, when she had no idea what might be waiting for her on the other side?

But she could see the suffering naked on his face. She'd done that to him, and he was begging her to go.

"Okay," she said. "I'll try."

Scott stood back up. "Good," he said firmly, and gave his wet cheeks an impatient swipe. "We'd better get to work."

Scott got out his notebook and explained the plan he'd come up with.

"The main problem is figuring out how to make our experiment work in such a small space. Exploding a generator just isn't an option down here. Even if we were resigned to destroying Dr. Schulde's lab, it wouldn't be safe—there's shrapnel to worry about. So, how do we get a high enough atmospheric charge without blowing anything up? Straightaway, I realized the best way would be to discharge a high-voltage capacitor in water. Capacitors are common and cheap, and if the voltage is high enough, they can give us the discharge we need."

Winnie nodded. The plan seemed solid so far—not as close to the events of her first trip as their original experiment, but a more elegant experiment design, in its own way.

Still, she needed to make sure it would be safe for her, and more important, for Scott.

"How do we get the capacitor into the water without shocking ourselves?" she asked.

Scott smiled at the question. "Good! Yes, that was the second problem. The safest thing is for it to drop while we're both in the Faraday cage—but how? We need some mechanism we can set in motion that will give us time to get into the Faraday cage before dropping and discharging the capacitor.

"Well, I thought of all sorts of complicated and difficult things, but then, in the end, I realized I was overthinking it. All we really need is rope and fire. Suspend the capacitor over a bucket of water; light the rope on fire; get into the Faraday cage and wait for the rope to burn through." He opened up his notebook and pointed at the page. "See?"

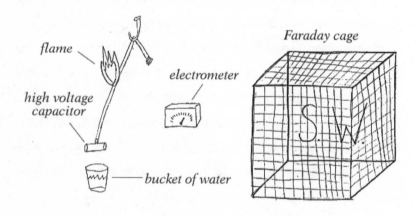

Winnie quickly examined the diagram. "I think it'll work," she said with relief, not because she was eager to leave him behind, but because this was the exact kind of thinking that would make him invaluable to Hawthorn's project.

Scott looked pleased with himself, as well he should.

"I did some calculations and figured out what voltage capacitor we need to give the discharge we want." He pulled a small bundle out of his knapsack and unwrapped it.

The capacitors Winnie was familiar with fit in the palm of a hand, ranging from the size of an aspirin tablet to the top two joints of a pinkie finger. This was by far the largest Winnie had ever seen—a cylinder about six inches long, the size of a fist in circumference. It made her nervous. Winnie had to remind herself they would be safe in the Faraday cage when it discharged.

"You're sure of your calculations?" Winnie asked.

"I checked them several times."

But this did nothing to ease her anxiety. They had been so sure before their original attempt at school, and it had gone so wrong . . .

But Scott's plan was solid and safe.

If the central hypothesis of their experiment was correct, it should work. She should be able to transport home. She had gotten herself here, after all. It made logical sense for her to be able to transport herself back. James had thought she could, and Hawthorn too.

But time travel?

That was a different thing entirely.

"If it works, and I go back in time—do you think maybe it will reverse the things that happened here? Make it like I never came? Just sort of undo it all, and then Winnie—"

"No," Scott said sharply, "I don't." He glanced over at her and must have seen the look on her face, because his tone was softer when he said, "I—I just can't pretend. She's gone. We have to accept it."

"What? You're the one who told me about time dilation.

How is this different? You're the one who said it meant I could save Scott."

He wouldn't meet her eyes.

Scott had told her that when she was refusing to try to go home. Winnie remembered it vividly.

"You *do* think that I'm going to be able to go back and save him, don't you?"

Scott paused for a long time.

"No," he said finally, "I don't. But I do think you can get yourself home."

Winnie felt the words settle on her. She slumped under the weight of them.

"Are you serious? You lied to me about that too? Jesus, Scott—is there anything you told me that was true?"

He sighed heavily. "Look. When you got here, and you told me it had been just this random thing, I was terrified! I've seen all the precautions Hawthorn takes in the lab when we transfer objects. He can be pretty cavalier about risks—obviously—but he has always been *very* careful about that. You refused to go to Hawthorn, and you were right not to, but you also refused to involve Professor Schulde. And then you were refusing to even let me help you go home! You were saying you wanted to stay!"

"You could have talked to me—"

"I knew that if I didn't get you on board immediately, Winnie would go to her father, and then it would be out of our hands. So, I lied. And I don't regret it. It wasn't even a *lie*, really. There is time dilation between different realities. But I don't know how it works, and I don't think it means you can time-travel."

"But . . . the Lichtenberg figure . . ."

"Winnie," he said gently, "Professor Schulde and I do all kinds of experiments down here. That could have happened anytime. I'm sorry. I know you wanted to save him. But sometimes we lose the people we love, and there isn't any fixing it."

"I know that! You think I don't know that?"

She'd lost enough people in her life to know the ugly truth.

They had *both* been through a lot, but she was so angry with him! Guilt and rage and grief mixed in one awful soup in her stomach, leaving her completely at a loss about what she should say or do.

"I know it's hard," Scott said, "and I know you're disappointed. That I am sorry for. But we don't have that much time before Professor Schulde gets home. We need to get the Faraday cage set up, and we need to try our experiment now."

"No!" Winnie said. "If leaving means losing you forever—if it means losing Mama *again*—I can't do it. I won't!" She could feel the anxious pounding of her heart in her chest. It was more of a declaration than she'd ever dared with her own Scott.

"It's more important for you to be safe than for you to be here. You'll grieve, but you'll get over it."

"I won't."

"Winnie . . ." Scott trailed off and sighed. He looked so exhausted. "We both know what Hawthorn is capable of. You have to do this. You have to try."

Winnie was tired too, and scared—but she was sick of feeling like prey. She was sick of being lied to, and sick of running.

"Look. Right now," Winnie said, "Hawthorn has all the cards."

Scott scoffed. "Don't I know it. All the cards, all the power—"

"Well, what if we get something on *him*."

Scott opened his mouth, but then closed it. He paused, head cocked, considering. "What are you suggesting?"

Winnie thought a moment.

An idea began to form.

"The Manhattan Project—making an atomic bomb—the military cares way more about that than any of Hawthorn's work, right?" She thought back to how snide Hawthorn had seemed about Fermi—the head of the Manhattan Project—at that party of his. "And Hawthorn resents Fermi for it, doesn't he?"

Scott nodded. "They're pretty well-known rivals."

"Exactly. And Hawthorn is the head of the department, but when the government came calling, it was Fermi they picked for their top project, right? Why do you suppose that is?" Winnie asked.

"Hawthorn pretends he wanted it that way—and multiverse theory has always been his pet subject," said Scott. "But most people think that Project Nightingale was just a bone the military threw him."

"So, what if someone broke into Fermi's office on campus and some of his papers ended up in Hawthorn's files—if the military found out, it would look like espionage, right? Since it's a military project? With the history between Fermi and Hawthorn, it would be believable. And they might even think that if James found out about it—maybe *that* was what got him killed."

Scott thought about it, and a hopeful smile began to spread on his face. She could tell he was intrigued by the idea.

"That could work, maybe," he said. "How on earth did you think of it?"

Winnie shrugged. "I got the idea from Hawthorn. If you come up with a story that's salacious enough, people will want to believe it. *Head of Columbia Physics Department Accused of Treason!*" Winnie could imagine the headlines now. "*Powerful Scientist Undone by Petty Jealousy!* The articles will practically write themselves. With a little bit of supporting evidence, I think the military will buy it, and the police too."

She thought about Muldoon—he hadn't liked Hawthorn any more than he'd liked her. He would be happy to see the wealthy elite indicted for his student's murder.

"They just might. I know that at least some of the faculty and students would buy it hook, line, and sinker."

Winnie smiled. "So, do you think you can get us into Fermi's office—tonight?"

He thought for a moment, then nodded. "Yes, I think I know a way. And there isn't any special security, other than the regular campus security guards. They've talked about putting in new locks around the offices and labs now that we're doing military work, but it hasn't happened yet. It's only been a few months since these projects started, and things on campus happen on university—not military—time."

Winnie felt a tentative excitement—a feeling she had learned to distrust.

"But if security is that weak," she asked, "do you really think Fermi will keep sensitive documents on campus—something it would make sense for Hawthorn to steal?"

Scott nodded. "I don't think *anyone* on these projects is conscientious enough to transfer their paperwork to headquarters as often as we probably should. I know Hawthorn and Professor Schulde sure don't. This could work, Winnie," he said.

"Then I think we should try."

They were putting their few eggs in an awfully rickety basket. She should be more frightened—Winnie knew that would come later—but for the moment, she was filled with relief. And if they accomplished what she hoped they would on campus tonight, then maybe, just maybe, she could stay.

It might not change the fact that Scott wanted her gone. And she'd have to hide her real self from her double's parents or risk losing them too.

It wouldn't be happily ever after, even if they successfully set up Hawthorn.

But maybe—*maybe*—she could at least be free.

CHAPTER THIRTY-FIVE

There were four informal places set around the dining room table, since Scott would be eating with them too that night, as usual. Back home, Winnie and Brunhilde took their supper at the kitchen table, and Father didn't eat dinner until quite late, if at all. Here, dinner was a family affair.

Mama dished out some Wiener schnitzel and buttered cabbage for each of them, and Father cut into his breaded pork and took a bite.

"Hmm—new recipe?"

Mama smiled ruefully.

"A rationing experiment—I left the eggs out of the breading. Not quite how Grandma used to make it, eh?"

"It's good! Just . . . different."

"Well, extra eggs means we can have cake with Sunday's dinner."

"Aha! In that case, this is the best Wiener schnitzel I've ever had!"

It was odd to see this levity from her double's parents. Her Mama and Father had certainly loved each other, but Winnie remembered there being so much resentment and arguing too.

Had her double been troubled by those memories? Or had those dark early days been papered over by the later, better ones?

Mama and Father seemed so happy with each other now, and so in love. People could grow together through shared tragedy—or be torn apart. If Winnie told them what happened to their daughter, would she be bringing those dark days back?

"Are you feeling better today?" her double's father asked. "No headaches? No double vision?"

Winnie glanced up from her plate. She felt so cut off from them, lost in her own unhappy thoughts, that she was surprised Father could even see her from across the gulf.

"No, sir," she said. "I'm feeling much better, thank you."

Father gave her a funny look and a little grin. Winnie reminded herself that here, Father was "Daddy."

"Good," he said. "That's very good to hear. Now, Scott, tell me more about this project you're working on?"

"Oh, I just constructed a Faraday cage for extra credit in Gilmore's class."

"And Winnie, you wanted to help? We just may make a scientist of you yet! I wonder if there are any summer programs we should be looking into for you for next year."

He seemed so eager for his daughter to show more interest

in such things. It made Winnie's heart hurt in ways she didn't quite understand. He thought he was seeing his daughter change, when in reality, she would never change again. Never develop new hobbies or interests. She would be forever sixteen. Stuck there, unfinished.

Winnie swallowed thickly, but her discomfort went unnoticed.

"Oh, Heinrich!" Mama said lightly, swatting at his arm. "Let the girl study what she likes."

"Correct me if I'm wrong," Father said to Mama with a smile, "but if *your* father hadn't encouraged your academics, we never would have met at university."

Mama shook her head in amusement. "True, but I'm not sure our daughter's interests are *purely* academic, in this case."

"Ah, but neither were ours," he replied with a wink.

Mama grinned, and she looked younger than Winnie had ever seen her look, even a decade ago.

Father looked at Winnie and must have misinterpreted her consternation, because he said, "I know, I know—your parents are a couple of silly-heads, and it's awfully embarrassing."

Winnie had never thought her father capable of such—such *lightheartedness*. She and Father were such a grim pair compared to their doppelgängers, although she knew her double had carried her own burdens too.

Winnie glanced at Mama. It was the loss of her that had done it—especially since rather than putting her death behind them, grief remained the engine that drove their work on the splinter machine.

Was that why Father had always kept Winnie at a distance—because losing his wife had schooled him to believe that love equaled loss?

It was a more generous interpretation than she had ever thought of before—generous to him, but also to herself.

This version of her parents seemed so comfortable. Their relationship seemed so strong. But was it strong enough to weather the loss of their child?

Should Winnie tell them now—who she really was, and what had happened to their real daughter? If she and Scott were caught that night, on campus, breaking into Fermi's office, she might end up being carted off to a military prison. This could be her final chance to be honest with them.

As Winnie was considering this course—its risks, her fear—she felt the stomach jolt of an oncoming splinter.

"I'm not your daughter!" a splinter-her confessed.

She told them what had happened. All of it, including the role Hawthorn played and the threat he still posed.

There was confusion. Then shouting. Then tears.

Finally, that splinter-Father grabbed his coat and fled the house to go confront Hawthorn, "the true author of my daughter's demise."

What happened to Father then was beyond the scope of the splinter she saw . . . but Winnie felt safe concluding it could be nothing good.

Winnie couldn't tell them.

Not until Hawthorn was no longer a threat.

"You look so deep in thought," Mama said with a frown. "Is everything okay?"

Winnie faked a smile. "Yeah, I'm just tired."

It was an odd family they made. Professor, wife, protégé—and the changeling who had brought about the death of their daughter.

Scott helped Winnie clear the table, then she walked him to the foyer to say goodnight. He paused in front of the door, taking her hand in his own. Winnie thought he was going to assure her everything would be all right, something anodyne and untrue like that, but instead he just gave her fingers a gentle squeeze and whispered, "I'll see you tonight."

He would be coming to get her at one o'clock—even Father should be asleep by then—and then the two of them would head to campus.

Winnie squeezed his hand back and tried not to think of all the things that could go wrong.

After he left, Winnie headed upstairs and dressed for bed. She lay down—it would be nice to rest, although she had no intention of sleeping.

After a little while, there was a knock on her bedroom door.

"May I come in?" Mama called softly.

"Yes," Winnie said, "come in," even though she dreaded the prospect of a conversation with her.

Mama was wrapped tight in a beautiful blue dressing gown,

and her golden hair was pinned up under a silk scarf for bed. She carried a tray with two steaming mugs.

"I brought you some drinking chocolate," Mama said. "Can I sit with you a minute?"

Winnie nodded, and tried very hard not to let the woman see that she was about to cry.

This was something Winnie's own mother had done for her when she was a little girl, whenever she was sick, or sad, or if Father had been particularly awful that day. Mama had told her once that it was something her own mother had done for her too, when she was a child.

Mama set the tray down on the bedside table and sat down on the edge of the bed. She opened her mouth to speak, but instead, she pulled Winnie into a tight hug. The sudden movement made Winnie's head throb painfully, but still, that embrace was the most wonderful thing to happen to her in recent memory.

Winnie closed her eyes and clung tight. Her mother's perfume was the same—verbena, rose, and some light musk. It took Winnie right back to Germany: picking wildflowers in the field behind their little house; carefully working on her block letters at the table while Mama prepared dinner; being read to in bed, tucked tight under the covers. Winnie hadn't even known she remembered that smell.

Winnie was much larger than she'd been the last time her mother held her, but the embrace gave her the same feeling it always had, the feeling that maybe nothing would ever go wrong again. But it had—oh, how it had!

Mama released her from the embrace and sat back. Winnie was surprised to see that she was crying.

"What's wrong?"

Mama shook her head. Tears poured freely down her face.

"I wanted to keep you safe, but . . ."

"You did—I am. I promise, I'm okay!"

Winnie would have told her even bolder lies, to make her stop crying like that.

"I was wrong—I see that now. Wrong to think seeing splits was something that could be suppressed."

Oh. What made Mama want to dredge all that up now? Winnie was startled by this sudden confession, but deeply curious too.

"Why did you?"

Mama sighed heavily. She seemed to hesitate, then finally she nodded to herself, and began to speak.

"When I was young, all I wanted was to be a scientist. And I was doing it! I was at the University of Zurich—the only girl in the physics department. I was studying, *hard*. But no one—*no one*—took me seriously. They just saw, well, this." Mama fingered a lock of her blonde hair, which had slipped loose of the curls she'd pinned it in for bed. "They just saw a silly girl. But then I was given an opportunity. A famous scientist approached me, and, well, because of my—of *our*—ability, I could really see what that choice meant."

Winnie had thought she wanted to hear Mama's reasoning, but not if it meant learning more about what had happened between her and Schrödinger. Winnie felt the same urge she'd had when she met Schrödinger himself—the desire to throw her hands over her ears. Because really, at its heart, the story of how Winnie was conceived was the story of how she'd ruined her mother's life, wasn't it?

But this woman seemed compelled to talk about it now, for god knew what reason, and considering what Winnie had done to her—in her own world, and here—the least she could do was listen.

"This professor invited me on a trip. I knew his reputation. I didn't trust him. I thought about saying no, but then I saw a split. A peek at what awaited me if I said yes. If I went away with him, I would be the inspiration for an incredible scientific discovery. Winnie, we haven't even seen everything that results yet, all from that one paper! It's—it's world-changing." She smiled and shook her head. "I'm proud of it, still, all these years later. Maybe that's wrong of me, but there it is. But being part of that work, it meant sacrifice, in all sorts of different ways."

It meant having her, Winnie knew. It meant leaving school. It meant being the only one to know that "Schrödinger's Equation" should have carried her own name too.

It meant marrying a man who loved her, but who never fully let her forget that severing ties with his mentor, marrying her, and raising that man's child had complicated his own career—at least in those early years. Winnie hadn't realized it at the time, but that was one of the things Mama and Father had argued about so much, wasn't it?

"Why are you—"

"I saw it, Winnie. I saw a split at the dinner table. The same one, I think, that you saw. I saw you telling us what happened to our daughter."

Oh god. Oh no. As soon as Winnie met this Mama, she understood she couldn't keep her—but she had *never* expected this.

"You must hate me."

Mama looked at her, brow furrowed, still crying. She gave a helpless shrug.

"How could I? It's Hawthorn's fault. And mine. I made her think she could never talk about seeing splits. If I hadn't, she could have called me and told me what was going on. She could have told her father. She wouldn't have had to try to solve it all herself." Mama gave a heavy sigh. "I just thought things would be easier if she could train herself to ignore them. At least until she was older. They just . . . they make the world so *big*."

"And you wanted her life to be—smaller?"

"Not smaller, exactly. Simpler. A simpler life, but a happier one. Because here's the thing. We don't get to see it all. We feel like we can see everything, because we can see more. But we don't get to see it all. I didn't see this."

Winnie understood what Mama meant. That splinter Winnie saw, when she saw herself meeting James . . . that put her on a path, one she didn't really understand. It had led her—it had led all of them—*here*.

"I wasn't able to keep her safe," Mama continued. "But I

will protect you. I'll figure out what to do about Hawthorn. We can't say anything to Heinrich yet—you saw, he'll go off half-cocked—but I'll come up with a solution. We can talk more tomorrow, okay? Now you should rest."

"I don't understand why you aren't angry with me. Why you don't *despise* me."

"It was an accident, right? And I'm your mother. There have been some forks in the road since then, but I gave birth to you."

Mama pulled the covers snug around Winnie's shoulders. She hesitated a moment, then kissed Winnie gently on the cheek.

Mama was so forgiving. How could she be so forgiving?

But it didn't make Winnie feel absolved. If anything, it made her feel even guiltier.

Mama wanted to protect her from Hawthorn. It made Winnie feel even more resolved to take him on herself, so Mama wouldn't have to.

No matter what Mama thought, Winnie understood that this was her mess. She would fix it.

Tonight.

CHAPTER THIRTY-SIX

Columbia's campus was completely empty, and more still than things ever got in the city. The night had the sort of bright, hard chill to it that seemed to amplify sound, and Winnie's and Scott's footsteps on the brick walkways echoed loudly across the quad.

"Should we be on the lookout for campus security?" Winnie asked nervously.

Scott shook his head. "We aren't doing anything wrong—yet."

Winnie wasn't as familiar with campus as Scott was, but she thought they were heading in the direction of Amsterdam Avenue, which was on the opposite side of campus from Pupin Hall.

"Isn't the physics building back that way?" she said, pointing toward 120th Street.

"It is—I'll explain in a minute."

Scott led her through an open wrought-iron gate toward a smaller brick building, less institutional than its surroundings, its peaked roof and dormer windows making it look almost like a large, stately home.

"Before Columbia was Columbia," Scott said, "it was Bloomingdale Insane Asylum. This is all that's left of it—aboveground. Underground, there's this labyrinth of tunnels. And that's how we're going to get into Pupin Hall."

These underground tunnels originally linked the various asylum buildings, he explained, and over the years these tunnels had been added to with infrastructure for all the new construction: steam tunnels, conduits for electricity, small underground rail tracks for transporting the coal that was used to heat the buildings.

This complex underground web now rivaled the centuries-old system of tunnels under the Kremlin, supposedly, and the passageways—some officially charted, some not—were a territory ripe for students' exploration. The administration frowned on it, but turned a blind eye so long as no one got too badly hurt or destroyed school property.

"Probably I should have asked earlier," he added, "but you aren't claustrophobic, are you?"

"Not that I know of," Winnie said.

The idea of prowling through some dark tunnels at night didn't thrill her, but what choice did they have?

Scott led Winnie around to the back of the old asylum building. There was an entrance to a storm cellar, its wide metal doors covered in ivy and secured with a padlock.

"Damn!" Winnie cursed. "We're going to need bolt cutters."

"It isn't really locked," Scott assured her, and true enough, the padlock's shackle hadn't been clicked down into the body of the lock.

Scott took a furtive glance around, but there was no one in sight. He opened the cellar door, and they descended into the dark.

THEY TURNED ON THEIR FLASHLIGHTS, WHICH SENT LONG SHADOWS UP the stone walls of the underground room.

"Do students really like to come down here?" Winnie asked, glancing around doubtfully. "It's kind of spooky." She put an exploratory hand against the brick wall. It was cold and thoroughly damp.

Scott laughed. "People come here *because* it's spooky. It's a whole thing—fraternity initiations, dares. You aren't really a Columbian until you've explored the tunnels."

"Ah, then you've been down here before," Winnie said, relieved. "You know the way?"

Scott scratched at his head in a failed show of nonchalance. "Oh, well, not exactly. But I've talked to students who have. And I borrowed a map."

He held up a crumpled, hand-scrawled piece of paper.

Winnie tried to remind herself that a wasp's nest of shoddily documented tunnels was certainly better than turning herself over to Hawthorn, which was the only alternative she'd been able to come up with, but she couldn't shake the feeling that they were in over their heads. This had been her idea; if it went wrong, it was her fault.

"You should stay here," Winnie said. He could give her the tunnel map and tell her how to get into Fermi's office. She would be able to tell which documents were important enough to use to frame Hawthorn.

"What? Absolutely not!"

"But what if there *is* night security posted in Pupin Hall these days? They wouldn't necessarily advertise that, would they? Why should we both get caught?"

"Whatever happens now," Scott said firmly, "it happens to both of us, together."

His words weren't some magic spell. The stakes were still high, the outcome uncertain, and Winnie was quite scared. But at least she wasn't in it alone.

THEY DESCENDED A LADDER WHOSE THIN METAL STEPS AND RAILS WERE slick with damp. Scott chivalrously went ahead of her, and at the bottom pressed a hand into the small of her back as he helped her off the slippery thing. Winnie's heart skipped a little at his touch. She felt her cheeks get hot. She was glad for the dark of the tunnels.

As soon as she had both feet on the ground, Scott quickly pulled his hand away, as if she were incendiary. She wondered if it was because he didn't want to touch her, or because he wanted to touch her too much.

Everything was all tangled up.

They had been frantically scrambling away from threat after threat these past few days. Winnie knew her double's death hadn't fully registered yet, not for her, and especially not for Scott. Not because it was so fresh, but because Winnie was still there, in front of him. Winnie knew this because she had experienced it herself. She had seen her Scott die, but here he was, breathing, moving, smiling at her. It softened her suffering.

Winnie shook off the thoughts and tried to focus on their mission.

Scott paused to double-check his makeshift map. "This way," he said, gesturing to a tunnel that branched off to the right.

Scott had told her the oldest tunnels were constructed in the 1880s, but Winnie would have easily believed them older still. The tunnel floor was made of crumbling brick, forcing Winnie to focus on each step or risk tripping—a welcome distraction from the danger ahead.

The tunnel quickly grew too narrow for them to walk abreast of each other. "Would you like to walk in front or behind?" Scott asked.

"Um, you can go ahead."

Winnie could feel the dark yawning behind her, the complete blackness a void at her back, urging her forward.

"We need to be careful not to rush, and watch out for the pipes," Scott said, motioning toward the fat metal pipes running over the tunnel walls on both sides. "They're quite hot.

Marcus told me he got a nasty burn on his elbow bumping into one, and that was through his shirt."

They traveled in silence for a few more minutes, until the path narrowed even further. Winnie estimated that the span of walkable space between the boiling hot pipes was perhaps no more than three feet wide.

"Careful, now—but this should be the worst of it," Scott said. "The tunnels are oldest here. Closer to Pupin, they'll open up a bit."

After a few hundred feet, they took a sharp left turn, ducked through a squat opening meant for the coal carts, and emerged into a much wider tunnel whose floor was threaded down the center with a slender line of railroad track. They followed Scott's map, and aside from some muck, a few rats, and a stomach-clenching moment when Winnie's flashlight flickered, died, and required a few slaps before it would light again, the rest of the way to Pupin was hardly more uncomfortable underground than it was above.

But even with the extra room, Winnie found it hard to take a full breath. The closer they got to Fermi's office, the greater the danger—and the more empty space around them, the easier it would be for some guards to hide in wait.

THEY ENTERED PUPIN HALL THROUGH A CAVERNOUS ROOM IN the basement. A massive machine filled about one quarter of the space, the U shape of it a magnet large enough to hoist a car and curved around two giant metal disks. Winnie recognized that it must be the cyclotron John R. Dunning had constructed a few years earlier.

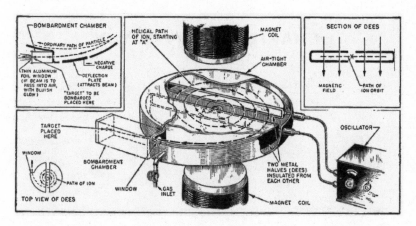

"I've never actually laid eyes on the atom smasher before," Scott said, voiced tinged with awe. "Funny seeing it down here, casual as a washing machine in a basement."

Winnie nodded, but really, she had no attention to spare. At any other time, she would be just as enthralled with the contraption—the most powerful particle accelerator on the East Coast, vital to the department's nuclear experimentation—but all her focus was attuned to the sounds in the building around them, anxiously awaiting the creak of a chair or a beat of footfall even though Scott had been certain there would be no guards.

"Where's Fermi's office?" she asked.

"Fourth floor," Scott answered, a bit distractedly. He went up to the cyclotron and laid his hand gently on the curved metal of its side as if he were steadying a skittish horse.

"Then let's go."

CHAPTER THIRTY-SEVEN

Scott and Winnie crept up the stairs to Fermi's office. Winnie made them pause and listen for guards at the top of each flight. By the time they made it up to the fourth floor, Winnie was convinced that no one was lying in wait, not even a lazy university security guard half-asleep at his post. She and Scott were the only ones in the building.

Scott led the way to a plain wooden door with a placard that read:

ENRICO FERMI

451

Winnie was struck by the banality of its appearance—just an ordinary door, nearly identical to countless others in the dusty hallways of academia everywhere. But behind this door lay state secrets, pieces to the quantum puzzle at the heart of the world, and—perhaps—the key to their freedom from Hawthorn.

By entering, they were committing espionage. To frame Hawthorn for treason, they had to actually commit it. She glanced up at Scott's face. She'd put him in so much danger that now *this* was their safest option.

He reached into his satchel and pulled out a screwdriver and the smallest claw hammer she'd ever seen.

"You're going to break the lock?"

He shook his head. "I'm going to remove the doorknob—we can reinstall it after. It will probably show some damage, but not so much that it won't be believable that Fermi didn't notice it."

Scott started to pop the metal collar around the knob.

"Wait!" Winnie said. She felt so sick to her stomach that she thought maybe she was about to see a splinter.

Winnie put her hand to the door and paused a moment, waiting for the splinter to strike, hoping it might give her some sort of insight into what this choice held for them.

There was nothing. The awful clenching in her stomach was just nerves.

In no world did they leave this door unopened. She should have expected as much.

THE OFFICE HAD A COZY, LIVED-IN FEEL. THERE WAS A HALF-EMPTY coffee cup on the desk, and next to the black Bakelite rotary phone was a day planner covered in squiggly abstract doodles and sloppy sketches of cats, mice, and hats. This, of all things, seemed deeply personal. For the first time, Winnie felt as though they were really trespassing.

Scott began searching through one of the five-drawer standing metal file cabinets, while Winnie scanned the papers on Fermi's cluttered desk.

Scott pulled out a green file folder, opened it up, and regarded the papers inside with a frown. "I can't figure out how his files are organized . . . if they're organized at all. Here are copies of his published papers on isotopes—filed under 'F.' "

"Hmm, 'F' for Fermi, do you think—filed under author name?"

"Perhaps. But there's an article by Heisenberg stuffed in here too."

Winnie opened a large, unlined notebook. Unlike his desk, Fermi's handwriting was tidy, his neat print running margin to margin, interrupted only by experiment diagrams.

When Winnie had imagined exploring Fermi's office, she stupidly thought she would be able to sift through all the notebooks and data as easily as she did her own father's research, but that was work she was directly involved with. Some of Fermi's notes might as well have been in Italian, for all the sense they made to her.

"How are we going to get through all of this?" Winnie asked.

Scott shrugged. "One page at a time," he said, and continued flipping through Fermi's files. "In a way, it's an advantage, not knowing what we're looking for—we don't need anything in particular, just something important."

That was true. If Hawthorn was found in possession of any of his rival's top secret files, things would look very bad for him. The content didn't matter—any sort of vital information about the Manhattan Project would do.

Winnie opened the top shelf of the filing cabinet next to the one Scott was searching. "Is it too much to hope there'll be a file marked 'Manhattan Project—Top Secret'?" she asked lightly.

Scott gave her a tired smile. "Probably."

"But you do think he'll have some of the papers here, right?"

Her whole plan relied on the hope that he would. So far, everything had gone so smoothly, but that wouldn't mean anything if they couldn't find what they were looking for.

"I mean, I think so—there has to be *something*." Scott gave her arm a reassuring squeeze. "It's a good plan, Winnie."

"I think so too," Winnie said. "But I thought that about our other ones also."

THEY DECIDED THE BEST PLAN OF ATTACK WAS TO QUICKLY SKIM THROUGH the files and pull anything that looked especially important, then set it aside for further review. It would be easier if they could make a mess, but the break-in was supposed to have happened before James's death a few days earlier, so they couldn't leave any obvious sign that things had been disturbed.

"Oh, now, *this* is interesting," Scott said. "It's a copy of Gamow's article on quantum tunneling. Fermi has marked up the margins everywhere. It looks like he thinks that quantum tunneling might allow not only energy but *matter* to pass through barriers—barriers like the ones between different realities."

"That is interesting. Does he say how?"

Scott frowned. "No, he doesn't mention a mechanism of travel. Not here, anyway."

"Let's take it," Winnie said.

"I don't think a published article is going to—"

"Not to plant on Hawthorn." Winnie gave him a faint smile and shrugged. "I just want to read it."

They continued to pore over materials, focusing on anything handwritten: mostly diagrams and scribbled experiment results.

They spent the next hour or so skimming Fermi's files, sorting the papers they pulled into three piles: the first, papers they were (almost) certain were worthless, but that contained some handwritten note from Fermi about the Manhattan Project; the second, experiment results that seemed important and needed a closer look; and the third, copies of memos that appeared to detail his results in more plain speech for the military higher-ups. By the time they were on the final file, Winnie's brain was starting to feel a bit mushy from scanning so many equations, and they had yet to find anything that seemed a fail-safe way to send Hawthorn to prison.

She tossed a folder onto Fermi's desk, a bit careless from exhaustion, and accidentally knocked the doodle-covered day planner off his desk. As she bent over to pick it up, she noticed a folded piece of draft paper lying on the desk—it must have been tucked under or inside the planner. As soon as she touched it, a sick frisson shivered up her arm, as if the paper were somehow charged not with electricity, but something just as deadly and far stranger.

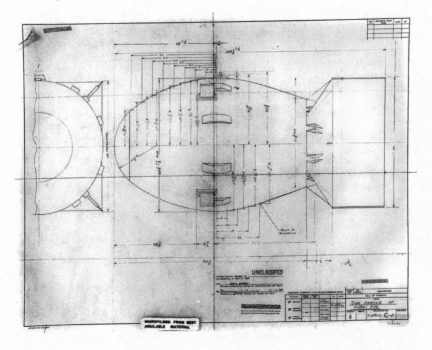

She laid the paper flat on the desk. It was a large sketch of some sort of pod, the bulb of it tapered then extending to a platform. The thing looked like a weapon—a torpedo, perhaps. She quickly scanned the specifications and began to shake.

"What is it?" Scott asked.

"The bomb," she whispered. "It's the schematic for the atomic bomb."

It was just a piece of paper, but it detailed a terrifying force.

This was exactly the sort of thing they'd been looking for.

Scott whistled low. "Now, that does look treasonous, doesn't it?" He gave a relieved-sounding laugh. "Yeah, I think that should do."

Winnie agreed that this must be just about the last piece of paper government officials would want in outside hands.

"This is the kind of thing that could be sold to the Axis for money that would make even Hawthorn blush," Scott said with a grin.

But Winnie found it impossible to return Scott's smile.

She passed the paper to him. She didn't want to touch it anymore.

"Did you see the output?" she asked.

Scott nodded. "A sixty-terajoule blast!" He sounded dazzled.

Winnie frowned at him. "Scott, an explosion like that . . ." She trailed off. "It's a terrible thing," she finished after a moment, unable to find the words to adequately express how it horrified her.

"Yes," Scott said, nodding seriously. "I'm glad it's ours."

"It shouldn't be anybody's. It shouldn't exist!"

"Well, that's debatable," Scott said, "but the fact is, it does exist—or it will. There's nothing we can do to change that, even if we wanted to."

Winnie frowned at him, trying to think of some way around the harsh truth of his words. There wasn't one. The plans for the atomic bomb were surely duplicated in other offices, and more irretrievably, in other minds. They couldn't eradicate them all.

"Winnie," Scott said gently, "this frees us. We found our ticket out of the whole mess, just like you planned."

Slowly, Winnie nodded her head.

"So, let's go," he said. "We'll plant this in Hawthorn's office. Then we can go home."

Winnie carefully folded the schematic and tucked it securely in the pocket of her skirt. She tried to shake the guilty feeling it gave her, using something so awful for her own ends. She was just one girl. She couldn't stop people from killing each other. She couldn't end war. But maybe she could save Scott. Maybe she could save herself.

They put Fermi's office back in order carefully. Winnie refiled most of the papers they'd pulled, but kept several of the more important-looking ones, in addition to the bomb schematic. They wanted enough evidence that it would be irrefutable that Hawthorn had stolen items from Fermi's files, not just stumbled on one vital piece of paper.

When they were done, Scott reinstalled the doorknob. Then he checked his watch. "My god! It's almost five!"

Winnie gave a tired laugh. "You sound surprised, but that feels about right."

"We need to plant these in Hawthorn's office quickly, so we can get you back home before Professor Schulde wakes up."

She hadn't thought about how long things might take when they were coming up with this plan. Father usually got up around six o'clock.

"You're right—we'd better hurry."

"At least for that, I have a key. Hawthorn's office is in the same suite as your"—he looked away guiltily—"as Winnie's father's."

"I didn't expect to just take her place," she said. "You know that, right?"

"I know," he said.

But he still wouldn't look at her.

CHAPTER THIRTY-EIGHT

The physics department's administrative offices were down on the first floor, close to the lab Winnie had so briefly seen when she met James. As head of the department, that was where Hawthorn had his personal office, along with the offices for Nightingale staff.

Scott unlocked the exterior door. As soon as they opened it, Winnie noticed a light was on—a small lamp on the receptionist's desk.

The two of them looked at each other nervously. "Do you think—"

The door to Hawthorn's office swung open.

It was him.

Hawthorn looked at them with surprise, then delight.

"It's her, Scott—isn't it? You've brought her to me!"

For a moment, Winnie thought she'd been tricked. If her own double could betray her—

But one glance at Scott showed he was as shocked as she was. And Hawthorn noticed.

She started backing toward the door.

"Stop right there," Hawthorn said. "All it takes is one call, and Scott's finished. I have evidence to back up my accusations, you know."

Winnie closed her eyes tight for a moment in frustration—the papers they had on them, the ones they'd meant to use against Hawthorn—if the police came now, she and Scott would be in more trouble than Hawthorn knew. Scott had some of the papers in his satchel, and the bomb schematic was right in her pocket. If she were frisked, the police would find it.

Winnie's heart began to pound even harder. If the night ended with her as Hawthorn's captive, that would be awful.

But if it ended with Scott in prison?

That prospect was unbearable.

Winnie had been so sure their plan was a good one. She felt like a fool.

Now she didn't know what to do, except try to stall and hope that some other idea for escape would take shape.

"What are you doing here so early?" she asked.

Hawthorn scoffed. "What, you think I would let Schulde start work before I do? There have always been jealous whispers, wondering how I lucked into my success. Well, there's no trick to it. I am always working harder than anyone around me."

Winnie looked over at Scott. She could tell he was thinking

hard, trying to puzzle out some way for them to slip this noose. Her own mind was a terrifying blank.

"The real question," Hawthorn continued, "is what are *you* doing here?"

"What does that matter?" Scott said quickly. "You've obviously spoiled our plans. So, what now?"

Hawthorn cocked his head. "I have a Faraday cage in my personal laboratory down the hall—very comfortable, I assure you. It has a bed, a toilet, anything she could need."

Scott clenched his fists. "She's not going in a cage."

Winnie was scared, but she was also a scientist. Her interest was piqued. Why was it a *Faraday* cage Hawthorn meant to keep her in?

They had utilized one themselves, and so had Father, but only as a way of protecting Winnie from the electricity necessary for their experiments. Hawthorn seemed to think that not just any cage would hold her—it required a cage that blocked electromagnetic fields.

Even though she was terrified at the prospect of being a prisoner, Winnie still felt excited to learn that they'd been on the right track with their experiment. Her abilities were electromagnetic in nature, and required an energy field to "activate," just like she had theorized.

Apparently, they were right in thinking that was all she needed. If her travel required additional equipment, Hawthorn wouldn't be so worried about keeping her isolated from atmospheric electricity.

But there wasn't anything for her to do with this information now. She and Scott were trapped.

"Don't make this more difficult than it needs to be, Scott," Hawthorn said. "We're taking her to the cage *now*. Like I said, it's comfortable, and I have no intention of harming her in any way. Why would I? She's—special. And I need her. With James gone, I need her now more than ever."

Winnie was scared, but she was also furious. How dare Hawthorn think he had some right to her just because she could do something he couldn't. She wasn't property. She was a person. Not a tool built for his use.

"Yeah, well, James might not have had any sort of powers, but he was special too," Scott said, "even if you didn't think so."

"Stop!" Hawthorn said fiercely, slamming his palm on the receptionist's desk. "I loved him like a son."

The worst part was, Winnie believed it.

"I had no idea his body wouldn't be able to withstand the serum," Hawthorn said, in a softer voice now. "But, Scott, don't you see? She can save him!"

Scott blinked in surprise. He looked back and forth between her and Hawthorn. If he was looking for answers, he was looking in the wrong place. Winnie had no idea what Hawthorn meant, although she was intimately familiar with the urge to undo a death you were responsible for—no matter how unintentionally.

Was Hawthorn just—crazy? If he was, what did that say about her?

Or was he onto something? Scott had already confessed

to lying about how time dilation worked, but he also said he didn't really understand it. What if Hawthorn knew something they didn't?

"What do you mean?" Winnie asked. "Save him how?"

Hawthorn sighed heavily. He shook his head, then let out a sharp bark of a laugh. "If there's a god, he's laughing at us. This incredible power—and he gives it to *you*! You could control the very fabric of space-time, and you don't even bother to learn how to sew."

Ah. A new verse for Father's old song. She didn't work hard enough to master her gift; she didn't deserve it. That had been the refrain all her life.

"My mother," Hawthorn continued, "she called it her 'intuition.' But when Father tried to get her to help him pick investments, she acted like he was asking her to rob a bank! She could have had the world on a platter, but she never accomplished anything."

What would Hawthorn make of Winnie's mother? Not much, she supposed. Because it was Schrödinger who took home the Nobel Prize—for a groundbreaking paper that never would have been written without her.

"Say whatever you want, but we both know the truth," Winnie said. "*I* got here. You have your state-of-the-art lab and government funding, but I'm the one who can travel between worlds."

"Then what are you still doing here?" he asked smugly. "Either you have no idea how to get home . . . or you have a home that's not worth going back to."

Or both.

He was right on the money, and boy, did it sting.

"You have the animal instinct," Hawthorn acknowledged. "But I can show you how to use it."

Scott glared at him. His face was full of loathing.

"You really think you're something, huh? You're a *murderer*."

"I already told you. She can bring him back! But if she won't do it—if you won't convince her—what does that make the two of you?"

What did Hawthorn know? Could she really bring back James?

Did that mean she could bring back Scott too?

. . . and her double?

She had to know.

"How," Winnie said flatly.

Hawthorn scoffed.

"You're not going to understand the mechanics of it."

"Well, I guess you'd better explain it very carefully, then," she said.

"You're going to be a real delight to work with, aren't you?"

"Just tell us!" Scott spit.

Hawthorn placed both hands on the receptionist's desk. "When you came here, that opening created a connection between our realities. The space-time of our respective worlds—it's stitched together at that point. It always will be. And that connection, it's a sort of fulcrum."

"Like on a seesaw?" Winnie asked.

"Yes! Very good!" Hawthorn said, like she was a puppy who'd learned a surprising new trick.

But Winnie was too distracted by this development to feel insulted.

When she had theorized that there was an inverse relationship between their timelines . . . could she actually have been right?

"So when we go forward in time—'up' on the seesaw—my world goes back?"

"The model of a seesaw is an oversimplification, but yes. When you crossed into our world, you didn't just connect our two timelines to each other. You linked them to yourself. You and the two timelines are connected variables now. Change the position of one timeline, and you necessarily change the other. We can use this connection—we can use you—to manipulate the timelines."

"How does that help James?" Scott asked.

Winnie knew the answer.

"When I return home," she said. "I could spring forward. And that would send you all back."

"You're a quicker study than I'd hoped," Hawthorn said, beaming.

She wished she weren't.

She wished she hadn't asked Hawthorn to explain.

She wished she didn't understand.

Scott had been lying when he told her about time dilation, but he had accidently hit on the truth. Hawthorn never would have told her any of this if he'd had any inkling that there was also a death in her own world she would want to undo, but now she knew. And now she had to choose.

She *could* go back. She *could* save Scott.

But that would mean leaving all her messes for this world's Scott to clean up. Leave her double dead. Leave James dead. Leave her double's parents without a daughter.

Or she could go forward. She didn't know *how* yet, but if Hawthorn said it was possible, she believed it. She trusted his expertise, if nothing else. It wouldn't take a big leap. Just a week into her own world's future, and they could go back to before she got there. Her double and James would be okay.

But her Scott would be gone forever.

And she would never see Mama again.

If she went through with it, would this Scott even remember what had happened? Would Hawthorn? What would stop Project Nightingale from continuing? What would keep Hawthorn from killing James again?

Winnie didn't have any answers, but she knew the right thing to do.

CHAPTER THIRTY-NINE

The realization of what she had to do stuck in her throat like a piece of dry bread.

She didn't want to go.

Of course, that assumed she could even figure out how.

"So, you're going to just let her leave?" Scott asked, voice dripping with skepticism. "You're going to send her into her own world's future so that we go back to before James's death? That's awfully selfless of you. But if that's true—why the cage?"

Scott thought Hawthorn was lying. But Winnie was sure he was telling the truth. She could feel the rightness of it in her bones. This wasn't like when she had jumped on Scott's suggestion of time dilation because she was so desperate to believe she could undo the past. This was making a sacrifice, moving forward, and fixing the mistake she'd made by coming here.

"Scott," Hawthorn said with a chuckle, and shook his head, "no. Of course I'm not letting her go! Not until I can create a tether. Some kind of leash—made of energy, not matter, of course—that lets me pull her back after she's gone."

Winnie raised her eyebrows. He said all this so casually! "A leash? Like for a dog?"

"A bit of advice, my dear. If you choose the most unpleasant interpretation of everything, life will be—well, unpleasant."

Winnie narrowed her eyes. "Unpleasant? Was that how things were for your mother? You used her body to make your serum—and it didn't even work!"

She had been prepared for this to make Hawthorn angry—she *wanted* him angry, to at least get some little dig in, if she could do nothing else—but all expression left his face. Those chilly eyes, blank . . . they were terrifying. She almost regretted her words.

"Is that really how you want to do this, Ms. Schulde?" Hawthorn asked, voice flat. He looked away and shook his head. "I can't believe he told you that," he muttered, as if *James* had been the one who wronged *him*!

"All right," Hawthorn continued, "you want to have control? You've got it. Cooperate with me, or Scott goes to prison for James's death. It's up to you."

Scott shook his head and grabbed her hand tight in his own. "No, Winnie. You're not going to be some sort of sacrificial lamb. I don't want that. Not for me. I couldn't live with myself."

He was well-intentioned, but this was no better than when he lied to her to convince her to go along with his plans.

Winnie was tired of being manipulated.

She would do this her own way.

"I'll go with you," Winnie told Hawthorn. "I'm not going to fight."

She was going to flee.

There was only one reason for Hawthorn to be intent on keeping her in a Faraday cage instead of just locking her in a room. He must know that she could escape their world at any time, as long as she had access to some electricity.

And she did—if she could get to it.

She grabbed Scott's arm. "It's okay," she said, and traced a spiral on the inside of his wrist with her thumb.

The cyclotron.

A spiral was how the mechanism was represented in diagrams. She had to hope he understood what she meant, because if she was going to get away from Hawthorn, she would need his help.

The cyclotron was in the basement, right below them. Winnie just needed to get down the hall, down the stairs, and it would be there, waiting for her. But if she was going to make a sudden break for it, she would need to convince Hawthorn he had already won, so he would let his guard down.

He didn't seem to think girls were capable of much. That gave her an advantage.

Winnie met Scott's eyes. His were bright with fear. She was sure hers must be too.

But she could do this. She knew she could.

"I can't do it, Scott," she murmured. "I can't keep getting

people hurt." She glanced over at Hawthorn. "He's a powerful man. He'll make you suffer. And if I can save James too . . ."

Winnie squared her shoulders. She wanted to seem brave but resigned.

"Show me to the Faraday cage. I'll do anything you ask if you promise not to hurt Scott or get him in trouble."

"Gladly."

"Say it."

Hawthorn rolled his eyes, but in a jolly, amused sort of way. "I promise."

Winnie was satisfied. She wanted him to see her that way—like a silly girl who accepted pinkie promises from murderers.

Hawthorn began guiding her down the hall, arm in arm, like a kindly chaperone.

"Keep back," he warned Scott, who trailed helplessly behind them, seemingly at a loss for what he could possibly do now, but obviously unable to just leave.

"Could you tell me more about your mother?" Winnie asked, half to keep him distracted and half out of sheer curiosity.

"My mother? She was a mystic," he said, voice dripping with contempt. "Completely uninterested in quantum matters, electromagnetic forces—the true source of her ability. Instead, she collected crystals and other poppycock. Called her gift the 'divine feminine.' She laughed at me for wanting to quantify and classify such things. Well, she wasn't laughing in the end."

Ah. Hawthorn's Faraday cage—built with every "comfort" in mind—had housed a previous occupant.

"Some people," Winnie said, shaking her head. "They refuse to see what's right in front of them."

Hawthorn released her arm to fumble in his pocket for the keys, then unlocked the door to his private lab.

"Scott, get the door," Winnie said, trying to sound ever-so-slightly put out by his "thoughtlessness" at not holding the door for them already.

Hawthorn was a man accustomed to being attended to. This didn't strike him as odd.

Scott grabbed the heavy wooden door to hold it open for the two of them.

Winnie quickly slid backward and shoved Hawthorn as hard as she could, pushing him through the doorway into his lab. Then Scott slammed the door shut behind him.

Hawthorn roared like an animal. The door had one small window of wire-reinforced glass, up above the handle. She could see him there, pushing at the door and fuming. His angry breath fogged the glass.

Hawthorn fixed his ice-blue eyes on her own. "You'll wish you were dead."

If he caught her? She didn't doubt it.

Winnie looked up and down the dimly lit hall frantically, searching for something to block the door.

Scott was braced against the door as Hawthorn slammed his body against it from the inside. He managed to shove it forward a few inches and snaked his fingers through the gap, only to have them get smashed with a sick crunch when Winnie helped Scott push it shut. He howled and jerked his hand back.

There were no heavy objects in the hallway just waiting to be part of a blockade.

"Should I—" Winnie began, then said, "Wait—Scott, give me your belt!"

His hands grasped the door handle, and his shoulder was braced against the wood.

"Better take it yourself."

Winnie felt her cheeks flame hot, but there was no time to waste. She grabbed for the buckle, unfastened it, and pulled the belt free of the loops on his trousers with one sharp yank.

There was a fire extinguisher set in the wall near the door, locked in a glass case. She looped the belt through the door handle and the little metal handle on the case, then buckled it.

"Winnie, no way will that hold—" Scott began, still braced against the door.

And she could see that he was right. When Hawthorn pushed against the door, the handle of the fire extinguisher case looked ready to break.

"You have to go by yourself," Scott said. "I'll stay here and hold the door."

Winnie couldn't speak. Her eyes welled with tears. She wasn't just saying goodbye to *this* Scott. She was saying goodbye to the idea of saving her own. Goodbye to the idea of ever seeing him again.

And goodbye to Mama.

Scott just looked at her. Tears were in his eyes too, and like her, he seemed to have no idea what to say. He was braced against the door, so he couldn't even hug her.

Scott wouldn't be able to hold the door forever. Winnie had stalled long enough.

She still didn't know if Scott would remember anything. That was out of her control. All she could do now was give them another chance. What they did with it was up to them.

"I love you," Winnie whispered.

Words she would never get to say to her Scott.

Then she ran.

THE STAIRCASE TO THE BASEMENT WAS JUST TWENTY FEET OR SO AWAY. Winnie flew down the hall, closing the space between Hawthorn's lab and the staircase in seconds.

The cyclotron was just one flight down.

Winnie clattered down the steps, and then she was in the basement work area. She skidded to a stop next to the cyclotron's control panel.

Winnie heard glass shattering from the floor above. The window on the door? Had Scott been hurt? Was Hawthorn still trapped?

She would have to be quick. Winnie examined the control panel. She was no stranger to lab equipment, and this seemed straightforward enough. She pulled a large lever, and the massive machine began to click. She hit another button, held it, then flipped a switch, and the cyclotron began to whine.

Inside the machine, a high-frequency oscillator was hurtling charged particles between the poles of an incredibly powerful electromagnet, generating massive amounts of magnetic Lorentz force.

There was some quirk in the makeup of her body's own particles that answered the call of these forces too. Her stomach fluttered. She felt like she was standing on the edge of a cliff, about to find out if she really could fly.

You've done it before, Winnie reminded herself. *You did it without even trying.*

Winnie remembered that day. How Scott's body looked crumpled there on the floor, like a marionette whose strings had been cut. She loved him so much, and he would never know.

That Scott was gone.

It was awful and it was unfair, but sometimes people died.

The accident that killed him had been just that—an accident.

So had the fall that killed her double . . . but that accident had been the result of the wrongness of her entering this world in the first place. *That* wrongness was her responsibility to fix.

The conditions were right, thanks to the cyclotron—she could practically *taste* it, like ions in the air before a thunderstorm—but she still had to harness her own ability to make the leap.

The border between worlds had always been blurred for her, but she couldn't force her transportation. Brute willpower didn't work.

That was Father's way.

Hawthorn's way.

She had to discover her own.

Winnie searched inside herself for the feeling that accompanied the splinters.

It took only a few seconds for her to find it: a sort of sickness in her stomach paired with an expansiveness in her chest, the nauseous feeling that she was bigger inside than out. She squeezed her eyes tight and focused. She followed that feeling down to its root.

All living things—plants, animals, people—were home to an electric charge. Galvani had dubbed this "animal electricity," which Mama had mentioned in her lecture that very afternoon. More recently, scientists had termed this living charge "bioelectricity." It wasn't unique to Winnie. But what she could do with it was.

Winnie visualized this living current of electricity as a river. It flowed through her. But it was outside her too, much bigger than her, reaching out to connect with the charged atmosphere the cyclotron had created. Those twin rivers—electricity outside herself, and within—they encompassed *everything*. All matter. All times. Hawthorn's mother had been right—this was beyond calculation and control.

It was miraculous.

Father had kept her in the Faraday cage during their experiments in an attempt to protect her, but now she realized it had also kept her from accessing this. Winnie was a sort of sailor by birth, and electromagnetic waves were the sea she traveled on. Father must have suspected the importance of these fields—that's why his experiments used electricity—but he had been too cautious about Winnie getting hurt. His care for her had undermined his own work all these years, Winnie now realized with a pang.

She returned her attention to the river of electricity. It had many, many pathways. It forked, and forked, and forked, an incomprehensibly complex Lichtenberg figure. It gave Winnie vertigo just thinking about trying to count all those paths. She focused on the one nearest to her. It forked into another path, one that pulsed faintly in time to the beat of her own heart. That river in her mind—it represented home, and it called to her.

But she was still tethered to the world she was in. Tied there by fear. Fear that her double's life was the best one she could ever have, and she was giving it up. Fear that she wouldn't be able to build a life for herself that she wouldn't long to leave.

It was her responsibility to try.

There was a wrenching crash from above, then the staccato of footsteps running down the hall. Hawthorn was coming for her.

It had to be now.

In her mind's eye, Winnie visualized traveling along that home current. She could go forward, along with the flow, or she could go back. She felt for a future spot. "Animal instinct," Hawthorn would call it. She found a place that felt right.

Then she jumped in.

Winnie didn't faint this time. She felt the moment of transportation like a stab of cold all over her body, almost unbearable, but over before she could really register the pain. There was resistance—to pull herself forward, she had to push that other world back.

Winnie shoved, and then—all at once—she was free of the current.

She opened her eyes. She was lying on the floor next to the cyclotron in the basement of Pupin Hall.

It was dark. The cyclotron was off, a sleeping behemoth. Hawthorn's footsteps and shouts were no more.

Winnie was back in her own world. She'd done it.

And now she was alone.

CHAPTER FORTY

Had it worked?

Winnie was home. It had worked for *her*.

But had it really worked for them?

There was no way to know. She just had to hope it had.

Winnie sat up, then stood. Her body felt heavy and slow. She had been scared for so long, striving for so long, propelled by fear—what now?

Winnie let out a long sigh. She could go to Dora's. She was sure her friend would be over the moon to see her. Winnie could hide out there. Come up with some plan. Run away. If she was very clever and very lucky, maybe she would never have to face Father.

But running away—that was what she'd been doing when she left their world before. And look how that had turned out.

No. Winnie would go home. She would face Father's wrath. Father's questions. After everything she'd been through, surely she could do that. And then, she'd tell him "no more."

She climbed the stairs up to the first floor of Pupin Hall—but before she could take even a dozen steps down the hallway, she heard the creak of a door opening.

Winnie looked frantically toward the sound, fearing Hawthorn—but the sound had come from farther down the corridor.

A figure stood there, perhaps ten feet away, hidden in shadow. A security guard? The custodian, come to open up the building?

"Winifred?"

It was Father.

"Oh my god. It is you. I heard a crash—it woke me up—mein Gott!"—he shook his head in disbelief—"you came home."

He ran up to her. Winnie flinched reflexively, but all he did was pull her into a tight embrace. Tears were streaming down his face, but what really surprised her was that his breath didn't smell of schnapps. What was he doing sleeping in his office if he hadn't passed out there?

"What are you doing here?" she asked.

"I thought I might never see you again," he whispered, tickling the top of her head with his breath. "I've been working nonstop," he said, gesturing vaguely down the hall toward his office, "trying to figure out how to get you back."

"How long have I been gone?" she asked urgently.

Father frowned in confusion, but he answered without questioning why she asked.

"Sixteen days."

Oh, thank god! By her count, she'd been gone ten. If what Hawthorn said was true and their timelines were attached, her jump of six days into her own future would have taken them six days into the past, back to a time when Winnie and James were both alive.

Father held her out at arm's length so he could look down at her, then smiled. "All my work, and I made no progress. But here you are. You came home yourself," he said, then frowned. "I'm surprised you would want to, after I—"

"I can't forgive you," Winnie said abruptly.

This Father, speaking to her so warmly, just like she'd always wanted—this was a trap the universe had set for her. It tempted her to take the easy route, but she wouldn't pretend like everything was okay any longer—not even if that meant provoking his anger.

If her sticking up for herself sent him into a rage, well, so be it.

"I know I have a lot to make up to you," Father said softly. "I've had nothing but time to think about all that I've done wrong . . . that empty house . . . but I *will* make it up to you, somehow." He swallowed nervously. "To you, and to Scott. I'll do everything I can to earn both of your forgiveness."

Father begging for forgiveness would have been enough to send her for a loop, but what he was implying about Scott—it was impossible.

Winnie had seen him die. Hadn't she?

"Wait. Are you saying Scott's okay?"

Father let out a heavy sigh. For the first time in her life, Winnie noticed there were lines around his eyes. "Oh, Winifred . . . the accident . . . he was seriously injured." Father's shoulders sagged. It was the guilt, Winnie realized, that made him look older. "The doctors are hopeful, though," he said, straining to sound more upbeat. "He's improving. Every day, he asks for you. He can't seem to remember you're gone." Father frowned grimly. "It will do him good, I think, to see you."

She couldn't focus. All this time when she'd been off in another world, messing things up for another set of them, Scott had been here. Waiting. Asking for her.

His body on the floor though—she had been so *sure.*

And she had been so wrong.

But that didn't matter now. Scott was here, alive!

"Can I see him?" Winnie asked. "Can we go see Scott right now?"

Heaven help any interloper who tried to take him from her.

"Yes," Father said, "yes, of course." He took her in his arms again and pulled her close. "I've been so foolish—so tied up in your mother's loss for all these years that I let myself lose you too. Things will be different now, Winifred, I swear it."

"You're the only one who calls me that, you know."

"What—Winifred? It's the name she chose for you. You wear it well."

"Maybe, but I prefer Winnie."

"All right," he said tentatively. "Whatever you like."

Would things really be different now? She knew they *could* be. She'd met that milder him already, and he did seemed softened by Scott's accident and her disappearance. Would that change last? Perhaps. But even if he changed back, she wouldn't. She would never be pushed around by him again.

THE HOSPITAL WOULDN'T OPEN UP FOR VISITORS FOR ANOTHER FEW hours, but the nurse on duty recognized Father.

"I promise we won't disturb him," Father assured her.

The nurse frowned, considering. She looked worn down by her job, but her eyes were kind.

"Please," Winnie said, "I just need to see him."

The nurse paused a moment, then nodded at Father. "All right, Dr. Schulde."

She walked them over to Scott's room, although Father surely knew the way, and opened the door.

"I don't want you going in right now," the nurse said. "He needs his rest. Come back later this morning, and you can talk to him." The woman put a gentle hand on Winnie's forearm. "You must be Winifred. It's good to see you here. Your father missed you."

Winnie was startled to hear that Father had talked about her, but before she could really register her surprise, the nurse stepped out of the doorway and Winnie could see past her to Scott, lying there in a hospital bed. Every other thought fled.

His head had been shaved, and one arm and leg were heavily

bandaged. Winnie leaned against the doorjamb to keep herself from falling over. Father reached an arm toward her and gave her support on the other side.

"Why did they shave his head?"

"There was swelling around his brain," Father said quietly. "They had to drill to relieve the pressure."

"And the bandages?"

"The entry point of the current, and the exit."

"Is he really going to be okay?" Winnie asked, her voice cracking. Father had already told her he should be, but seeing him like that, thin and pale and alone there in the dark, she needed to hear it again.

"Yes. The doctors feel optimistic about his recovery," Father assured her, but his expression was pained. "He can speak. He'll be able to walk, once his leg is healed." Father sighed heavily. "Will he ever be the successful physicist he was once certain to be? That, only time will tell."

"I don't care about that!" Winnie said fiercely. Scott stirred at the sound, but thankfully did not wake. "All that matters is that he gets well," she whispered.

"Of course," Father agreed quickly.

But they both knew it wasn't true. It would matter to Scott, and it mattered to Winnie too. She would help him. Help with research, help with school—whatever he needed. The two of them would be a team, like Marie Curie and her husband Pierre, like Émilie du Châtelet and Voltaire, like—

Like she and Scott's double had been.

She let herself think of that other Scott now.

She hated not knowing what had happened after she left, not knowing what was happening to him at that very moment, a world away. Not knowing, for sure, that what she had done had taken their world back to before James or Winnie died.

Should she go back, she wondered? Not forever—just long enough to figure out some way to make sure that they were okay, and stayed that way?

Winnie now knew how to transport herself, but the way alternate realities connected, the complex interweaving of space and time . . . she couldn't begin to pretend she understood it all.

Even with all that risk and uncertainty, she thought that if their roles were reversed, Scott would try to check on her.

Winnie pondered all this guiltily, wondering if she was being cautious or cowardly, but at the same time, watching the steady rise and fall of Scott's sleeping breath eased the ache of grief that had been so constant and familiar, she had almost forgotten it was there.

The nurse had told her to stay out of his room, but she simply couldn't. He was so close! It had been so long! Her heart felt almost painfully flooded. It had to discharge.

Winnie took a few ginger steps forward. The door swung shut behind her with a gentle *shush*; Father must have known better than to follow. She crept up to the edge of the bed and took Scott's hand in her own, stroking the back of it gently with her thumb.

She hadn't meant to wake him, but when his eyes fluttered open, she felt a surge of joy.

"Winnie?" he asked hoarsely.

She didn't feel the tears coming, but suddenly they were there.

"Hi, Scott. I'm sorry I haven't—I'm so sorry."

Scott frowned. He looked confused, and Winnie wondered how much of this was because she had just woken him, and how much was a lingering effect of his injuries.

"You were gone?"

Winnie nodded and quickly brushed away her tears. "Yes."

"But you're back now?"

"Yes."

He blinked up at her, sleepy-eyed as a child. "You'll stay?"

As soon as he asked, Winnie knew there was only one possible answer.

"Yes," she said. "I'll stay. Always."

And she knew she would never leave.

As Winnie got ready for bed that night in her own home—weary as she was, and desperately worried about the one Scott, while elated about the survival of the other—there was a certain delight to her every action. Slipping into *her* pajamas. Washing up in *her* bathroom sink. Pulling back the covers of *her* bed. And for the first time in forever, she knew that the next day held something predictable and good: going back to the hospital to spend more time with Scott, who was *alive*.

Winnie was surprised to hear Father's footsteps on the creaky attic stairs. She knew he couldn't possibly be coming to drag her down to the lab for one of his experiments, but the sound still set her heart thumping.

Once he reached the top of the stairs, he paused. "May I tuck you in?" he asked.

It was something he hadn't done since she was a small child.

Winnie nodded. She was already under her own beloved plain blankets, but Father pulled them up snugly under her chin, then perched on the edge of her bed. He reached out an uncertain hand, and when she didn't flinch, stroked Winnie's hair, tucking it behind her ear.

"It's so short."

"I like it," Winnie said.

"Well, it is the style of the time."

Father sighed and looked down at his clasped hands. He was nervous, and he was trying. That meant something to Winnie. It would take time to relearn how to accept affection from him, but Father finally seemed like he wanted to build a relationship with *her*, his daughter—not his subject. Winnie wanted that too.

He looked up suddenly, fixing her in his gaze.

"Winifred—" Father began. Winnie took a breath to correct him, but he quickly did it himself. "I'm sorry," he amended, "Winnie—where were you? When you disappeared, where did you go?"

The hungry look in his eyes frightened her.

How would Father react if he knew she'd visited a world where Mama was alive?

She would never tell him. She couldn't risk him thinking there was a way to regain what he'd lost. Winnie knew that folly all too well.

But she would tell Scott everything, when he was well enough to hear it. She wouldn't be like her double—she would never keep any part of herself from him again.

In response to Father's question, she just shook her head. "It doesn't matter," she said firmly.

And it didn't.

This was where she belonged.

EPILOGUE

Winnie opened the trinket box she kept on her dresser and pulled out a small embossed business card. She was glad now that she hadn't thrown it away, although she had considered it the night Schrödinger gave it to her, so angry with him for telling her terrible truths she could never un-know. That evening had set her down a dark path, but she could no more blame Schrödinger for that than she could blame James for disappearing, or Scott for caring that he had.

Winnie sat down at her little desk. She pulled out a sheet of her nicest stationery and her finest pen and began to write a letter. Three drafts later, she was pleased enough with the result to fold it up along with another sheet of paper, slip both into an airmail envelope, and address it to Schrödinger's office in Ireland.

• • •

"WHERE ARE YOU OFF TO?" FATHER ASKED AS SHE STOOD POISED NEAR the front door, tightening the belt of her heavy wool coat. The weather had turned in the past week. Late fall was now feeling more like winter, and the first snow of the season was forecast for that evening.

"Just an errand," Winnie said, "then I'm having dinner with Scott and Dora at the hospital."

With Winnie spending so much time at the hospital, Dora had gotten it into her head to start volunteering there. The work really seemed to be something of a calling for her, and not just because Scott's new roommate out of the intensive care wing was a dashing young man Dora was quite taken with.

Winnie knew it would be kind to invite Father to join her, but she didn't want him accompanying her to the post office. She hadn't told him about her plan to write to Schrödinger and knew he wouldn't approve. Here, Hawthorn knew her as nothing more than a plain girl he'd once met at a party—if he remembered even that. She was well and thoroughly out of that mess. And Father wanted her to stay out.

He was probably right. Winnie would be better off focusing on the future, not the past, and there was certainly enough to occupy her, between her new relationship with Scott and the extra classes she was taking so she could graduate early and enter Barnard next fall. Winnie was sticking her neck out with no way of knowing it would make any difference, but after hours of agonized contemplation, she had finally decided she must try.

Schrödinger was famous. He was well-connected. He was, technically at least, her father. He was an outspoken opponent of the Nazi party, so he must at least have *some* scruples, even if they didn't extend to his attitudes about seducing young students. And he was out of the country, safe from the reach of even military police. Perhaps he could help.

Even if it didn't work, Winnie knew she had to try.

Winnie wished Father a good afternoon and headed out. The nearest post office was just a few blocks away, an easy walk even on a cold day. She tucked her chilly hands deep in her pockets, the right one clutching her letter tight, and headed south on Sutton Place.

Originally, Winnie hadn't planned to do anything about Nightingale, uneasy as that made her. She could live with allowing Hawthorn's work to continue, if it meant keeping Scott—and herself, and Father—safe. So, she resigned herself to being a coward. Or she had, until a conversation with Father the night before changed everything.

Scott had been asking about James again. Worrying about him again, because that was who Scott was. Even laid up in a hospital bed, he still had the energy to worry about someone else.

It killed Winnie to hear him talk about James, about how he would resume searching for his friend as soon as he was released, when she knew James was dead. Sitting there and nodding made her feel like the worst kind of liar, but she didn't know if he was well enough for the truth.

So, she asked Father when he thought it would be safe to tell Scott that James was dead—much to his confusion.

That was how she discovered that, here, James's body had never been dragged from the cold Hudson.

This didn't necessarily mean James was alive. But, in that other world, Hawthorn hadn't hidden James's body when he died—he had been careful to dispose of the body in a way that practically guaranteed he would be found, and quickly. At first, Winnie had assumed it was a self-serving move on Hawthorn's part—that the discovery of a dead, "drug-addicted" James was less likely to implicate him than a missing research assistant—but Hawthorn had, in his own twisted way, loved James. She wondered now if disposing of James's body like that was a way to make sure he at least got a proper burial, and that his family was saved years of wondering.

Maybe James's body was submerged in the river still, waiting to be discovered.

But maybe not.

Maybe, here, James was alive. Alive, but trapped. Still being experimented on by Hawthorn, just like Winnie would be if she hadn't managed to escape.

Chances were slim, and on top of that, there was an even slimmer chance Schrödinger could help if James was alive—but if it were her in that Nightingale cage? She hoped someone would risk it.

Winnie paused outside the mailbox. The envelope in her hand didn't just contain a letter. Inside, in her own careful script, was a tidy copy of the atomic bomb schematic. How could she send her father the lock, and not the key? She already had the perfect ransom to exchange for James. With that, Schrödinger could go over Hawthorn's head, directly to the major general who Father had told her was overseeing both projects, and threaten to release the plan for the atomic bomb unless they searched Hawthorn's personal labs for James and then shut the project down.

It was a risky gambit, to say the least. But Schrödinger had never shied away from infamy, and she was his daughter. Perhaps he would let her use up her lifetime's worth of favors in one go.

What she was doing was treason—again—and Winnie did feel treasonous. And afraid. Not just of being caught, but of having the letter intercepted. It was an awful knowledge she was sending out into the world.

And for all she knew, she might be risking all this for a corpse decomposing at the bottom of the Hudson.

James wasn't unlike Schrödinger's cat now, both alive and dead until someone threatened Nightingale to find out for sure.

Winnie thought about Scott, in his hospital room across town. He would send the letter and the schematic, no hesitation.

Winnie weighed safety against cowardice, patriotism against governmental corruption, risk against reward. She thought about how Scott would never forgive her if he one day found out she'd had this chance and didn't take it.

And she thought about the boy she'd met in that other world.

How trapped he was, even while he was sitting across from her in that diner. Trapped, by habit and love and pride, just like she had been.

Winnie had freed herself from Father's work. She wanted James to be free too.

She opened the mailbox and placed her letter inside.

She thought it was the right thing to do.

She hoped it was.

ACKNOWLEDGMENTS

This book has changed and grown monumentally in the several years between first draft and final form. None of it would have been possible without my agents, Lara Perkins and Laura Rennert, whose keen feedback over several pre-sale drafts helped shape *When You and I Collide* from an idea to a book. Innumerable thanks to them both, and to the rest of the team at Andrea Brown Literary Agency.

I'm also deeply grateful to the team at Philomel, especially my editor, Liza Kaplan, whose insights helped this book become itself, and to associate editor Talia Benamy. And many thanks to eagle-eyed copyeditors Laura Blackwell and Krista Ahlberg! I'm in awe of everything this publishing team was able to accomplish, especially during a year as tragically challenging as 2020.

I completed the first draft of this novel over one summer break during my MFA program at the Ohio State University. As a writer, I owe a debt of gratitude to the faculty and classmates who helped shape my work during my three years there, and as a person, I'm so thankful for the friends I found there.